Praise for *The Rogue Pirate's Bride*

"Lovely and unexpected... Shana Galen certainly has a knack for turning a cliché into something fresh and lively."

—*USA Today Happy Ever After*

"Galen's latest old-school historical offers a nonstop, swashbuckling plot that will keep readers on the edge of their seats, while the passion-rich romance that develops between her bold, impetuous heroine and sinfully sexy hero will have them sighing with satisfaction."

—*Booklist Online*

"Enchanting... jam-packed with action, adventure, and the sort of passion that makes historical romance lovers swoon... Shana Galen has a unique talent for making a story come to life."

—*Romance Fiction* on Suite101.com

"Shana Galen has a superb talent for crafting the perfect characters that are strong, vulnerable, yet stunningly unique. This story has a splendid setting enriched with a vivid and captivating description that readers will adore."

—*Romance Reviews*

Praise for *Lord and Lady Spy*

"Lively, utterly delightful adventure romance."

—*RT Book Reviews*, 4 Stars

"The James Bond–esque heroics alternate with a surprisingly sensitive take on a young couple."

—*Publishers Weekly*

"Galen has a tremendous talent of writing action-packed, adventure-filled, sensual romances that leave a reader wishing the book went on forever. Well done!"

—*History Undressed*

"A fast-paced, blithe, and charming tale."

—*Historical Novels Review*

"Captivating… This book was everything that I wanted it to be, and then there were the little quirks that made it even better!"

—*Fresh Fiction*

"Seamlessly blends romance with mystery and intrigue… Sexy and full of danger."

—*Debbie's Book Bag*

Praise for *The Making of a Duchess*

"Galen's trilogy, the stories of lost brothers, begins with a fast-paced, action-packed, cat-and-mouse spy thriller that will leave you breathless. Her engaging characters and strong plotline enhance the spirited dialogue and sense of adventure."

—*RT Book Reviews*

"Galen strikes the perfect balance between dangerous intrigue and sexy romance in her latest deftly crafted Regency historical."

—*Booklist*

"Delightful reading! Shana Galen creates a captivating tale… the dialogue, charming wit, the intrigues, and the steamy love scenes make the novel a page-turner."

—*The Long and the Short of It*

"Vivid, intense, and had me ensnared from the first line… Galen's book had me up until all hours."

—*History Undressed*

"Exceptionally entertaining reading with a cast of brilliantly written characters… Galen's descriptive writing and wonderful dialogue make her novel impossible to set down… an all around delightful read."

—*Rundpinne*

"Intrigue, suspense, and romance wrapped neatly into a delicious story that will keep the reader going until the very last page."

—*Affaire de Coeur*

Also by Shana Galen

WHEN YOU GIVE A DUKE A DIAMOND

SHANA GALEN

sourcebooks
casablanca

Published by Sourcebooks Casablanca, an imprint of Sourcebooks,
Inc.
P.O. Box 4410, Naperville, Illinois 60567-4410
(630) 961-3900
Fax: (630) 961-2168
www.sourcebooks.com

Printed and bound in Canada
WC 10 9 8 7 6 5 4 3 2 1

For Tera, because you are—seriously—a brainstorming/ plotting genius, and because you're the kind of friend who knows what a wild roller-coaster ride this industry is and gets in the seat beside me anyway.

Prologue

Rumor held that the Prince Regent himself gave The Three Diamonds their sobriquets. Every gallant in London claimed to have been present when the three were knighted. One or two might even have been telling the truth. But no one, not even the scandal rags, who preferred to bestow their own nicknames, could argue with the prince's choices.

London's most sought after Cyprians were, in effect, treated like nobility. It was fitting that these diamonds of the first water be given titles reflecting their status among the demimonde.

Prinny knighted Juliette, striking with her pale blonde hair and ice-blue eyes, the Duchess of Dalliance. She broke hearts with a single smile and was never visibly affected either at the commencement or conclusion of a love affair. Her dalliances were legendary, and some claimed her lovers fell into a swoon when Juliette but disrobed.

The prince favored the enigmatic Fallon, she of the dark eyes and raven hair, with the title Marchioness of Mystery. Whispers swirled about Fallon like a crushed velvet cape from the moment she appeared in London Society. No one knew from whence she had come, though many liked to speculate. She was a princess from a foreign land, a gypsy queen, the daughter of a fallen maharaja...

And then there was Lily—witty, lively, and burning as bright as her auburn hair. The prince dubbed Lily the Countess of Charm. There were some who said she had certainly charmed Prinny, charmed him into ejecting the formidable Mrs. Fitzherbert from his bed. Others claimed she was far too discriminating to open her boudoir to the bloated, overindulged prince.

How the beau monde loved to whisper and conjecture. And nothing intrigued like The Three Diamonds: not the tempestuous liaison between Caro Lamb and Lord Byron, not the cut of Beau Brummell's coat or the knot of his cravat, not even the ménage à trois between the Duke and Duchess of Devonshire and Lady Elizabeth Foster.

Because, you see, The Three Diamonds knew something the glittering, attention-starved nobility of the *ton* had forgotten: The only thing more fascinating than an indiscretion is discretion.

Only a diamond can cut another diamond.

One

JULIETTE, THE DUCHESS OF DALLIANCE, LAUGHED when she opened her copy of the *Morning Chronicle*. She had turned directly to the Cytherian Intelligence column, as she always did. At the top of the column was her likeness facing a likeness of the Duke of Pelham, and the story below about their secret love affair was so delightfully wicked she almost wished it were true.

She lounged in bed, rumpled silk sheets pooled about her like an ice-covered lake. She sipped chocolate, popped a bite of scone in her mouth, and studied the image of the duke.

Juliette had never been introduced to Pelham, though on occasion, she had seen him from a distance. The artist in the *Morning Chronicle* had captured his dark eyes with their arrogant slant perfectly. The brown hair was too neat. Every time she had seen Pelham, his hair had been rumpled, as though he'd just climbed from a well-used bed. But the nose—that perfect Roman nose—the sculpted cheekbones and slash of a mouth, those the artist had rendered flawlessly.

She scanned the story again, well aware it fed the appetites of those in the *ton* who would like nothing more than a real liaison between the Duchess of Dalliance and the Dangerous Duke, so called because he gave the most contemptuous glances in London, perhaps all of England. He was rich, powerful, and influential. If he opposed another lord in Parliament, the man lost all support. And socially, if the Duke of Pelham cut someone, they were ruined forever.

She glanced at his likeness a second time. The artist had not managed to capture the cloak of danger surrounding the duke. But that was something one felt more than saw when near the man. Juliette shivered. She liked powerful men, had always been attracted to them. And not always with pleasant results.

How the *ton* did hunger for their gossip, and an affair between her and the duke would be enough fodder to feed the gossipmongers for weeks.

Juliette closed the paper then opened it again, having forgotten to study her own portrait. She frowned at it and closed the paper for good. The artist had drawn her to resemble an ice queen—cold, imperial, and haughty. She couldn't fault the work. The image did resemble her, but she didn't think any of her friends would have sketched her thus. They knew her merry, carefree side.

She climbed from bed, shed her clothing, and stepped into the warm bath waiting in her dressing room. She didn't linger but washed quickly. Rosie, her lady's maid, entered dressed in white. Female servants did not wear livery, but Juliette preferred that all of her servants match. Her maids were expected to wear clothing that complemented her signature livery—pure white with ice-blue piping. The Three Diamonds all dressed their servants in white to symbolize diamonds, but each used a different accent color. Lily used sapphire-blue, and Fallon used ruby-red. Rosie offered Juliette her blue silk robe, and Juliette donned it and returned to her bedchamber. Her maid glanced at the rumpled bed. "Anything of interest in the paper today, Duchess?" Rosie went about preparing the brushes, combs, irons, and other instruments of torture on Juliette's dressing table with a practiced efficiency.

Juliette sat in a dainty chair upholstered in cream silk. "I am embroiled in a scandalous affair with the Duke of Pelham."

Rosie lifted a brush and an eyebrow. "Are you now?" The round, pleasant woman of about forty grasped Juliette's waist-length pale blonde hair and applied her brush.

"Yes. His Grace and I are thinking of eloping via Gretna Green."

"Oh, dear." Rosie secured a section of hair with a pin. "Shall I set out your traveling clothes and pack your valise?"

"Not quite yet. I think I shall wait for an introduction to His Grace first."

Rosie nodded. "Wise decision." She pinned another section of hair. "What are your plans for today, madam?"

Juliette considered. It was already afternoon. She had been at a rout the night before and had not arrived home until after four. She had several invitations for this evening but had not yet decided which to attend. She would rather have stayed home. The *ton* would be surprised to learn their most celebrated courtesan preferred a quiet night with a book to the theater and musicales. They would also be surprised to learn how seldom her bed of sin was used for more than sleeping.

Her protector, the Earl of Sinclair—better known as the Earl of Sin—was not in London at present. Lady Sinclair, his countess, was ill and unable to make the journey to Town from their country estate, Somerset. Juliette had received a letter from the countess only yesterday and planned to answer it today, inquiring as to when she might call on the countess. It might not be socially advantageous to leave London at present, but Juliette didn't really care. And she doubted Fallon or Lily cared either. Both would be eager to accompany her.

If only the *ton* knew the truth about The Three Diamonds' relationship with the Earl of Sin.

Thanks to gifts from admirers and the Earl of Sinclair, Juliette had some funds, though she was far from wealthy. Of course, she would not remain London's most celebrated courtesan if she did not spend money. She must have the most fashionable Parisian gowns, a gleaming coach, matching horses, and a bevy of servants. As did all of London, she survived on credit. The mantua makers were eager to dress her because they craved an audience for their work and knew Juliette attracted attention. Every merchant clamored to be the one who dressed or furnished the horses or carriage or jewels for the Duchess of Dalliance. Few ever called in her markers, yet she felt the weight of the debts she owed.

She could not survive on credit forever. She was almost thirty. And there was always someone younger, someone prettier, someone more charming. Sinclair could not masquerade as her lover forever. His wife's poor health meant he rarely traveled to London anymore, and Juliette didn't want another protector. She accepted gifts and tokens from admirers who hoped to woo their way into her bed, and she had considered taking one as a lover. But she didn't want to *endure* a man's caresses. She didn't want to have to close her eyes and pretend he or she were someone else.

She wanted to fall in love. Forever.

She wanted a husband. She supposed that, as a divorced woman, she should swear off matrimony for good. But she had always been an optimist at heart.

Rosie was looking at her expectantly, and Juliette said, "I think I shall ride in Hyde Park." That was where she would likely find Fallon and Lily, and she was eager to speak with them privately—not that Rotten Row at four in the afternoon was private, but at least they would be able to speak without being overheard. And the *ton* would salivate at the chance to see The Three Diamonds together, heads bent in conference. Juliette smiled.

"Very good, Duchess," Rose answered. "The blue riding habit, then?"

"Yes. And do remember the hat I wear with it."

"Yes, Duchess. I know the perfect coiffure to set it off." And, true to her word, Rosie worked her magic.

Several hours later, after Juliette had been poked and prodded, powdered and perfumed, she drove her gig along the South Carriage Drive of Rotten Row, nodding to those with whom she was acquainted.

Some even nodded back.

She was careful not to acknowledge the gentlemen of her acquaintance if they were accompanied by wives, sisters, or fiancées. They would not thank her for causing them marital or familial discord. But she did stop to chat with several men riding alone. All the while, she could feel the fiery glares of the ladies of the *ton* burning into her back.

They hated her, and she understood why. It wasn't because she was bedding their husbands—she could all but guarantee she was not. It was because she had power they didn't. She was welcomed where they were banned, could speak when they were silenced, possessed knowledge when they were kept ignorant.

They hated her because they did not know where their husbands went when they bid them farewell of an evening. And because the wives didn't know, they hated Juliette because she did.

Juliette wondered if the women knew how much most of the men simply wanted to talk to her. Of course, they wanted an entrée into her boudoir, but if she was not amenable, they were more than happy to talk. They talked about their wives and children, their failures and successes, their plans for the future. They felt comfortable speaking with Juliette, felt they could trust her.

She was a friend in a time when most marriages were all but arranged. And that friendship was the real secret behind the appeal of the courtesan.

Juliette sat straighter when she spotted her closest

friends, surrounded as usual by male admirers. Under a grove of trees, Fallon, the Marchioness of Mystery, and Lily, the Countess of Charm, stood with parasols open but tilted to ensure their faces could be seen.

They wore riding habits, like she. Fallon's was a bold red, which offset her dark coloring, and Lily's was apple green so as not to clash with her auburn hair. As Juliette neared, her friends spotted her and smiled with genuine warmth. There were few true friendships among Cyprians. One's position was too precarious, too easily undermined by another of her ilk. But Juliette, Fallon, and Lily had been friends before they had become The Three Diamonds.

And as the three mistresses of the Earl of Sin, they had another bond, as well.

"You shall be applying for membership in the Four-in-Hand Club next," Lily said, speaking of the gentleman's club for superb drivers.

Juliette waved her hand. "Not I. I couldn't abide the strict requirements for dress."

Lily and Fallon's mounts grazed on the lawn. Nearby, the waters of the Serpentine rippled in the breeze, and a few ducks quacked as they waddled into the shallow water. All three women could seat a horse splendidly, but Juliette was also an excellent driver and liked to tool about in her lightweight gig in fair weather.

She slowed her conveyance, hesitating slightly when she noted one of the gentlemen was the Earl of Darlington, known as the "Darling of the *Ton*" because of his good looks and affable personality. He had been pursuing her for the last six months, and though she had made it clear in every way she knew how that his attentions would not come to fruition, he had not given up the chase.

The other man was Mr. Heyward. He was the son of a baron and known for lavish parties. Juliette had been to dozens of his routs.

Before the gig had fully stopped, Darlington was at her side, ready to hand her down. "Duchess, I had hoped to see you here!"

"Thank you, Lord Darlington." She accepted his proffered hand then released it as quickly as possible. She did not want to encourage him. One of Darlington's grooms stepped forward and took her horse's bridle, leading the animal in a slow walk to keep the beast's muscles warm.

Juliette watched idly then opened her parasol and stood beside Fallon, who moved aside to make room for her. The two usually contrived to stand beside each other, as Juliette's pale coloring contrasted nicely with Fallon's darker complexion and hair. The effect was striking.

Lily, with her auburn hair and jade-green eyes, was striking without any assistance.

"Good day, Duchess," Mr. Heyward said, tipping his hat.

"Good day, Mr. Heyward. Fallon. Lily." She smiled at her friends. "What a splendid spring day! I don't know how anyone can abide being inside on such a day."

"I couldn't agree more," Fallon said. Her voice was low and husky.

"I do love spring," Lily said, angling her face to the sun.

"Did you see the *Morning Chronicle*, Duchess?" Mr. Heyward asked.

Juliette took a steadying breath before answering. She was certain she would be asked this question a hundred if not a thousand times before the day was through. "I did." No use denying it. Everyone would know she was lying.

"Is it true?" Mr. Heyward asked. The man had no shame.

Juliette curved her lips in a secretive smile. "I'll never tell."

"Of course it's not true," Darlington said, his voice edged with annoyance. "Pelham arrived in London only last night."

"The papers claimed Juliette and the duke were secluded in the country," Lily said. Juliette had noticed she liked to antagonize Darlington when the opportunity arose. "Your observation only lends fuel to that speculation."

Darlington shook his head. His brown hair curled over his collar, and his cravat was askew, and Juliette thought—not for the first time—he needed a nursemaid more than a mistress.

"Anyone who knows Pelham knows what utter rot that is," Darlington said, tapping his walking stick to emphasize his words. "He came to Town solely for the opening of Parliament. The man has no interest in courting or elopements. The man has no interest in any type of diversion. If he makes an appearance at even one Society ball, I will stand on my head."

"I shall hold you to that promise, Lord Darlington," Juliette said.

He bowed to her. "I would expect nothing less, Duchess."

"Surely he will attend Prinny's fete at Carlton House tomorrow night," Fallon said, her smoky voice cutting off whatever Heyward had been about to interject. "It opens the Season."

"I would not hold my breath, Marchioness."

"Oh, I never do, Lord Darlington."

He bowed again to Lily. "Good day, Countess." He took Juliette's hand and kissed her glove. "Until we meet again, Duchess."

She nodded and pulled her hand back then watched as he strode toward his horse—a fine gray gelding—mounted, and rode on. He signaled his groom to continue walking her horse, and Juliette had to admit Darlington was courteous. She wondered just how well the earl did know the Duke of Pelham. She had never had any designs on Pelham, though she wouldn't mind if he took an interest in her. The *ton* wanted to see them together so badly, and she did like to give the public what they wanted. Of course, nothing would ever come of it. Pelham wouldn't want a woman with her reputation as his wife.

"I trust I shall see the three of you at the prince's tomorrow night," Heyward said.

"You shall," Lily answered. "And be prepared to be stunned."

Heyward clapped his hands. "Stunned? Really?"

Lily nodded, obviously pleased. She loved surprises.

"I don't suppose you will let me in on the secret," Mr. Heyward hedged.

"Not even a tiny hint," Fallon said.

"You are too cruel."

"And that's why you love us."

When he had taken his leave, Lily, Fallon, and Juliette glanced at one another. "Is your gown ready?" Juliette asked Fallon. It was a given that Lily, who loved fashion and planning grand entrances, had her dress pressed and ready to wear a week ago.

"I have one last fitting with Madame Durand," Fallon answered.

"As do I," Juliette said, linking her arm with Fallon, who linked hers with Lily. The three strolled on the lawn, quite aware of the fetching picture they made.

"What do you think of this business with Pelham?" Lily asked. "It's certainly made Darlington jealous."

"Heaven save us," Juliette said. "He's a puppy. A boy."

"Pelham's no puppy," Fallon added, pausing to study a wildflower. "If you could snag him, it would be the coup of the Season."

"I hear he's soon to be betrothed," Lily said.

Juliette had not heard this, and she frowned.

"That's of no consequence." Fallon squeezed Juliette's hand. "When have men ever been faithful to their betrothed, much less their wives?"

Juliette appreciated Fallon's efforts to reassure her. "You both know there's nothing behind these rumors. I've never even been introduced to Pelham."

"Perhaps he is the one spreading the rumors," Lily said, smiling at the Marquess of Cholmondeley, who was approaching on horseback.

Juliette paused as the marquess drew nearer. "I doubt it. I'd be more inclined to believe the papers fabricated the entire tale to sell more copies."

"And who cares if they did?" Fallon said. The

marquess slowed, and they both waved Lily away, knowing she would want to speak with him. She gave them a quick flick of her hand and tripped lightly to the path where he waited.

Fallon turned to Juliette. "You know my theory—all talk is good talk, whether it's true or not."

Juliette wasn't quite certain she agreed. She feared so much had been made of her tête-à-tête with the duke that if she disappointed now, she might fall out of favor. And that would make life difficult. Her finances were not yet quite what she hoped, and she did owe rather large sums to several modistes—including Madame Durand—who had supplied her wardrobe for the Season.

Perhaps she should begin looking for another protector.

"Come." Fallon turned her and started back. "Why don't we go together to the dress fitting? Then we can see if Lily's plan is as spectacular as usual."

Juliette nodded. A dress fitting was exactly what she needed to alleviate the vague unease lingering in the back of her mind.

≈

The Duke of Pelham strolled into his club at precisely twenty past six. He liked to eat at half past. That was an early supper by Town standards, but Pelham didn't care. He had always eaten at half past, he was hungry at half past, and he wasn't going to gnaw on his fist in order to wait until a more fashionable hour.

"Your usual table, Your Grace?" the club's steward asked as soon as the duke stepped through White's doors at 37–38 St. James's Street.

"Please." He handed Harrow his gloves, walking stick, and top hat, and the steward proceeded to hand those to a footman, who handed them to another footman. Harrow assisted in removing Pelham's great-coat, and there followed the same ritual handing of the garment from one man to another. Pelham pulled on the sleeves of his blue tailcoat and made certain his watch fob had not tangled. He was not fastidious about fashion—he was no Beau Brummell—but Pelham insisted on shined boots and a well-cut coat made by Weston.

"We have leg of lamb with potatoes and a white soup tonight, Your Grace," Harrow said as he led the duke to his table, which was situated in a particularly good corner of the dining room. The table was close to the hearth and afforded a view of the men coming and going. Pelham didn't know who sat at the table when he was in the country—he was certain it wasn't allowed to sit fallow—but for the moment it looked exactly as he had left it.

"Very good." Pelham took the chair pulled out for him by one of the waiters.

"We also have an excellent French sherry tonight. It arrived this morning." Harrow signaled to a footman to bring Pelham a copy of the *Times*. Pelham accepted the paper but shook his head at the offered sherry.

"Port for me, Harrow. English port."

Harrow nodded. "Very good, Your Grace." And he departed, leaving Pelham to peruse the *Times* in peace.

At least until Darlington plopped into the chair across from him. "Predictable as ever," Darlington said, lifting his glass of what appeared to be sherry.

Pelham raised the paper and tried to focus on an article about a revision to the current tax on corn. He also hoped to block out the sight of Darlington's bright green waistcoat.

"I don't suppose you've seen the *Morning Chronicle*," Darlington said, pushing down the top of Pelham's paper with his hand. Pelham frowned at him. That was usually enough to scare most men off, but Darlington was oblivious to the danger he was in.

"I don't read the *Morning Chronicle*. It's utter rubbish." Pelham raised his paper again.

"Thought not. Then you don't know you and the duchess are having a torrid affair."

How Pelham wished Darlington had sat on his other side, the side with his bad ear. Then he wouldn't have been able to hear him. But he had heard Darlington's ludicrous statement and now must make some response. Pelham lowered the paper. "What *are* you going on about, man?"

Darlington smiled, and Pelham had the urge to hit him with the paper. "I knew it wasn't true," Darlington said triumphantly.

"Knew what wasn't true?"

A waiter, closely supervised by the steward, arrived with the soup and the port, and Pelham set the paper on the table. Darlington leaned over, took a good whiff of the soup, and said, "Oh, that looks good. I'll have some of that myself."

"Very good, my lord." Harrow nodded to the waiter, who scurried away.

Darlington leaned over to smell the soup again, and

Pelham scowled at him. "By all means, find a spoon and have a taste."

"Mighty generous of you, Pelham," Darlington said, taking Pelham's own spoon and doing just that. Pelham sat back in disgust. He checked his pocket watch. It was now twenty-five minutes until seven, five minutes past dinner, and Darlington was eating his soup.

Darlington looked up from the bowl. "Quite good. Want some?"

Pelham ground his teeth. "No, no. You go ahead."

Darlington did. Pelham raised his paper again just as a hand clapped him on the shoulder. "Heard you were back in Town, Pelham." Warrick Fitzhugh, third son of the illustrious Earl of Winthorpe, sat in the unoccupied chair beside Darlington. In the future, Pelham was going to have to speak to Harrow about removing the additional chairs at his table.

"Fitzhugh," Pelham said, setting the *Times* aside again. Unlike Darlington, Fitzhugh's waistcoat was a reserved black with stripes. Also, unlike Darlington, Fitzhugh generally made sense when he spoke, which was—thank God—not overly much. Pelham had been at Eton with Warrick and admired the man's intelligence as well as his prowess with his fists, a necessary skill when finding one's place at Eton. Rumors circulated that Fitzhugh had worked with the Foreign Office during the war, perhaps as a spy. Distasteful business, that, but Pelham didn't believe every rumor.

Still, Warrick had a devious look about him.

"Hello, old boy," Darlington said to Fitzhugh

through mouthfuls of Pelham's soup. Pelham could not—and he had tried on numerous occasions—remember where or when he had met Darlington. It seemed one day the man was present, and Pelham hadn't been able to rid himself of the earl yet.

Truth be told, he hadn't tried overly much. Andrew was rather amusing, in his way.

And when he wasn't eating Pelham's soup.

As though summoned by that thought, Harrow reappeared with another bowl of soup. Without pausing to glance at Darlington, he set it in front of Pelham then motioned to the waiter to place the port and leg of lamb on the table, as well. "Will there be anything else, Your Grace?"

Pelham opened his mouth to say no, but Darlington interrupted him. "Another glass of sherry, Harrow."

"Very good, my lord. Anything else, Your Grace?"

Pelham looked at Fitzhugh. "I don't suppose you want anything."

"A glass of port, Harrow—since Pelham is paying."

"Very good, sir." Harrow signaled, the requested drinks were delivered, and Pelham was finally left in peace—almost peace—with his supper. He lifted his knife and fork.

"So this business in the papers with the duchess," Darlington said. Pelham lowered his fork again, but not before noting Fitzhugh's brows rose with interest.

"It's utter rot," Darlington continued. "Correct?" Darlington would one day be the Duke of Ravenscroft, but Pelham thought he had a lot to learn about stoicism before claimed the title. Pelham's father had drilled him in the tenets of his duty since birth. A duke was never uncertain, never faltered, never showed emotion. And a duke was most certainly never late. He resisted the urge to check his pocket watch again.

Pelham set his knife on the table and looked at Fitzhugh. "What the devil is he going on about? What duchess? What paper?"

Fitzhugh's face remained impassive, but Pelham could have sworn he was enjoying the moment. "You've been mentioned in the Cytherian Intelligence column of late. The writers of the *Morning Chronicle* have you paired with the Duchess of Dalliance."

"The who?"

"Don't pretend you don't know who she is," Darlington said, sipping his sherry. "Even a country bumpkin like you has heard of The Three Diamonds."

"Are you speaking of courtesans?" He should have known. Darlington was always chasing after some woman or other.

"Now you're following," Darlington said, raising his glass.

"Then why do you keep calling her duchess?"

Fitzhugh raised a hand before Darlington could speak again. Thank God. "The Prince Regent dubbed Juliette the Duchess of Dalliance. That's the one you're rumored to be madly in love with."

Pelham stared absently at the fireplace blazing behind Fitzhugh. On the mantel, an ancient clock ticked away the hours. Above it, a painting of a hunting scene in greens and browns dominated the dark-paneled wall. He thought he vaguely remembered glimpses of these Three Diamonds from afar. He tried to picture this Juliette. "She's the dark one?" he asked.

"No. That's the Marchioness of Mystery," Darlington informed him.

Pelham shook his head. Had the prince nothing better to do than invent titles? "Then she's the pale one?"

"Right," Fitzhugh said.

"I'd hardly call her pale," Darlington corrected. "She's blonde, but her complexion has quite the pinkish quality. Most fetching."

"Perhaps the papers should pair her with you," Pelham said, lifting his spoon and tasting his soup.

"He'd like nothing better," Fitzhugh said, swirling his port. "But the duchess won't have him."

Darlington scowled at Fitzhugh, and Pelham paused in dipping his spoon in the soup. Now this was interesting. He couldn't remember ever seeing Darlington scowl.

"Why won't she have you?" Pelham said, tasting the soup again. "She's a courtesan. I didn't realize they were overly choosy."

Darlington shook his head. "She's one of The Three Diamonds, Pelham. She picks her own lovers, and she's *extremely* choosy."

"And why don't you make the cut? Not rich enough?"

"No." Darlington looked away.

"Too ugly?" Fitzhugh asked with a laugh.

"Not compared to some," Darlington said with a pointed look at Fitzhugh, who shrugged.

"I'm not the one who can't get a woman."

"I will have her," Darlington protested a bit too loudly. "I simply need to prove that…" He mumbled the last.

"Say again?" Pelham asked.

"That I don't need a nursemaid."

Pelham lifted his napkin, covering his smile. Fitzhugh wasn't so kind. He laughed loudly. "Is that what she said?"

"Oh, stubble it."

"Listen, Darlington," Pelham said. "I have no designs on your pale duchess. I'd venture to say, she planted those stories in the *Morning Chronicle* herself."

"She's not like that," Darlington protested.

Pelham almost felt sorry for the man, besotted as he was. "Of course she is. Probably needs to be set in her place."

"I like her place," Darlington grumbled.

"Find someone else," Pelham suggested.

Darlington gave him a look of incomprehension. "I can't simply forget her. I'm in love with her."

"Oh, good God." Fitzhugh rolled his eyes and finished his port.

"I don't expect you two to understand. You have hearts of stone."

"That's not true," Pelham argued. "In fact, I have reason to celebrate tonight. I'm about to sign betrothal papers. In a few short months, I will have my own duchess."

"Lady Elizabeth accepted your suit?" Fitzhugh asked.

Pelham lifted his port and toasted.

"Lady Elizabeth." Darlington snorted. "You're not in love with Lady Elizabeth."

"You know my rule," Pelham told him.

"Ah, yes, Pelham's Cardinal Rule. Never fall in love. It's complete rubbish."

"It's sensible. Men and women in love make poor decisions and act like fools." He gave Darlington a pointed look. "It serves no purpose."

"But how can you marry a woman you do not love?" Darlington asked.

"I feel quite warmly toward her."

"You feel warmly toward the estate offered in her dowry. It borders one of yours in Yorkshire."

"That does add to her appeal," Pelham conceded, unabashed. After all, what was marriage but a business arrangement? One might as well make the most advantageous arrangement one could. He had not become the wealthy, influential sixth Duke of Pelham because his ancestors went about marrying commoners or—God forbid—courtesans. Lady Elizabeth was the daughter of a marquess. She was accomplished, intelligent, and dowered with a critical piece of land. She was not overly pretty, but she had a pleasing aspect. More important, they agreed on essential matters. They both liked routine. They liked to live quietly and with dignity. They avoided the theatrics and goings-on of the beau monde Darlington and his ilk so relished. Marrying Lady Elizabeth would guarantee Pelham a staid, settled, stately future.

And that was exactly what he wanted. And exactly what he would have once he took care of one small, distasteful detail.

Two

Eliza knew she was a fool. She shouldn't have come back; only a fool would return. But she didn't know how else to stop the shaking. She didn't know how else to staunch the gnawing hunger inside her. Neither food nor drink could satisfy it.

Only the game.

She gave her wrap to the squinting majordomo of Lucifer's Lair and strolled to her favorite hazard table. She could all but feel the eyes of the other patrons upon her. They knew who she was. She prayed to God they didn't know what she had done.

She prayed to the devil Lucifer didn't suspect her.

She spotted Lucifer at one of the faro tables and almost turned back. If she had any sense, she would run and keep running. Instead, she continued on her trek, as though guided by an unseen force. She couldn't resist the lure of the table, of the game.

Lucifer's dark brown eyes—so dark they were all but black—followed her. He didn't turn his head—framed by luxurious waves of black hair with a distinctive white streak—when she moved out of his line of vision, but she knew he tracked her every move.

She stopped at the hazard table, and Raphael, her favorite setter, asked, "Would you like to join the game, madam? Mr. Abernathy has just thrown out, and Mr. Canby is the next caster."

"Thank you. I think I shall simply watch." That was a lie. She would play, but she wanted to watch Canby first.

Canby put down a fiver and said, "Six." He lifted the dice.

"Six is the main," Raphael repeated. "The bet is five pounds."

Canby tossed the dice, and Eliza felt her heart beat faster. She hadn't even bet on the roll, and she could already feel her blood rushing. The first die rolled to a stop—a one. The second die teetered then turned up a two.

"Three," Raphael announced and scooped up the fiver. "Would you like to cast again, Mr. Canby?"

Canby turned to her. "Perhaps the lady might like a go?"

But before Eliza could nod her agreement, Gabriel, Lucifer's most trusted man, stood at her right arm. "My lady, if you would accompany me, please."

It wasn't a request. Dear God, she should not have come. She had no choice but to swallow and nod acquiescence, to follow Gabriel into the mouth of hell, Lucifer's private chambers.

A trickle of perspiration teased a slow path down her back. It was suddenly very warm in the gambling hell, made more so by the gazes upon her. But when she looked at the men watching her, none would meet her gaze. Her stomach churned, and her breath came in short pants. She could not tell if the feeling was excitement or fear.

But then that had always been her problem—fear produced excitement—and no one provoked either fear or excitement like Lucifer.

She followed Gabriel up the steep, narrow stairs to the floor above the gaming hell, where Lucifer's private rooms lay. Gabriel looked every bit the angel from whence he'd taken his name. He had long blond hair, a slim, chiseled face, and a smooth, melodic voice. He was too perfect, too polished, and he made her nervous. She had been to Lucifer's private rooms before and knew the way. But would Gabriel take her to Lucifer's library or his bedchamber? If the library, she faced certain death.

Of course, the bedchamber was little better.

Gabriel paused in front of the door to the bedchamber, opened it, and moved aside to admit Eliza. She gave him a smile full of confidence she didn't feel and stepped inside. The door closed in her face, and she heard the key turn in the lock.

Trapped.

She put her hand on the thick wooden door, painted black to match the décor in the rest of the room. The walls, the drapes, the furnishings—all were appointed in black silk. Only the bed, a monstrous thing, displayed any color. It was adorned in blood-red silk. She had lain on that bed, naked and trembling, feeling like a sacrificial lamb as Lucifer knelt over her.

And she had left him sleeping on that slippery scarlet silk. She'd walked away—but not empty-handed.

What had she done? Now she rested her forehead on the door beside her hand. The wood was warm to the touch.

Something cold and hard clenched her bare shoulder. "I didn't think I'd see you again."

Eliza stifled a scream but just barely. She had forgotten Lucifer's partiality for hidden entrances and exits. She had not even heard him enter. She forced herself to smile, even though she felt her lips quiver. "You know I can't stay away."

"Why do I have the feeling it's not me that keeps you coming back?"

"What else is there?"

"Indeed." He pried her hand from the door, turned her palm up, and kissed it. She sighed despite herself. "I've missed you," he murmured, looking at her from under those sooty black lashes.

"And I you," she breathed as he swept her into his arms. His mouth descended on hers, and his hands were rough on her bottom as he lifted her and pushed her against the black silk of the wall.

Eliza felt his fingers skate up her bare thigh and surrendered to the assault. Did he know? Was he simply toying with her before killing her?

No, he couldn't know. She'd been so careful, so meticulous.

She felt him shudder, felt his teeth sink into her flesh. She was always surprised he was human enough to climax.

He put his cheek next to hers. His skin was warm,

his breath hot against her ear. "Now that the pleasant-ries are over, I think it time we spoke of the diamonds."

Eliza jerked, but his hands held her fast, and she cringed as he laughed—long, low, and malevolent.

Three

JULIETTE COVERED A YAWN AND NODDED TO HER sleepy-eyed butler as he opened the door of her town house. To the east, the sun rose, streaking the sky with pinks and oranges. For once, London's omnipresent fog had fled.

"Duchess." Hollows nodded at her, closing the door. As was customary, the butler did not wear livery, but Hollows always managed to look distinguished in black with a white rose on his lapel. His height and stern expression gave him a dignified appearance.

"I'm exhausted," Juliette said, turning so he could take her wrap. "I want to sleep for a week."

"Yes, Duchess. Shall I rouse Mary?"

Juliette blinked, momentarily confused, and then remembered she'd given Rosie and most of the servants the night off. Tomorrow night—tonight, she amended—was the prince's ball, and she wanted them well rested before her preparations began.

But that was later. Now she wanted to sleep. She should not have stayed out so late, but the play had been witty, Vauxhall Gardens filled with the most entertaining men and women in London, and before she had realized, it was nearly morning. Rosie would have a difficult task ahead of her if Juliette was to look stunning at Carlton House tonight.

"Yes, Hollows, do rouse Mary and send her to my chamber." Juliette felt bad about waking the girl—she, Hollows, and Cook were the only servants not given the night off—but Juliette did not relish sleeping in her stays and gown, and she could not get them off by herself. Once she was undressed, she would send Mary back to bed and finish her toilette on her own.

Juliette started up the steps. "Off to bed with you, Hollows," she said over her shoulder. "I shan't need you for several hours."

"Yes, Duchess."

Juliette's feet felt like cannonballs—not that she had ever touched a cannonball, but she imagined they were impossibly heavy. Why had she agreed to so many dances? No, she had never been good at denying herself pleasure when it was to be had, and tonight the music had been lively, the gentlemen agreeable, and her spirits high. She could have danced until noon.

Thank God she hadn't. One day she would learn to think of the consequences before she acted.

She stepped onto the first-floor landing and started for the stairs to the second floor, where her bedchamber was located. The doors to the drawing room were closed, but Juliette paused when she heard a sound from within. She stopped, pressed her ear to the doors, and listened.

Silence.

She shook her head. She was so tired, her mind was deceiving her.

She started for the steps again and heard an unmistakable thump. Whirling, she did not hesitate but ran straight to the banister. "Hollows!" Her heart hammered in her chest. "Hollows! C—"

A hand clamped over her mouth, and she was propelled backward, losing one slipper as she was dragged.

Oliver.

He had come for her, as he'd vowed he would. She'd grown complacent, dismissing her additional footmen for the night. How could she have been so foolish? Now he would kill her. Hollows, who was rather hard of hearing, would never even hear her scream.

Juliette kicked and clawed, but she couldn't escape. The man—she assumed it was a man because the hands were so large—had grasped her about the waist to haul her back more quickly. His hand on her mouth tightened and began to cut off her air. She tried to gasp in a breath as the drawing-room doors slammed, and a man she did not know stepped before them.

"Hello, Duchess," he said.

She blinked and swallowed, still trying to catch her breath.

It wasn't Oliver. *Thank God.*

The man was dressed stylishly in black. His hair was the color of midnight with a streak as white as the pearls at her throat. He smiled at her, but his eyes were dark and menacing. Juliette thought perhaps she might reserve her thanks a few more moments.

"I'd like to have a brief chat," the man said.

"Gabriel, she's turning purple. Do lift your hand. You won't scream, will you, Duchess?"

She shook her head, having every intention of screaming as soon as this Gabriel removed his paw from her mouth. Even if Hollows didn't hear, the cook or Mary might.

"Good, because if you do, you won't like the consequences—for you and whoever comes to your aid."

Gabriel removed his hand, and Juliette kept her mouth clamped shut. Something about the man in black made her believe he could make her very sorry indeed if she did not do as he bid. She had been made very sorry before for disobedience and, subsequently, had become quite good at doing as she was told. For a decade, she had been her own independent woman, but now she felt seventeen again. All her survival instincts resurfaced.

She stepped away from the man called Gabriel and cut her eyes to take in the room. The usually stylish, immaculate room was in complete shambles. The expensive drapes had been ripped to ribbons, the newly upholstered chair cushions spilled their filling, antique lamps were overturned, and the heavy drawers scattered their contents on the rug.

Escape was her only salvation. She had to find a means to escape. But she couldn't allow these men to know she was afraid or planned to run. The punishment would come faster then.

"Looking for something?" she croaked.

The man in black smiled again, and this time it almost reached his obsidian-colored eyes. "Very perceptive, Duchess. May I call you Duchess?" He moved smoothly to a toppled chair, righted it, and sat as though he was perfectly at ease. As though this were his home, not hers.

Juliette bristled, but she was too adept at hiding her emotions to show it. The Countess of Sinclair had taught her well.

"I prefer Mrs. Clifton," she said, though no one had called her that in years. Oliver had used that name, and she'd come to hate it. But it seemed appropriate at this moment.

"Why don't I call you Juliette? It seems fitting, as we are going to be good friends, Juliette."

Her throat tightened. She had to get out of here. "And what should I call you?" she asked coolly.

"Lucifer, of course. Do you know what I want to discuss, Juliette?"

She shook her head. Dear God, she prayed he wasn't going to rape her. Her mind was racing, trying to place him. But he wasn't familiar to her at all. She didn't think she could have spurned him. She would have remembered, and she was always gentle with those whose attentions she rejected.

Could Oliver have sent him?

No, her former husband liked to do his own work. "Actually, I don't know what you wish to discuss, Lucifer," Juliette replied with strained politeness. "I'm afraid you have me at a disadvantage."

"Oh, come, come. We are friends. We can be honest with each other."

She shook her head, cutting her gaze to the drawing-room doors. If she ran, could she make it in time? Even as the thought occurred to her,

Gabriel—large and blond—stepped in front of the doors and crossed his arms.

"I am being honest with you," she said to Lucifer, panic rising in her throat now. "I don't know you." But even as she spoke she could see he didn't believe her. She could see she was doomed.

Lucifer raised a brow. "But *I* know *you*, and I know you have something of mine. Now, are you going to tell me about the diamonds, or am I going to have to find more creative methods of loosening your tongue?"

Juliette tried to steady her hands, but when she set her tea cup on the tray on her bed, the china rattled. She was so tired, and yet every time she closed her eyes, her mind raced with what ifs and should haves.

"Drink your tea, sweetie," Lily said. She was seated on one side of Juliette's bed, and Fallon was on the other. Juliette had sent Hollows to fetch them as soon as Lucifer and Gabriel had gone. The butler had wanted to fetch the magistrate, but Juliette refused. Lucifer had been rather explicit about what would happen if she went public about their so-called discussion.

"She doesn't need more tea." Fallon rose hastily. "She's had three cups. What she needs is three fingers of brandy."

Juliette shook her head. "No. What I need is sleep, but I'm too overwrought. I keep thinking about that man—Lucifer."

"And you're certain Oliver didn't send him?"

"Oliver had no part in this. This Lucifer didn't care about me. He kept hounding me about diamonds.

I cannot understand why he should think I would have them."

"Are you certain you don't want us to send for the magistrate?" Lily asked.

"Yes! I told you no magistrate!"

"But what if this Lucifer returns?" Fallon asked, pouring herself a splash of brandy from the decanter on the dainty table across from Juliette's bed. "Are you certain you convinced him you don't have the diamonds?"

"I'm not certain of anything. I tried to keep my composure, to reason with him and explain, but when he threatened to pull out my fingernails, I broke down."

"Of course you did." Lily hugged her. "That man was horrible and obviously has you mistaken with someone else."

Juliette shook her head. "No. He knew who I was, and he thought I stole his diamonds."

Fallon, who was an accomplished pickpocket, laughed. "You've never stolen anything in your life."

"That's what I told him. But he kept insisting we were friends, and I could tell him the truth." She shuddered. Juliette saw the look pass between Lily and Fallon, and shook her head. "No. Whatever you two just decided, no."

"I think you should stay home tonight," Lily said. "I think we should all send our regrets to Prinny."

"No." Juliette began to rise.

"You are in no state to attend a ball," Fallon argued, finishing her brandy. "You haven't slept, and you're upset. Let's stay home tonight, and the three of us will travel to Somerville tomorrow. I know the countess will rally when she sees us."

"I cannot miss the ball." Juliette stood, and her legs wobbled underneath her. She clenched her jaw and steadied herself.

"It's just a ball," Lily argued, taking Juliette's elbow. "There will be a hundred more."

Juliette shook her head. "Not like this one. The entire *ton* is expecting me to be there. They want to see what happens when Pelham and I are in the same room."

"You heard Lord Darlington yesterday," Lily argued. "The duke is unlikely even to attend."

"And if he disappoints," Juliette said, ringing for Rosie, "the beau monde will forgive him. If I disappoint, I'll swiftly fall from favor."

"Nonsense," Fallon said, waving to Rosie to wait outside while they finished their discussion. "If you don't attend, it will only fuel speculation."

Juliette gave her a level look, and Fallon notched her chin up. Juliette glanced at Lily, but Lily was looking at the toe of her pink slipper. "You know I'm right," Juliette said. "Both of you know I'm right. We three balance on a precipice. On one edge is our hard-won notoriety. It pays our bills—along with some help from Sinclair, which none of us wants to continue to accept. On the other edge is ruin. I, for one, don't relish spending the next dozen years hiking up my skirts in a back alley for any man with a shilling."

"We'd never let that happen to you," Lily said, green eyes burning with indignation.

"Then you'll be in the alley next to mine. We three have worked too hard to get where we are to lose it all now. I'm not going to let you ruin yourself for me, and I'm not going to allow some man who calls himself Lucifer to control me." And as soon as she ceased shaking, she would mean those brave words. She'd been controlled by a man once before and had vowed never again.

"At least have Hollows hire extra footmen for protection," Fallon suggested.

"It's already done, and I do think it's a good idea to quit the city for a short while. A sojourn to Somerville is exactly what I need."

Lily clapped her hands. "Splendid! I have the perfect dress to wear in the country."

"You would be thinking of fashion at a time like this." Fallon rolled her eyes.

"Speaking of fashion, we have a lot of work to do if we're going to dazzle the *ton* tonight. Rosie!" The door opened, and Rosie poked her head in. "I hope you can do something about these dark circles under my eyes."

"In no time, I'll have you looking like you slept twelve hours, Duchess."

Lily crossed to Fallon and linked arms. "I believe this is our cue to take our leave."

Fallon shook her head. "You, Duchess, are extremely stubborn."

Juliette smiled as she seated herself before her dressing table. "No more than you, Marchioness. I shall see both of you this evening."

"My coach will be here at half-past nine," Lily said. "We must arrive together to ensure the full effect."

"Then I shall see you at half-past nine."

When Lily and Fallon were gone, Juliette closed her eyes.

"I'm going to send for water for a warm bath," Rosie said. "Maybe you can sleep after you've soaked for a time."

"There's no time to sleep," Juliette said, stifling a yawn. "I have to look ravishing."

"Oh, you let me worry about that, Duchess. In the meantime, you rest in the bath. I think we'll scent it with lavender…"

Rosie left to fetch the water, and Juliette took a deep breath. Every muscle in her body ached. She did not know how she would make it through the ball tonight, but at least she'd have Lily and Fallon to support her. She closed her eyes again and shivered when Lucifer's dark eyes flashed in her mind.

If you're lying to me, Juliette, I'll kill you. Slowly. Painfully. One way or another, I will have those diamonds.

Four

"I HAVE SOMETHING FOR YOU," PELHAM SAID TO Lady Elizabeth.

"Oh?" She was seated demurely on the blue-velvet chaise longue in his drawing room, studying an antique Greek vase, which she held in her hands. She very carefully set the vase on the side table, her fingers lingering on the edge for a moment, then rose. He held out his hand to reveal the small wooden box inlaid with gold. "This was my mother's." He opened the box to show her a dainty gold necklace with a teardrop-shaped diamond attached.

"Oh!" Her hands flew to her mouth. Pelham gestured for her to turn around and secured the necklace on Lady Elizabeth's throat. He moved a dark curl of her hair aside to fasten the necklace and frowned at the mark he saw. "What did you say happened to your neck?"

Lady Elizabeth stiffened, but when she turned to him, she smiled and waved her hand dismissively. "My maid burned me with the curling tongs. I do think I shall have to let her go."

"I should think so."

Lady Elizabeth crossed to the mirror above the fireplace and turned from side to side, brushing her hair so it covered the mark on her neck again. "This necklace is simply beautiful, Your Grace. You say it was your mother's?"

Pelham nodded. He was not the sentimental sort, but his mother had died when he was ten, and the necklace was one of the few mementos he had of her. "Yes. My father gave it to her on the occasion of their engagement."

Lady Elizabeth's gloved fingers brushed the diamond reverently, and she gave him a tremulous smile in the mirror. "And now you are giving it to me as an engagement gift. I will treasure it always."

"Yes." Pelham cleared his throat, worried Lady Elizabeth might begin to cry. Emotional women made him nervous. He had thought Lady Elizabeth a bit more reserved in her expressions. He hoped he had not been mistaken.

He offered her his arm and led her toward the vestibule where a bevy of servants awaited them armed with hats, coats, and all the accoutrements necessary for attendance at a ball at Carlton House. Pelham donned his greatcoat and waited while Lady Elizabeth was helped into her pelisse, had her hair and hat fluffed, and was generally fussed over. Pelham thought he would go mad if he were ever subjected to so much fawning.

Finally, she was pronounced acceptable, and he led her to the waiting coach. A row of liveried footmen lined the walk, and the most senior escorted the duke and his future duchess into the coach. Pelham handed Lady Elizabeth up and paused to observe his horses. He had four matching blacks. They were sleek, high-strung beasts, and their coats shone in the flickering lamplight. The crest on his carriage was scarlet and gold, and he felt proud to belong to such a long, distinguished line of dukes.

Satisfied with what he saw, Pelham entered the carriage and took the seat facing backward. The soft velvet squabs reminded him he would rather be reclining in his library than dashing to Prinny's affair. Pelham could not abide the Prince Regent. The man was the biggest fool in England, if not the whole of Europe. Pelham found fools intolerable, but even worse than a fool—in Pelham's estimation—was a spendthrift. Prinny had huge debts and had even come to Pelham for a loan on several occasions. And though it was difficult to refuse the future sovereign anything, Pelham had managed to put Prinny off. He wasn't about to loan money to a man who would take the first opportunity to prance to Rundell & Bridge and buy his latest mistress a bauble.

Pelham sincerely hoped the man didn't intend to appeal to him for yet another loan. He preferred to avoid the prince when possible, but Lady Elizabeth had been adamant they attend the ball at Carlton House.

"My lady, you are certain our attendance at this function is necessary?" he asked, though he had asked previously and received a somewhat satisfactory answer. But he wanted to give his fiancée every opportunity to change her mind.

"You know my parents are old-fashioned. My

mother wants approval of our match from the prince. She would have rather had it from the King, but all reports are that he is severely indisposed."

The King was quite mad was what she meant, Pelham thought. George III's firstborn son was a pale substitute for the formidable King. Pelham could hardly argue with the wishes of his intended's parents. They had asked for very little from him, aside from substantial provisions for Lady Elizabeth and her offspring in the event he predeceased her. When Pelham considered the land he was receiving in exchange, this provision was paltry. He had plans for that land. He realized Lady Elizabeth was speaking and wrenched his mind away from thoughts of crops and soil improvements.

"—won't stay long. I should think if we dance twice that should prove sufficient."

Pelham almost balked. Almost. He was a duke and did not show his emotions. But he thought his deaf ear might have deceived him. "A dance?" he asked, keeping his voice level.

"Or two."

"*Two?*" He could not have possibly heard correctly.

He must have sounded choked, because she raised a dark brow. "Is that a problem, Your Grace?"

She had brown hair and brown eyes and was pretty enough. Pelham cared little about her looks, but he did care about her temperament. She was a serious sort—or so he'd always thought. But just now, he had thought she might be laughing at him. It was too dark in the coach—even with the carriage lights—to tell, though.

It must have been his imagination.

"Dancing is such…" *Torture.* "A frivolous pursuit," he managed.

"But surely you dance?" Lady Elizabeth asked.

He did and he had, but he did not enjoy it. It didn't seem dignified. "If you think it absolutely necessary." The evening had hardly begun and was already rapidly degenerating.

Lady Elizabeth did not comment, and Pelham wondered if it was too soon in the engagement to outline some rules. For example, in the future he would not be required to dance. Or attend balls. Really, he had little interest in most *ton* functions, but he did not want to be unreasonable. Perhaps they might attend one small soiree each Season…

The coachman announced their arrival, and Pelham peered out the window for a glimpse of Carlton House. It faced Pall Mall on the south, and the gardens were adjacent to St. James's Park. Palladian in style, the house appeared austere, formal, and classic on the outside. Inside was a different matter entirely. Henry Holland, the architect, had acquiesced to the prince's every whim, and the interior of the house was garish and ornate.

Horace Walpole, whose criticisms Pelham usually agreed with, had called the house "the most perfect in Europe." Pelham privately wondered if Walpole was going blind.

The coach sped past a small crowd of onlookers, eager to see the arrival of the wealthy or titled—as few possessed both wealth and title—they read about daily in their morning papers. Lady Elizabeth gave a small wave to the crowds, but Pelham ignored them. The coach joined a long line of other coaches, and it was a quarter hour before Pelham and Lady Elizabeth alighted and entered through the hexastyle portico of Corinthian columns. They entered a grand foyer graced by anterooms on either side, and proceeded to the entrance hall.

This hall soared two stories above them and boasted Ionic columns of yellow scagliola. Pelham was unimpressed, but Lady Elizabeth was turning her head this way and that, seeming to take it all in. He did hope she wasn't gleaning any ideas for remodeling his sober residence. He did not think he could stand yellow marble.

They were escorted to the ballroom and announced, and Pelham led his fiancée into the crowds. Her mother and father were the first to greet them, and Pelham spent a good quarter of an hour exchanging mindless pleasantries with them. He was informed the prince had yet to make an appearance, which meant Pelham might be here indefinitely. The thought depressed him, and he offered to fetch Lady Elizabeth and her mother, the Marchioness of Nowlund, glasses of champagne. There were footmen circling with trays, but Pelham needed a reason to escape.

He strolled away, immediately engulfed by the crush of people, and headed for the French doors opening onto the terrace. He had just stepped outside and breathed in fresh air when Fitzhugh joined him.

"I must be hallucinating," he said. "That's the only explanation I have for seeing the Duke of Pelham at Prinny's ball."

"Stubble it," Pelham growled.

Fitzhugh laughed. "Drink?" He handed Pelham a snifter of what appeared to be brandy, and Pelham took it, remembering why he liked Fitzhugh.

He drank a large portion of the brandy, which was admittedly very good, and said, "I suppose Darlington is skulking about somewhere. He'll plague me about this until the end of time."

"Actually," Fitzhugh said, his gaze on the gardens, "Darlington was called away. I understand his mother died quite unexpectedly."

"Good God. That's monstrous news."

"He left just this morning. I heard he was so distraught he didn't even stop to take his leave from the duchess."

"You mean his courtesan? He must be distraught indeed. I suppose that's understandable."

"Yes." Fitzhugh glanced at him, and Pelham didn't like the look on his face. "She'll be here tonight. And your presence... well, I don't have to tell you the speculation is rampant."

"I'm not interested in speculation. I'm here to present my fiancée to the prince and then take my leave. I could care less whether I see this courtesan or not." Pelham had to raise his voice over the commotion in the ballroom behind him. Fitzhugh glanced over his shoulder. When he turned back, Pelham frowned. Fitzhugh was smiling.

Fitzhugh rarely smiled.

"It seems you are in luck. The Three Diamonds have arrived."

Pelham spun around. Not because he wanted to catch a glimpse of the Duchess of Dalliance. No, he did not care one whit for her... well, perhaps he was mildly curious—as one is when one tours the Tower Menagerie to see the lions. He turned because the raucous ballroom behind him had suddenly grown completely silent.

At first he could not comprehend why everyone had stopped speaking and moving. Even the King, when he had been of sound mind, did not garner this much respect. For a full five seconds, Pelham puzzled at the crowd's reaction. And then he saw them.

Three women in gowns that looked as though they were made of jewels seemed to float into the ballroom. Pelham had missed their introduction, but these were the kind of women who did not need any. He had always claimed he was not impressed by female beauty. He had always claimed one woman looked pretty much the same as the next.

He was a colossal liar.

Pelham could not tear his gaze from these ravishing beauties. He knew their entrance was calculated to cause a sensation, and if there was one thing the duke detested, it was manipulation. And yet, logic—for once—failed him. He stared, in awe, with the rest of the crowd.

The three entered arm in arm. On the left was a dark-haired beauty with olive skin and dancing eyes. She wore a gown that resembled a lake of copper. It flowed over her body like water, and though the neckline and cut were modest, the silk flowed in a most revealing manner. The gown itself sparkled with ruby and diamond gems.

On the right, dressed in gold silk, was an auburn-haired vision with vivid green eyes. Her dress was prim, almost schoolgirlish in its embellishment. She smiled openly, almost laughing, but there was something sensual about the way she moved. Something that made Pelham's mouth go dry. Her gown was embroidered with sapphires and diamonds.

It took Pelham no more than a second to appraise two of The Three Diamonds, but when his gaze landed on the Diamond in the center, he found he could not dismiss her quite so easily. His heart actually thumped harder when it appeared her gaze met with his. But her ice-blue eyes slid away, and he realized he must have been imagining the connection.

Of the three, she was clearly the most classically beautiful. She had silvery-blonde hair coiled elaborately and sparkling with diamonds. Her light blue eyes seemed to look through those around her, rather than at them, and her figure...

Pelham could not quite tear his attention from the silver silk gown she wore. Unlike the other Diamonds' gowns, the blonde had no colored jewels as adornment. Her only accent was the sparkle of diamonds. Pelham could see why this woman was considered a diamond of the first water.

She was tall and willowy, her figure slim and graceful. Her cheekbones were high, her eyebrows winged elegantly on her brow. Her lips were impossibly red, her skin impossibly white with just a hint of pink on her cheeks.

Yes, Pelham knew in that moment he was a liar. He wanted this woman as he'd never wanted another in all his life.

"They certainly know how to make an entrance," Fitzhugh murmured.

Pelham had to turn his head to catch Fitzhugh's words. The man had spoken into his bad ear. "I'm not interested in courtesans," Pelham said as much to remind himself as to inform his friend.

"No, you don't look interested at all." Fitzhugh laughed. "The one you can't stop staring at is Juliette, the Duchess of Dalliance."

Pelham tore his gaze from her to peer at Fitzhugh.

"Yes, *that* duchess. And the more you stare, the more you fuel all those rumors. Ah, good evening, Lady Elizabeth."

Pelham blinked, coming out of his stupor as his fiancée and her parents approached. Fitzhugh was bowing and expressing his pleasure at seeing them. But Pelham saw Lady Elizabeth's gaze was on him. She'd obviously seen him looking at the duchess. Devil take it, he hoped he hadn't given tinder to spark the *ton*'s blaze of rumors. And he certainly didn't need his fiancée questioning his associations just as their engagement was formalized.

Pelham moved to stand beside Lady Elizabeth, turning his back to The Three Diamonds, who were now mingling among the crowd. The hum of voices had risen again, and Pelham swore he heard his name bandied about, but he was resolute in his decision to ignore the courtesans and all the conjecture surrounding them.

"I was supposed to fetch champagne," he said. It wasn't an apology. Dukes did not apologize. "Fitzhugh distracted me before I could return."

"It is good to see you again, Mr. Fitzhugh," Lady Elizabeth said.

"Do forgive me for detaining Pelham. I had no idea the importance of his errand. But I am glad to have this opportunity. I understand congratulations are in order."

Pelham was always amazed when a man like Warrick Fitzhugh, a man who by all accounts had a rather seedy past and an equally murky present, presented himself so properly and in such a charming manner. But Pelham supposed that as the son of an earl, Fitzhugh had the training, if not the desire, to live respectably.

Lady Elizabeth bowed her head in a show of modesty. "Thank you, Mr. Fitzhugh." She glanced at Pelham. "I am overwhelmed by happiness."

Pelham could feel more sentimentality in the air as Lady Elizabeth's mother began to speak, and he fled with the promise to return posthaste with champagne. He felt no qualms about leaving Fitzhugh alone with the women. After all, the man had brought it upon himself. No man even alluded to the topic of nuptials without expecting at least tittering, and quite possibly tears, from members of the fairer sex.

Pelham approached a footman carrying a tray of champagne, but before he could take three flutes, Lord Ridgebury, another of his school chums, cut him off. "Pelham, old chap!"

Pelham nodded stiffly. At school, Ridgebury had always tried to copy Pelham's answers. "Ridgebury."

"I see you were finally able to break away. If you hurry, you might still be able to claim a dance with the duchess."

Pelham stared at the man. "You cannot possibly

be suggesting I dance with a known courtesan in the presence of my fiancée and her parents, the Marquess and Marchioness of Nowlund."

Ridgebury shrugged. "My understanding is you've done a lot more than that."

"And do you believe everything you read, then, Ridgebury? Personally, I prefer my fiction in book form."

"Then you deny the relationship?" Lord Casterly, a viscount with whom Pelham had at best a negligible connection, asked. Pelham realized he had inadvertently attracted quite a crowd.

"I do deny it. Not that it's any of your affair. Now if you'll excuse me." Pelham reached for the champagne but not before he heard the Prince of Wales announced.

The Prince Regent, red-faced and waddling, entered, and his subjects bowed and curtseyed. All activity ceased for a matter of minutes as the prince greeted his favorites and exchanged quips with Brummell and Alvanley. The guests were beginning to mingle again, and Pelham reached for the champagne glasses a second time when Prinny called, "Pelham! Just the man I want to see!"

Pelham cringed, motioned to the footman to move along, then turned and bowed to the prince.

"Your Royal Highness."

"I didn't think to see you here tonight, Pelham," Prinny trilled. His rouged face was accented with a painted beauty mark on his cheek. Pelham couldn't stop staring at it. Why would a man want a beauty mark?

Come to think of it, why would a woman?

"I'd hoped to present my fiancée to Your Royal

Highness," Pelham answered coolly. "I think you know her, Lady—"

"Are you going to marry the duchess, now?" Prinny exclaimed. "Well, this is quite the *ondit*!"

Pelham frowned. He was not accustomed to being interrupted, nor was he accustomed to being the subject of rumor. "If you mean to imply that I might be marrying that strumpet—"

The prince opened his mouth and let out a small squeak. Pelham tried to speak again, but Prinny waved his hands frantically.

"That's quite all right."

Pelham heard a low, cool voice behind him.

"I've been called far worse."

Five

JULIETTE HAD SEEN THE DUKE OF PELHAM AS SOON AS she'd stepped into the ballroom at Carlton House. She was aware all eyes were on her and the other Diamonds, and she was careful to search the room for the duke without appearing too obvious.

Apparently Lily and Fallon had done the same. As soon as they had a moment alone, Lily gripped Juliette's arm. "He's here! I cannot believe it."

"Neither can I," Juliette said, though she was careful to tell herself his presence meant nothing. But it did mean she would remain the center of attention. The *ton* wanted something to happen between the two of them. This was exactly the situation she had wanted.

"You are going to be certain Darlington makes good on his promise, aren't you?" Lily asked.

Juliette frowned, trying to keep Pelham in sight as the crowds swirled between them. "What promise?"

Lily made a sound of exasperation. "He said he'd stand on his head if Pelham attended, and you said you'd hold him to it."

"Oh." Had Pelham always been so tall? Had he always been so handsome?

Lily was still looking at her. Juliette blinked. "Yes, I will hold Darlington to his promise."

"But not now," Fallon said. "Here's Prinny, and your opportunity, Juliette."

Fallon was right. She curtseyed as Prinny made his entrance, watched as he spoke to his favorites, and smiled when he nodded at her before making his way over to Pelham, who was standing near one set of the French doors leading to the gardens. So Prinny was anticipating her meeting with the Dangerous Duke, just like everyone else. Well, she couldn't disappoint her sovereign, now could she?

She felt a surge of excitement as she started across the room. In her mind, she was no longer Juliette, but the Duchess of Dalliance. She was not a divorced country girl pretending to be a beautiful courtesan in the big city. She was royalty; she was elegance; she was one of The Three Diamonds.

The crowds parted as the Red Sea must have done for Moses. As she stepped into the divide, she wondered if the Red Sea had as many sharks as the *ton*. If so, Moses had more bravery than she'd given him credit for. It was not easy to walk past those sharks and pay them no mind. But she kept her gaze on Pelham and was soon close enough that she could hear his voice—low and velvet soft—and Prinny's—high and far too feminine.

Prinny, as usual, was overly excited by the prospect of a scene to come and was blathering to Pelham about marriage. Juliette wanted to spin on her heel and retreat. Such a ridiculous statement gave the duke no choice but to deny it. Now was not the time to meet him, but she'd come too far to turn back now. She stopped behind Pelham and heard him say, quite clearly, "If you mean to imply that I might be marrying that strumpet—"

Prinny, of course, warned him of her presence. Juliette was actually sorry for that. She would have liked to hear how Pelham finished the sentence. She could have also used another moment to compose herself. If she was the blushing sort—and she hadn't been that sort since she was seventeen—her face would have been bright pink. Instead, she felt the heat but maintained her impassive expression.

"I've been called far worse," she said.

Pelham turned to her, and she took a short, quick breath. She had never been this close to him. She had seen him only across gardens and ballrooms. Usually men looked handsome from a distance, and when one drew closer, one noted the so-called handsome man had hair growing out of his nose or pockmarks on his cheek or food in his teeth.

But Pelham was perfect. He was dressed immaculately in evening wear, the cut of his coat tight over broad shoulders. His cravat was tied simply but impeccably, and his breeches were snug over muscled thighs. His skin was a rich bronze, indicating he spent some time outdoors. Perhaps that was where he'd acquired the streaks of red and gold in his thick, wavy brown hair. That hair was a bit longer than was fashionable, as though the duke had better things to do than sit idly for a haircut.

His eyes were impossibly blue. She didn't remember Pelham's eyes being quite so vivid a blue before. She did not think she had ever seen eyes so brilliant. Men often remarked on her eyes, but she thought they were too pale. Pelham's were dark and bright and... hard. No wonder he was called the Dangerous Duke. She was tempted to step back when his gaze swept over her.

She didn't. Instead, she notched her chin up, smiled, and ignored him. She focused her gaze on Prinny and curtseyed gracefully—Lady Sinclair would have been proud. "Your Royal Highness, I'm honored to be here."

Prinny giggled—probably because he had been trying to see down her bodice—and stepped forward. He took her gloved hand and kissed it. "Duchess, I am honored to have you in attendance. Might I say that you look exquisite?"

"You might. I should be disappointed if you didn't." Juliette focused her gaze on the top of Prinny's head, but she could feel Pelham's dark gaze on her. She didn't know why it should make her feel so warm and tingly when he was looking at her with such scorn.

Prinny giggled again. "You look exquisite, Duchess. As always. You know I could think of more compliments, but I'd like to give them to you in private."

Juliette was adept at maneuvering around the prince's suggestions for liaisons. She glanced markedly at Pelham, and said, "Your Royal Highness, do introduce me to your friend. Perhaps then he might cease staring at me."

"There's no need for an introduction," Pelham said in that low, velvet voice. "You know perfectly well who I am."

Prinny gleefully clapped his hands together. Juliette was aware the whole of the assembly crowded closer, hoping to overhear. "And Your Grace obviously knows who I am. I've read so much about us, it's a pleasure to finally meet the man with whom I'm having a scandalous affair." She thought his mouth might have quirked minutely. "I will say I'm happy to find you are even more handsome than in the sketches I've seen."

Juliette could almost see the *ton*'s collective neck craning to hear more. As one, their heads swiveled to Pelham. It was his turn to compliment her. What would he say?

"Your Royal Highness," Pelham addressed the prince. "If you'll excuse me, my fiancée is waiting."

The prince blinked. "Ah—I—"

Pelham began to move away, and Juliette almost choked.

Pelham was going to cut her!

In front of the entire beau monde.

Prinny was still stammering, trying to think of something to say to keep the duke from walking away, from ruining her.

Juliette couldn't leave this to the prince, and she couldn't allow Pelham to cut her. She didn't have time to think. She composed her face into an expression of ennui and remarked, "Too bad the papers didn't mention how rude you are."

The prince gasped. At least she thought it was

the prince. It might have been someone else in the crowd. But her statement worked. Pelham stopped. Slowly—her heart pounded at least ten times—he turned and directed those dark blue eyes at her.

"Excuse me?"

Her instinct was to apologize. Instead, she stepped forward to face him. They were standing toe-to-toe now. "I thought you had better manners than to be rude to a lady."

He raised a brow. "You are correct."

She was? Juliette almost smiled. She was saved.

"I would never be rude to a lady. You, madam, are not a lady. You are nothing more than a well-paid whore."

The silence surrounding them was as thick as London's morning fog. Juliette could all but hear the blood racing through her veins. It flowed fast and hot because she was truly angry now. How dare he? Who did he think he was? She had done nothing to him to deserve this.

Out of the corner of her eye, she saw Fallon and Lily approaching. No doubt they would intervene to save her. But Juliette didn't want to be saved. She wanted to bring Pelham down a notch or three. He had turned away from her again and was beginning to move through the crowd. Juliette cleared her throat. "I would rather be a well-paid whore, sir, than an insufferable ass."

He jerked to a halt and spun around. His fists were clenched and his face red with what looked like fury.

"One is a choice and can be changed," she continued, raising her voice so it would carry. "Whereas the other is a permanent trait of the personality. Not that you have much of one."

And with that, she turned on her heel and strolled away. She kept her head high and her face composed, but inside she was seething. And as she caught a glimpse of the faces of the members of the *ton*, she felt the first stirrings of panic. They were moving out of her path, their expressions full of pity. Juliette didn't mind the pity; it was the men who refused to meet her eyes that caused her stomach to tense and tighten. If she had just become unfashionable and unwanted, her career was over. How would she pay for her town house? Her clothes? Her carriage?

Her debts were not outrageous, but she did not have nearly enough saved to cover them. And she would not, could not, ask Sinclair to pay them for her. He had done more than enough for her already.

Damn Pelham! She wished she had never heard his name.

She was still walking, she knew not where, when Fallon and Lily appeared on either side of her. Somewhere in the distance she heard the orchestra begin to play a reel.

"That was magnificent," Fallon said. "You put him in his place."

Juliette shook her head. "Then why isn't anyone looking at me? Why are you two the only ones dashing to comfort me? I'm done for."

"Nonsense," Lily said, but she was a bad liar, and Juliette heard the tinny notes of false confidence in her voice.

"Who cares?" Fallon said.

"*I* care," Juliette hissed. "My creditors will care. How will I pay them?"

"Sinclair—" Lily began.

Juliette held up a hand. "No. I won't take his charity again."

"Calm down." Fallon put a hand on Juliette's arm. "We'll discuss this in the carriage on the way to Somerville. Lady Sinclair will know what to do if we three are unable to work out a solution."

Fallon was right, and Juliette took a long, measured breath. Her heart slowed its rapid staccato. "You're right. Perhaps it is a good time to leave London." First that business with Lucifer, and now Pelham.

"It is," Lily agreed. "A holiday is precisely what we need. In fact, let's quit the ball now and begin preparations."

"No." Juliette shook her head. She could see what her friends were doing, and she would not take them down with her. "You stay here. I'm sure you have dances reserved. I'm going to take in some fresh air and then sneak away."

"No!" Lily cried. "We'll go with you. You don't have to leave. You've done nothing wrong."

Juliette could have hugged her, and Fallon, too. They were such loyal friends. Their own good intentions would be their ruin. Juliette wouldn't allow it. "I need some time alone," she said, her tone harsh so Fallon would not argue. "I'd really prefer it if you afforded me some time to myself."

Lily frowned but nodded. "Very well. If that's what you wish."

Juliette started moving away, but Fallon caught her

arm. "I know what you're doing. I'll allow it this time, but we *will* stand by you."

When they had both been absorbed by the crowd and Juliette stood alone, she whispered, "Thanks."

For the first time in recent memory, no one clamored for her attention. No man was at her elbow with champagne or a request for a dance or a jeweled ornament he begged her to accept. No women were observing her, studying her mannerisms or her gown. She was an outcast and would be completely ignored.

The panic swirled again, and the room spun. She really did need some air. She managed to make it through a set of French doors and leaned her hands against the balustrade. The small balcony overlooked the prince's gardens, but Juliette was not interested in the view. She concentrated on filling her lungs with air and tried not to think about Pelham.

Breathe. Just breathe, she told herself. This was not how she had hoped the night would end, but it was not the end of the world. So her reign as one of The Three Diamonds was at an end. She'd had worse setbacks. She would recover.

She always did.

"Are you certain you prefer to wait out here?" a man's voice asked. Juliette shook her head. It sounded remarkably like Pelham. Now she was imagining him?

"Yes. I feel faint in this stuffy ballroom."

Juliette's head jerked up. She had not imagined the woman's voice. It must be Pelham and his fiancée. The last thing Juliette wanted was to be seen by either of them. She pushed off the balustrade and scurried into a shadowed corner then wedged herself behind one of the open French doors. It was scant protection if either of them looked directly at her, but it was the only place to hide.

"I'll fetch your pelisse and be back momentarily."

"Thank you," Pelham's fiancée said. She was pretty but not overly so. Still, Juliette could see the woman had grace and bearing. Her gown, her hair, and her face might be rather plain, but she was regal. She moved out onto the balcony while Pelham stalked away. Juliette breathed a little easier when Pelham's fiancée walked straight to the balustrade and peered out at the gardens. Now would have been an excellent time to sneak back into the ballroom. Unfortunately, she was trapped behind the door. If she had been wearing a dark-colored dress, she might have risked moving out of the shadows, but the silver was too conspicuous and shiny. She need only stay hidden for a moment. Pelham would be back, and then he would whisk his fiancée away.

Poor woman.

Juliette hoped she never saw the duke again.

"I know you're there," the woman said.

Juliette jumped. Had the duke's fiancée seen her step outside? Then why would she follow? Did she *want* to speak to her? Well, Juliette had nothing to say to the woman. She was about to declare this when a man's voice answered, "You've kept me waiting."

Juliette froze. There was something familiar about that voice. She shivered and pressed against the wall so hard she would have melted into it if possible. "Pelham is difficult to maneuver," the woman said. Her voice sounded rather husky more than regal now. "I was lucky to make our rendezvous at all."

The man dressed exclusively in black climbed over the balustrade. The balcony was low, and Juliette realized he must have been waiting under it for some time. Had he seen her?

He glanced up when he was firmly on the balcony, and the lights from the ballroom illuminated his face.

Juliette stifled a scream.

It was Lucifer.

For an instant, she thought he saw her, but then his gaze flicked to Pelham's fiancée, and he took her in his arms, bending her back and kissing her fiercely. Juliette could only stare in shock at the entwined couple. She definitely wanted to escape now. Why had she ever thought fresh air would invigorate her? She was scared senseless!

She did not even want to imagine why the Duke of Pelham's fiancée was kissing Lucifer, and she most certainly did not want to be present when the duke returned to find the two.

Thankfully, the kiss ended. "I don't want to go home with him," the woman said. "I'd rather go with you."

"Yes, we have much to discuss," Lucifer answered.

"I hadn't been thinking of actually talking," Pelham's fiancée said. Juliette recognized the sultry tone of her voice and had to cover her mouth to keep from exclaiming.

Pelham's fiancée was cuckolding the duke with Lucifer? This was information Juliette did not want. She closed her eyes and wished she could make herself invisible.

"I wasn't thinking of talking, either. The time for

that is over." Lucifer's voice had an undertone Juliette didn't like. She opened her eyes. Pelham's fiancée must have been worried, as well, because she took a step back, but Lucifer didn't release her.

"What do you mean?" The duke's fiancée tried to sound unruffled, but even Juliette heard the tremor in her voice.

"You lied to me, Eliza. You lied about the courtesan."

Eliza shook her head frantically. "No. No, I would never—"

"I need those diamonds. I've already sold them." He put his hands around her neck. "Tell me where you've put them."

"I don't have them. What use would I have for—?"

"Tell me. I warn you I intend to have the truth one way or another."

"Wait!" Eliza clawed at Lucifer's hands with her own. "Wait! I'll tell you the truth this time. The duke—" Her words were cut off as Lucifer hurled her to the ground.

"Do not dare lie to me again!"

"I'm not. I swear it."

Juliette shook, her whole body trembling with fear. She mouthed a silent prayer, swearing if she escaped this balcony alive she would read her Bible every day and give up brandy and help stray dogs and...

She stifled a scream when Lucifer lifted Eliza off the ground and threw her against the balustrade. Eliza stumbled back, tripped on her gown, and fell against the hard stone. Juliette cringed at the sickening crack. Lucifer stood perfectly still, watching Eliza's body. Blood trickled down her forehead and dripped on the stone beneath. The balcony was silent but for the sounds of a quadrille being played inside. Juliette held her breath as Lucifer approached the woman.

Please let her be alive. Please.

Lucifer knelt, blocking Juliette's view. But she heard his mutter clearly enough. "Bloody whore. Now what am I supposed to do with you?"

He crouched and lifted her body. Juliette was all but curled into a ball behind the French doors. *Don't turn. Don't turn.*

He didn't. In one move, he dumped the body over the edge of the low balcony. Juliette heard the soft thud as it landed in the grass. She stiffened, certain he would turn and see her now. Instead, he made a smooth leap over the balustrade and was gone.

Juliette did not dare move. She shook her head, trying to clear it of the horrible images she'd seen. She had to find Fallon and Lily. She had to get out of here. She began to rise then ducked down again as a shadow fell across the balcony. "My lady?" a velvet voice asked.

It was Pelham.

Go away. Go away.

He stepped onto the stone floor.

Go away!

"What the bloody damn hell are you doing here?"

Juliette started. How had Pelham seen her? "I—"

"Why are you crouching behind that door?" He pulled it closed and stared down at her, frowning. "What's going on?"

"I have to leave," she whispered. "I must go."

He moved aside. "I won't stand in your way."

But she stumbled when she tried to walk. She would have fallen if Pelham hadn't caught her. This was not the time to notice that he smelled like mint or that his chest was wonderfully broad. "I'm sorry," she mumbled, pushing away from him.

"Wait a moment." He caught her arm, holding her still and—though she wouldn't admit it—keeping her steady. "You're trembling, and you're too pale. Are you ill?"

"No." She didn't want to tell him what she'd seen. She didn't want to be the one to give him the news his fiancée was dead, to tell him his betrothed's blood was seeping onto the ground just beneath them. "I saw—"

A shot boomed through the night, and Juliette felt something hot zing past her cheek. Little chinks of stone scattered on the balcony at her feet. She blinked and gazed up at the sky. "Fireworks?"

Pelham grabbed her and pushed her down, crouching beside her. Inside the ballroom, the strings in the orchestra rose in a blazing crescendo.

"What are you doing?"

"That was a shot from a pistol, and if my guess is correct, it narrowly missed your head."

Juliette's trembling turned to violent shaking. "But—"

"Look."

She did. His finger indicated the side of Carlton House. A small lead ball was lodged in the stone.

"You're bleeding."

"What?" She touched her head, but he removed his handkerchief and wound it about her upper arm, just where her gloves ended. A few chinks of stone had embedded in her flesh, and tiny drops of blood marred her silver gown.

"We have to get out of here." She began scooting toward the ballroom. "Someone is shooting at me."

He glanced into the darkness beyond the balcony. "Why would someone be shooting at you?"

She blinked, having trouble concentrating.

"Who is shooting and why?" he said slowly, as though speaking to a small child.

"Oh. It's Lucifer. He must know what I saw." She would have dashed into the ballroom, but he held her good arm.

"The devil? Have you hit your head?"

"No. Not the devil, though I'm beginning to think he's a not so distant relation. Lucifer—the man who killed your fiancée."

Pelham's jaw dropped, and his hand on her arm opened.

Now free, she plunged into the crowds in the ballroom.

Six

PELHAM STOOD COMPLETELY STILL FOR SEVERAL moments. His ears rang with the duchess's last words.

Lucifer—the man who killed your fiancée.

He shook his head. Had his hearing failed him? It made no sense. Lady Elizabeth was alive and well. He'd left her no more than a quarter of an hour ago. Left her *right here* in this very spot. He glanced around the empty balcony.

So where was she?

She wasn't dead. Pelham didn't believe that for even a moment.

But the girl—courtesan—had looked quite frightened. And there was that pistol shot. He glanced at the stone wall, where the lead ball was still embedded. Certainly there was a reasonable explanation for all of this. Courtesans were notoriously dramatic. He would find Lady Elizabeth, and that would answer one question.

He bent to gather Lady Elizabeth's fallen pelisse and strode through the ballroom. The crowds were as thick as the locusts in an Egyptian plague, but they parted easily for him. No one wanted to be in the way of the Dangerous Duke. Not when he had a purpose so clearly in mind.

He scanned the ballroom, did not see his fiancée, and made his way to her mother. "Have you seen Lady Elizabeth?" he asked without preamble.

The marchioness's expression grew concerned, and she put a hand on her bosom. "Eliza? No, I thought she was with you. Oh, dear. I hope she hasn't run off again."

"Run off?" Pelham narrowed his eyes.

"I—oh—" The marchioness flapped her arms.

This would not do. Pelham couldn't conceive how the Cyprian might convince Lady Elizabeth to disappear, but he would not be trifled with. The woman needed to be shown exactly whom she was dealing with.

"I'll be right back." Pelham dumped the pelisse he still had strewn over one arm into the marchioness's hands and marched through the ballroom until he reached the hall. A footman in the prince's livery bowed to him, and Pelham demanded, "Have you seen the duchess?"

"Which duchess, Your Grace?"

Pelham clenched his fists impatiently. "The one they call Duchess," he ground out. "The courtesan."

"Ah." The footman smiled. "The Duchess of Dalliance."

Was that her sobriquet? Devil take her.

"Yes, Your Grace. She just took her leave."

Pelham was already striding for the doors. "Did she call for her carriage?" he called over his shoulder.

"I don't believe so, Your Grace. She arrived in the countess's carriage."

Pelham stopped. "Which countess?"

"The Countess of Charm."

Of course. Pelham stepped under the portico of Carlton House and ordered a groom to fetch his coach. "And be quick about it," he demanded. "If you can't be quick, bring me one of my horses."

Pelham paced while he waited, grunting out greetings to the ball's late arrivals. The duchess couldn't have gotten far on foot. He could easily catch her, if the damn groom didn't observe all the niceties of Society and allow every other carriage to go ahead of him. He would catch the courtesan and teach her to manipulate him as though he were one of the fools fawning over her.

Just as he was about to start off on foot, his coach thundered onto the drive. His coachman reined the horses in, but at Pelham's gesture, held them only long enough for the duke to jump in. "Drive to the gates. Slowly. I'm looking for a woman on foot."

"Yes, Your Grace!"

They reached Pall Mall without spotting her, and Pelham was about to instruct the groom to head for the park when he noticed members of the crowd outside the gates of Carlton House, craning their necks to stare along the street. Pelham followed the direction of their gazes and saw a figure in shimmering silver.

"Found you." He stuck his head out the window. "Fetch her." He ordered his footman and pointed at the duchess.

"Your Grace?" The footman looked horrified and understandably so. It was not every day his employer asked him to kidnap a woman off the street.

"Never mind." Pelham shoved the door open, not even waiting for the coachman to fully stop the carriage. He jumped out, landed easily, and went after her. The crowds outside Carlton House didn't part quite as easily as those inside the ballroom, and he had to shoulder his way through.

Until he was recognized.

"It's the Duke of Pelham!" someone shouted.

"The Dangerous Duke!"

And then everyone moved aside, and he had a clear shot at the duchess.

And an audience.

Several long strides later, he reached her. He grasped the flesh of her arm between her glove and the sleeve of her gown and released her just as quickly. Her skin was amazingly soft—a fact he wished he could erase from his mind. And where were his bloody gloves? He'd misplaced them somewhere, another indication the night was going to hell.

"You!" The duchess was staring at him. "Did you follow me?"

"You tell me my fiancée has been"—he lowered his voice—"murdered, and don't expect me to follow you?"

She shook her head. "I don't have time to discuss this. If he sees me, if he catches me…" She began walking away.

Pelham grasped her arm again and hissed. Devil take it if he didn't touch that velvet skin again. But he didn't release her this time. Only because he didn't want her to get away. Not because he enjoyed touching that silky skin.

And oh, what an accomplished liar he was becoming.

"You're coming with me," he told her. "I don't know what's frightening you, but you can explain in my coach."

"I'm not..." But she looked over her shoulder and seemed to reconsider. "Very well. You do realize, Your Grace"—somehow she made the title sound like an epithet—"that your actions tonight only confirm the rumors about us and incite new ones."

Reluctantly, Pelham looked over his own shoulder. A crowd of onlookers was watching them, most of them murmuring and whispering behind their hands. He scowled at them, and several scurried away. Others took a step back.

"I'll squash any further rumors," Pelham said between clenched teeth.

"Wonderful," she muttered.

He signaled to his coachman, and his carriage was beside them in mere moments. A footman opened the door and handed the duchess up. He was right beside her. Once inside, he closed the curtains and instructed his coachman to wait.

He turned his attention to the woman across from him and tried not to stare. The color was high in her cheeks, and her eyes were bright. He did not think it possible, but she was even lovelier than when he'd first seen her tonight.

His gaze—completely of its own accord—flicked to her mouth. She'd rouged it, because it was far too perfectly red to be natural. It reminded him of some exotic fruit, and he desperately wanted to sample it. One kiss…

He tightened his hands on his knees. What was wrong with him? He couldn't kiss her. She wasn't an acceptable kissing partner in the least. She was a courtesan—a whore. She seduced men for money, and he was falling under her spell.

She narrowed her icy blue eyes at him. "Why are you looking at me like that?"

He blinked. "I…" He couldn't think of an answer. What was happening to him? He was no schoolboy, falling over his feet or his tongue around a pretty girl. Come to think of it, even when he had been a schoolboy, he hadn't fallen over his feet or his tongue. Such behavior wouldn't have been tolerated.

She was still looking at him, so he blurted out the first thing that came to his, admittedly, befuddled mind. "What is your name?" Darlington had told him, but he couldn't seem to remember at the moment.

She shook her head slightly. "That's what you want to know? At a time like this? Lucifer is going to kill me. I saw—I saw—" She clenched her fist and took a deep breath. "Why are we sitting here? Let's get away. While we still can!"

"We are sitting here until you explain precisely what it is you think you saw. I will not be trifled with, madam. Now, I'd like to refer to you by some type of name, and I have an objection—I'm sure you understand why— to calling you *Duchess*. So what is your surname?"

She massaged her temples. "You are a vexing man, but if this is the game you want to play, I can play, too. Tell me your name, and I shall tell you mine."

"You know my name. I'm the Duke of Pelham."
He moved slightly, put his hand on the coach's squabs,
and felt the fine kid leather of his gloves. Thank God
something was going right.

"Oh, no. If we are going to sit in a dark carriage
and exchange secrets—"

He paused in the act of pulling on his gloves. "I
didn't say anything about secrets." But suddenly he
was wondering about them, wondering what hers
might be and how he might discover them.

"Then the very least you can do is reveal your
Christian name."

He stared at her. "I am a duke. The sixth Duke of
Pelham. That means you call me *Your Grace* or, if you
are one of my familiars—which you are not—*Pelham*,
or if you are a social equal—which you are not—
Duke. I do not have a Christian name."

She raised a thin brow at him. "I cannot believe
your fiancée's dead body grows cold by the moment,
and you sit here and argue etiquette with me."

"Then tell me your name."

"No! If I have to call you *Duke*—"

"I already explained—"

"—then you may call me *Duchess*."

She had cut him off! The nerve of the chit—to
interrupt him! He was of a mind to throw her back
out onto the street, but a tiny part of him rebelled
against the idea. What if what she said was true?
He hadn't been able to find Lady Elizabeth in the
ballroom. And his ears were still ringing from the
pistol shot.

He clenched his fists and steeled himself. His

association with this Cyprian would not be long-lived. He could tolerate her insolence for a few more minutes.

"I am William Henry Charles Arthur Cavington, Viscount Southerby, Marquess of Rothingham, and sixth Duke of Pelham."

She clapped. "Bravo! What a lovely recitation of your numerous names and titles. I think I shall call you *Will*."

He started, tried to stand, and bumped his head on the roof of the carriage. "No, you most certainly will not!"

She held out her gloved hand. "Hello, Will. I'm Juliette."

He gave her hand a scornful look. "I shall call you Mrs…?"

Her ice-blue eyes darkened to sapphire. "I'm afraid I can't tolerate my former husband's surname. If you wish to address me, you'll have to call me Duchess or Juliette."

She was divorced. He should have realized as much. He could not conceive what man, who once in possession of this Juliette, would ever divorce her—unless she drove him mad, which she was obviously quite capable of—but that was beside the point.

Divorced women were not accepted into Polite Society. A courtesan and a divorced woman. He shook his head. He must be rid of her quickly.

He cleared his throat. "Very well, madam. Tell me what you think you saw this evening."

"You keep saying that."

"Because you haven't answered the question yet."

"No." She shook her head as though he were the dimwit. "You keep implying I imagined what I saw. I did not imagine it, Will. I wish to God that I had."

He bristled at her use of the familiar address. In his whole life, no one had ever called him *Will*. Even his own father called him *William*, when he had called him at all.

"But I did not imagine it." She raised a hand, her gloved fingers playing with the velvet curtains. He wanted to tell her to let them be. They were tightly closed to keep the prying eyes of the crowds at bay. And he rather liked sitting here in the dim glow of the lamps with her. He liked the play of the candlelight on her pale, delicate skin.

Perhaps he *should* allow her to open those curtains. But she didn't. Instead, she caressed them, the action making him suck in a slow breath as he watched the path of her fingers and imagined she were touching him. He shook his head. He must find Lady Elizabeth and be rid of this bewitching courtesan.

"I was taking some air on the balcony when you and your fiancée approached. I heard you tell her you would fetch her pelisse."

"Eavesdropping."

She scowled at him, but somehow the gesture didn't mar the beauty of her face. "I was there before you, and I would not have been there at all had you not cut me." She held up a hand before he could reply. "But that is not the point."

She began to say something about a man jumping onto the balcony, kissing Lady Elizabeth, and asking about diamonds. Pelham tried to concentrate, but she wasn't quite making sense. Lady Elizabeth kissing Lucifer? And had this courtesan, this Juliette, really held up her hand a moment ago to cut him off?

"Mrs.—madam," he finally interrupted. "If my fiancée has been murdered, as you say, where is her body?"

She frowned. "I told you. He dumped it over the balustrade."

"Then it should still be there."

"I suppose. I don't know. I just want to get away. Please drive me home or allow me to get out." She put her hand on the door, and he covered it.

"Now wait just a moment, madam. You cannot leave the scene of a crime. You are a witness. We must call the magistrate." If she was lying, that threat ought to frighten her. But she only looked more tired.

"Rules." She shook her head. "You may call the magistrate and go back to the scene and do whatever you like. I am leaving."

He tightened his grip. "No, you are not. You will accompany me back to the balcony so I can see this body for myself. If there is indeed a body, then we will discuss our next step."

Though Pelham did not think any discussion was called for. Obviously the magistrate would have to be called.

Juliette blinked at him. "You expect me to go back? To look at a dead body? No. I will not do it. And if you had any sense, you would not go back either. He was shooting at us!"

"Who?"

She threw her arms into the air. "Have you not been *listening*? Lucifer! He must have seen me and realized I was a witness. That was why he was shooting. He doesn't want witnesses."

Pelham nodded. That would make sense—if the remainder of her story were true. But he was not convinced. "That might have been a shot fired from a pistol," he conceded.

"You said yourself it was. You showed me the ball." The color in her cheeks was exceedingly high now. She looked quite flushed.

"That doesn't mean you were the target."

She gaped at him. "You cannot be serious."

"We overlooked the park. It could have been poachers."

"Poachers?"

And before he knew what she was about, she thrust open the door of the carriage. He reached for her, expecting her to try and flee, but she pointed toward the street. "We are in *London*—do you see? There aren't poachers in the park!"

He had to admit it was far-fetched, but no more so than her assertion. When he said this aloud, she shook her head and let out a small scream. "You are completely daft. Completely!"

Behind her, the small crowd gathered around the carriage, closed in, trying to catch her words. "Madam, if you would lower your voice. You are attracting a crowd."

She jumped out of the carriage before the footman could even assist her. "Do you think I care? After what you did tonight, my reputation is in tatters."

"Interesting observation," he said, stepping out of the carriage after her. "You are a courtesan. I didn't think you need worry about your reputation."

"That's because you are daft."

There was a sharp gasp from the crowd, and she turned to them.

"That's right. Will here—the Duke of Pelham—is daft. He should be committed to Bedlam. But instead, I am going to traipse behind Carlton House with him and then admit myself to Bedlam, because only a daft person would go back."

She grabbed Pelham's hand and pulled him forward. "What are you doing?" he asked.

"You said you wanted to see the balcony. Obviously I shall not be allowed to leave until I prove what I said to you. So let us proceed." She tugged him back toward the gates of Carlton House. The crowds followed until they reached the men guarding the gates. At that point, Pelham and she were admitted again and the crowds barred.

Pelham noted the crowd did not take their exclusion happily. There were jeers and boos and several scuffles.

Mrs.—Juliette seemed oblivious to it all. She pulled him along, wending her way toward the back of the house rather than starting for the portico and the formal entry. Pelham tugged his hand free of hers, but when she looked back at him, he motioned for her to continue. He followed silently, the only sound the faint strings of the orchestra and the crunch of his shoes.

When they'd reached the back of the house and the prince's gardens, Juliette paused, ostensibly to study the house and determine which balcony they had stood on.

"That one," Pelham said, pointing to one in the middle. She nodded and started forward again. She took two steps and lost her footing. Pelham grabbed her arm, righting her before she could take a spill.

"Are you all right?"

"Yes. This dress is not made to traipse about in gardens."

He did not comment, but he kept his hand on her elbow as they made their way along the gravel path. No Chinese lanterns had been strewn about tonight, and the gardens were deserted. It was a cool night, and the prince had obviously not expected anyone to consider taking a stroll.

As they drew nearer, Mrs.—Juliette glanced about nervously, and he could feel her tremble. He drew her closer, shielding her with his body from the open park. He did not believe anyone was going to fire at them, so it was no heroic gesture. He wanted her to continue walking, not be overcome by fear.

When they stood directly below the balcony, she stopped. "I don't understand. I saw him toss her over the balustrade."

Pelham made no comment. It did not surprise him that the ground beneath the balcony was empty, the grass undisturbed. But if she were merely trifling with him, why would she lead him all the way back here? Why not admit her ploy in the carriage? "Perhaps you had too much champagne," he suggested as much to her as himself.

"No!" She turned to him. "I had three sips at most. I did not imagine what I saw."

"Madam, you are obviously overwrought."

She stomped away from him, closer to the balcony, skirting around it and bending in the darkness to get a closer look. "She fell here," she said, looking up at the short drop. "I was hiding on the other side, and they stood there." She stood on tiptoes. "Look! There! I see blood."

Dutifully, Pelham stood beside her and glanced up. There was indeed a dark smear of something on the balustrade, but he could not determine what it was.

She continued to stare up at the balcony, and Pelham looked down. Perhaps she had seen a lady's wrap or shawl fall and mistaken that for a body. He studied the manicured grass below the balcony for any sign of such a garment. The clouds moved away from the moon, and a weak shaft of light filtered through. In that moment, he saw a glint of... something.

He bent, but the clouds obscured the moon again, thrusting them back into darkness.

"What is it?" she asked. "You started."

He didn't respond immediately. Instead, he lowered himself to his knees and ran his hand along the dark foliage. He could practically feel grass stains forming on his breeches, and it bothered him a whole lot bloody more than it ought to have done.

And then his fingers closed on something cool, and he forgot about stains. He lifted the delicate diamond necklace out of the grass and let out a slow breath.

"What is it? A necklace?"

Pelham stood, the necklace clenched between his fingers. "My mother's necklace. I fastened it around Lady Elizabeth's neck tonight." He rounded on the courtesan, and she took a step back. "Where is she?" he demanded. "What have you done with her?"

Her eyes blazed. "Do not raise your voice to me, sir."

"Then tell me where she is."

"I told you what happened," she said quietly.

"You told me some rubbish about Lucifer. Now I want the truth."

"That *was* the truth! Lucifer killed her and threw her body over the balustrade."

Pelham gestured to the grass. "Then where is the body? Where is she?"

"I… I don't know. But I don't think we should stand about here searching. Lucifer might come back. He's already shot at me once."

"Do whatever the devil you want. I'm looking for more evidence." He bent again to search the grass, but even after the moon reappeared, he didn't find any other clues. Had Lady Elizabeth fallen, as the courtesan claimed, or had something else happened to his fiancée?

Or perhaps he was imagining this entire charade, and Lady Elizabeth had simply left the ball of her own accord. What was it her mother had said about running off? "I think we had better return to the ball," he said. "I want to question some of the guests." But when he turned, he was alone. He looked right and left, but there was no sign of the Duchess of Dalliance.

As he made his way back into Carlton House, he wanted to be glad he was rid of her, but something told him this was not the end of their acquaintance.

Seven

HER GOWN WAS RUINED, AND IT HAD BEEN A VERY expensive gown. But Juliette didn't care. She picked her way through the dark garden behind her town house until she came to the kitchen door. She rapped on it, hard, and then stood shivering in the chilly darkness.

She'd deliberately come from the back of the house, though it had been no small feat and rather scary to negotiate some of the dark alleys. But it wasn't as frightening as Lucifer. No, she would rather a dark alley than to encounter him again.

She didn't know if he was watching her town house, and she didn't want to take any chances. As soon as she could, she would get out of London. She had been planning to go to Somerville, but now she wondered if that was the best idea. She didn't want to endanger Lord and Lady Sinclair.

She rapped on the door again, harder, and prayed one of her servants would hear.

She wondered if Pelham was still climbing about on all fours under the balcony. She couldn't forget the look on his face when he'd found that necklace—amazement.

He really hadn't believed her, the obstinate man.

She was sorry about his fiancée, truly she was, but from what she'd seen, he'd be better off without the woman.

Not that she wanted him for herself. They would never suit—her being human and he a complete ass.

The door opened a sliver, and Juliette's cook peered out into the night.

"Thank God!" Juliette said. "Cook, it's me."

"Oh, Duchess!" The cook grabbed her shoulders and pulled her forcibly inside. Cook was a stout, red-faced woman with bright orange hair, ample hips, and the largest bosom Juliette had ever seen. The kitchen was overly warm as usual, but for once Juliette didn't mind. "You're freezing, Duchess! I'll get you some tea and a bit o' broth."

"Thank you."

The cook ushered her into a chair, and Juliette felt her muscles relax slightly. She ached from the strain and stress of the night. Everything in her was taut and rigid.

"I'm so glad you're here," Cook said as she put the kettle on and ladled vegetable broth into a bowl. She added a warm crust of bread to the plate and set it on the table in front of Juliette. "We were worried. A man came looking for you."

Juliette choked on her first sip of broth. "What?"

Cook immediately looked repentant. "I shouldn't have said anything. Rosie told me not to say anything. She said you were exhausted, and news could wait until morning, seeing as how the additional footmen you hired shooed him away."

Juliette blinked dumbly. Lucifer had been here. Looking for her. Thank God for those footmen, but how long would they be able to hold Lucifer off? If he could get to Lady Elizabeth at a ball at Carlton House, he could get to her. Footmen or no.

"Duchess?" Cook said softly. "Here's your tea."

Juliette rose. "I have to go."

"No, Duchess. Sit and eat your broth. You need something warm in your belly. You'll catch your death of cold or starve to death."

"I'm fine," Juliette said. "I'm far from starving, I assure you." She raced out of the kitchen and into the house proper, taking the steps to her bedchamber two at a time.

"Duchess!" Hollows called. "Is all well?"

"Send me Rosie," Juliette answered. But when she reached her room, she saw Rosie was already waiting for her.

"You know," Rosie said. "Who told you?"

"Shh. I have to think." Juliette paced the room. *Think, think, think.*

The answer came to her once, twice, three times, but she pushed it away.

"Duchess, let me prepare you a bath," Rosie said.

"That can't be the answer," Juliette muttered. "It can't be."

Rosie put her arm around Juliette. "A nice warm bath and hot tea. That's what you need."

It did sound heavenly, but Juliette shook her head. "I have to get out of here, Rosie. Before they come back."

"But, Duchess, he's gone and——"

"Pack a small valise and help me change. Is there any blunt in the house?"

"I… I think you have a few pounds in your drawer, ma'am."

"Pack it, as well." She gave Rosie her back, and the maid began to unfasten tapes and pins.

"Where are you going, Duchess?"

"I can't tell you that. The less you know the better. And, Rosie? Do me a favor. As soon as I'm gone, pack your things. Tell all of the servants to do the same. All of you, get out of London for a little while. Visit your mother or your brother. Just go away."

"All right," Rosie said slowly, helping Juliette out of the exquisite silver gown.

"I'm sorry about your wages," Juliette said, rushing to her clothespress in her stays and shift and quickly picking out a warm gown suitable for traveling. "I'll try to pay them. Somehow."

"Don't fret about it, Duchess. You'll be back soon."

Juliette turned to her. "I hope so, Rosie. I hope so. Now, hurry. Help me dress."

❦

Juliette stood on the Duke of Pelham's doorstep and stared at the large black door. It shone. Even in the cloudy darkness of London's night, it shone a gleaming ebony.

She did not want to be here. She did not want to knock on his door and ask for his help, but she didn't know what else to do. She wasn't safe at home, and she was afraid of going to Fallon's or Lily's for fear she might endanger them. She'd written a hasty note and had a footman deliver it to Fallon's residence before she'd departed. In it, she'd said she was going on ahead to Somerville tonight, and she would see them there. Hopefully, Fallon and Lily would follow without question. Then they, too, would be out of London and presumably safe.

Safe.

Juliette didn't know the meaning of the word. She couldn't remember the last time she had felt safe. It seemed ages since she hadn't had to look over her shoulder or could sleep without waking in a feverish sweat. And now Lucifer had come for her, as well.

No, she did not want to be standing on the Duke of Pelham's doorstep, but she did not know where else to go. The duke did not trust her, and she could hardly blame him for that. He was obviously a man of rote and routine. She'd churned up his placid pool.

Most of the dukes Juliette had met were used to having their own way. They had power, influence, and usually wealth. They expected to be catered to, and they always got what they wanted. And that was what she was counting on. Pelham could arrange for additional security for them. Not two more footmen to keep guard, but a small army, if he chose.

Now, how to make him so choose…

She would simply lay out the facts, and those were, like it or not, he was involved in this business with Lucifer. Before Lucifer had killed Eliza, he had asked about the diamonds. Eliza had said something about the duke before Lucifer cut her off. Juliette didn't believe the duke knew any more about these diamonds than she did, but if Lucifer couldn't find them elsewhere, he might come after the duke.

And that made them partners—or at least gave her reason to stick close to him. While he protected himself from Lucifer, he could protect her, as well.

But how to broach this with…

The door swung open, and a butler with pinched lips stood scowling in the doorway. He was younger than Hollows, her butler, and undoubtedly more arrogant. Butlers of dukes always were. His nostrils flared as though he smelled something unpleasant. "Madam, may I help you?"

"Oh! I…" She supposed she was going to have to ask to see the duke, though it was most inappropriate for a lady to call on a man at his bachelor residence. Not that she worried overmuch about propriety, but she could see this butler did.

"You have been darkening our stoop for the past quarter hour," the butler informed her. He did not merely speak; he *intoned*.

"That long?"

"Yes. I have kept the time." He indicated his pocket watch. "You have had ample time to think of what to say. I do not know what it is you want, but you will not find it here. Kindly remove yourself and your belongings"—he nodded at her valise—"from this illustrious doorstep."

Illustrious doorstep? She had heard of illustrious people, but doorsteps? The butler made to shut the door in her face, but Juliette pushed it open again. The butler might have closed it anyway. He was a robust forty with black hair, streaked with distinguished gray at the temples. He was handsome—or would be if his lips weren't pinched—tall, and immaculately groomed. He stared down at her with undisguised impatience.

"I need to see the duke."

"No." The door began to close again.

She shoved harder. "I must see him. It's a matter of life and death."

"Whose?"

"Mine."

"Good-bye."

Juliette blinked. The man was heartless, but she had years of practice dealing with servants. This butler was good; she was better.

"Sir!" she said in her most authoritative tone. The butler paused in the act of closing the door on her fingers. "What is your name?"

He straightened. "Richards."

"Very good. Richards, tell His Grace the duchess is here."

Richards stared at her. Juliette could tell he was digesting this new information and deciding whether she was to be believed. He shook his head. "I don't think so. Even if you were a duchess, which I don't believe you are, no duchess would come, alone, and knock on a man's door in the middle of the night."

"As I said, it's a matter of life and death. Mine, at present, but it could easily be Will's life soon. Now, please fetch Will—I mean, His Grace, immediately."

It was the *Will* that did it. She saw the change in the man's expression as soon as she called Pelham by his Christian name—her version of it, anyway. But he was a proud man, and he would not capitulate easily.

"Come inside and wait here," he said, opening the door just enough for her to squeeze inside. She set her valise on the marble floor of the vestibule—if one could call it that. The ceilings soared, and the butler's voice echoed in the tall, open space. Lavish marble stairs curled toward the first floor, and balconies embellished with carved columns waited for a princess or a king to walk their lengths.

"Do not touch anything," the butler warned her. "Do not sit. Do not move. Do not speak to anyone."

"Is it all right if I breathe?"

He gave her a dark look. "No." And he disappeared through a dark wood-paneled door nearby.

Juliette stood, waiting. The silence in the house surprised her. She could hear a clock ticking somewhere and the rasp of her own breath, but otherwise, the house was as silent as the grave. She saw a footman glide by on noiseless feet and noted Pelham's livery was red and gold.

It was a beautiful home. She had no doubt it was furnished tastefully and elegantly throughout. But it was a tomb. There was no life here. The servants were as quiet as mice, and unlike her modest town house, here no one dared make a sound. Juliette had always liked to hear the servants' banter and laughter when she was home. It made her feel less lonely. She supposed that made her a bit unusual, when most who employed servants preferred to pretend their maids and footmen did not exist.

But Juliette knew what it was to feel as though she were worth less than the rug on the floor, and she could never treat anyone else that way.

A door banged open, and Juliette jumped at the sound. She whirled, her heart in her throat. Seeing Pelham staring at her from the open doorway did not calm her. In fact, her heart kicked again.

He was handsome. She would give him that. He was handsome and not a little bit scary. His dark blue eyes took her measure, and his brown hair was wickedly disheveled. He was still dressed in ball attire, and except for that hair, he looked as though he had just left his valet, not been crawling in the grass with her mere hours ago.

But his hair... that hair would not cooperate with his attempts at order and rigidity. It had a stubborn streak, an unruly streak.

She liked it. It gave her hope.

"You," he said. The slash of his lips thinned.

She gave a mock curtsey. "Will, how good to see you again."

"I wish I could say the same, madam. What do you want?"

She cut her gaze to the butler who was standing behind Pelham. Without looking at the man, Pelham said, "Richards, leave us."

"Yes, Your Grace." And he was gone.

"I repeat, what do you want?"

"Is this how you treat guests? No offer of refreshment? You won't even show me into your parlor?"

"You are not a guest. You are an interloper."

"Did you find Lady Elizabeth?" Juliette asked.

His blue eyes narrowed. "You know I did not."

"And do you believe me yet?"

"No. I'm sure there is a reasonable explanation

for what you think you saw and Lady Elizabeth's absence. I have instructed her parents to send word the moment she arrives home."

"She won't be going home."

"Then that will be one more item to discuss with the magistrate in the morning."

Juliette stared at him. "Magistrate? You called for a magistrate?"

"Yes, but I didn't think this business important enough to drag the man out of bed. He will be here at first light. I will send him to you after I speak with him."

Not important to get the man out of bed? The man's fiancée had been murdered. Perhaps she had been wrong in assuming Pelham could protect her. He was obviously a complete numbskull.

"I thought I told you Lucifer has expressly forbidden me to go to the magistrate. He said he would hurt me and all I cared about."

Pelham scoffed at her. "A vague threat."

She closed her eyes. "I don't know why I thought you might listen to me. Why you might suddenly use your brain and realize we are in danger. I need your help, Will." She stepped closer to him, and he took a step back.

"I fail to see how I can be of assistance."

"When I arrived home tonight, my servants informed me a man had come looking for me. It must have been Lucifer. Now I know he saw me, and he means to kill me."

"Madam, calm yourself."

"Someone wants me dead. This *is* calm." She stepped

toward him, and he retreated again. They now stood in the parlor, a large, airy room with paper-hangings, wainscoting, and a liberal use of silk upholstery. "And like it or not, Will, you are involved in this as well."

"Stop calling me that."

"I heard her—before he killed her. They were arguing. He was incensed because she lied to him about the diamonds. I don't know what she told him or when, but I have to assume she told him I had them and that was the reason he sought me out." She stepped forward again, but this time he didn't retreat. She almost wished he would. She was too close for her own comfort. She could smell the mint soap he used.

"That makes no sense."

"It does if you read the *Morning Chronicle*. All of London thinks we are having a romantic liaison. Your fiancée obviously stole these diamonds and told Lucifer she gave them to you, and you, in turn, gave them to me."

"Rubbish. That's the most far-fetched—"

"But Lucifer came after me and his diamonds. He's not a fool—like some"—she poked Pelham in the chest—"and realized I had no notion of any diamonds. And so he went back to Eliza and asked again where they were. She was frantic, trying to save herself, and said something about you. That means you are involved in this, like it or not. And when Lucifer can't find the diamonds, he will come after you. That's why I'm here. You're a duke. I thought you, of all people, could protect me. Perhaps I was wrong."

"Eliza," he murmured.

She frowned. "What?"

"You called her *Eliza*."

"I—I did? I suppose that's because he called her Eliza."

Pelham sank into a blue silk armchair, his expression puzzled. "No one calls her that. No one but her parents and her closest friends. *I* don't even call her *Eliza*."

Had she finally gotten through to him? She'd at least made him pause to *consider* she could be telling the truth. "No offense, Your Grace, but I don't think you knew her very well." Juliette sat opposite him on a cream settee. She realized her legs were shaking with fatigue, and sitting felt wonderful.

"At least you called me *Your Grace* before offending me."

"Don't become accustomed to it."

He gave her what she thought might be a small—a very small—smile. Then he raked his hands through his hair, further disordering it. "I cannot believe I am doing this," he said.

Juliette sat forward. "Doing what?"

"If I allow you to stay the night—*one* night—you will not argue about leaving on the morrow?"

"Will you allow me to stay tonight?" She did not answer his question, and that was not an accident.

"Devil take it. Yes! The last thing I need is your blood on my conscience."

"I feel so… grateful," she drawled.

"Is your coach waiting?"

"No. I thought it too risky. I took a hansom cab."

He stood and leaned one arm against the fireplace, staring absently at a painting of an old castle.

"Is the likelihood of my death all that changed your mind?" she asked in an effort to distract herself from his fine form, displayed to advantage when he stood. How did he manage to wear such tight breeches? And that coat all but strained over his shoulders. She wondered what his bare chest looked like...

"I have questions I need answered," he replied, not looking away from the painting. "I believe you might have some of the answers."

"That and you want me present when you speak to the magistrate."

There was that whisper of a smile again—gone so quickly it might have been a wisp of smoke. "The possibility that you are a flight risk did occur to me." He pushed away from the mantel and rang the bell for a servant. "I'll have my housekeeper show you to the red room."

"The red room?"

"Yes, it's where I put all the courtesans who stay for the night."

She thought he was joking, but with him, she couldn't be certain.

The bedroom was indeed accented with silk and velvets in crimson, but as with everything else in the house, it was tastefully done. The bedroom was neither large nor small, which meant the duke did not consider her overly important or unworthy of space. The bed was large with crimson drapes, also in luxurious velvet. The housekeeper pulled them back and set Juliette's valise on the bed.

"I will send a maid to assist you with your toilette, madam."

"Thank you," Juliette said absently. She had gone to the window, parted the red-and-white damask drapes, and stared at the street below. Mayfair was quiet at this time of night—rather, morning—everyone was finally snug in their beds after a long evening of soirees and balls. She yawned. It must have been close to four.

"Before you retire, the duke wanted me to inform you of the rules."

Juliette turned, letting the drapes fall closed behind her. "Rules?"

"Yes. His Grace is very particular."

"What a surprise." Juliette wondered if the woman was weary. She did not look it. Her clothing looked fresh and clean, her cap starched, her hair perfectly coiffed in a simple bun. Juliette was also in a clean, pressed gown, but she'd had Rosie pull her hair into a simple tail tied with a blue ribbon to match her gown.

"Breakfast is at eight, precisely, and lasts thirty minutes," the housekeeper informed her. "Followed by a thirty-minute walk in the gardens. Next, the duke prefers to work in his library, but I have been informed the magistrate will arrive at nine, so the duke will have to put off his work for a quarter hour."

Juliette raised a brow. "How do you know the magistrate will finish his questions in a quarter hour?"

The housekeeper frowned at the question, her expression indicating it was impertinent. "Because he will be shown out at quarter past nine. The duke can hardly be expected to tolerate more than a fifteen-minute change to his routine. The duke prefers to eat a midday meal at—"

"It's past four now," Juliette interrupted. "Surely His Grace cannot expect me to be at the breakfast

table at eight, an ungodly hour by most anyone's standards. I will breakfast in my room while I complete
my toilette in preparation for seeing the magistrate."

The housekeeper shook her head vehemently.
"That is unacceptable, madam. The duke requires all
guests to keep to his schedule and to dine in the dining
room unless a dire illness prevents it."

Juliette crossed her arms. "Why?"

"Why? Because that is how it has always been done,
and because His Grace is a duke and he says it should
be so. I will send in a maid. Good night, madam."

"Good night. Not that I'm going to get much
sleep." She opened her valise, without waiting for the
maid, and found the simple, white-linen nightshift
she'd had Rosie pack. Next she loosened her hair and
shook it out. Her head ached, and it felt good to run
her fingers through her hair and massage her scalp.

"Oh, miss! You should allow me to do that!"

Juliette turned as a young girl rushed into the room.
She wore a starched uniform, bobbed an equally
starched curtsey, and set about fussing over Juliette's
hair. "I really only need help with this gown," Juliette
told her. "I can do the rest myself."

"Oh, no, miss. His Grace wouldn't hear of that."

"Well, then we shan't tell His Grace."

The girl shook her head, her curly brown hair
bouncing as she did so. "But he'll know, miss. He
always knows everything."

"I highly doubt that, but I'm too fatigued to argue.
And there's no need to call me *miss*. I haven't been a
miss for some time."

"Yes, madam."

"And what is your name?"

"Jane, madam."

She began unfastening Juliette's gown. "May I ask you an impertinent question, madam?"

Juliette smiled. "Is there any other kind, Jane? Go ahead."

"Is it true? Are you really a courtesan?"

"It's true. They call me the Duchess of Dalliance."

"And did the Prince Regent really give you that name?"

"Oh, Jane, I can't tell you all my secrets. At least, not on our first night together."

Jane laughed, the sound like a bell tinkling.

"Now, Jane, might I ask you a somewhat impertinent question?"

In the mirror above the dressing table, Juliette saw Jane bite her lips. "I suppose it's only fair."

"Why is the duke so particular about his routine? The housekeeper acted as though it were akin to treason not to dine with His Grace."

Jane helped Juliette don her nightshift and began brushing her hair. "I don't think I should speak of it, madam."

Juliette raised a brow. A secret? The Duke of Pelham had a secret? How utterly unexpected. "I promise to be the soul of discretion."

"That's not it, madam. It's just… I suppose… I feel sorry for His Grace."

Juliette spun around, knocking the brush from Jane's hand. "Why?" She could not imagine anyone less worthy of pity than the Duke of Pelham.

"It's not his fault, you see," Jane said, bending to

lift the brush. "He doesn't want to be so… so…" She waved a hand.

"Regimented?" Juliette offered.

"Yes." Jane nodded. "That's it. Regimented. But His Grace can't help it."

Juliette did not think she had ever been so intrigued. She did have a weakness for secrets, but she had not lied when she told Jane she would be discreet. She never told a secret not hers to tell. "Why can't he help it?" Juliette asked. She could see in Jane's face that the maid had already gone past what was comfortable for her. Juliette knew she should not push—that was not the way to unearth a secret. But she couldn't help it. She *had* to know. If the duke had some vulnerability, some Achilles' heel that would mean he was actually human, she wanted to know it.

Jane shook her head. "I've said too much, madam. Far too much."

"No," Juliette tried to reassure her. "You haven't. I promise you—"

"Is there anything else you require, madam?"

Juliette sighed, knowing when to admit defeat. "No."

"Then I shall see you in the morning, madam."

Juliette climbed into the bed with the velvet drapes and grasped one in each hand. "Jane?"

"Yes, madam?" The maid turned back.

"It's already morning." And she closed the drapes and fell back against the pillows. She expected to be assailed by images from the horrors she'd witnessed this evening. She expected to shiver in fear.

Instead, Juliette felt safe. The duke's house seemed

an impenetrable fortress against the terrors of the outside world. Even the street noise was muted. London seemed far away here inside the duke's crimson room, behind his crimson drapes, under his crimson coverlet.

She closed her eyes and felt the weight of exhaustion press down on her. And for the first time in years, she fell asleep in peace.

Eight

PELHAM PACED HIS LONG, RECTANGULAR DINING ROOM and checked his pocket watch again. Where the devil was she? He whirled on his housekeeper, who was standing at attention near the full sideboard, fidgeting with the frilly white apron she usually wore in the morning. "You told her breakfast was at eight sharp?"

"Yes, Your Grace."

"You informed her we have a schedule to keep?"

"Yes, Your Grace."

Pelham looked at his watch again. "It is five past eight, and she is not here. This is unacceptable."

"Yes, Your Grace. Shall I fetch her, Your Grace?"

Pelham let the question hang in the air for a moment while he surveyed his dining table. Everything was as it should be. His plate and teacup were in their usual place. His copy of the *Times* was folded in half and placed to the right of his plate. The correspondence he had asked to review the night before was stacked neatly to the left of his plate.

At the other end of the table, another place setting had been laid. He did not often have guests, and the anomaly of the extra plate drew his eye. He had requested a copy of the *Morning Chronicle* be placed to the right of that plate and a small vase of roses from his garden placed to the left. By God, he had thought of everything a good host ought. So where was his guest?

"I'll fetch her," he informed the line of servants waiting to serve him.

"Your Grace?" The housekeeper followed him out of the dining room and scurried up the marble stairs after him. The sound of his boots on the marble echoed through the house.

"You heard me."

"I did, Your Grace. Are you certain you wish to do this? She may not be dressed."

"Then I'll close my eyes." He'd do no such thing. He'd drag her stark naked to the table if need be. He quickened his stride—past busts of kings, portraits of former dukes, and tapestries from keeps long gone—and finally left his housekeeper to catch her breath.

When he reached the door of the red room, he knocked loudly. He did not need to knock. This was his door and his room, but he reminded himself he was a gentleman.

Behind the door, all was silent, and Pelham, growing increasingly impatient, knocked again.

Inside, he thought he heard a voice. He turned his good ear to the door and… nothing.

He rapped on the door a third time then tried the handle.

It was locked.

"Go away!" came a groggy voice from within.

"Open this door immediately," he roared.

Behind him he heard the scurry of footsteps and turned to see his housekeeper and a young maid approaching. "What's the meaning of this?" He pointed accusingly to the door.

The maid bobbed up and down like a marionette. "I'm terribly sorry, Your Grace. Please, please forgive me."

He looked to his housekeeper for an explanation. "Jane tried to wake the guest, Your Grace, but the lady was uncooperative. Jane was coming to fetch me in the hopes I could be of assistance."

Pelham pulled out his pocket watch. "It is now ten past eight. The time for assistance and cooperation is long past. Move aside." He prepared to kick the door down.

"Wait! Your Grace."

Pelham glanced at the young maid. She held a key out to him. Glowering, he took it. But just as he made to use it, the door opened.

Pelham was looking down, and the first thing he noticed was her feet were small, bare, and slightly pink against the reds and blues of the plush carpet. His eyes traveled upwards, noting the simple white shift she wore, until he reached the tangle of her hair falling over her shoulders. It was a cascade of moonlight over her porcelain skin. He tried not to stare at that bare flesh too long, tried not to notice how her sleeve was slipping farther, but his eyes lingered.

And when he finally looked at her face, he found he fared little better. Her heavy-lidded eyes, rosy cheeks, and plump mouth gave her a childlike appearance. She looked so young and innocent, without the icy expression she usually wore.

Pelham had the strangest thought. He wanted to sweep her into his arms and carry her back to bed. He wanted to hold her, tell her everything would be well. He would never allow any harm to come to her.

She had obviously driven him to the depths of madness. She was no kitten to be cuddled and petted. This cat had claws.

As if to prove his point, she said, "What is the cause of that infernal pounding?"

He glowered at her. In response, she yawned.

"Madam, it is"—he glanced at the pocket watch he still held ready in his hand—"eleven minutes past eight o'clock. You are late."

"Late?" She ran a hand through her hair. The night-shift she wore was voluminous, but the action outlined the curve of her breast. "Is the magistrate here?"

Pelham glared at the maid. "Did you not inform her of my schedule?"

She nodded furiously. "I did, Your Grace. I swear it."

He turned back to the courtesan and gave her an expectant look. She merely slid her errant sleeve back onto her shoulder and moved away from the door. "She's a good girl. Your Jane did tell me, but I'm afraid I am too fatigued to eat breakfast this morning."

From the doorway, Pelham watched in stupefaction as she padded back to the bed. She parted the curtains. "Wake me when the magistrate arrives."

The curtains closed, and all was silent.

Pelham stood rooted in place for three ticks of the clock. He shook his head, half expecting to wake at any moment. But this was no nightmare.

Fortunately, he knew how to deal with defiance.

He marched into the bedchamber, threw the bed curtains open, and stared down at the courtesan. She was lying on her back, her blonde hair fanned out on her pillow. She gazed up at him. "I don't recall inviting you to my bed."

"This is *my* bed," he said, punching the drapes with his finger. "And I have no intention of sharing it with you. I wouldn't touch you if you were the last woman on earth."

Her brows rose. "That's a bit drastic."

"Get up," he ordered.

"Why?"

"Get up and come to breakfast."

She didn't move. "Why? What is so important about breakfast?"

"It's how things are done. Now get up before I pick you up."

"I thought you didn't want to touch me."

"Devil take it!" he roared. "You are the most exasperating woman I have ever met."

"That's not the usual compliment I receive in my bedchamber, but I know you are out of practice."

"That's it." He reached down and lifted her, bedclothes and all, into his arms. She was a tall woman, and he was surprised she felt so light.

And so soft.

Even with the bedclothes between them, he could feel the curves of her body.

"Put me down," she demanded.

He marched toward the door, ignoring the startled stares of the servants standing there.

"You cannot really mean to carry me downstairs in this state."

"You brought it upon yourself," he replied.

"I am not a child, Will."

"Don't call me that." He started down the stairs.

"Put me down."

"No."

"This is beyond the pale," she seethed. "You do realize that, don't you?"

He did. He knew he was acting in the most ridiculous manner imaginable, and yet he seemed unable to stop himself. She had tested the limits of his patience, and she had won. He'd snapped. He deserved to be carted off to Bedlam. That was the only explanation for his present conduct.

He marched past the row of servants on the ground floor, all of them pretending to be quite busy with their dusting. Since when did footmen dust? He kicked the door of the dining room open, stomped to the far end of the table, and glared at the footman looking as though he wanted to melt into the wall.

"Chair," Pelham growled.

The footman jumped into action, pulling the courtesan's chair out. Without ceremony, Pelham deposited her into it then walked, calmly, to his own place, opened the *Times* and began to read.

A footman filled his teacup with hot tea—black as he liked it. He heard another footman offering the courtesan an assortment of refreshments. In a pleasant voice, she asked for chocolate. Of course she would want something decadent.

He continued reading his paper—or at least

pretending to. A moment later, the footman retreated to his spot against the wall, and the courtesan rose. He eyed her above his paper. She perused the contents of the sideboard, dragging the bedclothes behind her as though they were a train and she a queen. It did not matter that her feet were bare; it did not matter that her hair tumbled in an unruly mass down her back; it did not matter that that damned sleeve had fallen off her shoulder again. She acted as though being dragged out of bed, carried down the stairs, and dumped into a chair in the dining room were an everyday occurrence.

Perhaps it was.

He eyed his pocket watch. "It is now a quarter past eight," he informed her. "You have precisely fifteen minutes to eat."

He thought she would argue with him, but instead she said—without even glancing his way—"Do you ever cease looking at that watch of yours? I think it must be permanently affixed to your hand."

"Some of us must live our lives on a schedule," he answered.

She lifted a plate. "Eat on a schedule, sleep on a schedule, walk on a schedule. Tell me, do you visit the privy on a schedule, as well?"

He rose. "An inappropriate comment. I expect nothing less."

Now she did look at him, those blue eyes frigid. "You are the one who dragged me out of bed, Will. I expected quite a bit more."

He went to the sideboard and began to fill a plate without even looking at his choices. He piled food on the plate, sat, and ate mechanically. He couldn't say why this last barb stabbed him when so many of her others completely missed their mark. He did not want to care what this fallen woman thought of him. He didn't owe her anything. She had come to him. He should have turned her out.

He'd let her think he allowed her to stay because he wanted her present for the magistrate's visit this morning, but that was not the whole truth. He'd seen something in her eyes as she stood in his parlor—something he very much believed to be fear. How could he turn a frightened woman out on the street?

That would make him too much like…

He clenched his fist around his fork. He wasn't like him. He was nothing like *him*!

Except when Pelham thought of his behavior toward her—toward Juliette—this morning, he was reminded of his father. Not that his father would ever do something so outrageous as to carry an undressed woman down the stairs. In fact, his father would be appalled at Pelham's behavior. He would have berated him severely had he witnessed it.

But the lack of hospitality—that was not something his father had cared about overly much. Pelham looked down the long table at the woman sitting across from him. And wasn't that what had bothered him about her statement? She had called him out on his lack of hospitality. She—*a courtesan*!

She was frowning at the *Morning Chronicle*, and for a moment her face lost some of its icy veneer.

"What is it?" he asked.

Her head jerked up, and she hastily closed the paper. "Is it time for a walk in the garden?"

"No." But he wasn't certain. He resisted the urge to check his watch and eyed the paper. "What were you reading?"

"An article about fashion." She lied very smoothly, but somehow he knew it was a fabrication.

"Give me the paper." He spoke to one of the scarlet-and-gold-attired footmen, who immediately approached the courtesan. She snatched the paper out of reach and hugged it close.

"You don't want to do that, Your Grace."

"Your Grace? Since when did I become *Your Grace*?"

"That's right. Your name is Will. And I shall keep calling you *Will*."

"Give the footman the paper."

"But doesn't it anger you that I call you *Will,* Will? Don't you wish I would stop?" She was so obviously—and so desperately—trying to pick a fight.

"I wish you would give my man that paper."

She rose, still hugging the paper. "No, you don't, Will. You do not want to read what's in this paper."

He rose. "Why not?"

"Just trust me."

He pushed his chair back and marched to stand before her. Her bedclothes were still on the chair, and in the bright morning light of the dining room, her nightshift appeared very thin indeed. He tried not to look, but he could see the contours of her body outlined through the thin linen. "Give. Me. The. Paper."

"Very well." She handed it to him. "But don't blame me for this."

He opened the paper and perused the first page. He saw nothing of interest. He turned to the second page and skimmed it. It was complete fluff but nothing to make a fuss about.

He looked up at her. "Is this some kind of joke?"

"I wish it were." She took the paper, found the page she wanted, and handed it back. "Read the Cytherian Intelligence column."

"There's a Cytherian Intelligence column?" He looked down and saw it there in black print. He read quickly, passing an item about a courtesan's ball, one about Harriette Wilson, and another about the prince's latest ladybird. And then he stopped breathing.

> *Last night, dear Reader, the Duchess of Dalliance and her Duke were finally seen together publicly at the Prince of Wales's ball at Carlton House. But the rendezvous was not what was to be expected. The Duke of P— cut his lady in a most cruel fashion. Though our valiant Duchess held her head high in the face of such outright cruelty, it was clear the arrow pierced her heart.*

"Oh, good God!" Pelham exclaimed, looking up at Juliette. "This is the worst sort of exaggeration and melodrama."

"Keep reading."

"I—" He looked down. "There's *more*?"

> *The whisper at the ball was that the Duke was smitten with his newly betrothed, Lady E—, but if this is true, dear Reader, then why was the Duke of P— seen leaving the ball with the Duchess of Dalliance in his conveyance?*

We have it on good authority that though the Duchess left the ball alone, her Duke chased after her in his carriage, begging her on bended knee—

"*Bended* knee! What rot is this? I should sue for libel. For slander!"

"Keep reading," she said, sinking heavily into her chair.

—to return with him and to become his bride.

Pelham's hands shook with fury. If Lady Elizabeth saw this… if *anyone* saw this, he would be disgraced. But of course all of London was sitting about the breakfast table at this very moment reading this complete rot and believing it.

He looked down to read the last of the column.

We at the Morning Chronicle sought out the wronged Lady E— for comment but were unable to find her. The rumor is that she's fled to the countryside to mourn the loss of her Duke's love.

He lowered the paper.

"I told you not to read it."

Pelham could not speak. He could not even begin to form words.

"I hope you don't think I had anything to do with this."

He clenched and unclenched his fists.

"The interesting thing was that the writer was also unable to locate Lady Elizabeth. So it's not only you and

I who cannot find her. I think that should lend some validity to my statements about what I saw last night."

"You think this—" He wanted to say *paper*, but could not even give it that much. Finally he pointed to it. "Lends you validity? As far as I'm concerned, you orchestrated this entire farce in order to gain notoriety."

She sighed. "I knew you were going to blame me."

"Whom should I blame?"

"I don't know, but why blame me? How could I have possibly been responsible for this? Do you think—after what I saw last night—I want to be mentioned in the papers? No, I want to go into hiding. I want to be safe. Why else would I be *here*? With *you*?"

He narrowed his eyes. "To lend more weight to the article," he said, pointing to the paper again. Now it made perfect sense. She had wanted to stay the night to further the rumors they were romantically involved. If anyone questioned his servants, they could honestly say she had slept in his house.

And he'd contributed even more fodder through his actions this morning.

Pelham had always given his servants strict instructions not to speak of what occurred in his household, and he thought them reasonably loyal to him. But everyone had his or her price. If someone wanted his servants to talk, they would find a way to get to them.

"Do you really believe that?" she asked. "If what you claim is true, how did I convince Lady Elizabeth to disappear? How did I manage to have a pistol fired at me last night? How did I make you come after me in your carriage?"

These were all good points, but he wasn't feeling generous this morning and was not about to acknowledge them as such. He knew the whole of London was laughing at him right now. He would make the paper and the courtesan pay for this.

He looked at her again, and she drew back. "Why are you looking at me like that? I told you—"

"Do not speak. I want you out of here. Now. This minute."

"But—"

"Do not argue with me. And do not make me throw you out on the street. I *will* do it." His voice rang in his ears, echoing a voice in the past. But he would not listen. He would not back down.

A sharp knock sounded on the dining-room door, and his butler entered.

"What is it, Richards?"

"The magistrate is here to see you, Your Grace."

❦

Juliette didn't wait for Pelham to order her out again. Instead, she swept past him, her bedclothes trailing behind her. She was intent upon dressing and leaving as quickly as possible. She wasn't certain where she would go—somewhere far away. Somewhere she would be safe.

She wanted to be safe from murderers and gossipmongers and overbearing dukes!

She had jewelry she could sell. She was not entirely destitute.

She had almost reached the stairs when a gasp drew her attention. She turned and saw a short man with a dark mustache and monocle standing in the parlor doorway. "By Jove! You're the Duchess of Dalliance!"

Juliette could not have felt any less like a celebrated courtesan than she did at the moment. If only the *ton* could see her now.

Aware Pelham was probably directly behind her, Juliette made a show of curtseying and started for the staircase again.

"But wait!" The magistrate dove into the vestibule. "I... How are you?"

"She's leaving." Pelham's voice echoed and bounced off the marble.

"Your Grace." The magistrate bowed. Juliette noted he was wearing unrelieved black. In contrast to Will's stylish gray morning coat and snowy white cravat, the magistrate's coat was ill-fitting and his cravat wrinkled. "I cannot believe it's true. I read in the papers—"

"Silence!" Pelham smashed his fist on the newel post. Juliette winced.

"Nothing in that bloody paper is true," he stated, as though ordering it thus would make the article disappear.

"Of course not, Your Grace," the magistrate said, but his gaze traveled back to Juliette, and it was clear he did not believe the duke.

"You'd do better to say nothing," Juliette informed Pelham. "People will think what they want, no matter what the truth is." She knew this from long experience. "Somehow protestations of innocence only make one seem guiltier. Am I correct, Mr.—?"

The magistrate's monocle dropped onto his chest,

and he rushed forward to bow before her. "Mr. Sharpsly. And yes, Duchess, you are correct."

Pelham sighed. Loudly. "She is not a duchess."

"I'm sorry." Sharpsly never took his eyes from her. "What should I call you? I've never been this close to a cour—to someone of your stature before."

Pelham moaned. "She's not the bloody queen, man."

Juliette held out her hand. "You may call me *Juliette*, Mr. Sharpsly. It's what all my friends call me."

"Juliette." The magistrate breathed the word.

"But I'm afraid our friendship will be short-lived. Will has ordered me out."

"Will?" Sharpsly's brows rose.

"The duke." She angled her head in Pelham's general direction. "He thinks I had something to do with that piece in the *Morning Chronicle*."

Sharpsly gave Pelham an accusatory frown, and Pelham's expression of protest was priceless. Juliette thought it would be quite diverting to spend all day baiting Pelham, but she had Lucifer after her. She could not afford to dally.

"Good day, Mr. Sharpsly." She started up the stairs.

"Madam," the duke said.

Juliette paused. She couldn't help it. The authority in his voice all but compelled her.

"Come down and speak with Mr. Sharpsly about what you cl—what you saw last night."

Juliette looked over her shoulder, eyes narrowed. "I didn't take well to orders when I was married, Will, and I don't take well to them now." She lifted the sheets and started up the stairs again.

"Madam!"

Juliette kept walking, ignoring her every instinct to pause.

"Juliette."

With a smile, she stopped and looked over her shoulder.

"If you please." Pelham ground the last word out, like carriage wheels over seashells. "Come down and speak with the magistrate."

"You don't want me to leave?" she asked prettily. She knew she was pushing him, but if he wanted her to stay, she had no objection. Well, she did object on the grounds he was an ass, but at least he was not a murderer. She was safe here—safer than she would have been on her own.

"Come down."

So he wasn't prepared to go so far as to say he wanted her to stay. Very well. She would try to wrest an invitation somehow. Something told her to stay close to Pelham. But it was a strange experience—meeting a man who did not rush to fill her every whim.

Oh, she had met plenty of men like Pelham before she became the Duchess of Dalliance. When she was simply Juliette Clifton, no one gave her a second look. Pelham was a good reminder of what her life had been and would be from now on. Now that she would no longer be seen as the celebrated Duchess of Dalliance but a spurned fallen woman.

But if she were to stay here with Will for any amount of time, something would have to be done about his temper. She would not be yelled at or threatened. She'd had enough of that for a lifetime.

She descended the steps, more regally than she

might have, because she could see it annoyed Pelham. Then she waltzed into the parlor and took a seat on a couch upholstered in blue-and-white-striped silk. She arranged her bedclothes about her and folded her hands.

"We called you here today, Mr. Sharpsly," Pelham began, standing at the fireplace before the same painting he had stood before last night. Juliette was coming to think of this as his Lecturing Pose. "Because Juliette—I'm sorry for the informality, she refuses to tell me her surname—claims to have witnessed a murder."

Juliette was watching Sharpsly on Pelham's last words and saw his eyes harden. This man was not as silly as he had seemed in the vestibule. She could almost see the change in him. He was all severity and gravity now.

"I see." Sharpsly turned to her. "May I ask you a few questions, Duchess?"

"Please." She almost shivered. She did not want to think of the events of last night again. She would have rather teased Pelham or spent the day with Fallon and Lily or even at her own home. But she didn't have that luxury anymore.

"If you would, tell me what you saw last night."

She nodded. "I will, but it didn't begin last night." And she told him of Lucifer's visit to her town house, the events on the balcony at Carlton House, and her return with Pelham to the spot where Eliza's body had been dropped.

Sharpsly listened intently, asking for quill and parchment at one point, and asked her dozens of questions. By the time he was finished, she'd told the story more times than she could count and was drained. She glanced at the bracket clock on the side table and saw it was nigh ten. Pelham's schedule was in complete disarray, and yet he'd said nothing except to answer the questions Sharpsly directed to him.

Sharpsly made another scribble on his parchment full of them and looked up.

Pelham raised a brow. Juliette saw his hand pause before the pocket with his watch, but he resisted taking it out, and rested his arm on the mantel. "Well?" he asked.

Sharpsly's mouth was tight. "I'm glad you called on me, Your Grace. I understand why you were frightened, Duchess, but you should have come to us about the diamonds. I don't think it would have saved Lady Elizabeth, but it would have lessened the risk to your person."

"Then you believe her?" Pelham asked, unable to staunch the incredulity in his voice.

"I do." Sharpsly stood. "Firstly, because she has no reason to lie and gives no indication thereof. She's genuinely frightened."

Pelham glanced at her, clearly not persuaded. "She has reason to lie. Look at the papers this morning."

"I do not think even the duchess, who admittedly makes her living through her notoriety, would go to such extremes to feature in the *Morning Chronicle*. She is mentioned there almost daily, and all she need do is smile at a new man."

Pelham's lips thinned.

"I believe her secondly because I know of this Lucifer. He owns a gambling hell and is extremely disreputable. I have no personal knowledge of his clients reporting thefts of their jewelry or other valuables, but one never knows with a man like that. He has many vices. Thirdly, we had a report from Lord and Lady Nowlund that their daughter, Lady Elizabeth, did not return home last night."

"She is still not at home?" Pelham looked surprised, and Juliette wondered if he had even considered the possibility before this moment. He was so intent on believing she was lying, he had not even worried about his missing fiancée.

"Lady Elizabeth had not returned when I set out this morning. And that worries me. As does the missing body and the necklace you found, Your Grace."

Juliette watched Pelham's face. Finally—finally! He, too, looked concerned.

"We must search for Lady Elizabeth," he said. "I'll spare no expense, hire every available man—"

Mr. Sharpsly held up a hand. "I would appreciate the additional funds, Your Grace, but you must think of yourself and the duchess. If Lucifer realizes you saw something, he will come after you."

Pelham waved an arm. "I'm not afraid of this Lucifer. If anything has happened to Lady Elizabeth, I'll make him sorry he ever heard my name."

Juliette believed him. He had that dangerous glint in his eye—the one that had given him the name The Dangerous Duke.

But she was not the Dangerous Duchess, and she was afraid. She felt safe in the duke's home, but how long could she stay here? He had already ordered her out.

Was Lucifer lying in wait outside the duke's door?

Was he biding his time, knowing she had to emerge at some point?

Mr. Sharpsly rose and started for the parlor door. "I'm going to my office to see if any new information has been reported. Then I'll assign a man to Lucifer's Lair and sniff around there. If I can use your assistance, I will send word later today, Your Grace."

Juliette followed the two men into the vestibule, where Richards waited with his hand on the door handle. Sharpsly took her hand in his, kissed it. "The pleasure was all mine, Duchess. Please be careful."

"Thank you, Mr. Sharpsly."

The magistrate bowed. "Your Grace."

Richards opened the door, and Juliette screamed.

Nine

PELHAM PUSHED RICHARDS OUT OF THE WAY AND moved to catch the footman before he could fall. As the footman was dressed in Pelham's scarlet-and-gold livery, at first the duke did not see the blood. And then he felt the wetness and realized it was everywhere. The man gurgled, his eyes wide. Juliette screamed again, but Pelham heard Sharpsly's calm voice speaking to her, ushering her away.

Pelham knelt beside the man. Another footman rushed to his side, and Pelham ordered him to fetch a doctor. The duke glanced at Richards, uncertain of the name of the fellow whose head he held off the floor. The man was still gurgling, but he seemed to breathe easier with his head elevated.

"It's Davenport, Your Grace," Richards said, his voice low and anguished.

"Davenport," Pelham said. The man's unfocused gaze cut to him, seemed to sharpen. "I have a doctor coming. You hold on, do you understand? That is an order."

"Yerrrr—"

"Don't speak," Sharpsly said, kneeling on the man's other side. Pelham hadn't heard him return, and he hoped Juliette was somewhere far away from this. He did not want her to see it.

"Lie still, Davenport," Pelham instructed. "You're going to be fine." He didn't think the man would be fine at all. He didn't believe the man would last the hour. His fears were confirmed when Sharpsly parted the man's coat and shirt. The two men's eyes met, and Sharpsly shook his head.

"Would you like some water?" Sharpsly asked.

"Or something stronger?" Pelham inquired. After all, if this was the man's last drink, it might as well be a good one.

"Gin," Davenport whispered.

"Richards?" Pelham never took his eyes from Davenport.

"Yes, Your Grace. Right away."

Pelham held the man, noting with alarm that his breathing grew more and more labored. "Richards," he muttered.

A moment later, Richards rushed in with a glass and a bottle of gin. Pelham had no idea where the gin had come from. He never drank it, but he was thankful for whatever servant had donated it. Richards poured the gin, his hand shaking slightly, and handed it to Sharpsly. Sharpsly put it to the footman's lips. "Slowly, now."

The footman sipped, coughed, and sipped again. "Gud," he murmured. He tried to draw in another breath, and Pelham heard an awful gurgling sound. Blood and gin seeped out of the man's mouth, and his eyes closed.

"Davenport," Pelham said. He stared at the man's chest, waiting for it to rise again. "Davenport!"

Sharpsly put a hand on Pelham's wrist. "He's gone."

Pelham looked around. "Where's the doctor?"

"It's too late for that, Your Grace. The knife"—he pointed to the footman's bloody chest—"must have punctured his lungs. They filled with blood."

Pelham nodded, took a breath. Carefully, he laid Davenport's head on the cold marble. "Richards, bring me the tablecloth."

"From the *dining room*, Your Grace?"

Pelham glared at him.

"But, Your Grace, that was your grandmother's table—"

"Bring it."

Richards did as he was bid, and Pelham used the fine white linen to cover his dead servant. Immediately, scarlet flowers bloomed on the fabric. Pelham rose. His housekeeper stood nearby with a basin, pitcher, and fresh water. Pelham washed the blood from his hands, tinting the water pink. He frowned when he spotted Juliette standing in the parlor doorway. She was as pale as the white marble on the bust she stood beside.

"You shouldn't be here," Pelham said. "You shouldn't be seeing this."

"I—" She held out her hand. A slip of paper fluttered in it. "This fell to the floor when—" Her voice broke, but she rallied. "When you caught him. I think he'd been clutching it."

Frowning, Pelham took the paper. It was white with bloody fingerprints on the edges.

He opened it and read.

Regards, Lucifer.

Pelham clenched his jaw and rounded on Sharpsly. "What the hell is going on?"

"It's from him, isn't it?" Juliette asked. "Lucifer." She was shaking. He could see it, but he didn't know what to do about it. Who was he to comfort her? He'd never comforted anyone in his life. Hell, he couldn't remember ever being comforted himself.

Pelham shifted awkwardly, unsure as to whether he should make some attempt at… something. Pat her on the shoulder or some such thing. Instead, he took out his pocket watch.

It was now nigh eleven. His daily routine was shot to hell. Considering he now had a dead footman, a scared courtesan, and a cryptic note on his hands, he didn't think his day was going to improve.

"Is this someone's idea of amusement?" Pelham demanded, pocketing the watch and holding the note out to Sharpsly.

"I'm afraid so, Your Grace. I'm going to advise you to leave Town for the present."

"Leave Town? I have business to conduct. Parliament is in session."

"Will, stop being obtuse!" Juliette cried. "You won't conduct any business if you're dead."

Sharpsly nodded. "I agree with the duchess. I advise both of you to leave as soon as possible. Today, if you can be ready. Leave word with my clerk where I can reach you. I will try and keep you updated. Good day, Your Grace. Duchess."

Pelham watched Richards close the door on the

magistrate. He turned back to Juliette. "I suppose you think I orchestrated that, too," she said.

"No." He sighed. "But life was a lot simpler before I met you."

"You thought it was simpler only because you didn't know the truth."

"Perhaps I don't want to know the truth. Perhaps I *like* my life simple."

"Of course. I'll be gone directly. Then you can return to your simple life." She started up the stairs.

Against his better judgment, he followed. "Where are you going?"

"To the scarlet room and then…" She shrugged. "I don't know."

He continued following her, pausing only when she entered the bedroom she'd slept in. He stood in the doorway, not sure what to say or do next.

He was a duke. He knew all about obligations and dependents and responsibility. He had more than any one man should, and he did not want any more. But he also had a dead footman. That footman had been *his*, by God. And someone had cut him down.

Pelham couldn't help but see Davenport's death as a failure. He had failed to protect his servant.

He looked at Juliette. She'd thrown the bedclothes on the floor and was rifling through her valise, tossing out what looked like underthings. Pelham averted his gaze.

She did not belong to him. He didn't know whom she belonged to, but somehow she had become his responsibility. He knew the precise moment, too: when he'd seen her tremble.

She'd seemed so strong, so independent. But he'd seen the fear in her eyes. It aroused in him something besides lust for her. Something he hadn't felt in a long time. Something he vowed he'd never feel again.

"You're not going anywhere."

She whirled to face him. "What? First you want me gone, now you want me to stay?"

"It's not safe for you to set out on your own."

Her hands were on her hips. "Oh, really? When did you realize that? After I told you your fiancée had been murdered? When I told you Lucifer had been at my home last night? Only after your footman was killed? Do you finally believe me?"

"I don't know what to believe."

She threw her arms down and gave him her back. He could hear her muttering under her breath.

"Excuse me, Your Grace." Her maid was standing behind him. He moved aside to allow her entrance. He watched as the maid shook out a gown and held it up for Juliette's inspection.

"Regardless, you're not leaving. Yet."

"I don't have enough clothing for an extended stay." She didn't even look at him.

"I'll accompany you to your town house as soon as you're dressed. We'll take whatever else you require."

She glanced over her shoulder at him. Her jaw tightened, and he caught the hard glint of glacier ice in her eyes. Everything about her stance, her expression, her tightly reined fury projected loathing. She wanted to refuse him. She wanted to be done with him. "Fine."

He realized she must be frightened indeed if she was agreeing to remain in his company.

"Fine." He stood, watching the hatred radiating from her. He could almost feel its icy fingers reaching out to poke him. Yes, hers was a cold fury—unlike his father's. That had been white hot.

"Are you planning to stand there and watch me undress?" she asked, shaking him out of his thoughts. "Is that your fee for protecting me?"

He frowned. "There's no fee."

"Are you certain?" A look of seduction crossed her face. Cold seduction. "Because if there's something you want, you should tell me now. I like to be up front when doing business."

He took a step back, revulsion flowing through him. "I'm sure you do. But as I think I have made perfectly clear, I am not interested in your *services*."

She raised a brow. "And yet you're still standing in the bedroom doorway." She raised the hem of her nightrail. "Are you certain you don't want at least a glimpse of what you're refusing before you do so?"

"No." His voice was husky as his traitorous gaze dropped to her white ankles and calves.

"No, you're not certain?"

"Yes." He looked at her face, reminded himself to stare at those glacial eyes. "Yes, I am certain I want nothing from you." And he strode away, but he'd be damned if the image of those shapely calves wasn't forever etched in his mind.

Ten

JULIETTE STOOD IN HER BEDROOM AND STARED AT THE destruction around her. The draperies had been slashed, the clothespress emptied, her velvet jeweled pillows ripped open. Feathers and silk and stuffing littered the floor.

"I take it this is not your usual style of housekeeping."

She cleared her throat, uncertain whether she could force her voice to work. The entire macabre scene was so familiar, it was almost as though she had gone back in time. She had to remind herself she was no longer Juliette Clifton. Oliver was not going to step into the room and strike her at any moment. She swallowed. "No, it's not."

"And that on the bed?"

She stared at the bed, shivering. Her bed was virtually untouched. She could see a corner of her blue silk sheets peeking out from beneath the luxurious cream coverlet. Stabbed through the center of the bed was a knife pinning a slip of blood-red parchment. Oliver had never done anything like that. "Not mine," she said.

Pelham crossed to her bed and peered down. "It's

signed, *All my love, Lucifer*." He looked at her, hands in his pockets, expression haughty and holy. How she hated that expression. She notched her chin up, building her wall of protection a little higher.

"Could this Lucifer have been a lover?" Pelham asked.

"No," she said immediately.

"No?" He gestured to the bed. "Surely you don't remember every one of your lovers. There must have been dozens."

She wanted to laugh—or cry. "Dozens?" Or perhaps she should hit him. Right now she was so angry and frustrated and scared she wanted to pound her fists into this unsympathetic duke's chest until he gasped for breath. But there was more than one way to do that. She sidled up to him, put her hand on his chest. He wanted to step away; she could see it on his face. She made him so very, very uncomfortable. "Oh, I think it has been more like hundreds. But as I told you, Lucifer was in my drawing room the other night. I had never seen him before."

"Then why?" He gestured to the bed again. He was all but itching to move away from her. She would have liked nothing better. She could smell his scent. The mint fragrance was familiar to her now. She wanted to see if this man would break. Oh, he wanted her, but would he give in to temptation? She needed to know what kind of man he was. Could she trust what he said, or would his baser instincts lead him?

"Symbolism, I suppose," she answered. He began to move away, but she lifted a gloved hand and traced it down his cheek. He froze. "I know this must be a disappointing picture of my famed boudoir. And I so hate to ruin your fantasy."

"I never fantasized—"

"No? You never fantasized about me lying on this bed?" She sat. "Naked and breathless. Calling your name?" She lay back on the bed and gave him a catlike smile.

He stood stiff and unbending. "You should rise. Sharpsly will want to see this, and you should leave it undisturbed."

"Sharpsly already knows who's responsible for Lady Elizabeth's death. This won't make any difference. Come here," she purred. "Just one kiss."

He was tempted. She knew the look of desire in men's eyes. It was there in his and was just as dangerous as every other look he'd given her.

"Get up." He turned away from her. "Take what you need and meet me downstairs." He walked away, and Juliette rolled off the soiled bed. She knew she'd never touch it again. She was like that bed to Pelham. Irreparably soiled.

And if he knew the truth?

But why should she tell him the truth? He wouldn't believe it. Let him think what he would. Let him judge her as so many others had done. She didn't need or want his approval. She frowned as she righted a chair and piled petticoats onto it. Well, she didn't need his approval anyway. Why she wanted it, she would never know. A lingering weakness from the silly girl she had once been.

The door slammed open, and Pelham rushed in. Juliette jumped. "What is it?"

"The men I stationed spotted someone suspicious. There is a man in the alley behind your house. They fear there might be trouble. I want you to close the door and stay in this room. Do not leave."

He turned, and she caught his arm. "Where are you going?"

"I want to see this Lucifer."

"No!" She yanked him back. "No. That's what he wants. He wants to lure you out. Once he does so, he'll kill you."

Pelham frowned at her. "No. He wants to break in and get to you."

She shook her head. "*Think*, Will. If he wanted to get in without your men noticing, he could have done it. He managed to kill your fiancée on a balcony at Carlton House in the middle of a ball. He can gain access to my town house."

Pelham considered for a long moment. "What am I supposed to do? Hide in here with you?"

Yes! she wanted to shout. Why did men have to be so utterly ridiculous and rush into danger at each and every opportunity? But she knew how to deal with men. She'd had years of experience. "You're supposed to protect me."

"You?" He raised a brow. "You'd give him one of your icy glares and slay him on the spot."

"You say the most romantic things."

There was that ghost of a smile again. "We're not staying in here," he said, taking her hand and starting for the door.

"Too tempting?"

"Too obvious." He stood in the corridor and looked left then right. "Do you have an attic?"

"I suppose." She didn't really know, though she had vague recollections of instructing servants to put this or that in the attic. None had ever contradicted her.

"Where's the access?"

"I… ah…"

"Isn't this your house? Didn't you inspect it before purchasing it?"

"I didn't purchase it. The Earl of Sinclair did."

Pelham's dark slash of brows came together. "Ah, your protector." Without waiting for her assistance—not that she could offer much—he started up the stairs to the upper floor. When he reached it, he found a hatch and lowered the ladder to the attic. She'd expected the attic to smell musty and the ladder rungs to be covered in dust, but everything smelled fresh, as though it had recently been cleaned.

She was thankful for her wonderful servants and glad she had sent them away from all this danger.

"I'll go first," Pelham told her.

She watched him ascend the ladder. He had long legs, muscled legs. He probably rode horses at his country estate. He obviously spent some time outdoors. He wasn't pasty white like most of the men she knew. He had a nice backside, too. She had a good view of it from below. It looked firm and solid, not saggy or all but nonexistent.

He disappeared for a moment, and then his face reappeared in the hatchway. "Come on up."

She lifted her skirts and climbed the ladder. The action reminded her of her childhood, playing in the stables and on neighbors' farms. That was a world away from who and where she was now. She gazed about while he pulled the ladder aloft and closed the hatch. There was a small window to one side, and she supposed if she'd had enough servants, one could have slept here. It was not large enough for two, especially not with a man of Pelham's size taking up so much room. A trunk had been shoved in one corner, and she opened it, curious as to what it contained.

Pelham was at the window, looking down, probably wishing he was there with his men. "Can you see anything?" she asked.

"Not much." He glanced at her. "If I put that trunk over the hatch, no one will get up here without us allowing it."

She stood, and he closed the trunk and shoved it over the hatch. When he had it positioned just so, he opened it again. "What's all this? Something the previous owner forgot?"

She shook her head. "No. This is mine."

He frowned and held up a sober brown dress and ugly half boots. "These are yours?"

"In a different life," she said, pulling out a drab gray dress and a horrid hat. He was watching her, obviously trying to imagine her wearing these conservative gowns. She set them aside and lifted something wrapped in linen. She opened the linen and immediately wished she hadn't.

"That must be you," Pelham said, angling his head to see the two framed pictures. "But who is the man? Your father?"

"Mr. Oliver Clifton. My former husband."

"Oh." He shifted and stepped back, obviously uncomfortable.

"I told you this was from a different life." Looking at the clothing, the pictures, the few treasures she'd managed to take with her when she'd fled, made her sad. She missed her mother and her brother, too, even though he cared more about his reputation than he did about his sister. She hadn't seen either of them in years.

She pulled out another linen-wrapped item and unwound it to stare at a portrait of her mother and father. She angled it so Pelham could see. He was going to hurt his neck trying to crane it unobtrusively. "These were my parents."

"Are they dead?"

She stared at the picture. "My father is. I don't know about my mother. I haven't seen her in eight years. But even if she's still alive, I'm dead to her. When Oliver filed for divorce, she and my brother told me they never wanted to see me again."

"So your husband divorced you?"

She nodded. That wasn't the full story, but it was true nonetheless.

"Why?"

"Why else? Criminal conversation."

Pelham's eyes widened, and she shook her head, surprised anything she should say or do would shock anyone anymore. Surprised he didn't already know she'd been divorced for crim. con., otherwise known as adultery. But he didn't spend much time in London and spent no time that she could recall with the denizens of the demimonde.

She wanted to tell him the stories of her adultery weren't true, but that would require her to reveal the full truth. And that she could not do. She hadn't told anyone but Fallon and Lily and Lady Sinclair. Pelham was not exactly offering a shoulder to cry on.

"He looks a great deal older than you," Pelham said, obviously trying to break the awkward silence.

"He is. I married when I was seventeen. He was forty-one."

"And I suppose you fell in love with a younger man."

"Mmm." She tossed the portrait of Oliver back into the trunk without wrapping it again. Then she tossed that of her parents in, too. She would burn the contents of the trunk when she was done. Burn it all except...

She stared at a dirty white piece of fabric, grasped it, and gently tugged Mr. Whiskers from under a stack of dingy shawls.

"What the devil is that?"

She smiled and hugged the much-loved stuffed rabbit. "Mr. Whiskers, of course."

"It looks like a dirty rag."

She rolled her eyes. "You, sir, have no imagination. Mr. Whiskers—who is a rabbit, since you have no imagination—was a good friend for many years. My mother made him for me when my father had forbidden me to have dog. And then even after I did have a dog..." She trailed off, remembering the chocolate puppy Oliver had given her as a wedding gift. He'd been so soft and warm, so wriggly, and his big brown eyes had looked at her with such trust, such love from the first moment she held him.

How was she to know she was bringing him into a nightmare?

"Your father finally relented?"

She glanced up at Pelham. He was sitting on her trunk now, an indulgent look on his face. "No. My husband gave me a puppy, the sweetest creature." She could feel the sting of tears burning her eyes and then, to her horror, one of the salty tears dropped onto her skirt.

"What is the matter?" Pelham asked, sounding horrified. She glanced up at him. He looked ready to bolt.

"Nothing." She swiped at the tears. "I was just thinking of the puppy."

"What happened to him?" Pelham asked warily. He obviously feared a fresh outbreak of tears.

"I don't know. When he was angry, Oliver always threatened to kill Brownie. I didn't think he'd actually do it. I didn't think he'd go that far." She was weeping now, unable to stop herself and mortified that she should make a scene in front of the last person who would be even remotely sympathetic.

And then to her shock, he was kneeling beside her on the floor, and he set Mr. Whiskers gently on the trunk and put his arms stiffly around her.

She was so surprised, she stopped crying and looked up at him.

"Did he kill the dog?" Pelham asked quietly. Something in his eyes made her think he understood.

But how could he? How could anyone who had not lived with a man who took pleasure in terrorizing everyone around him and who sought to control his wife through any and every means necessary?

"I don't know. I—I made him angry. Something silly. I had disturbed his papers or some such thing."

She gave a half laugh. "You would probably have sided with Oliver and not thought it silly at all. But I was so young and so careless about small matters. I didn't think. Even though I knew the consequences, I didn't think."

She remembered it had been a beautiful spring morning. She'd gone out to help their housekeeper hang the laundry, taking the frisky dog with her. They'd played tug on the rope and fetch, and he'd chased her through some nearby wildflowers.

Oliver had been gone that morning, and she felt free and happy. After an hour or so, she and Brownie stormed into the house, and she hadn't even looked at her shoes. She'd tracked mud onto the floors, and the dog's paws were dirty as well. She'd poured herself a glass of water from the pitcher and watched Brownie happily lap water from his bowl. Then she'd stupidly— stupidly—set the pitcher on the table without looking. Oliver always had their manservant lay his papers on that corner of the table. He liked to look over business at meals. She'd put the pitcher on top of the papers, ruining them when the condensation ran down the sides of the cool pottery.

"What happened?" Pelham's voice was quiet, steady. He didn't ask what she meant by *consequences* or agree that a man's business papers were sacred. He simply encouraged her to continue.

"Brownie disappeared, and I never saw him again. I searched for him. I looked everywhere, but I never found him."

"Did you ask your husband about him?"

She nodded. "He never said a word, but he smiled."

She put her hands over her eyes. "Oh, I don't know how to describe it. It was a small, sardonic smile that let me know he had gotten rid of my dog. I suppose he saw it as payback. I ruined something he cared about, and he took something I cared about."

"A dog is not the same as papers—no matter how important."

She was acutely aware of the warmth of him now. His arms had relaxed slightly, so he wasn't holding her quite so tensely. She smelled the wool of his coat and the clean, soapy smell of the linen of his shirt. She looked into his eyes. They were a deep blue, such a pretty color, and mysterious, like he was. "I never said Oliver was a fair man," she said.

"What kind of man was he?"

Her gaze flicked down to Pelham's lips. "The kind I don't wish to discuss." She felt warm, safe, and beneath that, the faintest hint of yearning. How long had it been since she had kissed a man? *Been* kissed by a man?

Pelham disliked her. Somewhere deep inside she knew that. She wanted to detest him, too, but how could she when he held her while she cried over a dog lost years before? How could she hate a man who sat on a rough attic floor with her, probably ruining trousers that cost more than one of her best gowns? How could she hate a man who had treated Mr. Whiskers—who really was little more than an old rag now—so tenderly?

She rose slightly on her knees so their faces were level. She waited for him to push to his feet, but he didn't move. She could have sworn he didn't even breathe.

Slowly, ever so slowly, she leaned forward and brushed his lips with hers. The frisson of skin on skin sent a shiver through her, but she checked her impulse to seize him and devour him hungrily.

She was not an impulsive child any longer.

Well, she was no longer a child, anyway.

Instead, she traced the strong plane of his cheek with the palm of her hand, feeling the first hints of stubble on his bare skin. Vaguely, she remembered taking her gloves off and setting them on her dresser in her room. Now she was glad. She liked the feel of his skin. It was actually warm, proving he was indeed human.

She breathed in his scent, the taste of tea and jam on his lips, and then brushed her lips over his again.

He was a statue. Her gaze flicked to his, and his eyes were wide but dark, so dark. With a half smile, she flicked the tip of her tongue out and scraped it across his lower lip.

He inhaled sharply, and his arms tightened around her.

"Shall I stop?" she whispered. "I know this is wildly inappropriate."

"There's little about you not inappropriate," he answered, his voice husky.

"And I think you might just like that about me."

"No. I—"

She didn't give him time to answer. She slanted her mouth over his, claiming his lips in a kiss that made heat pool in her belly and her entire body tingle. She was certain his face must be tingling where her fingers still touched him. He didn't resist her, but neither did he return the kiss. She'd had enough of men forcing themselves on her to want to avoid doing the same at all costs.

She pulled back and took a deep breath. "I'm sorry. I shouldn't have done that."

He stared at her. How could his eyes be so dark and so lovely? Blue velvet, she thought. They reminded her of her favorite riding habit.

"Why did you?" he asked.

"Why does anyone do anything?" She pushed back, broke his hold on her. "Because I wanted to." She stood and felt her walls drop back into place.

He was still stone. "I've given you no encouragement."

"No," she reassured him, raising her chin. "You have actively discouraged me. And I can understand why. Your fiancée is dead. To kiss me—to kiss anyone—a day after her murder would be callous indeed." She strolled to the window, hoping to God they could be out of here soon so she could stop feeling like such a dolt.

"And yet you kissed me." His voice came from behind her and sounded steady and logical. Everything she was not.

She waved a hand. "Momentary lapse of reason. Your manly charms overwhelmed me."

"Is this a game to you?" He stood, and she heard the swish as he dusted off his trousers.

She spun back to face him. "No. But I should think before I act. I wanted you, and so I took you. It won't happen again."

He stared at her. "Bloody hell but you're frank."

"You seemed to want the truth, and I gave it to you. Do you want me to act coy and pretend I didn't kiss you? To pretend I don't feel anything when you put your arms around me, when I touch your skin, when I look in your eyes? I feel something between us, and God knows I don't want it any more than you do."

She spun back to the window, but his hand caught her elbow and pulled her into his arms. "What are you—?"

For a moment she considered fighting. She didn't like to be taken off guard. She didn't like to be handled roughly. But then his hold softened, and he pulled her against his chest. She held her breath, wondering what would come next. She half expected a lecture about how he was a duke and she was a courtesan, a speck of dirt, beneath his notice…

And then he took her face between his hands, looked into her eyes, and said, "I'm certain Brownie was given to another family. He's probably still chasing rabbits." His thumb caressed her cheek. "And with regard to your husband, you're well rid of him."

He released her, and she all but toppled over. He, on the other hand, walked calmly to the trunk, pushed it off the hatch on the floor, and proceeded to leave her in the attic alone.

She didn't expect him to explain all his actions to her, but a simple "by your leave" wouldn't be amiss.

She sank down to the floor and almost laughed. Amazing how the man could arouse her, stun her, and anger her all in the space of two minutes. She thought of his words again. Did he realize he had just condoned her divorce? He, a duke and a paragon of Society, had just told her she was well rid of her former husband.

And the way he'd done so... He'd been so gentle. She had not thought Pelham capable of any emotion, but he'd actually seemed to feel compassion for her.

The man was an enigma, and the more he confounded her attempts to understand him, the more she wanted to know him, the more she was drawn to him. His maidservant had spoken of secrets. What were they? And why did she feel that despite the huge—no, *enormous*—gap in their social stations, he understood her?

Pray God Lucifer was caught soon. The sooner she and Pelham parted ways, the better.

She—

She heard the creak of the floor below her and the scrape of a boot. It was too late to pull the ladder up or close the attic door now, so she scrambled behind the trunk and held her breath.

The floor creaked again, and then she heard the sound of a man's boot on the first attic step.

Eleven

SHE'D BEWITCHED HIM. THAT WAS THE ONLY EXPLANATION for why he, the Duke of Pelham, had allowed a courtesan to kiss him.

Or perhaps it was because he'd felt sorry for her, he considered as he walked quickly through the town house and down the stairs to where he'd stationed his men. Except that he hadn't felt sorry for her. He'd understood how she felt and what she'd been through.

And he didn't want to understand, and he didn't want to know what she'd been through. The damn woman made him think *too* much.

He'd had a Brownie, too—oh, he hadn't named his dog anything so sweet as *Brownie*. His dog was Hunter, and he'd been a birthday present when Pelham turned six. Of course, he hadn't been Pelham then. He'd been Master William, the future Duke of Pelham.

And he'd never had a dog, never had anything that was his own. Master William had loved that dog, and the dog had loved him.

It was a wondrous feeling to have something love him—to have something lick his face and stand at his side and seek him out. Pelham had had so precious little love in his short life.

But he should have known how it would end. He should have known!

He paused at the town house's door and slammed his hand into the wall beside it.

He'd been six, devil take it! How could he have known? And why did he allow her to make him think of those days again?

They were done. Over. He was no child. He was no scared little boy. He was a man. He was a bloody duke, and heaven and hell and everywhere in between knew the duties associated with that title were weighty enough without a courtesan stirring up murky memories from the past. The past didn't matter. What mattered was that Pelham had become a duke his father would approve. He had done his duty.

He threw the town house door open and startled a footman standing directly on the other side. "Your Grace, I was sent to seek you out. We've searched the area and found no sign of anything untoward."

"Good. Tell the coachman to prepare the coach. We're leaving directly."

Pelham went back inside and took the stairs two at a time. He stopped outside Juliette's bedroom, but she wasn't inside. His gaze rested on her bed, on the knife piercing the bedclothes. What if he'd turned Juliette out last night? Would the knife be plunged into her heart?

He didn't want to care. He didn't want to take responsibility for one more person, especially a brash courtesan who made him feel... too much. But what could he do? She was his now. Somehow she'd elbowed her way under his wing. The trick would be to keep her safe without succumbing to the temptation she offered.

His eyes rested on the bed again.

He shook his head and stepped out. No, the trick would be not to allow her to upset his life, his routine. Yes, Lady Elizabeth was probably dead. That was unfortunate. He could not help but wonder if he shouldn't feel it was something worse than merely *unfortunate*. Shouldn't he be grief-stricken? Shouldn't he be hell-bent on exacting cold revenge?

But every time he tried to conjure a feeling of sorrow for Lady Elizabeth's death, his mind wandered instead to the change her death would require in his plans—all of the adjustments. Firstly, he would have to adjust to the presence of this courtesan, this Duchess, and a killer, Lucifer, into his life. He did not like the disruptions these people and events made to his routine. And devil take him if he was thinking about his routine again when he was supposed to be feeling anguished.

Pelham shook his head and checked his pocket watch. It was after noon. He was late for his midday meal. But he swore this was the last time he would allow his routine to be altered.

He poked his head in the town house's other rooms and failed to find Juliette. Wonder of wonders, she'd actually done the intelligent thing and stayed in the attic. His look about had also satisfied him no interlopers were lurking in the house.

Pelham stood under the attic hatchway and started up the steps. He'd barely cleared the hatch when something whooshed at him, and he ducked, narrowly avoiding tumbling back down the steps. "What the devil!"

"Oh, it's you." Her ribbon of blonde hair slid over the top steps as she peered down to where he hung onto the ladder.

"Who did you think it was?"

She shrugged. "I didn't want to take any chances."

He climbed back up and eyed the candlestick sitting next to the hatchway. "Is that what you almost hit me with?"

She gave a sheepish smile. "It makes a rather good weapon, I think."

He swiped the candlestick and moved it out of her reach. "No more weapons for you. Come and finish packing. We leave directly."

"For?"

"My town house." He climbed down the ladder and made a point of keeping his eyes on the floor. He would not chance looking up and seeing a glimpse of her leg.

"And after that?" she said, stepping off the ladder and standing beside him.

"There is no after that."

"Then we're not taking the magistrate's advice and leaving London?"

"No." He started for the stairs leading to the vestibule, intending to leave her alone to make preparations.

She hurried after him. "But why not?"

"Because the dukes of Pelham don't run away."

For a moment, he had almost forgotten that key point. "We stand and fight."

He thought she'd keep after him, but when he looked back, she was standing outside her bedroom door, her expression inscrutable.

❧

Perhaps running was her problem, Juliette thought as she stuffed the last of the belongings she deemed absolutely necessary into her trunk. It was the second of two, and she hoped Pelham didn't argue with her about how much she was taking. He had already come to check on her three times, pocket watch in hand. She was obviously keeping him from some pressing matter. Probably a meal. Men were always wanting to eat.

But she didn't know when she would be back, or even if she would ever be back.

And, of course, that meant she was doing what she always did. She ran.

But Pelham had said he wouldn't run, and she honestly could not understand why. It seemed all she'd done her entire life was run. She'd run from the death of her loving father into the arms of an abusive husband. She'd run from Oliver to the Earl of Sin, which had actually been the only good thing that had ever come from running. Then she'd run to London and into the life of a glamorous courtesan. She'd thought if she became the Duchess of Dalliance, she could forget all she'd been and all that had happened to her before.

But she couldn't. It was all still there, waiting in her attic.

And she'd never really escaped Oliver, either. She

was always watching for him, waiting for him to turn up. Deep down, she knew as long as he lived, she'd never be free of him. He'd promised her that much and more. And now she had to watch for Lucifer, too. And she feared that even if both men were somehow exiled to the New World, she would never really be rid of them because she hadn't stood up to them, hadn't fought—figuratively or literally.

She'd simply run.

But not everyone could fight. Not everyone had the prestige of being a duke of Pelham.

Except Juliette had seen something else in Pelham when he'd touched her cheek in the attic. And she thought perhaps being a duke didn't shield one from all of life's unpleasantness. Unfortunately, that little peek into his heart—his vulnerable heart—had touched her own. Perhaps he wasn't such an ogre after all.

"Ahem."

She turned and saw the ogre himself standing in her doorway, pocket watch open in his hand. With a flourish, she closed the trunk. "There!"

He raised a brow. "Is that all? Are you certain you don't have dishes or a couch or a servant or two you'd like to stuff in there?"

"You're very amusing."

They took his coach back, and her trunks followed behind on a cart that had turned up when Pelham had but said the word. He was quiet as they rode through London. Juliette peeked out the carriage curtains and watched the expressions of the people they passed. She saw reverence and awe on their faces as they noted the ducal crest.

She'd always garnered attention when she rode through Town, as well, but the stares were far from reverent. People respected Pelham, admired him. No wonder he held so tightly to his name and reputation. He had much to protect.

As they neared his town house, her brows drew together. Pelham must have been watching her, because he asked, "What is it?"

"I don't know. There's a carriage in front of your house, and your servants are outside. It looks as though they are arguing with the coachman."

Pelham was immediately beside her, drawing the curtains apart. "Damn it." He glanced at her. "I'd beg your pardon, but I'm sure you've heard worse."

Of course she had heard worse, but that didn't excuse Pelham. Then again, why should she expect him to treat her as he would a lady? "Far worse," she said. "Who is it?"

"The Marquess of Nowlund, Lady Elizabeth's father. And... yes. That's her mother, as well." He swore again then gave her a hard look as his coach drew to a stop. "Stay in the coach. Do not, under any circumstances, show yourself."

"Yes, sir." She saluted, making light of the situation. She would never let him see how it hurt her to have to hide. But she could do nothing but shame and embarrass Pelham. She'd thought she'd come to terms with these facts of her life. She was an independent woman. She was the toast of London. So what if decent men and women pretended she didn't exist and crossed the street when they saw her coming?

It hadn't really bothered her before.

She hadn't even thought about it until now. Until she was with Pelham.

He climbed out of the coach, and she drew back into the shadows. The door closed, and she heard him hail the marquess. The two men's voices sounded like a low rumble, and then they were joined by a woman's voice—high-pitched. Upset.

Eliza's mother.

They must have moved closer to the ducal coach, because slowly their words became clearer.

"—even care about our daughter?" Lady Nowlund was asking.

"Of course I do, my lady. I've already spoken to the magistrate this morning."

"So have we," Lord Nowlund said. "He doesn't know anything. We searched the house three times over for some diamonds or other and found nothing."

"They said that… that duchess woman saw her murdered." This came from Lady Nowlund. Inside the coach, Juliette pulled back. The scorn in the marchioness's voice was enough to make her cringe.

"But I can't believe that. This is just another of Lady Elizabeth's lapses in memory. Surely she forgot to tell us she had plans." That was Lord Nowlund. Apparently, it was not so unusual for Lady Elizabeth to disappear.

"Yes!" That was Lady Nowlund. "Just like when she ran off to Yorkshire not long ago. No one knew why she would want to go to Yorkshire. Did she say anything to you, Your Grace? Give you any indication of where she might go?"

"No."

"Oh, I told Eliza she must stop being so flighty. I told her a man like you wanted a wife who was reliable. Now I suppose you will want to call off the engagement."

Juliette tried to imagine Pelham's face as the marchioness spoke. She was certain it was granite.

"Let us not speak of such things now," the duke said. "Let us bring Lady Elizabeth home. That is our first and only concern at the moment."

A long silence followed, and Juliette had to stop herself from parting the curtains. Had the three walked away? Then Lord Nowlund's voice exploded. "I will not be silenced. I will ask!"

Silence from Pelham. Juliette imagined he stood stiffly, waiting.

"Are the rumors true, Your Grace?" Lord Nowlund asked. "Have you taken up with that… *courtesan*?"

"I won't dignify that question with an answer," Pelham said.

Good evasion tactic, Juliette thought. It might even work for him.

"Is that woman, the harlot, the reason my daughter ran away?" Lady Nowlund asked.

Or perhaps not.

Juliette rested her head on the squabs. How had she stepped into this nightmare? It simply could not get any worse.

"No. I assure you I've done nothing that would account for Lady Elizabeth's disappearance. The courtesan and I have no ties," Pelham said. Even in the coach, Juliette could hear the undercurrent of danger in his voice.

"But that doesn't exactly answer the question, does it?" the marquess demanded. "Are you or are you not involved with that woman?"

"I am most certainly not," Pelham said.

And then Juliette heard it—the rattle of wheels on the street. It sounded like a cart. She drew in a breath as she saw in her mind a cart with two trunks lumber to a stop in front of the duke's town house.

She closed her eyes as the door to the coach flew open. When she opened them, Lady Nowlund was staring at her with undisguised disgust. "There! There's the harlot right there."

Over Lady Nowlund's head, she could see Pelham. He was angry, furious if the vein throbbing in his neck was any indication.

"How do you explain this... this *slut*?" Lord Nowlund wanted to know after gawking at her as well.

Lady Nowlund looked at Pelham, and Juliette looked, as well. She imagined everyone within half a block was looking at Pelham. She held her breath. What would he say? A tiny, tiny part of her wanted him to defend her. Wanted him to say, *How dare you call her a slut? How dare you impugn her? You know nothing about her. Under that icy shell, she's warm and funny and loving and has wishes and dreams just like you.*

Pelham said, "I told you I was doing everything in my power to find Lady Elizabeth. If that means I must associate with the worst of Society—with the pick-pockets, drunks, and sluts—then I will. But do not ever, *ever*, accuse me of being involved with that woman."

Lady Nowlund and her husband stepped back at the vehemence in his voice. "Is that understood?"

Oh, Juliette thought. She understood all right. She understood perfectly.

Twelve

PELHAM SAT IN HIS LIBRARY, A GLASS OF PORT IN HAND. It was late, very late, and he was weary. It was not his habit to sit alone drinking. He liked to be in bed at eleven and up with the sun.

But eleven had long since come and gone, and here he sat. And drank.

It was the woman keeping him awake. The look on her face when he'd put Lord and Lady Nowlund in their places had rent him in two.

Oh, it had been a fleeting look—there for no more than a second and then quickly replaced by her cool exterior. But he'd seen it. He'd seen the vulnerability just for a moment.

He'd hurt her.

Bloody damn hell. He did not want to care about hurting her. The one thing he liked about her was that she wasn't the emotional tidal wave most women were. They'd been through several disturbing events together, and she hadn't broken down. She hadn't dissolved into hysterics.

But she was no block of stone, either. Clearly, her

former husband had hurt her. He doubted this was information she had shared with other men.

But she had shared it with him.

And now he'd hurt her, too.

He downed the port and poured another glass. He was good and drunk now. Why not have another?

And what did the woman expect, anyway? She was a Cyprian, for God's sake! She took men to her bed for money. She and her two friends were famous for servicing the Earl of Sinclair. He didn't know if they took turns or all frolicked together, and he didn't care.

She *was* a slut.

What choice did she have?

Pelham drank again to still that small voice in his head. Oh, where was his father's voice when he actually wanted it? "There are always choices," he muttered. "One doesn't have to sell one's body to survive."

What do you know about it? You're a man and a duke.

"That's right. I am a duke, and I bloody well don't have to listen to you."

"I haven't said anything yet."

He all but jumped, sloshing a measure of port on his loosened cravat where it streamed down his linen shirt.

He blinked when she came into focus, and he sniffed his port. Had someone added more than port to the decanter? He was seeing visions.

"You look as though you've had enough." She was standing in front of him, and before he could respond, she plucked his glass from his hand and sipped.

She shrugged. "Not bad. I prefer brandy, but I recently had to give it up."

"How did you get in here?"

"Through the door." She looked back at it, and he took the opportunity to blatantly peruse her. She was wearing a silk robe over what looked like a simple white nightshift. Her feet were bare, and her blonde hair was caught with a blue scrap of satin and tumbled over one shoulder like a silver ribbon.

She wasn't the picture of a courtesan. Oh, he supposed the silk robe could be seductive, if she wanted it to be, but it was hardly arousing over a linen nightgown. Free of adornment and with her hair down, she looked young and pretty, not exactly a Duchess of Dalliance.

She turned back to him, and he quickly looked away.

"I couldn't sleep and wanted a book."

"You read?"

She laughed. "Sometimes." She gestured to the empty spot on the couch beside him. "May I?"

"I don't think that's a good idea."

"Why?" she asked, taking the seat anyway. He felt the silk of the robe brush his hand and shivered. "Because you're foxed and might take advantage of me?"

"I'm not foxed."

"You're slurring your words." She set the glass of port on the floor beside the leg of the couch. "And your eyes are bleary. If there's one thing I know, it's when a man is foxed." She said it matter-of-factly.

"I'm not foxed." He was, but he had already said he wasn't. A duke was decisive. He had decided something earlier this evening. What was it? "We're leaving in the morning."

Her brows rose. "I thought dukes didn't run away."

"I'm not running." He stumbled over the *r* in

running, but he went on anyway. "I'm investigating. It's not the same thing."

"Of course. Now I see the difference. Is this *investigation* outside London?"

"Yorkshire."

"Yorkshire? The seat of your country estate?"

"It's near Nowlund Park, where Lady Elizabeth grew up. The marchioness said something yesterday that piqued my interest."

She tucked her legs under her and sat forward. "Pray tell. I'd love to know what piques the interest of a man like you."

And this was why she was a notorious courtesan. Pelham didn't think he'd spoken so many words together since… well, very rarely. But she had him talking. Despite that icy veneer, she was easy to talk to.

That's because she's not icy. You can feel how warm she is.

"Stubble it."

"Pardon?"

"Nothing. The marchioness mentioned Lady Elizabeth had made a quick jaunt home a fortnight ago. Claimed she wanted to see her dowered land one last time before agreeing to the betrothal."

"Ah, so she came with land."

"What's your point?"

"I don't know exactly. I thought you were in love with her, but then I realized you weren't. I suppose I wondered what would entice a man like you to marry."

"I am a duke. I have to produce an heir."

"Exactly, but why Lady Elizabeth for your heir? Now I know. Land."

Why did he feel that, in the guise of these compliments, she was actually disparaging him?

"And I want to know why Lady Elizabeth would go to Yorkshire. She didn't care about that land."

Juliette's eyes widened. "You think she hid the diamonds there?"

"I don't know. I know your theory is before the events on the balcony at Carlton House, Lady Elizabeth told this Lucifer you had the diamonds. And this is what precipitated his visit to your home. But I can't think why she would do such a thing."

"Because you and I had been linked. She probably told him you gave me the diamonds." She nodded. "Yes, that makes sense. That night, Lucifer kept saying to me, *I know he gave them to you.* He must have been referring to you, Will."

Pelham ignored the completely inappropriate use of his name. *Will* wasn't even his name. It was William. "Why would I have these bloody diamonds?"

"Eliza told him you had them. I don't know what lie she concocted. It could be anything—you'd caught her with them and forced her to confess. She'd asked you to hold them for safekeeping…"

"I don't have them."

"But Lucifer doesn't know that, and if he thinks you have them, you're in danger."

"Then I suppose it best we find these diamonds."

"Will you return them?"

"No. But I want to know what I'm being threatened over. I want to know what Lady Elizabeth died for."

She clasped his arm with her bare hand. He realized he'd discarded his coat. All this time he'd been talking to her he'd been without a coat, and his cravat was undone. There was no excuse for such slovenliness. "Then you believe she's dead."

"I have no reason to believe otherwise." He glanced at her hand on his arm, and her gaze followed. "I'm not going to take advantage of you."

"No." She withdrew her hand. "You wouldn't."

"I called you a slut." He knew he was stating the obvious. Moreover, he knew he was bringing up a matter that, were he sober, he would never mention.

She laughed without humor. "I know. I heard."

"It upset you."

She pressed her lips together, the haughty reserve coming down again. "It didn't please me, but it's not the first time, and I suppose it won't be the last."

"You're not made of ice."

She gave him a puzzled look. "What strange things you say when you are foxed." She looked away, appearing to study the books behind his desk. "No, I'm not made of ice," she said quietly. "Neither are you, but we both have hard outer shells." She gazed at him, those blue eyes penetrating like icicles, only far, far warmer. "You know where my shell came from. What about yours?"

"I'm a duke. I'm expected to be—"

"Pompous?"

He frowned at her. "Formidable."

"Oh, you are that, but I have the feeling you want to apologize to me."

He blinked. "Why would I do that?"

"Because you hurt my feelings."

"Dukes don't apologize."

"No, they are far too arrogant." She rose, and he realized belatedly she intended to leave.

He also realized he didn't want her to go. It wasn't a mental realization. It came to him when he noted he'd caught her wrist with his hand.

She looked down, as cool as a winter day. "Your hand is wrapped about my wrist, Your Grace."

"Don't call me that."

He blinked. *What* had he just said? Something was wrong. Something was very wrong indeed. His body—his mouth—was not obeying his mind.

"What would you have me call you? *Your Highness?*"

"Will," he said.

She stared at him, something flickering in her eyes. Amusement? Surprise? "Are you going to take advantage of me, Will?"

"I might." He pulled her back on the couch beside him. "And I won't apologize for it later."

"No, I'm sure you won't."

He stared at her, amazed this beautiful creature was beside him. She'd kissed him in her attic this morning, and he hadn't been able to forget the feel of her lips on his. The smell of her, the taste of her. He wanted more.

And he could not have it. He was a duke. She was a courtesan, and he didn't want a mistress.

Anything more than that could never be.

She blinked at him then raised one of those sweeping eyebrows. "Well? I thought you were going to take advantage of me."

He could. He could kiss her, touch her. That was hardly taking advantage, considering who and what she was. But he didn't think he could leave it at that, because the more he knew her, the less she was the Duchess of Dalliance and the more she became Juliette.

She sighed. "Are you thinking about it, Will?"

"I'm weighing my options."

She rolled her eyes.

"Would you have me pounce on you like some sort of animal?"

"That's what most men do."

"And that's what you want?"

"Will." She took his shoulders. "I don't want to be attacked, but a woman likes to feel desired. As it is now, I can see you making lists in your head. Next you'll pull out your watch and check the time." She stood. He was losing her. "All your contemplation has given me time to contemplate. And do you know what I've contemplated? You insulted me today. You've insulted me on several occasions and all but called me a liar. You dragged me out of bed and humiliated me in front of your staff."

He stood. "*I* humiliated *you*?"

"Yes! I kissed you this afternoon because I was feeling vulnerable… and because"—she clenched a hand as though her next words were distasteful—"you were kind. For once. But I don't want to kiss you again. And I certainly don't want to share your bed. You probably look at that dratted pocket watch when you're making love!" She whirled, and he stood there, prepared to let her go.

And then his pride bubbled to the surface, and he took three steps, caught her about the waist, and swung her around.

"Oh, now what?"

"Now this." He lowered his mouth to hers and kissed her. He meant the kiss to prove to her that he could be spontaneous, that he was not as she'd painted him. But of course, as soon as he kissed her, he started wondering if this had been a mistake and if he shouldn't just go to bed—alone—to prepare for the early morning departure.

And then she kissed him back.

Her mouth moved under his, and she made a small sound like a satisfied cat. And Will forgot all about time and mistakes and everything but the woman in his arms. Her mouth was soft and sweet, her lips ripe under his, her breath tasting slightly of the port she'd drank. The silk robe she wore was thin, and he could feel her curves beneath it as he wrapped his arms about her and pulled her closer. She was warm and feminine and just the right height. He did not have to bend to reach her lips.

His hand moved up the silk on her back and wrapped about the silk of her hair. It was thicker than it looked and softer, as well. He could imagine it spread beneath her on her bed of blue silk. He could imagine her making those little kitten sounds she made now in his bed as he pleasured her.

Her hands grasped his hair and pulled him nearer still. He couldn't seem to get enough of her, and he slanted his mouth over hers, kissing her deeply and thoroughly. She broke away and murmured, "Will."

The sound of her pet name for him broke his last barriers. He was hard for her, and he nipped her neck, smelling the scent of lavender. Kissing his way to her ear, he felt her shiver and moan.

But she wasn't moaning. She was speaking. "Touch me," she whispered. "It's been so long. Touch me."

Her hand guided his around her slim waist, up her rib cage, and to the fullness of her breast. He cupped it, feeling the hardness of her nipple through the thin layers between them. He remembered the soft flesh of her arm that night he had touched her at Carlton House. Would this flesh be even softer?

Don't think, Pelham! he chastised himself and did what his body urged. He tugged the robe open, saw it flutter and pool on the floor, then gazed at the porcelain shoulder revealed by the loose nightshift. He put one finger in the neckline and inched it down.

His gaze met hers, and she wet her lips. Everything in him strained to rip the nightshift off her, but he held on to the last vestiges of control and was rewarded with the plump flesh of her breast. A moment later, her pink areola came into view, and then the hard nub of her nipple.

His finger skated over it, over flesh so soft he could not begin to describe it, and the way the skin contracted further drove him to the edge of maddening desire. He teased the hardened flesh, and her head fell back slightly, as though she offered herself to him.

He took. Without thinking, he took, lowering his mouth to that impossibly soft flesh and that exquisitely hard nipple. He took her in his mouth, tasting, lapping, sucking gently until she was crying out. He moved her toward the couch, wanting to feel her beneath him, wanting to see her supple body inch by inch.

They took two steps, three, and then there was a crash.

She jerked, and he was instantly on alert. Had Lucifer somehow managed to gain entrance to the house? Pelham had posted additional men to guard the perimeter. He didn't believe the man could make it through his security, but he was taking no chances. He pushed Juliette behind him and looked about for something to use as a weapon. The fire poker was closest.

"Will."

He could lunge for it and—

"*Will.*"

He turned.

She pointed to the floor. His glass of port was upturned, the dark liquid spreading on the floor in a small pool. "It was only the glass. I knocked it with my foot."

"I see." He looked up at her, and she pulled the bodice of her nightshift up to cover herself. The moment was awkward, and he remembered why he avoided entanglements with women—hell, with anyone—there was always that awkward moment when one fears one has revealed too much.

What was he supposed to say now? What was he supposed to do? Why the bloody damn hell had he kissed her in the first place?

"Since now would be the appropriate time to apologize"—she bent and retrieved her robe—"and we both know you won't do that, I suppose I should take my leave." She wrapped herself in the robe and tied it securely. She didn't appear the least disturbed he'd just had his hands all over her—not to mention his mouth and tongue. His hands were still shaking with arousal, but her fingers were as steady as a tumbler on a high rope.

It came to him this meant nothing to her. And why should it? She was a courtesan. This was her nightly routine. Had she felt *anything* when he touched her?

"We'll make an early start tomorrow," he said, his own voice sounding surprisingly calm in light of the pounding of the blood in his ears—and other regions.

"Yes, and I know what happens if I'm not dressed and ready on your schedule." She gave a laugh and waltzed from the room.

Pelham watched her go then sat and put his head in his hands. Now that she'd gone, he could not understand what he had done. He could be logical and reasonable and tell himself touching her was a mistake. Kissing her was an egregious mistake. Anything further was utter catastrophe.

But when she was near...

He raked his fingers through his hair. When she was near, he knew he was making a mistake, and yet he did it anyway.

He glanced at his desk, at the portrait hanging to the right of it. There was really no excuse for it, he thought, staring at the portrait of his father. It was weakness and behavior not befitting a duke.

It would cease now. Tonight.

He would not touch her again.

But that didn't mean he could stop wanting her.

⁓

The man was stone, Juliette thought as they raced along in the well-sprung ducal carriage. He sat across from her, reading the *Times* and completely ignoring her. He'd been doing so for the last six hours.

True, she hadn't tried to make conversation, but then she was playing the role of the Duchess of Dalliance. She was supposed to be used to this sort of thing, not be clamoring for attention the morning after a liaison. Not feeling insecure and wondering what she had done wrong.

She'd been wondering since last night. As soon as they'd been interrupted, he'd looked at her with such ferocity it had scared her. She'd thought it best to make a hasty retreat, all the while hoping he would stop her.

Hoping she'd been wrong about him.

Hoping…

She could picture Lady Sinclair's face in her mind, and the countess was frowning. Hoping was what naïve young girls did, not independent women. Hoping for something did not make it come true.

She could hope Pelham felt something for her all she wanted, but his actions said something very different. His very words said something completely different.

Why had she even kissed him? From the start, he'd done nothing but insult her. Lady Sinclair would raise a brow and ask, "Now Juliette, why would you kiss a man who obviously detests you?"

Because he didn't detest her. He just thought he did. Really, he needed her, needed someone to wrench him from his mind-numbing routine and introduce some fun into his life. He said he did not want her, did not like her, but his eyes said something altogether different.

When he looked at her, his gaze—hard and dangerous as it was—made her ache. Suddenly her skin was so sensitive even her softest silks itched and chafed. And she might be standing in the cold morning—arguing with him as to whether or not they should take a carriage with a ducal crest when they were trying to be inconspicuous—and he could look at her, and she would feel as though she were in the middle of a desert.

And…

I know! I know! I know! she told Lady Sinclair in her mind. This was folly. She wanted him to need her, and she wanted his gaze to reflect what she felt for him. But it was nothing more than lust.

It was not love, not even romance.

She had been celibate too long. Spent too many long, lonely nights wishing she had someone to hold her. Pelham had made it clear he would not be that man.

And she didn't want him to be. She wanted a man who loved her, who accepted her for who she was, not one who would judge her.

And most certainly not a duke, who was the center of attention wherever he went. She would never be able to live down her past married to a duke. Though she often wondered if she could live it down regardless of whom she married.

And Pelham was so cold, obviously completely unaffected by all that had passed between them last night. Did he know how rare it was to feel that kind of spark, that kind of passion? She'd talked to dozens of courtesans, and very few actually felt anything at all when they bedded a man. It wasn't something that happened for everyone. She herself had kissed her fair share of men and usually felt only mild disgust at their slobbering all over her.

She could not have said what Pelham did differently. She could not have said why his touch, his kiss, his very voice made her melt inside. But they did, and it wasn't right.

"It's not fair!"

He lowered the paper. "What was that?"

She pressed her lips together. Had she spoken aloud? He blinked at her, those dark eyes working their spell on her. She took a shaky breath. She would not be a foolish woman any longer. "I said, are we almost there?"

He raised a brow. "We're traveling to Yorkshire."

Perhaps she would be foolish, but she would not behave like a lovesick ninny. "But we will stop for the night, won't we? We've only paused at posting houses, and I've been out of the carriage once in six hours, and that was for all of five minutes."

"It was almost a quarter of an hour," he said.

"You should know, as you had that ridiculous watch in your hand the entire time."

He frowned. It was the kind of frown that would make even the prime minister relent. But Juliette wasn't afraid of him. She'd been married to Oliver, and she'd been threatened by Lucifer. A mere *Dangerous* Duke didn't scare her.

"Someone must keep us on schedule," he said. "Clearly, it won't be you."

"You and your schedules and your routines!" And your cold, cold heart, she added silently. "Do you ever vary from your routine? Have you ever asked your coachman to simply stop the carriage so you could get out and walk through a field of wildflowers?" She swept the drapes apart and pointed to a pretty meadow. There were no wildflowers, but there was a low fence and a brown pony craning its neck to reach the tender grass on the other side. "Why not stop now and go feed that pony some apples? The sun is out." She pointed to the sky, which was actually rather cloudy and gray, but at times the sun had peeked out. "The day is warm." If one wore a warm spencer. "We might never have this chance again."

He was looking at her as though she were mad. And she was. She was completely mad. She needed to get out of this carriage before she said or did something she would regret.

"We will not stop the carriage and feed that pony because—" He held up a finger. "It is bad for the horses to stop and start. They have to be cooled off and rubbed down and walked. One cannot just stop and start at will on a long journey such as we are taking." He held up another finger, and Juliette sighed. "We have no apples to feed the pony." He held up a third finger. "We are not on a pleasure ride." He slammed the curtains closed again and lifted his paper.

Juliette huffed and lifted the book she had taken from his library. It was *The Knights of Calatrava*, and she should have been enjoying it, but then nothing was enjoyable in Pelham's presence. As if to prove her point, a half hour later it started to rain. Not a small shower, but a gusty, thundering downpour of a storm. At the first crack of thunder, Pelham lowered his paper.

Juliette gave him an accusatory look. "Now see what you've done."

He tried to make some response, but she raised her book and ignored him.

Insufferable ass.

Thirteen

PELHAM STOOD IN THE RAIN AND SUPERVISED THE INN'S grooms as they stabled his horses. An hour in the storm, trudging through thick mud to reach the inn, had left the horses tired and hungry. Pelham himself was soaked through, chilled to the bone, and annoyed beyond measure. He'd wanted to travel the better part of the day and evening, and now his carefully planned schedule was ruined.

And Juliette saw fit to blame him for the storm. He would just as soon pin it on her. After all, his life had been perfectly scheduled, perfectly routine before she entered it.

When the horses were tended to his satisfaction, he clomped through the muddy inn yard. It wasn't a bad inn. He didn't typically stay here, because many members of the *ton* did, and he didn't relish their company. The inn was far from luxurious, but he could trust the proprietor would provide a warm bath, hot food, and a clean bed. He had the urge to check his pocket watch, because he was not certain if it was time for a meal, but he resisted. He would eat no matter what the time.

And Juliette said he couldn't be spontaneous.

Pelham pulled open the door of the inn and stopped short. When he had escorted Juliette into the public room, it had been quiet and subdued, a few men and women sitting quietly over cups of tea at small wooden tables. Now raucous voices and—was that singing?—assailed him. He stared at the group of men in the corner of the room. Most of them had a leg propped on a wooden bench, and from the looks of them they were vying for someone's attention.

The rest of the room was empty except for a few serving girls.

He looked back at the group then back at the room.

Not a single woman remained in the room, if one didn't count the serving wenches. Not even Juliette. Pelham marched to the group of men, knowing what he was going to find before he even saw her.

With his height, it wasn't long before he spotted her. She was seated, pretty as a picture, on a chair surrounded by half a dozen or more men. They offered her food and drink, clamored for her attention, and she bestowed it on each with a smile and a moment's glance.

He would have been suitably impressed at her management skills if he hadn't been furious. His fury must have radiated from him, because several of the men closest to him took steps back, and Juliette's gaze met his. "Will!" she said and smiled.

His fury turned to rage as all attention focused on him. "What are you doing?" he ground out.

"Waiting for you," she answered, as though this were patently obvious.

"And what is this?" He gestured to the men surrounding them.

"Oh, these are friends. Surely you know Lord—"

"I told you to wait for me, not to ply your trade."

Her face went pale, and her eyes narrowed. She rose, slowly. "I beg your pardon. I was conversing with friends. Nothing more."

He stepped closer to her, aware they were making a scene, and though he abhorred scenes he was too angry to stop himself. "And all of these *friends* want to take you to their beds."

"What do you care?" she said, hands on hips. "You don't own me. You have no say in what I do or do not do. Whom I do or do not bed." Her expression told him into which category he had been placed.

He opened his mouth to respond, but no words came forth. She was correct. But just because he didn't want her—which was a bald-faced lie—didn't mean he wanted another man to have her. He glanced at the men surrounding them. It seemed to Pelham they were smirking, waiting for him to give up his claim so they could step in.

Well, he wasn't going to do it.

He grasped Juliette's arm, pulled her to him, wrapped an arm about her waist, and kissed her. She sputtered a protest against his lips, but he silenced it with the flick of his tongue. She didn't go limp as she had in his library. He could feel the indignation in her rigid spine, but she did surrender to the kiss.

When he broke away from her, applause and cheers erupted. He kept his gaze resolutely on her face. She gave him a look that would have made a lesser man burst into flames and descend into hell. "Innkeeper!" he called.

"Yes, Your Grace." The man scurried beside him, ready to do his bidding. "Escort the duchess to my room. I'll need only one chamber after all."

"Yes, Your Grace."

He didn't expect Juliette to argue or fight. That wasn't her way. She was a duchess in the truest sense of the word. She kept her head high and made a regal exit, following the innkeeper with cool, measured strides.

She was a much better duchess than he was a duke. His father would have been proud of her comportment and mortified at his own son's behavior. Pelham shook his head to silence the ringing in his ear.

A hand slapped him on the back, making him stumble forward. "That's the way, Pelham. Show her what's what."

He turned to the man, ready to put him in his place, when he realized he knew the gentleman. It was Viscount Marfham, an inveterate gambler. He'd all but depleted his family's fortune.

Since he had no reply, Pelham moved toward the steps—and was accosted by another man, the reprobate son of an earl. They'd been together at Eton. Was the whole *ton* here tonight? "You're a lucky man, Pelham. When you're done with her, you know where to find me."

"And me!" another man piped up. Pelham felt sick. What the devil was wrong with these men? She was a woman, not a hat one tired of and gave to someone else when one was through with it.

Was this her life? Being passed from man to man? His lip curled in disgust, and he pushed his way through.

"I don't suppose you're the type to share?" another man asked, and Pelham turned and hit him. He hadn't meant to strike the man. It seemed as though his fist acted of its own accord. Pelham stared as the man went sprawling across the floor, knocking a chair over and landing against a table leg. Blood poured from the injured man's nose, and Pelham stood, feeling as though he were a mere bystander.

And then the injured man sputtered and jumped to his feet. "Who the devil do you think you are?"

The earl's son rushed to his friend and held him back. "He's the Dangerous Duke. You'd best hope that's all he does to you."

Pelham looked at the other men. Several took a step back. "We didn't mean to offend you," Marfham said.

"In the future, try some respect," Pelham said and marched away.

He was halfway up the stairs before he realized what he'd said. *Respect* and *courtesan* didn't belong in the same sentence. And why did he expect anyone to respect her when he'd shown her the worst disrespect of any of them a few moments ago?

He met the innkeeper at the top of the stairs, and the man offered to show him to his room. Pelham declined, nodded when the innkeeper directed him, and ordered a bath and a hot meal brought to the room.

His feet had never felt so heavy as he made his way down the hallway and stopped outside the chamber.

He heard nothing from within. Not a scrape, not a rustle, not a whisper.

He wondered how much of a fool he would appear if he asked the innkeeper for his own room. But no. He was a duke. He need not worry about some courtesan's hurt feelings or avoid her wrath. And it was better if she was near him. He could keep her safe from the wolves below.

Of course, it appeared she'd been doing just fine without him, but that was beside the point.

He tugged on the handle and pushed the door in. Juliette was standing before the fire. She glanced over her shoulder at him then back at the fire.

He shrugged off his greatcoat and pulled off his gloves, and still her silence continued. He should have been glad she was not speaking to him, but he found he wanted her to say something. He was primed for battle.

"Aren't you going to chastise me for treating you like that in the public room?" he asked, sitting on a chair to work on his boot. It was completely inappropriate for him to undress before her, but what was the sense in propriety now? The entire *ton* was going to hear about the incident below and assume he was bedding her. If she saw his feet, it was nothing compared to the rest.

"I've been treated worse," she said, not looking at him. "It doesn't affect me."

"I don't believe that."

"Are you saying I have feelings?"

"Of course you do." He held one boot and stared at her back, not certain where this conversation was going or why he was taking it in that direction.

"I'm a courtesan, a woman of pleasure." She turned

to him, gave him a quick, seductive look. "What I feel doesn't matter."

Pelham clenched the boot in his hand. "How can you let men like—like that"—he gestured to the door—"touch you? Kiss you? Come to your bed?"

"Does it offend you? And this after you disgrace me in front of those men and then order me to your room?"

He began loosening his other boot so he wouldn't have to look at her.

"And what will you order me to do next? Take off your boots?" She crossed to him, presented her back, bent, and easily pulled off his boot. He tried—not very hard—not to admire her backside.

"Loosen your cravat?" She inserted a finger and loosened it with a quick flick. The material tumbled down his shirt. He was about to speak when a knock thudded on the door.

"No, no!" she said, hurrying to it. "I shall answer." She pulled it open and gave him a look. "A bath. Perfect. Now I can scrub your back. Put it near the fire," she directed the men. It was a huge copper tub, not the hip bath he was used to. It took three men to carry it, followed by a bevy of maidservants. The men clunked the tub down, and the women filled it with enormous buckets of steaming water. One handed Juliette a towel and soap, bobbed, and exited. "Well, at least you shall be clean when I service you. I—"

"Cease!" he roared.

She started, blinked at him.

"You're not going to service me or scrub my back." He crossed the room to her. "I wanted you with me to keep you safe."

"Ha! You wanted me with you because you were jealous."

"Jealous? *Jealous?* I am a duke. I do not feel jealousy."

To his utter amazement, she put her hands to her ears and screamed. "If I hear you say *I am a duke* one more time, I will not be responsible for my actions. Dukes are not gods, Will. They are people. They make mistakes, apologize—or at least they should—and feel all sorts of emotions."

"I suppose you are the expert on such matters."

"I have known several dukes."

"Yes, and I am a duke—"

Her eyes widened, her lips pursed. "I." She shoved him. "Warned." Hard. "You." Backward.

"Juliette—"

She shoved him again, and he stumbled against the lip of the tub, faltered, and fell, sloshing warm water all over the floor and soaking his clothing worse than the rain had done.

He stared up at her, water dripping in his eyes. He expected her to apologize, to look horrified, to beg his forgiveness.

Instead, she laughed.

❧

Juliette knew she shouldn't laugh. She knew it would affront Pelham's dignity, and he clung to it so tightly, but what else was she supposed to do? He looked like a waterlogged rat with his hair plastered in his eyes and his clothes soggy and limp about him.

He sputtered, tried to rise, and slipped back again. She laughed harder.

And then she felt his hand clamp on her wrist, and she stopped laughing. She glanced at him, saw the glint in his eye, and shook her head.

"No."

He tugged.

"Will! *No!*"

He tugged harder.

"Your Grace!"

"Oh, that won't save you now."

He gave one last hard tug, and she fell, splashing into the water on top of him. She got water up her nose and sputtered a curse, then dissolved into a fit of coughing. Finally, she pushed back and managed to sit, rather awkwardly. Her bottom was on Pelham's lap, and her legs were around his waist.

"See," he said, slicking the hair back from his face. "How do you like it?"

"I think it's wonderful."

He gave her a look as if to say he knew she was daft and this only proved him correct.

"Will, you're being spontaneous! Doesn't it feel refreshing? Doesn't it feel wonderful to do something unplanned for once?"

"I'm soaking wet," he grumbled.

"Of course you are. You're in a bathtub." She gave him a quick kiss on the forehead. "I believe you are making progress. One day you might even go an entire hour without looking at your pocket watch."

"My watch!" He fumbled under the water for it. He pulled it to the surface, opened it, and gave her a dark look. "It's ruined."

"I'm sorry," she said.

"No, you're not."

"No, I'm not! This is exactly what you need. A break from your routine. I'm only sorry Lucifer and poor Lady Elizabeth had to be the reason for it."

"You're the reason for it," he said. It was an accusation, but his tone wasn't accusatory. In fact, it made shivers race up her spine. Her gaze flicked to him. His eyes were on her, and she could have sworn the water temperature increased ten degrees.

"Are you blaming me again?"

"I'm giving you credit," he said. His hand caressed her arm, leaving tingles in its wake. "You have brought me out of my routine."

"Kicking and screaming."

"I didn't say I liked it, just that I'm giving you credit." His hand was on her shoulder, tugging the sleeve of her gown down so her skin was exposed.

"Do you think—?" Her voice was husky in her ears. "Do you think you might come to like it? To like me?"

"I do like you, Juliette. I like you far too much." He kissed her bare shoulder, and she had to suppress a moan.

"Far too much?" she whispered. "Because I'm a courtesan and you're a duke, and I'm oh so far beneath you?"

"There might be ways in which you're the superior."

She raised a brow. "You mean in intelligence?"

He laughed. It was a full, throaty laugh, and she admired it. She'd do anything to make him laugh like that again. "No. I mean, I have rather limited experience with this sort of thing." He gestured at the tub.

"With bathing?"

"With women. I'm not one of your gallants."

Juliette stared at him, not comprehending for a good long minute. And then she gasped. "You mean you've never"—she gestured at the bed—"before?"

"I have. Once or… twice." He looked away, and she could tell that though he held onto his dukely arrogance, the subject was embarrassing him. Oh, if only he knew the truth about her. But, of course, he expected her to be the expert. Who wouldn't? She was the Duchess of Dalliance.

In truth, she had been with a man more than once or twice. She'd been married. But that had been a long time ago. Still, she supposed making love was one of those things you never forgot—or two people figured out as they went along.

Her heart pounded as she considered what she and Pelham were about to do. Was this what she wanted? She wanted a husband, a family. Pelham was unlikely to ever consider marrying her. He was a duke—as he reminded her every other minute.

But when she looked back at him, she saw, once again, that vulnerability. There was more to this man than his bluster and arrogance. He had secrets. She wanted to know what they were.

She wanted to know him.

She put her hands on the sides of his face. "Why don't we both forget what happened before and just think about what is happening now?"

"You're very good at that."

"Yes, too good sometimes." She bent and kissed him. It was a gentle kiss, slow because she wanted the fire to build. And slow because it had been a long time since she had been with a man. She wanted to remember the feel of his lips against hers, the roughness of the stubble on his cheeks under her fingertips, the hardness of his thighs under her bottom.

Their lips met and parted, met and parted, and she was only vaguely aware of the smell of fresh linen, the crackle of the fire, and the patter of rain outside the window. She memorized the taste of his mouth, the texture of his hair when she ran her fingers through it, the sound of his breathing—still steady, though she was already half panting with desire.

For a man who had little experience, he knew how to kiss her until her toes curled and her lungs ran out of air. She could feel him hard and straining at the junction where their bodies met. If she freed him, it would be an easy matter to have him inside her. And while her body called for immediate satisfaction and her heart warned her against doing anything that would fuel her infatuation with him, she ignored both of them and pulled Will—awkwardly—to his feet.

"Let me help you out of these wet clothes."

She undressed him, and he stood still, assisting her in the way he might a servant. He was used to being served. Used to having people cater to him.

What if she turned the tables? What if she made him serve her?

Oh, it was a delicious thought, and not simply because she liked the idea of a duke playing servant to her duchess. She wanted to challenge him. She wanted to see who he was when he wasn't in his element.

She pulled his shirt over his head and took a

moment to steel herself. This was worse than she thought. She'd known he was an attractive, athletic man and he kept in shape, but she hadn't expected his chest to be quite so muscled, his shoulders quite so broad, or his waist quite so trim.

She swallowed. Hard. His bronze flesh gleamed in the flickering firelight, and she had the urge to lick every inch of it.

But no. *He* was going to service *her*. And even undressing him was for her benefit now.

"Are you having second thoughts?" he asked.

Juliette realized she'd been standing and staring at him for too long. "No." She shook her head. "No. I was admiring you."

He frowned and looked down at himself as though he had never seen his own chest.

"You're beautiful," she whispered.

"I believe I'm supposed to say that to you."

"Oh, you will," she said with a smile. "Just don't swoon."

"Swoon? I'm a—"

Before he could say *duke*, she loosed the fall of his trousers and pushed them down over his hips. That shut him up, which was her objective exactly. When she had the trousers off, she threw them over a chair and stood back to admire him.

"Those are going to wrinkle," he said, "not to mention soak the chair through."

"Mmm-hmm." She nodded absently. Yes, he was a very nice male specimen. Muscled legs, shapely calves, and though his comments about wrinkled clothes belied it—his interest for her was evident.

Quite evident.

"You know the rumor is that men swoon when I but disrobe."

He raised a brow.

"I don't know where that started, because it's never happened, but right now I feel as though I could swoon from looking at you."

"I'm not precisely certain what to reply to a statement like that. I feel rather… like an object."

She laughed. "I'm sorry. I know the feeling, and it's not altogether pleasant. But I suppose fair is fair. Your turn to ogle."

She gave him her back, and when he didn't move for several seconds, she glanced over her shoulder. "Are you going to undress me?"

"I—"

"I can't do it myself. Oh, but you're not afraid of swooning, are you?"

"No." He gripped her shoulders and straightened her, then set about undressing her. He'd obviously never undressed a female before, because he was completely unfamiliar with the laces and tapes and pins securing her garments. But she didn't give him instructions. Men hated that. She simply allowed him to flounder until she finally—*finally*—stood in only her silk chemise.

"How the bloody damn hell do you get into all of that each day?" he asked.

"I have a lot of help." She turned to face him and saw his gaze flick to her shoulder, where one sleeve of the chemise had fallen down. "But this"—she indicated the silk garment—"is fairly easy to remove. Simply tug on this little string, and it pools at my feet."

His eyes were so dark they looked indigo as he reached for the string. She caught his hand before he could tug it. "Don't swoon."

He gave her a murderous look, and when she released his hand, he tugged. He kept his gaze on her face, which surprised her, and then took a slow, leisurely perusal of her from teeth to toes and back to her eyes again.

"Do you feel faint?" she said with a smile.

"I wouldn't be averse to the idea of lying down."

She took his hand, led him to the bed, and lay on her side. He followed, and when they were face-to-face, he bent to kiss her. She put a hand between them. "What *would* you be averse to, Will?"

He gave her a look that was part undisguised interest, part horror.

"Because, you see, I have a rather extensive library, and I read something I would like to try."

"In a book?"

"I believe we have had this discussion before. I do read."

"Of course."

"More than the *Morning Chronicle*."

"Obviously. Do you always talk this much?"

"No. Let me be brief. I want you to give me pleasure."

"I believe that is the general idea."

"With your tongue."

His brows went up. "What sort of books are you reading?"

"The sort I hope you will benefit from as well." She cupped his cheek. "You can say no."

"Why the devil would I say no?"

And then he kissed her, and she realized her plan was turning against her. She had thought to control him, but she'd failed to consider she had been in control thus far.

Now he was taking over—something he made all too clear by the way he kissed her—taking everything, leaving her unable even to catch her breath before the next assault. And when he took over, she feared she might lose herself altogether.

Their lips met again and again, and then he rolled on top of her, bracing his weight on his elbows and pinning her under him. The feel of his skin on hers was a heady mixture, like drinking too much of the finest brandy. Her head swam, her senses reeled, and the earth seemed to tilt. When his mouth left hers, she wanted to cry out. Instead, she arched as his lips brushed the skin of her neck and his teeth scraped the tender flesh of her earlobe. She dug her fingers into his back, feeling the taut muscles and the smooth, wet skin under her tingling fingers.

"How am I doing so far?" he whispered.

"I…" She wanted to give him some pithy, amusing answer—after all, she was the so-called expert—but she was having a difficult time forming a coherent thought when his hot breath fanned against her neck.

"I'll consider your stuttering a positive sign."

He still sounded so cool, so composed. She wanted to break that composure, but she needed to think to do so.

And then his mouth closed on her breast, and she could barely remember her name, much less that she wanted to shake Will to the core. She dug her hands into his hair and breathed, "Please. Yes, please."

His tongue flicked her nipple, rolled over it, and she was in exquisite agony. His hands cupped her breasts then made long, lazy paths down her belly, teasing the fine blonde hair at the juncture of her thighs.

"Juliette," he murmured. "May I tell you something?"

"Yes, anything. Just—" She didn't even know what she wanted anymore—more of the same, much, much more.

"You're beautiful. I see why men swoon."

She opened her eyes and met his gaze. He was looking at her so intently, and the moment their gazes met, she felt something pass between them that was more than physical attraction, more than this physical act between them. She could not have said why those words from him meant so much to her. She'd been told she was beautiful thousands of times. But this was a man who gave compliments rarely, if ever. This was a man who meant what he said.

She felt beautiful when he looked at her. In his arms, as she was now, she felt the rest of the world was far, far away, and she was safe in this world of their own making. Somewhere far away she was the Duchess of Dalliance and he was the sixth Duke of Pelham. But here they were Will and Juliette. And in this moment, she didn't have to pretend.

"I…" she began, uncertain what she would say.

"Shh." He put a finger over her lips. "Don't speak. Simply feel."

His mouth meandered with torturous slowness down her belly, pausing to kiss and tease her in all the most sensitive spots. When he reached the apex of her thighs, he nudged her legs open. Juliette didn't know why she should resist or feel suddenly shy. He gave her a questioning look, and she wanted to tell him she'd never done this before. But that would elicit only skepticism or confusion, and she didn't want him to stop.

He brushed his stubbled cheek against the tender skin of her inner thigh. She moaned as he pressed soft kisses against her leg, inching ever closer to her core.

And when his mouth touched here there—at her heat-filled center—she wanted to burst into flames. She arched into his lips, crying out when his tongue darted out to touch her. She was certain he must be appalled by her behavior, but she couldn't seem to stop herself. She clenched the bedsheets and held on as the ecstasy reached higher and higher crescendos. She thought she might die from the intensity of sensations, thought she might expire from craving what he promised her with each touch from his tongue. And now his fingers had plunged inside her, and she was aching and all but sobbing for release.

When it came, it took her breath away. The sound of blood rushing in her ears deafened her, the world went bright white, and she all but broke open. She gripped his hair, holding on to her anchor in the tempest of sensation.

Fourteen

PELHAM WATCHED JULIETTE'S EYELIDS FLUTTER CLOSED, watched the rise and fall of her breasts as she struggled to calm her breathing. He didn't need to ask if he'd pleased her. If he'd pleased her much more, they would have alerted the entire establishment to their lovemaking. As it was, he feared those in the rooms closest to theirs had a pretty good idea what they had been doing.

For once, he didn't care. Her pleasure had given him pleasure, and when he looked down at her flushed face and her long, willowy body, he wanted to do it again. She was beautiful. Her body was perfect in every way—soft and curved as a woman's should be. Her legs were long, her breasts full, her glorious hair in a tangle on the pillow.

And he'd pleased her.

He, who had so little experience with women, had pleased London's most celebrated courtesan. It wasn't that Will had no experience. He'd been as curious as any young man and found willing women plentiful. He'd tussled with one or two, and found the experiences satisfying physically but still strangely unfulfilling. As he grew older, he thought he might enjoy the act a bit more, but he was always so busy. And most of the ladies to whom he was introduced were not the kind one dallied with.

He might have paid a woman for her services, but he found the thought distasteful. And then he had met Lady Elizabeth, and he need only wait until after the wedding and he could have her as often as he wished.

Of course, Juliette was teaching him relationships with members of the fairer sex weren't quite as simple as he'd imagined them. Nor was he such an innocent as to believe that every man and woman experienced the passion he had with her. When he'd looked into her eyes, there was something there.

Something he did not want to examine too closely.

He glanced down at her, meeting her light blue eyes when she peered up at him. "Apparently, you don't require any books to tell you what to do."

He smiled. She made him laugh. Even when he didn't want to be amused by her, it was difficult not to smile. The cold, imperial Duchess of Dalliance was warm and amusing and all but infectious. God knew he couldn't seem to get enough of her.

"I do enjoy reading."

She sat, her silver-blonde hair falling around her. "So do I." She gave his chest a small shove, and he supposed she wanted him to lie down. He complied, curious as to what she would do next. "Let me tell you what I've been reading about."

He was hard for her instantly. He'd been hard, didn't think he could want her much more than he did, but suddenly he was all but aching for her. "Why don't you show me?"

"Why don't I do both?" Her gaze never left his, but her hands stroked him slowly. Up and down, then a pause. "I've read that a man is most sensitive here." She circled him with her thumb, teased. "Would you concur?"

"I might." His voice sounded strained, and he cleared his throat. But then she began stroking again.

"And that a little pressure here…" She paused and applied exactly the right amount of pressure. He groaned, shocked the sound had come from him but seemingly unable to stop it. "Or cupping a man here…" He groaned again and began to sit up.

She pushed him lightly. "Not so impatient, Will. Good things and all that."

Her hand on his chest was a feather. He could have tossed her down and been inside her within moments. He could have found release and perhaps given her pleasure again, as well. But he was a patient man. A disciplined man. He eased back down as she stroked him again.

She was driving him mad, and he fisted his hands at his sides and tried to keep his gaze on her face. But she licked her lips with that small pink tongue, and so he had to look away. At her breasts. The nipples were pink and hard, and he wanted to take one in his mouth, suck gently…

She bent, her soft, full breast rubbing again his thigh. "What are you–?"

And then her mouth closed on him—hot and wet and taking all of him in.

"Oh, good God!" he exclaimed, and then words

failed him as she stroked him with her mouth, teased him with her tongue, and sucked long and hard. He felt he would explode inside her. He didn't want to, but he knew he would not be able to stop himself.

And then just when he was about to cross over, she released him and sat. There were no words for the need he felt. He reached for himself, but she caught his hand and put it on her breast. And then she climbed on top of him, straddling him.

She was the most exquisite creature he had ever encountered. Her skin, her hair, her shape were all painfully exquisite. She took hold of him, guiding him into her wet core. Slowly. Inch by punishing inch.

She was tight around him, and he fought hard to control the urge to plunge into her hard and fast. Finally, she sheathed him to the hilt. She waited a moment, until he opened his eyes and met her gaze.

Those eyes. Those cool, clear eyes. He would never forget them as long as he lived. She moved, and he moved with her—as one. He was part of her and she of him, and he could all but read her mind, know when she wanted more pressure or less, and she seemed to know when she should move faster or slower. He caressed her, memorizing every slope of her body, marking it as his, taking note of her every reaction.

And then her head fell back, her hair brushing his calves, and her hips began to move furiously. Will could stand it no longer.

He grasped her waist, and without breaking contact, flipped her over. Fast and hard, he plunged into her. Every thrust slaked him of his need and seemed to double it, as well. She was calling out his name and meeting him thrust for thrust. His hands were shaking, his hair falling in his eyes, but he opened them and stared at her as he came, hard and completely. She clenched around him and shuddered. Her arms came up, her hands cupped the back of his neck, and he lowered his forehead to hers.

She kissed him, softly, sweetly, as he emptied himself into her. And then, as one, they rolled to the side and fell into an exhausted sleep.

༺৵

Pelham woke some time later—hours or minutes, he wasn't certain. He was alone in the bed and heard the sound of someone moving. He rose on one elbow and peered into the darkness of the unfamiliar room. "Juliette?"

"I'm here." There was enough light from the fire for him to see her outline. She had stepped behind a screen in the corner.

"What are you doing?"

"Washing. We didn't take any precautions to prevent a child. I don't think simply washing will help, but I didn't think it could hurt."

Pelham lay back on the pillows and put an arm over his eyes. He'd never even thought about the possibility Juliette would conceive a child, his son or daughter.

What an entanglement that would be. He could imagine Juliette's sweet body heavy with his child. She would be beautiful—even more than she was now.

But he didn't want her to carry his child. A courtesan would not be the mother of the seventh Duke of Pelham. How would he even be certain he was the father?

He heard something rustle and moved his arm to see her standing beside the bed. She was wearing a white dressing gown and looked almost virginal.

"You don't have to worry. I don't think it's the right time for me to conceive. Or perhaps I'm unable. I was never able to conceive with Oliver."

"What precautions do you take with your... protectors?"

She gave him a blank look and then seemed to remember herself. "Oh! I..." She trailed off, seemingly at a loss for words. "I don't want to talk about that." She slid into bed beside him. "I don't want to think of other men."

But the spell—and it must have been a spell for him to act as he had—was broken. He could not stop thinking of the other men she'd been with. Was he just another in a long line?

He slid out the other side of the bed, and she frowned at him. "What's wrong?"

"Nothing." But everything was wrong. He'd been intimate with a courtesan! He'd known he had a weakness for her, and he'd allowed himself to succumb.

And the worst of it was—He turned his back to her and tugged on his trousers, which were still wet and uncomfortable—another transgression he could blame on her. But he wasn't really angry about the trousers. He was angry because what they'd shared had meant something to him. For that brief time when he'd been kissing her, touching her, moving inside her, he'd forgotten he was a duke, forgotten he was a member

of the House of Lords, forgotten he had a dead fiancée
and stolen diamonds to find, and he'd just been Will.
He hadn't thought about what time it was or if he
was missing dinner or how the rain had thrown off
his schedule. He had thought only of Juliette—her
scent, her taste, the feel of her hair running through
his hands.

He'd never lost himself like that before. Never.
Every action he took, every step he made, every single
thought was analyzed and justified and considered.
His father had drilled method and precision into him.
Routine. Punctuality. Dignity.

Pelham swore he could still hear his father's voice
when he slept. He dreamed of the sadistic old man.

But just for a moment, in Juliette's arms, he'd been
someone outside the man his father had made him.
He'd been his own man with his own desires and
needs and preferences. His father, that skeleton he
carried with him always, had been vanquished.

But now the former duke was back, and he was
weighty. Pelham couldn't stand to look at Juliette and
think of what a disappointment he'd be if his father
was alive to see him today.

"Will?" she said quietly.

He pulled his shirt over his head. It, too, was
wet, but he didn't want to take the time to find dry
clothing. He shoved his feet into his boots, which,
thankfully, had escaped the tub.

"Tell me what's wrong."

"I need some air." He started for the door without
looking at her.

"Is it something I said?"

He'd seen her out of the corner of his eye and cursed himself. She was on her knees, her hair tumbling over her shoulders, the white of her dressing gown and the sheets pooled around her, making her look like an angel.

She was no angel.

"Will?"

He opened the door.

"It's storming out—"

He closed the door on her words, cutting her off. There was pain in her voice. He'd heard it. He'd caused it.

He was no better than her Oliver.

He was no better than his father.

Fifteen

THE NEXT DAY DAWNED CLEAR AND COLD, THE weather chilly even for this time of the year. It was equally frosty inside the carriage, as Will had neither looked at her nor said a word to her in the two hours they'd been en route to his home in Yorkshire.

Juliette was a reasonable woman. She'd lived with an unreasonable man for almost three years and then been tutored in the ways of men by the Countess of Sinclair for another year. And then she'd spent the last six years in London, fending off the advances of scores of men and playing the part of a glamorous courtesan.

She understood men.

She understood Will wanted her but was not prepared to admit he wanted her, because he was A Duke. She understood what had passed between them last night had shaken him, because it had shaken her as well. And she was smart enough to know something else was bothering him, but she didn't know what it was.

Perhaps he wasn't ready to share it yet, but the time for politeness and consideration—not that either of them had been particularly polite or considerate until now—had passed. It had fallen to the floor with the last of her soggy clothing in the inn chamber last night.

Juliette had no illusions that she and Will had any future together, but she did think she was owed some kind of explanation for the way he'd behaved last night after he'd made love to her. She did think she was owed a few words the morning after, so she would not feel as though she were a common whore.

But of course Will probably thought of her that way, while she... she was half in love with him. And she was a monumental fool for allowing this to happen with a man like Pelham. She wanted a husband and a family, not a lover. Clearly, Will was prepared to be neither to her.

"I don't mean to intrude on your brooding silence," she said, her voice splitting the tense stillness, "but I do think you owe me a few words this morning."

He glanced up at her, his eyes shuttered and wary. What did he think she was going to do to him? Attack him? Seduce him? Neither and both sounded agreeable.

"Good morning, madam." He had a copy of the *Times* in his hand, and he pretended to read it again. She knew he pretended, because he hadn't turned the page in half an hour.

"Ah, so I'm *madam* again. What happened to Juliette?"

He glanced back up at her and steeled his features. "I'm sorry to say I believe last night—"

"—was a mistake," she finished for him. "I knew you were going to say that."

"You agree, do you not?"

"No."

He frowned. "No?"

"No. The mistake was in you leaving my bed and spending the night in the stable—at least I assume that's where you slept, as you smell suspiciously of horse and leather."

He bristled. "If I have offended your sensibilities, madam, I—"

"Oh, stubble it. I don't want your perfunctory apologies."

His eyes went hard. "Stubble it? I am a—"

"—duke. Yes, I know, and I'm sure you know what you're about in affairs of the House of Lords or matters dealing with... dukely things." She waved a hand to indicate whatever those dukely things might be.

"*Ducal* matters is the term you're seeking," he corrected.

"Precisely. You see, you know all about dukes and ducal things, but you don't know anything about relationships. You don't know anything about emotions, and, if I may be so bold as to say it, you don't know yourself."

"And you do?" His tone was icy.

"No! But I want to." She crossed the divide between them and sat beside him. He pushed himself into the corner. "Don't you see, Will? I *want* to know you. Not The Duke. I want to know Will, but every time I get close, you push me away."

He looked away. "There's nothing to know. I *am* the duke."

"You're pushing me again."

"What happened last night was a mistake," he argued.

"You've already said that, and it's a futile effort to push me away."

He lifted his paper again. No, no. She was not going to allow him to shut her out.

"Will, why was last night a mistake?"

He didn't answer.

"Because you enjoyed yourself? Because you took pleasure from and gave pleasure to a—" She gasped. *"Courtesan?"*

He cut her a glance, and she grabbed his hand, forcing the paper down.

"Because for one instant, you forgot you were a duke and could just be a man?"

"Madam—"

"Juliette. Call me Juliette. You don't have to be the duke with me. You can simply be the man."

"Madam—Juliette, I don't want to talk about this."

"Why? Because I'm correct?"

"Yes!" He all but yelled the word. Juliette almost flinched but resolutely held his hand. He was not Oliver.

"You are correct. Is that what you want me to say?"

"I want you to be honest with me."

"Honest? Fine. Bedding you last night was a mistake because I am the Duke of Pelham. I cannot afford to forget who I am. I cannot make the mistakes others do."

"Why not? Are you not human?"

He shook his head as if to say this was not the point. "Of course, but my behavior was... not acceptable. I must be better than everyone else."

"Because you're a duke?"

"No, because I'm William Henry Charles Arthur

Cavington, Viscount Southerby, Marquess of Rothingham, and Duke of Pelham. From birth, I have been tutored in three fundamental tenets—dignity, decorum, and honor."

"Don't forget a tedious routine and an obsession with punctuality," she mumbled.

He ignored her. "I violated all three of those tenets last night with you."

"You certainly know how to flatter a woman, and I would be deeply offended if it wasn't all complete rubbish." *And if I wasn't falling in love with you.*

"Rubbish?" His mouth gaped open. Clearly, no one had ever spoken to him thus.

"Yes. Who told you to follow these tenets? Who made all these rules you adhere to—no, *cling* to as though they were the last piece of shipwreck debris in shark-infested waters? You keep telling me you're a duke. Well, *act* like a duke! Make your own rules."

"Act like a—" He stared at her, not blinking, not moving, not breathing. After two minutes she was afraid she had shocked him into some type of coma. And then he reached for her. She drew back, taken off guard, but he pressed a hand to her cheek. "Make my own rules." His tone was incredulous.

"That was my suggestion."

"Might I make a suggestion?"

"Of course."

"Stop blathering and kiss me."

Before she could argue that she was not *blathering*, he cupped her chin and brought her mouth to his. Tenderly, so tenderly she wanted to weep, he kissed her.

She kissed him back, wrapping her arms around

him and pulling him tight against her. Why couldn't he be this man all the time? Why did he have to retreat back to Pelham and his stupid dukely—or ducal—or dukefied—ways?

He broke the kiss and leaned his forehead against hers. "It was my father," he said, his voice so low she almost couldn't make out his words over the clatter of the carriage wheels. "My father was the man who ingrained these ducal tenets into me from birth."

He didn't apologize, didn't say she was right—had she really expected him to do so?—but he was making an effort. She didn't speak, wise enough to know that anything she said now might hinder him from continuing.

Oh, don't think, Will. Just speak. Just tell me.

"The fifth Duke of Pelham was a hard man. Serious. Dignified. Strict."

In other words, unapproachable and incapable of love. Juliette's own father had spoiled her, doted on her. Perhaps she'd been too spoiled. Perhaps that was why her brother hated her and had turned his back on her. Family could be a curse and a blessing.

"And your mother?" she asked.

"She died when I was ten," he said, then clenched his jaw. "No, that's not true. My father threw her out of the house. I never knew why and never knew what became of her. I heard a few years later she died on the Continent, alone and penniless."

"Oh, Will!" She reached for him, but he moved away.

"She'd been dead inside long before that. My father was like your Oliver in some ways. Things must be done his way or not at all. She disappointed him, and one did not want to disappoint my father. Before me, three children had died at birth or shortly before. She mourned those children, but mostly I think she mourned the girl she had been—beautiful, lively, full of life. I saw paintings of her when they were first married. She was radiant." He looked at Juliette. "She shone, like you. People told me when she walked into a room the light and sound clustered about her. She was a lodestone. But once my father got his hands on her, secluded her in the country, she withered away."

Juliette clutched his shoulders and felt sorrow and pain for the little boy with a mother too dead inside to love him, and a father who did not tolerate even the slightest disappointment. She could barely imagine a childhood like that. Her parents had been so indulgent of their only daughter when she'd been young. If she'd grown up as Will had, would she have realized the way Oliver treated her was wrong? Would she not simply have accepted there was no love in the world, and this was the way life was meant to be?

"I had a dog," Will said quietly, leaning his head back against the squabs and closing his eyes. "Like your Brownie, but I called him Hunter. And he was a hunting dog from the best stock."

"How old were you?" she whispered, fear coiling in her belly. She knew what was coming. She did not want to hear this, but she had pushed him to reveal his secrets. She steeled herself and raised her gaze to him.

With his eyes closed and his head tilted back, she could scrutinize his face. She loved the rich bronze color of his skin, the arrogant set of his mouth, the flat planes of his cheeks, and that classic Roman nose. He had long eyelashes, and they were auburn like the glints in his hair. She remembered he'd had a smattering of auburn hair on his chest, and then she shivered because she remembered the scratchy feel of the hair when it rubbed against her body.

"I was six. My father gave the dog to me as a gift, and I shouldn't have trusted him. But bloody hell, I was six!" He opened his eyes and sat forward, anguish in his face. "I wanted something to love me, and that dog was the first thing that did."

Juliette wanted to hold him and tell him she loved him. She would love him enough to make up for the little boy who hadn't known any love. Instead, she asked, "What happened to Hunter?"

"I was late," Will said simply, as if this should explain all.

"Late?"

"Late to dinner. We always ate at half past six. Always. Not a minute before and not a minute after. I arrived one minute late. My father was furious."

Juliette didn't like the look on Will's face. She clenched her hands in her lap.

"He stalked out of the dining room without a word, marched to the kennels, took Hunter by the scruff of the neck, and threw him so hard against the wall it killed him. Then he stomped the dog's head into the floor with his boot."

Juliette wanted to gag. How could anyone do anything so cruel? How could anyone do that to the beloved pet of a little boy? "Oh, Will." She reached for him. She thought he might refuse her touch again, but he allowed her to hold him. "I'm so sorry."

"I did everything in my power never to be late again," he said. "Until I met you."

And she hadn't understood. She'd mocked his reliance on the pocket watch. He looked up at her, and she kissed him gently. "You're free now. You can make your own rules and set your own time. No one can ever hurt you like that again."

He took her into his arms. "Of that I'm not so certain."

His mouth descended on hers in a slow kiss that left her absolutely breathless. When he pulled away, she took a long moment to compose herself before opening her eyes. "You should do that more often."

"I will." He reached up and began pulling pins from her hair. When it tumbled down, he brought it to his nose and inhaled. "Your hair smells like... something. I can't place it."

"Lavender," she whispered, loving the feel of his hands in her hair.

"Is that it?" He leaned down and brushed his lips across the skin of her neck. "It suits you." He slid the sleeve off her shoulder, and she sighed in anticipation. He had such a tender mouth, and it was so skilled. He nipped and licked and kissed her until her skin burned with need for more.

"Will?"

"Hmm?" His mouth traced her shoulder as he slid her sleeve lower.

"You're not going to..." She had to think for a moment, because his mouth was driving her to distraction. And now his hands were on her breasts, and she didn't want to speak so much as feel. "You're not going to shut me out again, are you?"

He paused, and she wanted to cry out in frustration. His dark eyes met hers. "No. I won't shut you out again. I've given up."

"Given up?"

"I can't resist you. I've tried. In vain, I have tried. It's no use."

Her lungs tightened, and she found she could not draw a breath. "It's not?" What did that mean, precisely? Did he feel about her the way she did about him? Did he think he could love her?

"I want you. I want you naked and writhing beneath me. I want you on your hands and knees in my bed. I want you above me, your hair spilling over your breasts." He stroked one as he spoke, and she felt her nipple harden. "I want you here." He pushed her gown and undergarments down, baring her. "I want you now."

"I want you, too." And when his mouth closed on her nipple, desire was all she could think of and all she knew. Need like she'd never known possessed her, drove her mad with a frenzy to take him, have him inside her, touch him until he begged for release.

She pushed him back against the squabs, freed him, and stroked him until he was all but panting. And then she raised her skirts and taunted him, taking him so slowly he was cursing her before she finally thrust her hips and engulfed him fully.

She moaned, thrilled at the way he filled her so completely. His hands were on her waist, but he allowed her free rein. He allowed her to set the pace, and she did so until she finally raced to an exquisite, blinding pleasure. She felt him swell, and then he cried out a moment later.

Finally, she laid her head on his shoulder and tried to breathe. He put his arms about her and held her tight, and she thought, *This is enough. This should be enough.*

But it wasn't.

&

It was late by the time Pelham recognized the markers indicating they were close to Rothingham Manor. The country house had been built by the first Duke of Pelham when the man was still the Marquess of Rothingham. He'd left the house named for his marquisate and proceeded to outfit it in a style fit for a duke. He'd been a wealthy man, had married an heiress, and left his eldest son a fortune. The second duke had increased that fortune, married well, and so on.

Until now. Until me, Pelham thought.

Juliette was curled against him, her hand on his chest, her head on his shoulder. She hadn't complained when he told her he did not want to stop for the night. She hadn't complained when he gave her only ten minutes every four hours to stretch her legs and use the privy.

Come to think of it, she rarely complained.

She hadn't even complained about his treatment of her the night before. She'd simply tried to understand why he'd acted as he had, and to his shock, he'd found himself telling her.

He supposed this was why she was a good courtesan. Men liked to talk with her. And men liked to bed her. There was no mystery as to why there. She was beautiful, uninhibited, and clearly knew what gave a man pleasure.

He couldn't seem to get enough of her. How had he thought he'd be able to resist her? But this was a temporary indulgence. He would enjoy her until this business with the diamonds was over, and then he would get back to the business of finding a duchess from among the eligible young ladies of the *ton*.

Yes, the *Morning Chronicle* and its ilk would make the most of his romantic liaison with the Duchess of Dalliance, but there was always someone else doing something more scandalous—one could count on Darlington to scandalize, for example—and the papers would soon forget about Pelham once he forgot about Juliette.

The niggling feeling that he might not ever be able to forget Juliette—the softness of her hair, the fullness of her breasts, the sweetness of her lips—rose within him, but he pushed it down. Of course he would forget her. She was a woman and a courtesan, and courtesans existed because men tired of women all the time.

His primary task now was to search for information about the diamonds. Had Lady Elizabeth hidden them somewhere in Nowlund Park? And if so, could he ascertain why? Why had she felt the need to steal diamonds from a man like Lucifer? Why had she been involved with such a man at all?

Pelham glanced down at Juliette as they turned into

the long drive of Rothingham Manor, and the carriage ride smoothed as the wheels crunched over gravel long worn down by decades of carriage processions. She was stirring now, and he would have liked nothing better than to carry her to bed and make love to her for the rest of the night.

But he was a duke. And he must act as befitted his station.

He hated to wake her, but she would have to be presentable for the servants. His one solace was that she could relax here at his home and not fear Lucifer. She might spend the day idly while he made inquiries about Lady Elizabeth's last visit to Yorkshire and these diamonds.

And then the nights they would spend together. He expected to conclude his business in Yorkshire quickly, so he and Juliette might have no more than a handful of nights together, but he would make the most of them.

He shook her gently. "Juliette."

She smiled. "I was having the most wonderful dream." She wrapped her hands around his neck and pulled him in for a kiss. "Come here and make it a reality."

She had the ability to make him desire her instantly, but now was not the time. He untangled her arms from his neck and righted her. She opened her icy blue eyes, now considerably warmer when she looked at him. "What is it?"

"We're almost to Rothingham Manor."

"Oh." She parted the curtains farther and peered outside. "It's still dark."

"I don't have my pocket watch, but I think it must be close to three in the morning."

She began coiling her hair and feeling around the squabs for pins with which to secure it. He admired the way she could do this without even the use of a mirror. Her fluid, graceful movements entranced him.

And he must be besotted to be marveling at the way a woman styled her hair. Pathetic.

He straightened his cravat and attempted to brush the wrinkles from his coat. "My staff will greet us at the front drive."

She lifted her all-but-forgotten hat from the squabs and positioned it. "At this hour?"

"Of course. Is there anything you require? Anything I should request for you?"

She watched him as her hands arranged the hat so it framed her face. "What will you tell them about me?"

"They are my staff. I need not explain myself."

The carriage was slowing, and he could see the footmen's torches burning bright as the staff lined up to greet him. The gold piping on the scarlet livery gleamed in the firelight.

"But they will talk. Servants always do. You realize word of our... involvement will travel back to London, if it hasn't already."

He thought of the men at the inn they had stopped at the night before. News had definitely traveled back to Town.

"Let London think what it will. We have more important matters to attend to."

"The diamonds?"

"What else?"

"Yes, what else?" she murmured, staring out the window as Rothingham Manor finally came fully into view. Her gasp of surprise pleased him. He couldn't say why. He didn't want or need her approval.

"It's magnificent. I can only imagine how it appears in the sunlight."

The house *was* magnificent, especially lit as it was by lamps and torches. The servants always had word when he would arrive and made sure every window facing the drive beamed bright with light. Pelham preferred this view of the house. It was graceful and noble in the daylight, but at night its grey stone façade seemed to turn to alabaster and float ethereally on an overlook facing the wild moors of Yorkshire.

The carriage slowed and turned in the gently curved drive, stopping in front of a line of servants fanning out from the top to the bottom of the stone steps leading to the door.

A footman opened the carriage door, another lowered the steps, and a third offered his white-gloved hand. Juliette paused before taking the footman's hand, and a gust of frigid Yorkshire wind blew about her skirts and fluttered the ribbons in her hat. Pelham had thought she would seem out of place here. She was so obviously a woman of London and the city, but when she took the footman's hand and descended the carriage steps, he would have sworn she had always lived here.

He exited next and, offering his arm to Juliette, led her to the housekeeper. If she had been his duchess, he would have introduced her to the staff. But she was not his duchess. Though his servants were unfailingly formal and not one moved even minutely to glance his way, he knew they noted the absence of Juliette's introduction.

"Your Grace." Mrs. Waite made a deep curtsey. "How wonderful to have you back again." She didn't add *so soon*, but Pelham thought it in his head.

"Thank you, Mrs. Waite. I will be here for a few days on business. This is Mrs.—" He wasn't certain what to call her. He knew she would not want to be referred to as Mrs. Clifton. He certainly couldn't introduce her as the Duchess of Dalliance. And he didn't want his staff going about calling her *Duchess* as she was referred to in London. That would lead to rumors of their marriage.

As usual, Juliette stepped in. She held out her hand. "I'm Miss Juliette. I'm a friend of the duke's."

"Miss Juliette." Mrs. Waite nodded, and Pelham thought he detected the slightest twist at the corner of her mouth to indicate disapproval.

"Put her in one of our best rooms," Pelham instructed.

"Yes, Your Grace." He started up the stairs, and Mrs. Waite followed. "I'll make certain everything is done to your satisfaction."

Pelham stopped at the door and turned to face her. "I don't think I shall break my fast at eight, Mrs. Waite."

Her jaw dropped open. He had rarely, exceedingly rarely, deviated from his routine.

"That is too early for Miss Juliette." He turned to her. "Would ten be agreeable?"

She smiled, not looking surprised in the least. "Most agreeable."

"O… of course, Your Grace," Mrs. Waite

stammered. "Breakfast shall be ready at... ten. Anything else, Your Grace?"

"Yes. I don't have my pocket watch. What time is it?"

If one of the blustery Yorkshire gales had chosen that moment to whip through the courtyard, it would have surely blown Mrs. Waite over. "I... I... I—" She fumbled in her apron. "It is quarter past three, Your Grace."

"Thank you." With a smile, he escorted Juliette inside.

Sixteen

JULIETTE HAD EXPECTED THE RESIDENCE OF A DUKE TO be grand. She had often visited Somerset, the ancestral home of the Earls of Sinclair, and it never failed to impress. But Somerset was a cottage compared to Rothingham Manor. She supposed she might have given Rothingham the advantage because of its location. The moors of Yorkshire, covered with cotton grass and bilberries, were a stunning backdrop for any house, especially one that stood out so starkly against the ravaged landscape. She could imagine the landscape was breathtaking when the heather was in bloom.

Rothingham was a perfect rectangle—long and sleek with more windows than she could count. The grounds were meticulously maintained and as lovely as any in London. Somerset also had lovely gardens, but it was situated in Hampshire. It was not difficult to cultivate a lovely garden in Hampshire.

And yet even with so impressive an exterior, it was Rothingham's interior that caused her to gasp with pleasure. The corridors were endless with painting after painting of illustrious personages exquisitely framed along every wall. The rooms were wide, and their ceilings soared. Every item, from the smallest figurine to the molding on the ceiling, was tasteful and elegant. She had never been in so beautiful a home, and she doubted she ever would be again.

She'd been so intrigued by her quick tour the night before, she actually could have joined Pelham for breakfast at eight. She was awake and exploring before that dreaded hour.

But she had not seen Will. He had left her in the capable hands of his housekeeper before retiring to bed. She had thought he might come to her room, but he did not. She tried not to let that bother her. In fact, she rather hoped it would extinguish some of the feelings she had for him. But no. She was still falling in love with him—and his beautiful home. Her explorations this morning had turned up three parlors, a drawing room, a ballroom, a dining room, a music room, a billiards room, and a map room. But it had not turned up Will.

In fact, he was nowhere in the house at all. He might have been one of those personages painted in the endless corridors, but she had yet to come across the painting. His father she had seen. His likeness had been present in several rooms, including the bedroom to which she'd been shown the night before.

When she'd asked her maid about the man in the painting over the large fireplace, the maid had said he was the duke. Juliette had squinted at the portrait. The man certainly bore a likeness to Pelham, but his eyes were brown and cold. Will's were warm blue. And this man's hair had streaks of gray in it. Will's was still richly brown, and certainly any artist worth his or her salt would have painted the auburn and gold glints of Will's hair, given the opportunity.

"You mean that is the duke's father," Juliette said.

"Yes," the maid answered, looking rather thoughtful. "I suppose after knowing His Grace's father, it is hard to think of anyone else as the duke."

But Will was the duke now, and as far as Juliette could tell, he had done nothing whatsoever to put his mark on his home.

Oh, everything was tasteful and beautifully maintained. Not a scrap of carpet appeared faded, not a section of upholstery looked even remotely worn. But the selections reminded her of those of the Countess of Sinclair. And while she was also a woman of taste, she preferred the fashions she had grown up with, which meant Somerset always looked a little old-fashioned.

Juliette was standing in one of the corridors, staring at one of Will's ancestors, when a clock somewhere chimed ten. She supposed she had better make her way to the dining room or face Will's wrath. The house, though large, was easy to navigate, and she found the room quickly.

But when she arrived, Will was not there. Two footmen stood to either side of the door, but they offered no explanations as to the duke's whereabouts. With a shrug, Juliette poured herself tea and sat at one end of the table. She stirred sugar into her tea and looked at the empty chair at the other end. It was not an exceedingly long table, perhaps long enough to seat eight. This was obviously more of a breakfast room than the formal dining room she had peeked at earlier. Will's place was set, his paper in its usual position. But Will was not there.

Juliette sipped her tea and glanced at the sideboard, trying to decide what to eat and wondering who else was expected to dine, because the cook had prepared mountains of food.

She was about to rise when Mrs. Waite poked her head in. She glanced at Pelham's empty chair, her eyes went wide, and she ducked back out again. Juliette sipped her tea again, decided she wanted a scone, and was about to rise again when the housekeeper poked her head in the door a second time.

"Mrs. Waite," Juliette said.

The housekeeper, in the process of ducking back out, paused. "Yes, Miss Juliette?"

"It appears I am all alone for breakfast this morning. Won't you join me?"

The housekeeper gaped. "That would be most inappropriate, madam."

"Very well." Juliette rose. "Then join me for a brief walk."

The housekeeper shook her head. "I am very busy this morning—"

"Then I shall accompany you on your errands."

Mrs. Waite pursed her lips, obviously realizing Juliette was prepared to be persistent. "I will join you for a walk."

Juliette rose. "I would adore a tour, if you don't mind."

"Of course." When they had left the dining room, Mrs. Waite began to point out the various rooms, all of which Juliette had seen. When they reached the music room, Juliette paused, arm on the pianoforte. "Does His Grace play?"

"I believe he had instruction as a child, madam."

Juliette circled the pianoforte, lifting the lid and running her hands over the keys. "Have you been at Rothingham house that long?"

"For thirty-seven years, madam."

Juliette played a few bars of Beethoven's *Piano Concerto No. 3.* "Then you must know all there is to know about the duke and his father."

"Yes." The housekeeper looked decidedly uncomfortable now. She glanced at the door. "Shall we continue the tour, madam?"

"Of course." Juliette played a little of Mozart's *Variations on Sonata K331.* "In all the time you have known Pelham—thirty—?"

"Thirty-four years, madam."

"In those thirty-four years, have you ever known him to be late?"

The housekeeper narrowed her eyes. "Once or twice."

Juliette played a scale. "That's a remarkable feat. Only once or twice to your knowledge, and never to mine, though I confess I have known him only briefly. And yet"—she played a bit of Bach's *Celli Suite Solo Piano Music,* which always sounded mournful to her— "he is late to breakfast this morning. Is it safe to assume that was why you peeked in on me?"

"Yes, madam." The housekeeper's hands wrung her apron. "I was concerned. The duke is not in residence, and no one seems to know where he has gone or when he will be back. I cannot believe he would be late. He did say ten."

Juliette gazed at the keys, though she didn't need to look at them to play this piece, and smiled. Finally Pelham was breaking free of his father's tyranny. She understood how he felt—scared and elated. She'd felt that way when she'd escaped Oliver.

"I'm certain he is fine," Juliette told the housekeeper. The poor woman looked overwrought.

"But he is never late. The last time he was late—"

The housekeeper paused, and Juliette's fingers stilled. The expression on Mrs. Waite's face was an equal mixture of horror and concern.

"What happened the last time he was late?" Juliette rose. "Was that when the last duke killed Will's dog?"

"He told you about that?" Mrs. Waite looked surprised.

"His father sounds like a monster, and I suppose His Grace and I have that in common. I was married to a monster."

The housekeeper nodded then glanced at the music door again. "That was not the last time His Grace was late." Her voice was a mere whisper. "He was late again a few years later. I think he was eight or nine. It wasn't his fault." She glanced at the music door again. She was speaking so softly Juliette wanted to move nearer, but she dared not do anything that would cause the housekeeper to pause.

"His Grace—he was Master William then—was taking his daily ride. His father insisted upon it. The Dukes of Pelham have always been known for their excellent horsemanship. The horse went lame, and

Master William had to walk him back to the house. To do otherwise might have crippled the animal."

"And so he was late."

Mrs. Waite nodded.

"And what did the duke do?"

"Beat him," Mrs. Waite whispered. "Beat him so badly Master William was in bed for a week. And his hearing never returned."

Now Juliette did move around the pianoforte, for Mrs. Waite was speaking very softly. "His hearing? But he seems to hear perfectly well."

"Yes, in his right ear. He's deaf in his left."

Juliette stared at her. "His father did that to him?"

The housekeeper nodded.

"And what did his mother do?"

"She never left his bedside, but if you mean did she reprimand the duke, the answer is no. I was employed a year after they married, so I do not know what their first year together was like, but if you want my opinion, the duchess was terrified of her husband."

Juliette leaned back against the pianoforte and sighed. She glanced about the airy music room with its wispy draperies and its curling music stands. Such a beautiful home to house so many ugly secrets.

"Why is no one eating breakfast?" Will's voice boomed through the rooms to the music room, and both Juliette and Mrs. Waite jumped to attention. The housekeeper looked as though she were about to run and apologize to the duke, but Juliette put her hand on the woman's arm and shook her head.

Juliette's heart was heavy. She wanted to go to Will, take him in her arms, and kiss away all the pain he'd suffered. She wanted the love she felt for him—the love she kept hoping would go away—to heal all his wounds. But she knew Will would take these gestures as pity. So instead, she put on a frivolous expression and tripped lightly out of the music room. Juliette caught sight of Will outside the breakfast room. "There you are!" she said.

He cocked his head. Had he always done so? Was it because he could not hear her?

"Here *I* am?"

"Oh, I've already been to breakfast, but when I saw I would dine alone, I decided to explore instead." She took his arm. He'd offered her his right, and the gesture seemed natural. But what if she had taken his left? How would he have compensated? "You, sir, are late. And might I add that it's about time?"

He frowned. "I don't follow. And I'm not a *sir*—"

"I mean that it is about time you were late to something. You're far too punctual for my taste."

He led her into the breakfast room and pulled out her chair for her. "I do my best to please."

"I like that in a man." She lifted her tea and sipped. It was almost cold, but she barely noticed. What she had noticed was that Will had not apologized. Any other man would have apologized for keeping a lady waiting, even if that lady gave him every forgiveness and sign of understanding.

But then she was not a lady in Will's eyes.

Now that Will was here, Juliette asked for a cup of chocolate then fetched a scone as well as clotted cream from the sideboard. She believed if one was going to sin, one should do so completely. She took a bite then looked down the short table at Will. He was having tea and toast. "And might one inquire as to why you were late?"

He glanced up at her, and something flickered in his eyes. Something akin to guilt. She narrowed her eyes and set down her fork. "Will?"

"I had business," he said, looking down at his paper.

"You were supposed to have been in London. The only business you have in Yorkshire at present is the diamonds."

He ate a bite of toast. "Precisely."

She glared at him from across the table. "You were investigating the diamonds without me?"

"I thought it best."

"For whom? I'm in just as much, if not more, danger from Lucifer as you. How could you leave me behind?"

He tugged at his cravat and flicked his paper. Juliette decided he looked particularly uncomfortable, which was unusual for him. "It was best for everyone involved. I visited the Nowlund estate, and I thought it rather gauche to bring you."

She opened her mouth then closed it again. "I see. And did you discover anything?"

"Obviously the marquess is not in residence at present, and their steward was not amenable to allowing me access to the house without asking Lord Nowlund's permission first. He sent a message. Now I wait."

"Now *we* wait. I won't be left out of this search."

He frowned at her. "I'm perfectly capable of conducting this investigation on my own. And I knew Lady Elizabeth. I might be able to deduce where she hid the diamonds, if indeed she hid them at Nowlund Park."

"And I have met Lucifer and had him question me extensively about the diamonds. I have a better idea what we are looking for."

"What we are—I assumed—"

Juliette shook her head and glanced at the footmen. She dared not say any more in front of them. "So we are in the country," she said to cover their sudden silence.

Will nodded. "It would appear so."

"What is there to do in the country besides take walks? I was never a great walker."

"Ah…" Will raised his brows as though never before considering what one might actually do if one was at one's leisure. "I suppose you could ride."

"Excellent idea." Juliette stood. "Let's go for a ride."

"I didn't mean—"

Juliette marched to his end of the table and took his arm. "We'd better not dally. It looks as though it might rain. Or is it always so cloudy and overcast in Yorkshire?"

Will looked as though he would protest further, but finally he sighed. "Very well. I'll have the grooms saddle two horses."

"Oh, good. I shall change into my riding habit." She pulled away from him, toward the room she'd been given. "And Will?"

He glanced back at her, wariness in his eyes. Juliette almost laughed. The man was obviously not used to having his days taken up with entertaining. Good.

The more she could move him out of his routine, the better. He needed to have fun.

"Don't give me some old, plodding mare. I want to ride fast."

"Of course you do."

Juliette couldn't stop a tinkle of laughter from escaping her lips.

Pelham watched the sway of her hips as she made her way up the stairs to her chambers. He hadn't sought her out last night, and perhaps he should have. He found himself wanting her again. In fact, his body had made it difficult for him to think of anything besides wrapping his arms around her soft curves, stripping off her clothing, and burying himself inside her.

He was definitely bewitched by her.

But that did not mean he had lost control of his senses—well, not all of them anyway, he thought as he turned toward the door to the stables. He would have been insensitive indeed to take her to Nowlund Park. He didn't much care what the servants thought, but his neighbors would talk. And he did have respect for Lord and Lady Nowlund. More respect than to bring his… He didn't want to call Juliette his mistress, but he wasn't precisely certain what she was.

In any case, he hadn't thought it prudent to bring her along. Besides, she should rest and recuperate. There was no need for her to involve herself further with these diamonds.

Of course, he hadn't considered he might be part of her recuperation. He had thought to take care of business—there was always business—while she rested. But now it appeared he would have to ride with her.

Ride fast.

He chuckled as he waved at the groom. The man gave him a surprised look. Probably had never seen him laugh before. But he was laughing thinking of Juliette's horse cantering. That would be fast enough to please her.

Once again he was wrong. It was annoying how often he was wrong about Juliette. He would have preferred she canter, because the breakneck pace she set frankly frightened him. The surrounding landscape was flat and covered with grasses and sheep. The sheep trotted out of their way with bleats of protest. And they scared a few red grouse from their hiding places. Pelham rode a faster horse, and Juliette still managed almost to beat him to the old crofter's cottage, a landmark she'd spied after she'd kicked her horse into full gallop.

She'd only almost beaten him because he hadn't wanted to encourage her to ride so fast. He didn't want to see her injured. But when it looked as though she would win, he urged his own horse on and won, pulling his mount up short and giving a quick wave to the family who came out to see what all the commotion was about.

Juliette charged up behind him. Her hair had come loose of its pins and whipped about her pink face. "I demand a rematch!" she yelled over the wind. "We race back to the house, and I'll beat you this time."

In the distance, thunder boomed. It had been

drizzling for the last quarter hour, but now the rain started in earnest.

"Your Grace!" the crofter yelled over the thunder. "You and your new duchess are welcome to shelter with us."

Pelham blinked. *Duchess?* They thought Juliette was his duchess? He looked at her. She sat a horse well, and her riding habit was stylish and complimented her figure. But her hair, her eyes—they were wanton. No duchess—no real duchess—would ever look so... so tempting.

She was looking back at him, amusement in her eyes. "I'm perfectly capable of riding in the rain," she told him.

"Oh, no, Your Grace!" the crofter's wife said. "You'll catch your death of cold. We don't have much, but we have a warm fire and tea."

Pelham wanted to ride back. He never knew what to say to his tenants. Never felt at ease with them. But Juliette was already accepting the crofter's hand. She dismounted and swept one of the small children running about into her arms.

"Your Grace, would you allow me to rub the horses down?" the crofter asked.

Pelham tore his eyes from Juliette. "No."

The man took a step back.

"What I mean is we are partaking of your hospitality. Go inside and warm yourself. I'll see to the animals."

When he'd walked and rubbed the horses down, then situated them in a covered area next to the house, he knocked on the crofter's door. No one answered, and so he opened the door.

The family of five was seated around the fire, cups of tea in hand. Juliette had her back to him, but from the rapt gazes of the others in the room, she was telling a vastly entertaining story. Devil take it. What kind of stories would a celebrated courtesan have to tell to a crofter's family?

But as he started forward, the entire group burst into laughter. He paused, closed the door, and heard Juliette speaking.

"I hid the piglet in the barn's loft and told my father he'd escaped. Unfortunately, this conversation took place in the barn."

Pelham moved into the room. Her voice sounded different. Not quite so cultured. Not quite so formal. And she had one of the mop-haired children on her lap. And the child appeared to *want* to sit there. "What happened then?" the little girl on her lap asked. Pelham assumed it was a girl, because she was wearing a dress of some sort. The child couldn't have been more than three—though he was no judge of children.

"What do *you* think happened?" Juliette asked, rocking the child back and forth on her knees. "I bet you can guess."

"Pig Pig went *wheee*."

Pelham raised his brows. It was a good imitation of a pig's squeal.

"That's right!" Juliette bounced the girl up and down. "Just as I had convinced my father Pig Pig had escaped, she said *wheee* and *oink oink*!" Juliette tickled the little girl, who squealed herself. "And I was found out."

"Did you get in trouble?" one of the boys asked.

He was older and taller but had the same mop of brown hair as the little girl.

"Yes. I had to go to bed without dinner for lying." Juliette's face was serious.

"And was Pig Pig sold to the butcher to make ham?" the little girl asked.

"That's the good part of the story."

Pelham rather thought hearing Juliette make pig noises was his favorite part.

"The next day when I woke up, Pig Pig was in her stall with a red ribbon around her neck. My father said I could keep her as a pet."

"And do you still have her?" the little girl asked, clearly excited at the prospect of seeing this Pig Pig.

Juliette shook her head. "No, she grew up and had her own family. Just like you will one day."

"And you married His Great." The little girl pointed at him, and Pelham couldn't help but smile.

"His Grace," her mother corrected gently.

"Oh, but he is very great," Juliette said, her gaze on him. Suddenly he felt warm, despite being wet through and through.

"Maybe one day I'll marry His Great."

"Oh, don't be putting those notions in your wee head," her father said.

"Oh, but why not, John?" the crofter's wife interjected. "If Her Grace, a farmer's daughter, can marry a duke, why, anyone can."

Juliette's eyes slid to the floor, and she gave the family a shaky smile. Pelham cleared his throat. "It looks as though the rain has slowed. We had better get back while we have a chance."

"Of course." Juliette gave the girl one more bounce then set her on her feet. "It was a pleasure meeting you." She shook all of their hands and gave the children quick kisses on the forehead.

Pelham nodded gruffly, feeling like a foreigner witnessing some exotic ritual. What did he know of bouncing children on his lap or sitting by a fire surrounded by family? His childhood had been made up of governesses and tutors, regiment and routine.

When they had mounted again and were riding back, more slowly this time, as the ground was muddy and the rocks slippery with moisture, Pelham said, "I didn't know you had grown up on a farm."

"It's not something one wants advertised when one is the Duchess of Dalliance," she answered.

"No, I suppose not." The sky was a perfect blue now, and the sun had come out, warming the land. "Do you ever wonder what your life would have been like if you had married a good man? Would you still live on a farm and have three of your own small ones?"

She gazed at him, her blue eyes clear as the sky ahead of them. "No. You can't go back, Will. I made my choices, and I don't regret them. I loved being a courtesan. It was fun, much more fun than living on a farm. You can't allow your past to dictate your future. You can make your own future."

He was silent for a long time. He could see how she had made her own future, and from difficult circumstances. Could he do the same? Could he step out of his father's shadow and live life without regret?

When they were in view of Rothingham Manor,

he said, "And what will you do when"—he gestured to the house—"this is over?"

"I don't know. I don't think I can go back to being a courtesan. I'm not sure I want to. I was tiring of it even before you cut me at Carlton House."

Pelham pulled his horse to a stop. "Really?"

She nodded. "I want a home and a family. I love balls and dancing and fun, but even London becomes tedious after a time. And besides, beauty, fashion, celebrity—those things are fleeting. I want something real. I want something forever." She looked away from him. "I want someone who loves the farmer's daughter and the Duchess of Dalliance and everyone I've been in between. And I want someone I can love, as well."

Now she looked at him, and Pelham saw tears sparkling on her lashes. They glittered in the sunlight. "Juliette—"

"Damn you, Will. Damn you."

He gaped. "What have I done?"

"You made me fall in love with you, and I know you can never, ever love me back."

He knew his mouth hung open. He knew he should say something. But words failed him. Juliette didn't seem to expect them anyway. She kicked her horse and rode ahead without him.

Pelham let her go. There was nothing he could say to comfort her, because she was right.

He could never love her.

Seventeen

JULIETTE LAY IN BED, LISTENING TO THE RAIN AGAINST her window. Shortly after they'd returned, the rain had begun again and not let up. It rained all afternoon, and she was forced to wander the house alone, gazing at the pretty gardens that were too wet to explore.

She finally found a book and decided to read, but she never found Pelham. The housekeeper told her he had decided to dine in his room, something Juliette deduced from Mrs. Waite's shocked expression he did rarely, if ever.

And so Juliette had eaten in the dining room alone. She'd eaten many, many meals alone and knew she would probably eat many, many more in that fashion.

But she was disappointed. She had not thought Pelham so much of a coward. Yes, it was probably not every day a woman told him she loved him—especially not one so completely wrong for him as she was.

But then *was* she wrong for him?

Juliette didn't think so. He had fun with her, something he sorely needed. Something completely lacking in his life before her, as far as she could tell. He was finally changing his routine, and perhaps one day he might even change this house so his father was not everywhere one looked.

But she would not be here to see it. She did not know why she even thought of Pelham's future. It didn't involve her, and Lady Sinclair would have told her she was a fool to hold onto dreams that would never come true.

Reality, Juliette, is all you can cling to. It's a hard pillow to lay your head on, but it will still be there in the morning. She fluffed the soft pillow under her head and shifted until she was again comfortable. She was sleeping in Pelham's house in one of his—she didn't know how many—large, inviting beds. He could find her if he wanted her. Obviously, he didn't want her.

And she hated that she still wanted him. If she went to him now, what was the harm? She was already in love with him. She might as well enjoy him for the short time they had together. She supposed if she had more pride, she might turn over and try to sleep. But where had pride ever gotten her?

She rose and found a dressing gown. She put it on then hastily took it off, removed her nightrail, and donned the gown again. The fewer clothes, the better. When she reached her door, she considered that Pelham might have decided it was best if he no longer bedded her. But she had yet to meet a man who held on to his scruples for long when a naked woman slipped into his bed.

Not that she had ever done so. But she had lived among courtesans for the last few years, and she'd learned something from all their chatter.

She opened the door and stepped into the dark corridor. She knew where Pelham's rooms were. She'd seen the maids cleaning them when she'd passed by earlier in the day. She'd caught a glimpse of the large tester bed and the plush rug, and had known immediately it was the duke's room. It was too grand, too ornate for any mere guest.

It was close to hers, a few doors away, and she tiptoed down the corridor, watching her shadow in the flickering flames of the candle she held. When she reached the door, she raised her hand to knock then thought better of it. She tried the handle, found the door unlocked, and moved silently inside.

The royal-blue curtains on the bed were drawn, but she could hear Pelham's soft, regular breathing. Just like a man to sleep while a woman agonized over their relationship. She took a moment to study the room. The tester bed was by far the largest piece of furniture. It looked as though it had been built for a king. There was also a sitting area by the window with two armchairs upholstered in blue. A small desk completed the room's furnishings. She spotted an interior door and supposed it led to the dressing room and the empty duchess's chambers beyond.

Juliette blew out her candle and quietly set it on a table near the door. A low fire burned in the huge hearth across from the bed, and her eyes were already adjusting to the darkness. With a fortifying breath, she slipped her robe off and felt the cold air brush her naked body. Oh, but it felt deliciously scandalous to pad, naked, across the soft rug, push open the bed's heavy draperies, and crawl in.

Pelham didn't even stir. She took a long look at him, his dark hair framing his stern face. Even in sleep, he had a serious expression. One hand was on the pillow beside his cheek, and the other rested on the bedclothes at his chest.

His bare chest.

She bent and kissed that chest. He was warm and smelled like sleepy male. She tugged the bedclothes down to reveal his taut stomach and the indentation of his waist. He stirred slightly, and she smiled as she ran light fingertips down to circle his navel then followed with her tongue.

That elicited a low moan from him, but a peek at his face told her his eyes were still closed and he continued to sleep. His body was waking, though. She could see the hard bulge at the edge of the covers, and she inched them down, revealing him. Her hand wrapped around him, sliding up and down his hardness. Now he moaned in earnest, and she heard a muffled, "Wha—?"

Before he could wake fully, she leaned down and took him in her mouth, sliding as much of him as she could between her lips and sucking lightly.

"Oh, good God!" he groaned. "Juliette?"

With a teasing lick, she released him. "You were expecting someone else?"

"I wasn't expecting anyone. What are you doing here?"

She sat up, revealing her nudity. "What does it look like? Seducing you."

"How did you—?"

She took him in her mouth again, and his words

turned into a groan. His hands fisted in her hair as she moved up and down, loving him with her mouth. Finally, his hips bucked, and he pulled her shoulders back. "Wait."

"For?"

"I'm not even awake."

She glanced down. "You look awake to me. Is there something else you'd like me to do?" She straddled him. "This, perhaps?" She slid him inside her, and his hands clenched on her hips. She rode him slowly, torturing him as he made every effort to quicken her pace. But she could feel her own pleasure rising now, and she wouldn't be swayed. Finally, her hips began to race of their own volition, and just as she was about to climax, he flipped her onto her back.

"Will!" she sputtered.

He grinned down at her, that unruly hair of his brushing his forehead. "Tit for tat, I always say. And speaking of which…" He leaned down and tasted her nipple, taking one then the other into his mouth. She arched beneath him, pushing his hand between her legs. But he moved it back to her breast without giving her satisfaction. He teased her, pinched her, and she fisted her hands in his hair. "Will, *please*."

He traced a wet path down her belly with his tongue. She rose for him, but the man maddened her by tickling her thigh. And then his hands spread her legs wide, and she felt his tongue on the inside of her thigh. "Yes," she breathed.

He lapped at her, lightly—far too lightly. "Is this what you want?"

"More," she moaned. "More."

He licked her, rolled his tongue over that sensitive nub.

"Yes. Yes!" She was already convulsing, bucking as he played her, sucked her, devoured her. She came hard and fast, exploding into a thousand white-hot shards. She'd never felt pleasure like that before, couldn't begin to catch her breath. And then just when she thought she might survive, he plunged into her, and she bucked with pleasure again.

She wrapped her legs around him, pulling him deep as he thrust hard and fast. "You feel so good," she moaned.

"I feel good," he panted. "You're hot and wet. I—"

She clenched around him, and he made a guttural noise and swelled within her. He collapsed on top of her, his body shuddering.

They lay like that, two lovers entwined, for what seemed hours. Finally, he rolled off her. "I didn't mean to flatten you." It was probably the closest to an apology the duke in him could manage.

"I'm fine," she said. "I like feeling your weight on top of me." She reached over and traced his chest.

He grabbed her hand. "Woman! Give me five minutes."

"Only five? Now that's impressive."

He quirked his mouth in a half smile, and she couldn't resist kissing that mouth. Couldn't resist kissing his cheeks and his eyes. He was so beautiful, so perfectly male. If only he could have been born someone else, and she could have—

But she'd sworn she'd not have regrets. Her life was

her choice these past few years. She'd had precious few choices, but she'd made those she did with full knowledge of the consequences. Now she would have to live with them.

"What are you thinking about?" he asked.

She smiled. "All the wanton things I want to do to you. With you. On top of you. Under you…"

"I like that train of thought."

"I thought you might."

He touched her hair, rubbed it between two fingers. "It's like moonlight. Silken moonlight."

She raised a brow. "I didn't realize you were a poet."

"I'm not." He touched her face. "I missed you tonight."

"And I you. I had to eat in that enormous dining room all alone, waited on hand and foot. It was awful."

"It sounds perfectly monstrous."

She swallowed. "You didn't have to avoid me."

"I thought it best." His face changed into an expression she liked to think of as The Duke. Suddenly, he was solemn and paternal. She wanted to kiss The Duke away and lie in the arms of the man.

"Because I'm in love with you?"

He shifted, tried to sit. "Juliette—"

She pushed him back down. "Do you think avoiding me will make me fall out of love? I'm no ingénue, Will. I don't fall in love easily. In fact, I'd say with the exception of John Miller when I was thirteen, this is the only time. If all of your efforts thus far haven't swayed my emotions, I don't think hiding from me will."

"I wasn't hiding. I'm a—"

"Man. Men at times prefer to avoid women's emotions. But I'm not going to pelt you with tears or sentimentality. I know you don't love me."

"Juliette, I…"

She raised her brows, waited. "You're very fond of me?"

"Yes, but I feel more than that." He put a hand over his eyes, scrubbed at his brow. "I don't know what to say. I'm no good at this."

She took his hand. "You needn't say anything. John Miller didn't."

He furrowed his brow. Oh, how she loved the little lines that formed when he furrowed his brow. "Did you tell this John Miller you loved him, too?"

"Of course."

He laughed. She'd heard him laugh so rarely, she laughed as well. "You're no coward, I'll give you that. And what did John Miller say in return?"

"Why, nothing. He grabbed me by the shoulders and kissed me. It was my first kiss."

"A romantic story."

"Hardly. His breath smelled like onions, and I vowed never to kiss a boy again. Needless to say, I fell right out of love with poor John Miller."

"I'm sure he died of a broken heart."

"No, he married Sally Johnson, and they had six children at last count. Apparently, she likes the smell of onion breath."

He shook his head. "I've never met anyone like you."

"That's because you spend too much time with *ladies*. I guarantee you Fallon, Lily, and I are more fun than any real countess or marchioness."

"I don't doubt it. You three have an interesting friendship."

"Why?" She knew why, but she wanted him to say it.

He shifted uncomfortably. "Well, considering how you know one another."

"You mean how we met? What story have you heard?"

"No story. I…"

"You mean you haven't heard that the Earl of Sin invited me to his bed, and when I arrived, I found Lily and Fallon already servicing him?"

He opened his mouth then closed it again. Apparently, that was not the story he'd heard. He looked rather shocked.

"Or perhaps you heard that we have adjoining suites at Somerset House, and he alternates his nightly visits between us?"

"Juliette."

"So that is the one you'd heard. And do you believe that?"

"It's not true?"

She sighed, feeling disappointed. "I'm a courtesan, Will. The truth is whatever you want it to be." She sat and scooted away from him. "I find I'm rather more tired than I thought. If you don't mind, I'll find my own bed."

He caught her arm before she could hop off the bed. "But I do mind."

She looked down at his hand on her arm. "One aspect of marriage I never could tolerate was being owned. You don't own me, Will. I'll sleep where I wish."

"I don't want to own you." He softened his grip but didn't release her. "You're not the Duchess of Dalliance to me. You're Juliette. I care about you."

Her gaze jerked from his fingers to his face. She saw softness there, a sincerity of emotion. He hadn't apologized for anything he'd said—now or before. He hadn't told her being a courtesan didn't matter. Most important, he hadn't said he loved her.

But could this perhaps be the first step?

Oh, she could all but hear Lady Sinclair grinding her teeth in frustration.

Juliette knew she was a fool. But what could she do? She loved him.

She turned back to him, and Will took her in his arms. The feel of him, of his skin, warm and naked against hers, made her shiver. She wanted to stay in his arms forever, curl up there, close her eyes, and know she belonged. She wanted to be safe and loved and to know she would always be safe and loved.

She wanted Will to love her.

He kissed her, cradling her head in his hand, whispering she was beautiful.

Tonight he was offering her his gentleness, his care. It would have to be enough.

～∞～

Will was gone when she woke. It didn't surprise her. Any man who voluntarily breakfasted at eight, even in London, was obviously a man who enjoyed mornings. She lolled about in his bed for the better part of the morning, drank chocolate, and nibbled on several delicious pastries, and then decided the day was too fine to spend indoors. The weather had vastly improved overnight, and the day dawned bright and sunny. It was still crisp and cold, but with her spencer over her warmest dress and a muff for her hands, she was quite comfortable in Will's well-tended gardens.

There were two. One was manicured and shaped to perfection. It had been laid out precisely to conform to the standards of what an English garden should be. She spent all of a quarter hour there, admiring the flowers and forsythia shrubs and staying on the graveled walk. There was much to admire—pink and red Lenten roses; Solomon's Seal with its white flowers swaying from arching branches; pansies in blue, purple, orange, and more. She saw violas, dog's tooth violets, and the crocus and daffodils were coming in, too. And she adored the hyacinths, especially in blue. No tulips yet, but she knew another fortnight would bring those.

Finally, she wandered to the wild garden behind the house. It too had been planted and maintained, but it was not sculpted; instead, it retained much of the natural landscape. A small brook ran through it, shadowed by scrubby trees, and Juliette found the whole atmosphere quite peaceful. Of course her boots and hem were a muddy mess, but after yesterday's rain, that couldn't be helped.

She found the remains of an old Roman wall and sat on top, kicking her feet to and fro and staring up at the cloudless sky. Nearby, the brook babbled and birds chirped. She closed her eyes—and fell backward.

Juliette started, but the hand clamped about her mouth muffled her scream. And then she hit the ground and the air was knocked out of her lungs. She gasped and tried to focus, but the man holding her hauled her up and moved behind her, out of her sight.

"I could kill you right now," he hissed, his voice low and disguised and yet familiar. Lucifer? "I've been watching and waiting for this chance, and you, like a fool, gave it to me. Where's your lover, little whore? Where is he now that you need him?"

She shook her head, tried to free her mouth, but he held fast. To her horror, she realized he had her arms pinned behind her back.

"So now the question becomes, how should I kill you?" The rasp of his voice made his words difficult to decipher, but she understood *kill* well enough. "Should I murder you now or rape you first?" His hand clenched painfully on her breast. "Hmm. I think rape first."

"No!" she managed, though the sound was hampered. She writhed and squirmed, and he was forced to use both hands to subdue her.

"Help!" she screamed. "Help me! *Will!*"

He hit her hard on the back of the head, sending her sprawling forward. Her vision dimmed briefly, but she refused to lose consciousness. She could feel his hand on the back of her leg, feel his weight on top of her. He was pulling up her skirts to take her from behind. He had one arm pressed into her neck, holding her head down, and even though she tasted dirt, she screamed again.

He jabbed something into her back—his knee perhaps—and she let out an *oof*. And then he yanked her head back and slammed it down. The world dimmed then, and the sound of the brook seemed too loud as it rushed in her ears.

She felt his hand on her bare thigh and closed her eyes.

Eighteen

"YOUR GRACE, I BELIEVE SHE IS WAKING."

Pelham turned from his steward and crossed to the bed where Juliette lay. Her eyelids were fluttering, and she moved slightly.

"Lie still, madam," the doctor admonished her. "Open your eyes but don't move as yet."

Pelham stood over her, frowning. She looked so deathly pale. He thought he could see the bluish tinge of her veins under her eyelids. And even though she was tall for a woman, she looked tiny lying immobile in the guest bed.

Her eyes opened slowly and focused on the ceiling. Pelham wanted her to look at him, wanted to see the flicker of mischief he was used to, but she didn't turn her head. "Where…?" she began. Her voice was hoarse and low. She had what would be a nasty bruise on one side of her face. Now it was red and swollen, but the doctor had told him it would yellow and then darken to blue-black.

She reached up and touched her cheek gingerly. Pelham clenched his fists. If he could take the pain from her, he would. This was his fault. He glared at his steward, who looked down at the floor.

"Will?"

Pelham started and jerked his attention to Juliette.

"Are you all right?" she asked.

He knelt beside her, partly because her voice was raspy and partly because he wanted to be close to her. "I am fine. You are the one who has been injured."

"Do you remember anything, madam?" the doctor asked.

"Yes. I was in the gardens and… he tried to rape me, but I hit my head, and I don't remember."

"Devil take him!" Pelham roared. "When I get my hands on him, I'll reach down his throat and rip his lungs out."

The doctor patted Juliette's arm. "Your screams were heard before the man could do his worst. Your face is bruised, but otherwise you are fine."

Juliette smiled at Will, her lips a little crooked where it obviously hurt her to curve them. "Will. You heard me. You came for me."

How he wished it had been he who had saved her. He would have murdered Lucifer and disemboweled the man on the spot. "It wasn't me," he said through his clenched jaw. "The gardener heard you."

"Oh." She glanced about. "Thank God. Is he here? I want to thank him."

"I will make sure he knows of your appreciation."

Pelham's steward stepped closer to the bed. "Madam, I want to offer my most abject apologies."

She blinked at him. "Why? I'm sorry. Who are you?"

"This is my steward," Pelham said. "Mr. Cargrove."

"I don't know how he got past us, madam," Cargrove said. "His Grace instructed me to have sentries stationed along the roads and at the posting houses. No one saw a man meeting this Lucifer's description."

"I'll be questioning each of those men," Pelham said. "I'll find out who was asleep instead of doing his duty and have his head."

"Wait a moment." Juliette put her hand on his arm. Her fingers were cold. "Mr. Cargrove?"

"Yes, madam?"

"Is there any way Lucifer might have found a way around the men?"

"Madam," the doctor said, "you should not overtax yourself. This is not your concern."

Her brows shot up, and Pelham was glad he was not on the receiving end of the glare she gave the doctor. "Excuse me, sir, but I believe I was the one attacked. That makes it my concern."

"As you wish, madam." The doctor shrugged as though washing his hands of the matter.

Juliette glanced back at Cargrove. "As I was saying, perhaps the men are not entirely at fault."

"I did put my best men on this job, my lady— excuse me, madam. I don't understand how Lucifer could have gotten by them. Yorkshire is rough terrain in these parts. It's unlikely he would have been able to travel off the main road."

"And yet he managed not only to evade the sentries on the road but also make it onto my estate. How do the men I have on the perimeter explain that?" Pelham demanded.

"Good grief!" Juliette exclaimed. "I had no idea we were living in a veritable fortress."

"Apparently, we are not." Pelham eyed Cargrove.

"But surely someone would have seen Lucifer," Juliette said, "and reported it."

"Unless he came in disguise," Cargrove added. "A man who did not match Lucifer's description might not rate a mention. Could you see his face at all, my la—I mean, madam? Was he in disguise?"

Pelham watched as Juliette considered. His steward knew she was a London Cyprian. Why did the man continue to mistakenly address her as a highborn lady?

"I didn't see him," Juliette said finally. "He grabbed me from behind."

"Then he very well could have been in disguise," Pelham said. "We shall have to change the orders. Anyone not known should be reported."

"Yes, Your Grace," Cargrove said. "I will relay the change immediately." He bid Juliette farewell, and soon thereafter, the doctor left.

Pelham gave the maids a frosty stare, and they, too, found occupations elsewhere. When it was the two of them, Pelham sat down beside her.

He expected her to say something, one of her witty quips, perhaps, but she was staring distractedly at the window. After several minutes, he took her hand. "Are you tired? Should I leave?"

She didn't answer or turn her head.

"Juliette?"

She glanced at him. "Yes? Oh, I'm sorry. I was lost in thought."

"What were you thinking?"

"Nothing. Only…"

He waited, and she returned to staring at the window again.

"Only… the mention of disguise made me think." She glanced at him, her gaze meeting and holding his. "What if the man who attacked me wasn't Lucifer at all? What if it was… someone else?"

Pelham frowned. "Who?"

She shook her head. "I don't know. I just thought…" She shrugged. She didn't even know why the idea it was Oliver crossed her mind. Their divorce had been so long ago. Why would he come for her now, after all this time? And why in Yorkshire? Oliver had never even been to Yorkshire.

"Who else would want to attack you? The gardener didn't recognize the man, though he admitted he didn't get a very good look. But he would have known the man if he was local. It must have been Lucifer."

She nodded. "You're right, of course." She glanced about. "Where is everyone?"

"They found other places to be."

She smiled. "Do you intend to scare me away as well?"

"Can you blame a man for wanting a little time alone with you? Besides, you need your rest."

"I'm fine. I have a slight headache but am otherwise unharmed. Perhaps you could climb into bed beside me?"

He would have liked nothing better, but she should sleep now. "Why don't I sit here"—he pulled a chair beside the bed—"while you rest."

"That's not quite what I had in mind," she said.

"It will have to do for now. Close your eyes and sleep."

She laughed. "I can't just go to sleep at the snap of a finger. Perhaps you could tell me a bedtime story."

"I don't know any stories."

She frowned at him. "Then make one up."

He opened his mouth, closed it again, at a loss for words.

"*You* wanted me to rest."

He sighed. A story, a story…

"I'll help you begin. Once upon a time…"

He stared at her.

"Once upon a time," she prompted.

"Once upon a time." He cleared his throat. "There was a young boy named…" No name came to mind. He was horrible at storytelling.

"Named Will," she supplied for him then yawned. At least that was a good sign. She might fall asleep and save him from continuing. "Will lived in a fortress." When he didn't speak, she said, "Now you continue the story. Good grief, Will, I can't do everything."

And it was a good thing she was incapacitated, because once she felt better, he was going to throttle her. "There was a boy named Will."

She yawned again and motioned for him to continue.

"Will lived in a fortress. He'd lived there all his life, and he liked this fortress. Until he met…" He glanced at Juliette. Her eyes had been closed, but she opened them now. That ice-blue gaze seemed to look right through him. "A princess."

She raised a brow in a skeptical expression and closed her eyes again.

"The princess showed Will he didn't have to live

in this fortress. He could exist outside its walls." He leaned back into his chair and stared at the ceiling. The firelight flickered in oranges and yellows. "He could laugh. He could have fun. He'd never had fun before, because this Will was a duke. And dukes were supposed to be serious and act in a manner that befitted their stations. Dukes do not have fun."

He thought about his childhood and tried to remember if he'd ever done anything fun as a boy. Surely he must have played games at some point. All children did. He did have a vague memory of a nanny who smiled a lot and clapped for him, but that memory was brief. Mostly, the image of his father rose up. He touched his bad ear. No, his childhood had not been *fun*.

"But this princess was always smiling and laughing, and she loved to have fun. Will was skeptical at first, but he gave in to her cajoling, and soon he had fun as well." He glanced at Juliette and saw her eyes were still closed. Her breathing seemed regular, and he thought she must have fallen asleep. He lowered his voice to a murmur.

"And then one day the princess told Will she loved him. That was even more confusing than trying to have fun. No one had ever loved Will before. He didn't know why anyone should love him. He didn't understand why the princess loved him. She was beautiful and witty and popular for her dazzling personality, while he was dull, dreary, and sought after only because of his title." He leaned forward and took her hand in his. She didn't stir, and her hand was limp. He stroked the soft skin.

"Will wanted to deserve this love, and so he tried to protect her. He tried to keep her safe. But he failed even at that simple task." Will lowered his head and touched his lips to Juliette's hand. "I vow I'll keep you safe from now on. I'll find the diamonds and stop Lucifer. It's the least I can do after you've given so much to me."

෧෨

Juliette's heart ached at Will's words. How could he think himself so unworthy of love? How could he think he had to repay her in some form or fashion for her love? All she wanted in return was his love. He didn't have to protect her or find the diamonds. She wanted him to love her.

But she didn't think Will understood what love was. How could he, after the way he'd been raised? Perhaps if she'd been the daughter of a viscount or baron, he might have been able to accept her and one day love her. Perhaps if she'd never become a courtesan, they might have had a future. And she so desperately wanted a future with this man who vowed to keep her safe, who pressed his lips so gently to her fingers, who laid his head on her hand as though asking for absolution.

At some point, she must have fallen asleep, because when she woke up, the room was dark and the fire low. She blinked and winced at the pain in her head. The wince only made the side of her face hurt more, and she turned to try and find a more comfortable position. Beside the bed, sitting with his head lolled to one side, was the Duke of Pelham. He'd fallen asleep in that uncomfortable chair and presumably stayed at her side for hours.

For a long time, she watched him sleep, memorizing the line of his eyelashes on his cheek, the curl of his unruly hair on his forehead, the softness of his mouth, which he usually held in a proud slash. He looked extremely uncomfortable. The man had a dozen or more beds in this home, but he'd forgone all of them to sit with her.

She wanted to cry, to reach out to him, to scream for joy. He *did* care about her.

Mostly, she wanted to wake him and insist he come to bed, but she knew he'd only refuse. And then he'd lose the little sleep he'd found. Poor man. How she loved him. How she wished he could see himself as the sweet, thoughtful man she did.

But all he saw was the duke.

The next morning, Juliette insisted upon rising from bed, assuring everyone she felt fine. One glance in the glass told her she did not look fine. She looked a fright. Nothing short of a veil would cover the yellowish-green marks on her face. But since she had not brought one, she did her best to ignore the damage. She had the maid dress her hair simply and donned a plain gown.

And then she went in search of Pelham. One of the footmen outside the library informed her that His Grace was within and was not to be disturbed. Juliette ignored the man, opened the door, and marched inside. Will looked up, rose hastily, and let out a long-suffering sigh.

The man who had been seated across from Will rose as well. He'd been speaking, but his voice died away. When he turned to her, his jaw dropped open.

"It's not as bad as it looks," she said.

"Yes, it is," Will answered. "You should go back to bed."

She wasn't about to be drawn into that argument. "Aren't you going to introduce us?"

Will sighed. He had that beleaguered look she was so familiar with. The look that meant she had won this time. She took a moment to glance about the library, as it was the one room she hadn't been able to explore previously. As she expected, it was a bastion of maleness. Libraries usually were. They were intended to be a man's sanctuary, his refuge. Her father had spent hours in his every week. Juliette did not know what he did behind those closed doors, but as soon as a caller knocked on the house door, he'd retreated to his worn leather chair.

Her favorite memories of her father were when he invited her inside and allowed her to sit on his knee at the desk. She'd practice writing her letters, and he'd praise her every effort. She remembered going to the library after his funeral and sitting in his chair. She'd no longer been a child, but she'd felt small in that chair. She'd felt safe.

The chair—the room—smelled like her father, and everything in it reminded her of him.

This library was male in its furnishings, but it did not make her think of Will. It could have been any man's library, with its shelves of books in perfect rows, spines lined up exactly; its large oak desk, clear of any personal effects; and its perfectly serviceable bookshelves, chairs, and similar other trappings.

And then, of course, there was the portrait of the

last duke above the mantel. He frowned down at the room and her, as though daring her to change something. She glanced at Will.

Or someone.

"This is Mr. Pittinger," Will said. "He is the steward of Nowlund Park. Mr. Pittinger, this is…"

Juliette raised her brows.

"A friend."

Coward, she mouthed.

"Y… you're t… the—"

"Duchess of Dalliance? Yes. You may call me Duchess if you'd like." She sat in Will's empty chair so the men might sit again, as well. "Have you news from London, Mr. Pittinger?"

"Y… yes, madam." The duke sat, and Pittinger followed. "Lord Nowlund has given permission for His Grace to search his property here."

"I see. May I assume that Lady Elizabeth has not yet been found?"

"No one has seen her or had any contact from her," Will told her. "Her parents are desperate for any clue as to her whereabouts. They don't wish to leave London, as that was her last known location, so they have authorized me to search for any clues here."

"Good. I'll search with you."

"No, you won't."

She gave him a catlike smile and turned to Pittinger. "Any word about Lucifer?"

"He's still not been found, madam. Bow Street Runners have been stationed outside his gambling den, but he has not been seen in Town. His Grace tells me you have reason to believe him in Yorkshire."

Juliette touched her cheek. "Yes. It is a possibility. You should make sure the entire staff at Nowlund Park is on alert. He might try to break in and search the place himself."

"What precisely is he looking for? Perhaps if I knew, I might be able to help in the search."

Juliette and Will exchanged glances. Juliette shrugged. What could it hurt?

"We're looking for diamonds. The man called Lucifer was acquainted with Lady Elizabeth and believes she took diamonds he claims are his."

"Diamonds?" Pittinger frowned. "Loose diamonds, or were they set in some way?"

Juliette shook her head. "We don't know, Mr. Pittinger. I suppose we assumed they were loose, but they could be in a necklace or a bracelet."

"Obviously, we don't expect diamonds to be lying about Nowlund Park," Will said. "But we'd like to search in case Lady Elizabeth secreted them there. If we have the diamonds, we might be able to use them to lure Lucifer out and seize him once and for all."

"Very good, Your Grace." Pittinger nodded. "Lord Nowlund did not put any restrictions on the search, so you may look where you wish. Do you wish to begin today?"

"No," Will said at the same time Juliette said, "Yes."

"You're not coming," he told her.

"Yes, I am. Mr. Pittinger, we will see you within the hour."

Pittinger rose, seeming eager to be away. "Very good, madam. I shall take my leave."

When he was gone, Juliette held up a hand. "Do not argue with me. I am going with you."

"You're not well."

She blew out a breath. "You're arguing."

He crossed his arms over his chest, looking formidable behind the large oak desk. "Because I don't want you to suffer a setback."

"Setback? I'm not ill. I bumped my head." The man was impossible. He seemed unable to stop giving orders. And he was so serious, so grave again. Perhaps if she tickled him. She could tie him to a chair and tickle him unmercifully. She rose, and he rose, as well.

"Sit down."

"No." She rounded the desk.

"You shouldn't be out of bed."

She reached him and put her hands on his chest, began untying his cravat.

"What are you doing?"

"Showing you exactly how well I feel."

"Juliette, this is neither the time nor the place."

She allowed his cravat to fall in a snowy heap against his linen shirt and began on the buttons at his throat. "Then stop me." She finished with the buttons and tugged the shirt from his trousers. When she glanced at his face, she saw his gaze was centered across the room. She followed it to the portrait above the mantel. "I suppose we had better do something about that."

"About what?"

"Him." She pointed. "We can't do this with him frowning down at us."

"Juliette—"

She tugged off his coat, ignoring his protests. After

all, he could easily have stopped her. But he hadn't. When she'd freed him from the garment, she walked to the portrait, laid the coat over a nearby chair, and began to tug the chair toward the hearth.

"What are you doing?" Will was instantly at her side. He took the chair from her hands. "Allow me. If you're thinking of removing the portrait, you should know it's far too heavy for you or I to do alone."

She could see that herself. "I don't want to remove it." *Today.* "I had planned to cover it with your coat."

Will looked at the coat, looked at the portrait, looked at her. She could see he wanted to argue. Instead, he climbed on the chair, took the coat, and hung it over the portrait.

Not even one argument.

The man was learning.

Either that or he wanted her as much as she wanted him.

He stepped down, and she pushed him back onto the chair. "Do sit, Your Grace."

He obliged, and she left him and crossed to the draperies. Heavy cords held them back from the windows, and she released them and carried the cords back to the chair. "Hold these, please."

With an amused look, he took them. She pulled his shirt over his head and tossed it aside.

He frowned. "You could at least drape it over something."

"Oh, I assure you much more than your shirt is going to be mussed when I am through."

"Should I be concerned?"

"Only if you value your dignity."

His brows came together. "What the devil does that—?"

"Hands behind your back," she instructed. She had no idea what she was going to do with him once she secured him. She wasn't going to tickle him, but she was going to make him forget he was A Duke for a little while. She stood behind him, but he didn't immediately offer his hands. "Will, hands," she ordered.

She could all but hear his teeth grind, but he gave her his hands. She tied them behind the chair and secured the cords tightly. He could escape if he really wanted. She was no sailor and knew very little about tying a good knot. But she didn't want him immobile for long.

She moved to stand in front of him and could not help but smile.

"Was all this for your diversion?" he asked.

"Of course. I'm excessively diverted." She brushed her fingertips lightly over his shoulders. "By your broad shoulders." She skimmed lower. "Your muscled chest." She paused on his hard, flat abdomen and allowed her fingertips to brush the waistband of his trousers. "Your firm stomach."

That, of course, was not all that was firm, and she ran her hand over him before she stepped back. His lips were pressed tightly together now, and she aimed to soften that expression. She remembered how he'd looked last night, so relaxed.

Juliette reached for her own clothing, tugging at the sleeves of her morning gown. She couldn't possibly undress herself. It had taken a maid half an hour to wrestle her into her clothing. But she could tease him a little. She pulled the gauzy fichu from her bodice and allowed it to flutter to the floor. Will's gaze followed the garment's winding trek then darted back up to her breasts. The morning gown had a modest neckline, but now she allowed the loosened sleeves to fall off her shoulders, revealing the swell of her breasts.

She heard Will inhale.

She wore long stays with a busk down the center. At the top of the busk, the maid had tied the securing ribbon into a little bow. She undid the bow, and though the stays remained in place, she was able to push the materials down so that her breasts, with their hard nipples, were visible.

"And I am tied to this chair because?" Will's voice was low and husky.

"Would you like to touch me?" she asked then stroked her own nipple playfully.

Will groaned, and she saw the muscles of his biceps strain.

"Oh, but I forgot your hands are useless." She cupped her breasts, lifted them. Will's eyes grew impossibly dark. "Fortunately, your mouth is free." She moved to straddle him, pulling her gown up so he might catch a glimpse of her thighs. She leaned close to his mouth, brushing first one nipple then the other over it.

Will's eyes closed, and when he opened them, the longing she saw pierced her. She had to steady herself with her hands on his shoulders, and he took the opportunity to take a nipple into his mouth.

"Oh!" The sudden shock of pleasure surprised her. She didn't know if the sensation came more from his skilled mouth or the way his dark blue eyes devoured her. As she watched, he moved from one breast to the other, running his tongue over the sensitive flesh.

She moaned again when he took her in his mouth, and she wanted nothing more than to free him from the trousers and sink down onto him.

But this was only the beginning. The time for that would come.

"I'm feeling very well indeed," she said.

"You should be in bed."

"As much as I like that idea, I have you here. Now. At my mercy." She stepped back and ran her gaze over him. "Now, where to start…"

"Why don't you untie me, and I'll show you."

"Why don't *I* show you?" She stepped forward, leaned down, and kissed his cheek, brushing her lips over the faint hint of stubble. She kissed her way to his ear, inhaling the scent of mint. Gently, she kissed his ear, nipping the lobe playfully and whispering what she wanted to do to him.

"Juliette, this is torture."

"And you thought I was feeling unwell." She kissed his bare shoulder, his chest, and ran her tongue down to his abdomen. Then she knelt between his legs and kissed his belly.

"Juliette, if a servant should enter…"

"No servant would dare enter when you're within. The footman outside will ensure that. Of course, he's probably deduced what we're doing." She flicked open the fall of his trousers. "I imagine that will be the source of gossip at the dinner table tonight."

"Wonderful."

She moved the fabric of his trousers aside, and his erection sprang free. "Do you wish me to stop?"

He glared at her. "No."

"I didn't think so." She dipped her head and touched her mouth to the tip of his erection. He inhaled sharply, and she licked him, teasing and tantalizing. "Will, has any other woman ever done this to you?"

"No." His voice was ragged.

"I'm going to tell you a secret. I've never done this to another man." She glanced up at him, took him inside her mouth. He blinked, his expression a mixture of pleasure and confusion. "It's true," she said a moment later. "I'm not even certain I'm doing this correctly."

"You're doing just fine."

"Oh, good. But perhaps you might like it if I used my hand like this."

He groaned an answer as she pleasured him, then groaned again a moment later. "What was that you said earlier about dignity? I think the entire household heard me."

"I can stop."

"Why don't you untie me? I want to be inside you."

She rose. "I don't need to untie you for that." She straddled him again, hiked her skirts up, and guided him into her.

"Yes," he breathed against her neck. His lips kissed her softly, brushed her chin. She was surprised at his gentleness and kissed him back. Their mouths met again and again as she moved over him. She could tell he was holding back, waiting for her, and she felt her own pleasure mounting. She clenched his shoulders as her hips pistoned, and she kept her gaze on his face. His eyes were so impossibly blue. She thought of all the things she would remember about him, but it was the blueness of his eyes she would remember the most.

Pleasure surged within her, and she rode it to the end. At some point, she heard Will moan and felt him swell inside her. Then she laid her head on his shoulder and attempted to catch her breath. She felt his hands on her back, stroking languidly, and frowned. "You're free."

"Mmm. I let you have your fun, but now I want to hold you."

She closed her eyes and burrowed into his arms.

Nineteen

WILL WASN'T CERTAIN HOW SHE HAD MANAGED IT——HE supposed the seduction hadn't hurt—but Juliette was with him when he arrived at Nowlund Park. They took his carriage because, although she claimed to feel perfectly well, he didn't want her jostled about on horseback. The enclosed carriage was also more protected, especially as he'd enlisted half-a-dozen men to accompany them.

Juliette peered out the window as they approached. "It's an impressive house, but not as large as yours."

"This is not the earl's primary residence."

She nodded, studying the reddish brick structure. It was small but well maintained. The real value lay in the tenants who farmed Nowlund's land. It was prosperous land with soil good both for growing barley and grazing livestock. He supposed now Nowlund would sell it, as he had no daughter to dower it upon.

Will still didn't understand how he could have been so wrong about Lady Elizabeth. He found it difficult to believe the sensible, proper woman he'd been betrothed to was carrying on with a man like Lucifer.

And she had stolen diamonds? Why? Why would she need to steal, when she was to marry one of the wealthiest men in England?

"This is the property that would have been yours," Juliette commented.

"Yes. That was part of the marriage contract."

She nodded and glanced at the drive as the carriage pulled to the door.

"Why do you mention it?"

"I saw in your face you were thinking of her. You associate this place with her."

"This is where we met," he admitted as the carriage slowed to a stop.

"Will it upset you to return?"

He hadn't even considered the idea, but he did not have to think about the answer. "No."

He did not elaborate. How could he explain Lady Elizabeth had meant virtually nothing to him? It would sound as crass as it was. He hadn't understood that only days ago. He hadn't understood what it meant to care for someone, to want to be with them, to look forward to their smile each day.

He hadn't known what torment it would be to worry for their safety and health. To know the pain of losing them would be all but unbearable.

He understood now what Darlington had meant that night at White's. He'd claimed Pelham didn't love Lady Elizabeth, and Will had responded by saying he felt warmly toward her. And he thought that had been the truth. But he'd felt nothing. Now that he knew what it was to… not love someone… but *care* a great deal. He understood what he'd felt for

Lady Elizabeth had been no more than what he felt for his solicitor.

He supposed that made him a cold, hard man. But it also meant he did not have emotions to deal with. Emotions that would get in the way of finding out why Lady Elizabeth had stolen Lucifer's diamonds—if indeed they were his—and why. More important, he wanted to find those diamonds. They had not been recovered in London, so this was the next most logical place. Her parents said Lady Elizabeth had recently made a trip here, and Juliette said his fiancée told Lucifer Pelham had them. Lady Elizabeth hadn't been to Rothingham Manor in months and months. That could only mean she'd left them here—on what would become his estate as soon as they were wed.

He followed Juliette into the house, where they were met by Mr. Pittinger. The man bowed and welcomed them, then asked where they would like to begin.

"Lady Elizabeth's private chambers, I think," Pelham told the man.

Juliette nodded her approval, and the two were shown up a flight of steps to a large suite of rooms. Pelham had no notion of whether the rooms were furnished stylishly, but he approved of the staid color choices and the general austerity of the place.

Mr. Pittinger left them, and Juliette shook her head. Will raised a brow. "You disapprove?"

"I wouldn't go that far, but this room is sterile. There's no color, none of the woman here. It reminds me of your rooms."

Will frowned. "What does that mean?"

"It means you didn't decorate the house yourself. There's none of you there."

Will crossed his arms. "Rothingham Manor is an old, distinguished home. It has been outfitted elegantly, as befits the rank of the Duke of Pelham." He could tell she didn't like his answer. Her lips thinned.

Hell, he didn't even like his answer. He sounded like a pompous prig.

"Don't start being ducal again," she said, coming to stand before him. She took his face in her hands and pulled his head down so she could kiss his nose. "Your home is lovely. I was merely observing that there is no Will in the home. I believe the house would still be elegant if you added a bit of yourself."

"What do you mean? A portrait?" He had the uneasy feeling the following conversation was going to force him to think along lines he did not particularly care for.

She laughed. "Heavens, no! But you might consider taking down one of the thirty-nine portraits of your father."

"Thirty-nine?"

"Yes. I had a footman count for me. There are thirty-nine. Why not replace those with artwork you enjoy? Your father is certainly far from deserving a shrine." She touched his deaf ear, and he drew back.

"You know." He did not know why he felt suddenly ashamed. It was not as though he could have helped what had happened. And his deafness did not hinder him, unless he was in a noisy situation and had to rely too much on his good ear. But it was a reminder of how his father had punished him. It was a reminder of his far-from-perfect childhood.

"Yes. Mrs. Waite told me what your father did. It's appalling."

"It's over and done. Not everyone had a perfect childhood like you."

"I was fortunate in that, but I can guarantee you if my father had ever hurt me, I would not want to remember him with portraits in every room. How can you stand to look at his face each and every day?"

Will never considered that he had a choice. The manor had always housed those portraits of his father. He never even thought of taking them down. But Juliette had a point. Why didn't he make some changes?

Because he had no idea what or how to change it. That was why. Juliette told him to replace the portraits with artwork he enjoyed. What, precisely, did he enjoy? His father liked the Dutch masters—Vemeer, Rembrandt, van Harlaam. Will had never particularly cared for this art, but he knew it was valuable. His father had impressed upon Will the value of the work.

What did it matter that Will thought the images homely? What did it matter that the colors left him feeling vaguely irritated?

"You have changed since I met you," Juliette said to him. "You can change your life, as well. You don't have to be a man like your father. You don't have to be the Dangerous Duke. You can be the Dashing Duke."

He raised a brow, and she laughed. She was always laughing. "You're right. Perhaps *dashing* doesn't quite fit. But you see my point, don't you?" She took his hands, held them in her warm ones. She was always touching him, smiling at him. No one had ever treated him this way. He didn't know how to react. "I've remade myself a half dozen times. I was a farm girl and then the Duchess of Dalliance. And when all of this is over"—she waved her hand to indicate the room—"I'll become someone else. You can make your own destiny."

"*You* can," he said before he had thought it through.

"But what does that mean? You have far more resources than I ever did. You can do whatever you like." The side of her face had turned a greenish-purple where she'd been hit by Lucifer. The swelling was going down, but the mottled colors marred her otherwise perfectly porcelain complexion. He found himself staring at that bruise, knowing it would fade and she would be perfect again. Why couldn't she have more imperfections? Maybe then he wouldn't be so drawn to her. Maybe then it wouldn't be so easy to forget about her one glaring imperfection.

She was a Cyprian.

"It means I come from a family with a long history of tradition and duty. I can't simply do whatever I choose."

"I'm not suggesting you run off to China. I'm suggesting you hang a few paintings, maybe change the draperies."

He gaped at her. "Now I must change draperies, as well?" This was too much. He stomped away from her, began searching Lady Elizabeth's room. He started with the small escritoire in the corner.

"Will?"

"We should begin searching. This may take some time."

"Will, what is it?" She placed her hand on his back. "Did I say something wrong?"

"No." He smashed his fists on the desk and leaned on them heavily. "You're right. I should make changes. I should make Rothingham Manor my own, but I…" He looked down at his hands. He knew every scar, every ridge, every line on his hands. The same could be said of his arms, his legs, his face. Why then did he know so little about the man inside the body? He sighed. "I don't know what I like." He closed his eyes. "I don't really know who I am."

He expected her to laugh. It was an appalling revelation. He'd never admitted this to anyone. He hadn't even dared think it, except at times of extreme vulnerability. He was no poet. He didn't have the time or the inclination to dissect his soul.

He felt Juliette's arms come about him. "*I* know who you are. You're kind and brave and handsome and strong."

He turned to her. "I'm none of those things."

"You are to me, and before you protest again, you should take the compliments, because you have plenty of shortcomings, as well."

He laughed. What else could he do? No one else ever dared talk to him this way.

"Why don't I help you make some changes?"

He drew back, and she held up a hand. "Small changes. Maybe a few paintings. Perhaps a new rug. We could have the footmen take down a dozen or so of your father's portraits and simply enjoy the empty space."

When she spoke of it, the task didn't sound quite so monumental. And he thought he might like having her input. At least she would give him her honest opinion. "All right," he said.

She smiled and clapped her hands. "Oh, good! This will be fun."

"Juliette, small changes."

She rolled her eyes. "I know, I know." She looked around the room, and he had to admit it was rather spartan. "I suppose we had better begin searching. I know we'll have no fun until you can tick it off your mental list."

He didn't bother to argue. Lucifer was out there somewhere, and he'd proven over and over he'd kill for these diamonds. Will wanted to find them. Before anyone else was hurt.

❧

Juliette collapsed on the chaise longue in the drawing room—or was it the parlor?—and let out a long sigh. "I cannot search one more nook, Will. Not one more cranny. We've been here two days. My back hurts, my neck aches, my eyes are crossed. There are no diamonds anywhere in this house. If Lady Elizabeth had a hiding place and she put Lucifer's diamonds there, I have no idea where it is."

Will looked up from across the room. He was on hands and knees, checking under a settee. "Perhaps my assumption was incorrect. Maybe she hid them in London. But I know her parents have searched her things and found nothing."

"It's hopeless," Juliette said, staring at the ceiling. There was a brownish water stain a little to her left. It looked a bit like an apple. "No one could have done more than we have. I think Mr. Pittinger is ready to be rid of us."

Her view of the water stain was obscured by Will's face—a much more pleasant view. She smiled. "Why don't we go home and find other methods of entertaining ourselves?" She'd been wanting to kiss him for the last hour. And she couldn't wait to get rid of the draperies in his drawing room. She had the best idea for color and material—not that she'd shared it yet.

She didn't want to scare Will. Much.

She'd cautioned herself not to become overly excited about the prospect of decorating his home. It was not as though it were her home. It was not as though she would ever live there. In effect, she was probably decorating for another woman. But Juliette didn't want to think of that. She simply wanted to help Will make some changes.

And she loved redecorating, especially with someone else's money.

"I can certainly think of several ways to entertain you."

"Can you?" She curled a hand around the back of his neck and pulled his lips to hers. "Why not begin now?"

He kissed her softly at first, and she allowed herself to sink into the pleasure of his lips meeting hers. There was always a little thrill when she touched him, a frisson of excitement coursing through her. She loved his lips. She loved their shape, their texture, their taste. She loved how he used them, how he brushed them against her mouth, once, twice, then kissed a slow path from her mouth to her temple. He kissed her ear, and she laughed and pulled his mouth back to hers.

He was smiling as well, and she loved the curve of his mouth when he smiled. He did so far too infrequently.

His mouth slanted over hers as he deepened the kiss, and the world swirled around her. She heard only his breathing and the persistent thumping of her heart; she smelled the scent of mint she always associated with him; she felt only Will, always Will. Heat curled in her belly and licked through her body like a small wildfire.

"I want you," she moaned when he moved to kiss her neck. "Let's go." She stood and then pulled him off the coach to join her. She was already thinking of the wanton things she could do to him in the carriage on the way back.

He stood, and she saw the reservation in his eyes. "I was thinking—"

She put a finger to his lips. "Stop thinking. I want you inside me, Will. I want your hands on me. All over me. There's nothing to think about."

His eyes had darkened, and his expression was that of a man torn. Good. She took his hand and began to pull him toward the drawing-room door.

"But I wonder if we did a thorough enough search of the stables."

She stared at him. "The stables? Will, she didn't hide the diamonds in the stables."

"But we've searched everywhere else and haven't found them." He placed his hand on the small of her back and began to usher her out of the drawing room. "I want to be certain there's nowhere we've over-looked." Instead of heading toward the main entrance, where they could summon the carriage, Will guided her toward the back and the stables.

"But Will," she protested. "It could take hours to search the stables."

"Then we'll be back in time for dinner."

He walked resolutely now, and she knew her objections were futile. She could not believe they were going to search the stables—horse manure and feed and hay. She'd mucked out enough stables in her life to know she did not care to spend more time in them. But she had told him she would not be left behind. She could not bow out now.

But she might put the inevitable off for a few more minutes. She paused as they reached the door that would lead outside and to the stables. "I'll join you in a moment. I want to use the ladies' retiring room."

He frowned. "Do you want me to wait for you?"

"No, go ahead. I'll be there directly."

He leaned down and kissed her lightly then walked outside. She watched him go, almost too stunned by his actions to move. Who was this man who kissed her so easily, laughed with her, and teased her? Surely this was not the rigid, arrogant duke she'd met at Carlton House not even a fortnight ago.

She took her time finding the retiring room, seeing to her needs, and setting her hair to rights. When she felt another moment would cause Pelham to send a search party, she started for the stables. Once outside, she was assailed by a brisk northerly wind. The skies promised rain, and thick gray clouds rushed overhead. She wished she had dressed more warmly and crossed her arms over her middle to keep in body heat.

Perhaps Juliette's crossed arms made her slow to respond. Perhaps it was because she was staring at the sky or thinking of Will's kisses or wishing she was back at Rothingham Manor with a hot cup of tea.

Whatever the reason, she never even saw the man until he had taken firm hold of her and was dragging her away from the stables and the protection of the house.

At first, she was so taken off guard, she stumbled and had to focus on moving forward without tripping over her feet. And then she realized what was happening, and she tried to wrench her arm from his grip. Lastly, she began screaming, but she knew that was all but futile. The wind was too loud and the stable already too far away. With the horses pawing and stamping, and Will busy searching in and around, he would never hear her.

"Release me!" she screamed and pulled away. But Lucifer's grip was iron. Her hair was blowing in her eyes, and she had yet to see his face, but she knew it must be him. How had he managed to get to her? Will had taken every precaution. "I don't have the diamonds. Release me, and you still have time to get away."

"Get away? Without you? Why would I want to do that?"

Juliette's blood turned to ice in her veins. She angled her head into the wind so that the loose locks of hair blew back and away from her face. She finally caught a glimpse of the man dragging her into the moors.

It was not Lucifer.

～

Will reached for his pocket watch and swore with frustration when it was not there. As soon as he returned to London, he would purchase another. Devil take him if it made him less than spontaneous.

He needed to have some notion of time. He cut his gaze out the doors of the stable and tried to judge by the darkening skies. He wasn't certain how much time had passed, but it was more than he liked. Where was Juliette?

He stepped outside and looked toward the house, hoping to see her, but the path was empty. A raindrop fell on his hand and another on his cheek. One of the grooms stepped out beside him. "It's going to storm, Your Grace. Should I ready your carriage so you can be home before the worst of it hits?"

Will looked back at the stables and frowned. He'd like to search them more thoroughly, but he didn't want to be stranded on the road back to Rothingham in a rainstorm.

"Yes, prepare the carriage," he said to the groom. He started back toward the house, noting that a light drizzle was falling now. The temperature had dropped, and the wind had a definite chill. When he stepped into the house, Pittinger was there to greet him.

"Might I be of assistance, Your Grace?"

"I'm leaving. Where is Miss Juliette?"

Pittinger frowned. "I thought she was in the stables with you."

Will scowled. "No, she's still inside. She wanted the ladies' retiring room."

"Yes, but I saw her head toward the stables a full quarter hour ago, Your Grace. At least that's where I assumed she was headed when she walked out the door."

A slow panic spread through Will's body. It was as though an iron fist closed on his lungs. He could not seem to breathe, and he could not seem to speak.

"What is it, Your Grace? Did the duchess not make it to the stables?"

Will swallowed and fought back the panic. "No, she didn't." She had been wearing a dark red dress today, and the color would stand out against the drab yellows and browns of the moors. He stepped to the windows but did not see any sign of red. The rain was beginning in earnest, though. Heavy drops fell on the ground and pattered against the window as though seeking entrance.

Will clenched his hand. If Lucifer had her—no, he would not think such thoughts. Nothing had happened to Juliette. Nothing would happen to her. He whirled to face Pittinger. "Get every man, woman, and child you can find. I want everyone searching for Miss Juliette. Search the house, the outlying buildings, the gardens, the moors."

"But, Your Grace, it's raining."

Will grabbed Pittinger by the collar and all but lifted the man off his feet. "I don't care if it's bloody snowing. I want her found. *Now*."

"Yes, Your Grace." The man rushed away, and Will did not wait to see if his orders had been followed. He yanked the door open and stepped into the howling wind and sluice of rain. He pulled the collar of his coat up against his neck and started running.

◈

"Oliver," she said, her voice shaking. Her feet had stopped working, but he was still dragging her. She stumbled, and he scowled at her.

"Clumsy cow. Come on!"

She complied, staring at him as though he were a specter. He had aged in the last—what was it? Seven years? His brown hair was salted with white. His face drooped, and he had lost at least a stone, perhaps two. His skin seemed to hang off his jowls, and his clothes were too big on him.

He had never been a particularly tall man. They were of the same height, but now it seemed he had shrunk. Or perhaps she had made him seem bigger in her mind. His hands were still thick and red, his grip still punishing as it dug into the tender flesh of her upper arm.

And suddenly she looked ahead and realized Oliver was leading her away from the safety of the house, away from Will.

She wrenched her arm, but he held on fast. Digging her heels in, she screamed, "Will! Will!"

"Shut up!" Oliver screamed. "Your lover will never hear you, and your voice grates on my nerves." He all but carried her up a small rise. For a wiry man, he was strong. She knew she would have bruises on her arm to match those on her face.

Her face!

She gaped at him. "It was you. It wasn't Lucifer at all. It was you who attacked me."

He shoved her down the rise, and she had to fight to keep her feet under her. She tumbled to her knees at the bottom, and Oliver stood over her. Juliette knew she could not be seen from the house now. And it had begun to rain. Would Will think she had waited inside for the rain to abate? If so, he would never find her before it was too late. She had no illusions about what Oliver would do to her. This time he would kill her.

"Who did you think it was? The fallen angel Lucifer? You might prefer hell to what I'm going to do to you. I've been waiting for my opportunity for a long time. And then just as I'm about to strike, you seduce Pelham. Mighty inconvenient, but then when you're a whore who beds half of London, what can a man expect?" The rain sloshed over the rim of his hat and dribbled onto his shoulders.

Juliette was cold and shivering and feeling hopeless. There was nothing and no one anywhere in sight. In the distance, she saw several sheep huddled together, but with the rain, no person was likely to venture out.

"Let's go." Oliver reached down and grabbed her arm, pulling her to her feet. "Keep walking. I want more distance."

Juliette knew she was on her own, knew no one was coming to help her. Perhaps she could run. She was younger than Oliver, and she might be faster, even though she had heavy skirts and flimsy slippers to contend with. But if she could outrun him, she might just have a chance. She began walking, knowing each step took her farther and farther away from Will.

"You thought you got away from me," he was saying. "You thought you were rid of me. But you'll never be rid of me. I *own* you."

He was right. She'd always known he'd come back for her. She'd always known this day would come. But she was not giving in—not this time. She wasn't the same girl he'd married. She was stronger, braver.

They started up another rise, and Oliver clenched

her arm tightly, but he was watching her and not where he was going, and he stumbled, losing his grip slightly.

Juliette grasped her chance, yanked her arm free, and staggered into a run. She ran blindly, wildly, but as fast as she could.

Behind her, she heard Oliver scream and then the sound of his booted steps pursuing her.

❧

Will paused, hands on knees, and studied the landscape before him. The rain was coming down heavy and hard now, obscuring his vision and making anything more than a few feet away impossible to make out. He'd already run headlong into one of Nowlund Park's footmen. It encouraged him that the staff was searching, but he was beginning to think the effort futile. He had the bad feeling he was simply covering the same ground over and over.

But he was not going to give up. He could not lose Juliette. Not now. Not when...

He did not want to consider his feelings right now. This was not the time or the place. When he had her safe, when he had her in his arms, then he would take a moment to examine what he felt for her.

He started running again, a slow jog up a slight rise. He did not remember this rise and took it as a good sign that he was making progress. At the top of the rise he stood and scanned the moors before him. The rain made it difficult to distinguish details, but he swore he saw a flash of red in the distance.

"Juliette!" Was that a figure? A woman? If so, she was running away from him.

Will wiped the water from his eyes and squinted. No, not away from him—away from another man chasing her. "Juliette!"

But he could already see he would be too late.

❧

Juliette stumbled on a rock, caught herself with her hands, but the moment's pause cost her. She was cold and stiff, and her muscles were not hers to command. Her knees buckled, and she went down, scraping her hands painfully on the rocks beneath. With a cry of pain and terror, she lurched to her feet and limped forward. Blood mixed with water, making her hands appear pink.

She could hear Oliver's rough breathing behind her. He'd stopped cursing her, probably to save energy for catching her. She was still ahead of him, but he was not far behind. She had to keep going. She had to keep running...

Suddenly Will's words—words that it seemed he spoke a lifetime ago—flashed into her mind. *The Dukes of Pelham do not run away.*

She was no Duke of Pelham, but hadn't she tired of running? Hadn't she run far and long enough? Perhaps it was time to face her problems and suffer the consequences, even if those consequences were death.

She spotted a fist-sized rock ahead, stooped to grasp it in her hand, and swung to face Oliver. He was close, so much closer than she had anticipated. She realized she would never have beaten him. In another moment, he would have caught her hair or shoulder, yanked her backward, and that would have been the end of her.

At least now she would die fighting. She raised the rock. "Come on!" she screamed. "You want me? I'm right here."

Oliver gave her a wary look and slowed. He was breathing hard and squinting at her. That was her one advantage. The wind was behind her, blowing rain into his eyes, while she faced away.

"You're going to pay," he yelled. He was not far from her, but the wind made it all but impossible to hear.

"Fine. Do your worst. I'm not running from you anymore, Oliver Clifton. You don't scare me anymore. You don't control me anymore."

"We'll see how scared you are in a moment, you worthless slut." He was coming for her, and her hand itched to throw the rock she clutched tightly. The rough edges cut into her flesh, the pain keeping her mind clear.

Wait, she cautioned herself. *Wait until he's close enough.*

She would have one chance, one shot. She could not miss, or she would die.

"Worthless?" she spat. "You tried for years to make me believe so. You belittled me and tried all you could to break my spirit. And you almost succeeded, but you couldn't break me completely, Oliver. Deep down, I knew I was worth something. And now I've proven it. I'm a celebrity. I'm in the papers. Everyone knows who I am. I dine with the Prince Regent!"

"You take him to your bed. You're nothing more than a glorified slut."

"And what are you? No one and nothing. A warped old man who was bested by a slut. I got away from you. I forgot you. But you couldn't ever forget me."

"And now you'll *never* forget me!" He charged her, and she raised her arm and flung the stone. She watched in horror as it went off course, hitting him in the cheek instead of the center of the forehead, as she had hoped.

And still he stumbled forward, surprised by the action and the impact. Juliette hit him over the head. It probably hurt her as much as it hurt him, but she wasn't going to die without a fight. He plowed into her and knocked her over. She fell hard on the rocky ground, and for a moment, the world dimmed. Rain mixed with fresh tears of pain, coating her face. And then Oliver's face came into focus. He was bleeding from a gash on his cheek, his teeth were bared, and there was murder in his eyes.

She did the first thing she could think of, which was to strike at him. She hit his nose with her hand, and he reared back. She rolled over and tried to climb to her feet. Oliver caught her shoulder and pulled her back down. He wrapped his hands around her neck, and she tried frantically to catch her breath. But he was squeezing hard, strangling the life out of her.

She tried to claw at him, but he was above her, out of arm's reach. She flailed and writhed, and the world went gray then charcoal. He was straddling her now, leaning in close as her movements began to weaken. He wanted to be close when he squeezed the life from her. She opened her eyes and measured their positions. And then she took one last chance, brought her knee up hard, and caught him between the legs.

He howled but didn't release her. She dug into her reserves, into every last ounce of strength she possessed, and fought him. His grip loosened, and she rolled away. When he didn't catch her immediately, she began crawling. Her fist closed on another rock, this one long and jagged. She rose to her knees then climbed to her feet. Slowly, she turned to face Oliver. He was staggering toward her, his face a mask of pain and rage, his bloody cheek making him look grotesque and evil. He reached for her, and as his hands closed on her throat, she brought her hand up, stabbing the rock through his jaw.

He stilled, his eyes widening, and then he released her and grabbed for the rock embedded in his flesh. He fell to the ground, clutching the rock, and she stood over him, feeling no pity, feeling no triumph.

Feeling nothing but the hard rain pelting her back.

Twenty

WILL SAW LUCIFER COMING FOR JULIETTE. HE SAW HIM reach for her, and Will knew he would be too late. He was running now, running through the punishing rain and sliding on the wet grasses. He heard someone screaming, "No, no, no!" over and over. After a moment, he realized it was he engaging in this completely undignified behavior. It was not the kind of behavior one would expect from a duke.

And he didn't care. He ran and he yelled, and it was entirely futile, because he saw Lucifer had her. And then he was afraid he imagined what he saw next, because Lucifer fell to the ground and Juliette stood over him, fists clenched, face set in a mask of stone.

"Juliette!" he called. He was close enough for her to hear him now, but she didn't turn, didn't acknowledge him whatsoever. "Juliette!" He reached for her, touching her shoulder, afraid to believe she was real and not a figment of his imagination.

She jumped when he touched her, hissing and turning defensively. He put his hands up, shocked at the anger and coldness in her eyes. And then all of that melted away, and she was Juliette again. "Will?"

He didn't have time to respond before she fell into his arms. She was cold, but she was solid. She was alive. He held her tightly, whispering words she could not have possibly heard, words he did not even understand himself. She buried her head on his shoulder, and he caught a glimpse of Lucifer over her bright hair.

Except it wasn't Lucifer. He didn't recognize the man, and not only because he had a large chunk of rock protruding from his chin. "Who the devil is that?"

Juliette lifted her head and peered around. "It's Oliver, my former husband."

"I don't understand."

"All this time we thought it was Lucifer who attacked me, only Lucifer who was after me, but it was Oliver, too. The night of Lady Elizabeth's murder, my cook told me a man had come looking for me, and I assumed it was Lucifer. But it must have been Oliver. And then the day we went back together, the day we were in the attic. Your men saw a man lurking about the alley. Again, we assumed it was Lucifer, because he had been there earlier, but your men didn't see any man matching his description. Because it *wasn't* Lucifer that time. It was Oliver."

"Then where is Lucifer?"

"I don't know."

Oliver made a moaning sound, and Juliette shrank away. Will pulled her close, turning at the sound of another voice. "Your Grace!"

Will wrapped his arms around Juliette's waist and started back toward the house. "Let's go."

"We can't leave him here, like this."

He pointed toward the house. The rain was still steady and strong, but it no longer pelted them with a vengeance. Mr. Pittinger trudged toward them. "We'll give him over to Pittinger," Will told her. "You needn't think of him anymore."

She gazed at Will. "I stood up to him. I didn't run this time. I stood and fought."

He thought of the man's bloody face. "I never had any doubt."

"I stood and fought, Will," she said again, swaying on her feet. "Just like the dukes of Pelham. I didn't run."

"Juliette—" She swayed again, and he caught her before she could fall.

❧

Juliette woke to the sound of snoring. She didn't know where she was, but she knew she was warm, comfortable, and safe. Something heavy lay over her midsection, and she reached up gingerly to touch it. Her arm muscles were sore. Every part of her body was sore. She touched an arm—a man's arm. And then she knew, before she even opened her eyes, it was Will's arm.

She opened her eyes slowly, smiling when the first thing to greet her was Will's face. He was asleep beside her, fully dressed, lying on the counterpane. Though the drapes had been drawn, she could see strips of sunlight on the ceiling and knew it was full day. A quick glance about told her she was in the ducal chambers at Rothingham Manor. Why should she be here? She was not the duchess.

She had no recollection of how she had come to be in the bedchamber. She didn't even recall how she had come to travel from Nowlund Park to Rothingham Manor. She did remember Oliver. She shuddered at the memory of the rock jutting from his flesh, and Will pulled her closer. She smiled. Even in his sleep he comforted her.

She traced a finger over his stern cheekbones, so perfect even when he was in repose. She touched his eyelashes lightly, marveling at how they lay so straight and still on his skin. She traced his eyebrows, the slope of his nose, the curve of his lips.

His lips moved. "You're awake."

"I don't remember falling asleep."

His eyes opened, and she felt as though she could stare into their dark blue depths forever. "You fainted."

She blinked. "I don't think so."

"I know so. I was the one who caught you."

She shook her head, tried to sit, but he held her down with light pressure from his arm. "But I've never fainted. I'm no delicate flower."

"I think it's safe to say you were exhausted and traumatized. I had you brought back here."

To his bedchamber, not her room. Did that mean there would be no more pretensions? No more acting as though they would occupy two chambers and then sneaking in to see each other? She was afraid to hope that it might mean more.

She swallowed. "And Oliver. Is he…?"

"He's alive, unfortunately," Will said, lifting his head and leaning toward her to kiss her cheek. "You didn't kill him, but I dare say he will have a nasty scar to remember you by." He caressed her hair as though she were a child to be comforted.

"Where is he?"

"Jail, I should hope. Pittinger called the magistrate, who said he would take care of the matter. I don't believe you will need to give a statement. There were enough witnesses. I imagine he'll be tried and hung. We'll keep it quiet. No need to have the news reach London. You're finally rid of him." He kissed her again. "No need to think of him again."

Juliette stared at the ceiling. She was rid of Oliver. He would not bother her ever again. She would never have to look over her shoulder for fear of finding him coming for her. Suddenly, she felt as light as one of those balloons that lifted people high in the sky. She felt so light she thought she might fly.

"One of the footmen I brought with me from London recognized him."

Juliette glanced back at Will. "How?"

"You were right. He was the man at your town house in London. The footman saw him outside that day we waited in the attic. He didn't match Lucifer's description, so they didn't stop him or question him, though his appearance in the back alley caused them enough concern so that they notified me. But he gave them some story about a coal delivery, and they let him go."

"All this time we thought it was Lucifer after us."

"I don't think we're rid of Lucifer yet. He may still be in London, biding his time."

"He knows the diamonds are there."

"Well, they sure as hell aren't in Yorkshire," Will said. "We searched everywhere."

"Then where are they? If we didn't find them at Nowlund Park, and Lord and Lady Nowlund didn't find them at their London town house, and the diamonds are obviously not hidden at my town house, where are they?" Juliette asked.

"Only Lady Elizabeth knows that. We may never find them, but we won't have to contend with Lucifer forever. The magistrate will apprehend him. If I need to supply additional men and funds, we'll catch him."

Juliette nodded. Then they were going back to London, back to their old lives. She knew this couldn't last forever, knew she was a fool to allow herself to fall in love with Will. She took a deep breath. "So what now?"

"Now? I was thinking we might try some of this." He rose on one elbow and kissed her gently on the mouth. She responded, but her mind was still conjecturing. Will must have known she had been asking about returning to London, but he'd evaded the question. Did that mean he wasn't anxious to return either?

She would have loved to continue kissing him, but she had to know where they stood. "Will, wait."

He pulled back, looked down at her. "What is it? Are you still feeling unwell? I should have—"

She put a finger over his lips. "I'm fine. But I was wondering, do we return to London?"

His brow furrowed. "I'm in no hurry. Are you anxious to get back?"

"Not exactly."

"Good. Then for now, we stay right here."

She stared at him. "You mean, you have no plan, no schedule, no timetable?"

"Oh, I have a plan," he said, pulling her tight against him. "I plan to seduce you."

She stared at him, and he raised a brow.

"Am I growing horns?"

Who was this man who was suddenly amusing and carefree? What had happened to the rigid, stodgy duke? "No. But I'm amazed at how much you've changed."

He grinned. "Perhaps I can amaze you in other ways, as well."

"Do you think so?"

"A man can hope." He kissed her again, and this time she put all thoughts of London and the future aside. Oliver was gone. She was free of him forever. She was in Will's bed, in Will's arms. That was all that mattered. He moved on top of her, careful to support his weight so she would not bear it. He kissed her nose, her chin, her eyes. He was so tender, so gentle, and then he kissed her cheek and whispered in her ear, "I thought I'd lost you. I saw him reach for you, and I thought I'd lost you." His voice sounded so raw and anguished.

"You didn't lose me, Will. You'll never lose me," she said.

"I don't think I could bear it."

For a long moment, they simply held each other, and Juliette thought she had never been happier. This was what she wanted; this was what she had dreamed of—this closeness, this tenderness, this love.

She had a moment of doubt, but it was fleeting. She pushed it away just as Will kissed her again. It was so easy to get lost in Will's arms, in his mouth, in the caress of his fingers. It was easy to forget everything but the two of them.

Slowly, carefully, Will stripped off her nightshift until she was laid bare before him. The way he looked at her, with such reverence, made her catch her breath.

"He hurt you," Will said, tracing the bumps and bruises she'd garnered during her fight with Oliver. He touched her knee, her hip, her elbow, her neck. She winced. "That looks tender."

"It's nothing." And it wasn't. She didn't even feel the lingering ache from Oliver's fingers when Will looked at her this way. She was eager to look back. Will still wore a linen shirt and trousers. She pushed up slowly and sat with her legs crossed. Reaching for his shirt, she pulled it up, revealing that hard bronze abdomen little by little. She allowed her fingers to skate along Will's flesh, teasing both of them. He lifted his arms, and on his skin, she saw the play of the streaks of sunlight escaping the wall of curtains. And then she pulled the shirt off, and he was naked to the waist. She touched his broad shoulders, his muscled chest, his flat abdomen. "How is it you are so tan? Do not tell me a duke works outside without his shirt."

"I think it is that you are so pale. Either that or it is from my mother. I'm told she was part Italian."

"Ah, then that explains why you are sun-kissed here." She tucked her fingers into the waistband of his trousers. "I had images of you outside in nothing but your boots."

"I'm sorry to disappoint." His voice was husky as she released the fall of his trousers.

"Oh, you haven't disappointed me yet." She worked the trousers over his hips, and he sat back so she could pull them off. She tossed them on the floor in an unorganized heap, glanced at him, and raised a brow in challenge.

He smiled and tossed his shirt on the floor after the trousers. She laughed. "You are too wicked, sir."

"Let me show you just how wicked."

He loved her. He hadn't said the words, but Juliette knew he must love her. The way he kissed her, touched her, held her. Will loved her—she was sure of it. And when they lay, sated and spent, in each other's arms, Juliette was happier than she'd ever been in her life. She fell asleep to dreams of their future together.

And woke to a nightmare.

Twenty-one

WILL STARED AT A GHOST.

He was no fanciful child—had not been fanciful even when he was a child—but the man's resemblance to his father was striking. Will's shock began when Richards, who had finally arrived from London, stepped into his library and announced the arrival of Lord Henry Cavington.

"Who?" Pelham asked, looking up from his ledgers. He'd been up since six, and it was only half past eight at present. To the best of his knowledge, Juliette was still asleep. He would have preferred to stay in bed with her, but they had spent the afternoon, evening, and night talking, eating, and making love. If he stayed by her side, he would want her again, and he knew she needed her rest.

And so he had decided he would work until she woke, and then they could make plans for the day together. It was a strange feeling—not knowing what he would do that day, not having it planned out—but he was gradually getting used to the idea. He was even considering what artwork he might like to hang in place of his father's portraits. Juliette had been correct. There were far too many images of his father gazing down, with disapproving eyes, at him. Will idly looked over his ledgers, checking the accuracy of his steward, and thinking of Juliette's lovely mouth, her long legs, the freckle on the third toe of her left foot...

He had been imagining kissing that freckle when Richards knocked then entered, announcing a guest. "Lord Henry is your uncle, Your Grace," Richards said. "Your father's brother."

"Of course." What was his father's brother, a man Will had last seen at his father's funeral over ten years ago, doing at Rothingham Manor at half past eight in the morning? The man must have ridden all night. "Show him—"

"I don't have time for these formalities," Lord Henry said, pushing past Richards and shouldering his way into the library. Will had been in the process of standing, but he all but sat again when Lord Henry entered.

The man looked almost exactly like the fifth Duke of Pelham. Will felt as though he was seeing a ghost. Immediately, he stood, straightened, and reached for his pocket watch, worried he must be late for something.

Richards gave Will a look, indicating he would show Lord Henry right back out if Will wished it, but Will shook his head slightly.

"I have been riding all night," Lord Henry was saying. "I came as soon as I heard. And I want to know what the devil you think you're about."

Will opened his mouth to respond then closed it again. First of all, he had no idea to what his uncle referred. Second of all, *he* was the Duke of Pelham, not this interloper. He should begin to act as such. Slowly, with deliberate casualness, Will sat back in his seat, leaving his uncle to stand before him. "Hello, Uncle. To what do I owe the pleasure of this unexpected visit?"

Will made a gesture dismissing Richards, and the butler left, leaving the library door open slightly in case Will should call for his return.

"It is no pleasure, I assure you. No pleasure at all. I have come from London to find out for myself whether the rumors are true."

Will noted his uncle did not address him as *Your Grace*, did not give him any courtesies at all. In his belly, a slow fury began to simmer. Will steepled his fingers, showing none of his emotions on his face. "Rumors? I don't really have time to discuss all of London's rumors. If that's all you came for, you might as well go back again. I am happy to provide you a fresh horse."

Lord Henry frowned, and the little boy Will had been wanted to cringe. His father made that same expression when he was displeased, and it usually led to violence. Will shook his head and could have sworn his deaf ear was ringing.

"Even if the rumors concern you and a certain courtesan?" Lord Henry gave a slight smile.

He should have known this visit would be about Juliette. He could not deny his relationship with her, and yet he did not want to confirm it. Will looked away.

"I see it's true, then. These aren't rumors at all. You have taken up with a Cyprian." The disapproval in his uncle's face was clear in the heavily etched lines about his mouth. Will opened his mouth to—he knew not what... give excuses?—and then closed it again. What was happening here? *He* was the duke, not his uncle. And while Will had respect for Lord Henry, he did not answer to him.

"I fail to see how what I do in my private life is any concern of yours."

"Allow me to enlighten you, then," his uncle said, placing his hands flat on Will's desk and meeting Will eye to eye. Will did not blink. "I am a Cavington, as was your father, my father, my grandfather, and his grandfather before him. My sons are Cavingtons and third and fourth in line for the dukedom, after myself. What you do reflects not only on the Cavington name but also the future dukes of Pelham. You have a responsibility to honor and distinguish the name, not disgrace it by taking up with a harlot."

The fury began to boil. It was true. It was all true, but that wasn't Juliette's fault. He stood. "She's not a harlot."

"What is she, then?" Lord Henry raised a brow.

Will didn't answer. What, exactly, *was* she to him? His mistress? His lover? His savior?

"Good God, she's called the Duchess of Dalliance," Lord Henry sputtered. "Don't try to tell me she's a blushing virgin."

Will clenched his fists. "Her name is Juliette."

"William—"

He slammed a hand on his desk. "You may call me *Pelham*. I have not given you leave to use my Christian name." And he would not. His uncle needed a reminder that Will was the sixth Duke of Pelham, not he. Lord Henry's disrespect annoyed him, but it wasn't the real reason for his fury. No. Will knew too well it had far more to do with the topic of his uncle's conversation. And he, Will, had no excuse. He *had* taken up with a courtesan.

"Very well, *Pelham*. Here is another juicy morsel I learned while in London. The body of your fiancée has been found."

Shock jolted through him, and Will all but fell into his chair.

Lady Elizabeth's body had been found. She was really dead. It was the last thing he expected his uncle to say, and the words seemed to echo and spin through the room. Will's heart was heavy for Lord and Lady Nowlund. They had lost their daughter, their only child.

Lord Henry's expression was smug, but Will didn't care at the moment. Why had he ever doubted Juliette?

"My understanding—and this has not yet been released to the papers—is she died from blunt force to the head."

"She fell against the balustrade at Carlton House," Will murmured. Juliette had been telling the truth. But he'd known that. He'd always known and simply had not wanted to accept the difficult truth—he had no idea who the woman he was betrothed to was. He had known what she was—the daughter of a marquess—but not the woman herself. And he knew exactly who Juliette was. He didn't want what she was to matter, but it did. It mattered far too much.

"I do not think the examiner can be that specific as to her demise," Lord Henry said, "but that is not all."

Will glanced up at him. "What do you mean?"

"This Lucifer, the man suspected of murdering Lady Elizabeth, has still not been found. The magistrate suspects he's fled to the Continent. His place of business, if one may call a gambling hell named Lucifer's Lair a business, was thoroughly searched. The registers have been found and studied. The magistrate believes Lady Elizabeth is the same Eliza listed in the register."

Will frowned. "Why would Lady Elizabeth be listed in a register for a gambling hell?" It made no sense. None whatsoever.

"Witnesses have been questioned, Pelham. These include the regular patrons of Lucifer's Lair, many of them gentlemen. Several of them describe a woman meeting Lady Elizabeth's description as frequenting Lucifer's Lair. It seems she preferred the game of faro."

Will shook his head and stood. "This cannot be true." He paced the carpet behind his desk. "She was a lady, the daughter of an earl. Why would she patronize a gambling hell?" It made no sense. None at all.

"Perhaps she enjoyed gambling? According to the register, she had lost over three thousand pounds at Lucifer's Lair."

Three thousand pounds? Will swallowed. It was a small fortune. How did she plan to pay her debts? Perhaps with his money.

Or perhaps she had thought to sell some diamonds…

Will looked at Lord Henry's face and saw the undisguised glee in his uncle's expression. The man was enjoying this. He was all but gloating. Will would have liked to smash the grin off his uncle's face, but he exercised restraint. He was not his father.

"I never saw her gamble," Will said almost to himself. "I never saw her act in any way even remotely inappropriate. Her behavior was always impeccable."

"Yes, but as we have established, you are not the best judge of character. After all, you are bedding a prostitute who has been with half the men in London. That is when she is not busy entertaining the Earl of Sin with her two friends—"

Will bolted around the desk, grabbed Lord Henry's coat, and slammed him against the bookshelf. Two large volumes toppled down, and Will jerked to the right to avoid being knocked on the shoulder. "I don't want to hear another word from you about Juliette." In fact, he didn't want to have to look at the man for another moment. "You said what you came to say, now get out."

Lord Henry shook his head. "Your father would turn in his grave if he could see you now."

Truer words were never spoken. "Good," Will said and meant it. "I hope he is shocked straight to Hell."

"You are a disgrace to the title," Lord Henry said, pushing Will back. "I am disgusted with your behavior."

He didn't want his uncle's words to matter, but they stung. "Get out," Will ordered, loud enough for Richards to hear.

"Answer me one question first. Do you intend to marry this… this Juliette? Do you intend to sully this house and the title of Duchess of Pelham by wedding that woman?"

"That's none of your business."

"It is my business, and the business of my sons. We have a right to know from whence the next duke will come."

Will gritted his teeth. There was no point in dissembling. "No. I'm not going to marry her."

Lord Henry nodded. "Good." He straightened his coat and moved toward the door. "Remember who you are and your duty to your title and your family." He pushed the door open, and Will saw Juliette standing on the other side. Her face was pale, her eyes shuttered, her posture rigid. She looked like a queen of ice.

Lord Henry gave Will a smile. "Good day, Your Grace." He swept past Juliette without even a nod.

Richards stood beside Juliette, and his expression was torn. Finally, he scurried to catch Lord Henry and escort him out. Will stepped forward. "Juliette—"

She held up a hand. "Don't. Don't say a word. I have heard more than enough."

He went to her, but she stepped back as he advanced. As he reached for her, she jerked away. "Juliette, I didn't mean—"

"What?" she demanded. "You didn't mean what you said?" She waited, he didn't speak. He didn't have the words. "So you *are* going to marry me?" She stared at him then looked at the floor before him. "Very well, then, kneel down. Ask me to be your wife."

Will was acutely aware that several of his servants were pretending to go about their duties nearby and were witnessing this scene. "We should speak in private."

"What need is there for privacy? If you love me and want to marry me, then say so." Color bloomed in her cheeks, making the harsh bruises on her face and neck less obvious. But still he was aware of them. He could not stop staring at them. He had almost lost her. But now he realized Lucifer—Oliver—had not been his greatest threat. He was his own worst enemy.

"Juliette," he said quietly. "I have a duty you cannot possibly understand." Damn his uncle, but he could not put duty aside so easily.

"Oh, I understand all right." She laughed bitterly. "I know dozens of men like you. They claim to love me, but to them, love is paying me for my favors, setting me up in a house with servants and a clothing allowance. But then you never even claimed to love me, did you?" She took a step back. "All the more fool me for falling in love with you."

He reached for her again, though he knew the gesture was futile. "No."

"Good-bye, *Your Grace*. Our time together was most diverting, but I suppose now I will take my congé and go." She turned and walked away, the shush of her slippers echoing in the silence that followed her.

Will wanted to yell *Don't go*. Everything in him wanted to race after her. She was the only person who had ever loved him. The only person who cared about him, not his title, not his wealth.

And she was walking away.

And he was allowing it.

What else could he do? Fall to his knees and beg her to marry him? He was the bloody Duke of Pelham. He did not fall to his knees. He did not beg. His uncle's words rang in his ears. He could hear his own father saying them.

You are a disgrace to the title. Why have I been cursed

with a disappointment for a son? Better you died at birth than act as you do.

Juliette disappeared up the steps, and Will turned. He went into his library and closed the door.

⤳

Tears ran down her cheeks as she stormed up the steps to her room. Angrily, she swiped them away. She would not cry. He had never said he loved her; he had never said he would marry her. She was a fool, and there was no sense in shedding tears over him now. He was not worth it. She should be too old and too worldly to fall in love so completely with a man who made it perfectly clear not only did he not love her, he didn't even respect her.

Had he ever apologized to her for cutting her at Carlton House? For calling her a slut or a strumpet? For embarrassing her at the inn after they'd left London? What had he said at the prince's ball? She was not a lady but a well-paid whore?

Well, she supposed she was a whore, but he certainly hadn't paid her.

She reached her room and threw the doors open, startling the maids cleaning the chambers. "Good day, madam," one of them said.

"No, it's not," Juliette answered. She spotted her trunk at the end of the bed, flipped the lid open, and began piling clothing into it. Her second trunk was still at Pelham's residence in London. She'd send a servant for it when she returned to Town.

Oh, but she didn't have any servants at her town house...

Well, then she would send one of Lily's servants or Fallon's. She was going home. She'd heard Lord Henry say Lucifer was gone. She needn't worry about him anymore. She really had nowhere to go but London, and she wanted to be with her friends right now.

"Is there anything we might help you with, madam?" one of the maids asked.

"No." Juliette swiped at an errant tear. "Yes. Fetch a footman and tell him to carry this trunk downstairs. And I need to know where the nearest coaching inn is located."

"Yes, madam." The girl hurried away.

Juliette emptied the clothespress and pushed the top of the trunk down. It wouldn't close, and she pounded it fiercely until she could latch it. She had to admit, the physical aggression had made her feel a little better, especially as she imagined Pelham's face where her fists landed.

Finally a footman arrived and informed her His Grace had offered the use of his carriage for her return trip. Juliette shook her head. "How magnanimous of the duke," she said. "That makes my departure all the more convenient."

She donned a spencer and hat and breezed out of the room. Coming down the stairs, she half expected— perhaps even hoped?—the library door would open. She wanted Pelham to beg her to stay. She wanted to tell him she'd rather sleep in a rat-infested hovel than under his roof. Oh, she could think of a great many things to tell him.

But the library door did not open, and Pelham did not tell her good-bye.

❦

Will had known the precise moment Juliette was gone. It wasn't simply that the bustle associated with her departure quieted or the hooves of the horses pulling his carriage faded away. It was Rothingham Manor that alerted him.

Without Juliette, the house felt colder, emptier, darker. He kept expecting to hear her tinkling laughter or see her open his door and admonish him not to spend so much time inside. He expected to see her around every corner—her captivating eyes, her contagious smile, her glorious hair.

Slowly, as the day wore on, little realizations came to him. He would never kiss her again. He would never touch her again, sleep beside her, dine with her, tickle her toes. He might have a passing glimpse of her in London, but even that possibility was remote. She would not stay in Town now. She said she wanted to start over.

His one solace in allowing her to go was that she was safe from Oliver and Lucifer. Oliver was going to prison, and from all accounts, Lucifer had fled the country. Whatever she did with her life, she would be safe doing it.

He'd been wandering the house rather aimlessly and ended up in the drawing room. He stood there, looking at the drapes on the windows. Were these the draperies she had wanted to change? He had to admit the heavy brocade in gold silk was rather outdated. He glanced at the hearth and noted the large portrait of his father staring at him. The duke's mouth turned down in a frown.

"I suppose you approve of my letting her go," Pelham said to the portrait. "She wouldn't have made a suitable duchess." He moved closer to the painting, noting the small details, like the signet ring on his father's hand. Will wore it now. He looked down at that finger, knowing the ring he wore had been passed down for generations. "I suppose you finally won." He looked at the portrait again. "Because now I'm as much an ass as you ever were. More of one. You threw your wife out, and I allowed the only woman I ever loved to walk away." He took off the signet ring and flung it at the portrait. "God help me if I'll become a barbarian like you. Richards!" Will marched to the door. "Richards!" he bellowed. He looked back at the portrait. "I don't want to look at your face ever again. I've sold my soul for your bloody duty and title. The devil take me if I have to look at your face every time I turn around. Richards!"

"Yes, Your Grace." Richards was running. Will did not think he had ever seen the man run before.

"There are thirty-nine portraits of my father in this house."

"Are there, Your Grace?"

"So I have been informed. I want every single one taken down."

Richards' brows lifted slightly. "Every one, Your Grace?"

"Yes. Get the staff and begin now."

"Now?"

"This minute. You may begin with this one." He pointed to the portrait in the drawing room. Richards stood looking at it, and Will clapped his hands. "Haste, Richards! That is what we want."

"Yes, Your Grace!"

Several hours later, half of the portraits had been removed, and Will was supervising the removal of one in the music room. The entire staff seemed to be enjoying the activity. Maids and grooms would rush in to inform him they had found another portrait in the yellow room or the conservatory. Will had tallied the total as closer to fifty than the thirty-nine Juliette claimed. He stood and watched as three footmen wrestled with a large portrait of the duke. While he supervised, Will listened to the chatter and laughter of the servants around him. He did not recall ever hearing them laugh or talk around him before.

"You've almost got it," he said. "Lift the left side."

"Redecorating, Your Grace?" someone asked.

"Hmm? Now the right side," he directed.

"It looks like a mammoth project to me. Perhaps that explains why no one answered your door."

Will turned to stare at the woman standing beside him. She was at least sixty and very likely older. Her white hair coiled neatly on her head, her sharp blue eyes were clear and assessing, and her small frame bony and frail. But she held her shoulders back, even as her hand trembled on the walking stick she held. Will's first thought was that she had been a handsome woman in her time. She was still a handsome woman.

He voiced his second thought. "Do I know you?"

"I don't think we've been introduced." She held

out her hand. "I am the Countess of Sinclair. I believe I'm better known as the long-suffering wife of the Earl of Sin."

Twenty-two

WILL DID NOT KNOW WHAT HE HAD DONE TO BRING this deluge of visitors upon him. He knew Juliette must take some of the blame. After all, before he met her, he never had visitors he didn't specifically invite. And since he almost never specifically invited anyone—save Fitzhugh once or twice and the odd cousin or nephew—two unexpected visitors in one day qualified as a deluge.

He was at a loss as to what to do with the Countess of Sinclair, and fortunately, Richards stepped in to aid him. "Your Grace, shall I show her ladyship into the drawing room?"

That sounded like the correct thing. "Please. And have Cook…" He waved his hand around.

"Of course, Your Grace. Tea and cakes will be brought immediately."

Richards led them to the drawing room, and Will wondered why he suddenly felt as though he were a guest and this was the countess's home. She sat in one of his blue silk chairs, and he sat across from her on a couch with similar upholstery.

"So," she began after perusing the room, her gaze pausing on the empty space where his father's portrait had hung. "Where is my protégé?"

"Your protégé?"

She tapped her walking stick. "Pay attention, Pelham. Where is Juliette?"

He leaned back. "She's not here."

"I've deduced as much, which is why I asked where she was. Really, Pelham, I had been told you were an intelligent man."

Will opened his mouth but wasn't quite certain he could make any response that wouldn't get him into more trouble. The term *protégé* was a strange one to give to the mistress of one's husband, but Will could definitely see where Juliette had adopted some of her brashness. Finally, he said, "I don't know. She left this morning."

"I thought as much." The countess leaned forward, her weight on her gold-tipped walking stick. "And what precisely did you do to make her leave?"

"I?" He had the urge to glance at his signet ring to remind himself he was still the Duke of Pelham. Unfortunately, he had thrown it at his father's portrait. "I did nothing to her." Perhaps doing nothing was exactly the problem.

The countess gave him a long look. Will wondered how she managed not to blink for such a lengthy period. Her blue eyes never left his face. Will squirmed. He had not squirmed since he was eight, but he was squirming now. She raised a brow.

"She might have overheard something that upset her."

The countess tapped her stick once. "Continue."

Will didn't particularly wish to continue, but he didn't see as how he had any choice. He could not exactly throw the countess out. She was a woman, and she was elderly. "My uncle paid me a visit this morning."

"Lord Henry," she interrupted.

"Yes. Do you know him?"

"He's an insufferable ass, much like your father. Much like you." She pointed the stick at him. "Unless Juliette has been able to bring about any change in you."

Will shook his head. "My lady, we have never before met. I do think characterizing me as an *insufferable ass* is a bit premature."

"Oh, really." She raised her brows, her blue eyes piercing him through. "Did you or did you not run off my lovely Juliette?"

"I didn't run her off, I—"

"Then, pray tell, where is she?"

Will frowned. "I didn't want her to go. I tried to explain."

"Did you now? How hard did you try?"

Will clenched his jaw. Truth be told, he had not tried very hard at all. Could he have tried harder? And if he had?

The countess sat back. "That's what I thought."

The door opened, and Mrs. Waite brought in the tea service. While his housekeeper fussed over the sugar and cream and made sure the cakes were placed just so, Will wondered how the Countess of Sinclair should know his father. Will had never heard this woman mentioned until he met Juliette, and he had never seen her at any of the house parties his father held. Admittedly, those had been rare.

"How did you know my father?" he asked when Mrs. Waite had left them alone again.

"Oh, I met him here and there. We ran in the same circles. He was even a suitor of mine for a short time."

Will blinked. It was difficult to imagine the hard, angry man he'd known as any lady's suitor.

"Of course, he didn't stand a chance, seeing as he was an insufferable ass."

"And your current husband?" Will knew he was pushing the boundaries of propriety, but the countess did not seem to observe the social niceties anyway. And he did wonder how a woman whose husband had three mistresses and who had been given the nickname the Earl of Sin by the *ton* could call *his* father an ass.

"Oh, no, no, no," she said, waggling a finger. "I see where you are going, and I admire you for it, but that is Juliette's secret to tell."

"What secret?"

"We are discussing you. Allow me to conjecture as to what occurred." She studied him. "You are a man who grew up under the thumb of a cold, heartless man. I can imagine that experience did not leave you completely unscathed."

Will bristled. He was no victim. "I beg your—"

"Shh. I am speaking. Now where was I?" She tapped her chin. "Oh, yes. Knowing my Juliette, she fell in love with you. She not only has a weakness for powerful men—a detrimental weakness considering her former husband—she also has a propensity to want to save animals, plants, and people. You needed saving, and she decided she was the one to do it. Along the way, she fell in love with you because, presumably, you have some charms." She narrowed her eyes at him as though this was a matter of some dispute. "And you fell in love with her."

He started. "I never said—"

She snapped her fingers, and Will clenched his jaw.

"I am *still* speaking. Now where... oh, yes! You fell in love with her. Don't deny it."

He narrowed his eyes. He was *not* in love with Juliette.

He liked her. A great deal. But love her? He thought of those bruises on her cheek and the consuming fear he'd felt when he'd seen Oliver move to strike her down. Very well, he was a little in love with her.

"Everyone falls in love with her," the countess was saying. "But you were too proud to tell her you loved her and too proud to offer her marriage because she is a courtesan and you are a duke, and so she left. Is that correct?"

Will glared at her. "Oh, am I allowed to speak now?"

She pointed a bony finger at him. "Do not be insolent with me!"

Will knew he was fighting a losing battle. "Your synopsis is more or less correct," he said through clenched teeth.

"I know. Now, what are you going to do about it?"

Will shook his head. "I'm not going to do anything about it. She left me."

"Can you blame her?"

"Yes!" Will stood. "I never made her any promises.

I never told her I loved her. I made it very clear I could never marry her. Why should she be upset when I say as much to my uncle? She's no green girl. A courtesan shouldn't fall in love, shouldn't expect marriage." Will paced the room, fists clenched.

"No, a courtesan shouldn't," the countess said quietly. "But Juliette... is different. She wants a husband, a family, a man who will be a father to children they might have together."

"I am not that man. I made that perfectly clear." And he had. He had been perfectly direct on this point with her.

"Well." The countess rose. "I suppose there is nothing more to say."

"You came all this way to tell me there is nothing to say? Could you not have written a letter?"

"Do you want to hear what I have to say?"

Did he? Not particularly, but he might as well. Devil take him, but he wanted Juliette back. Perhaps the countess could speak to her, tell her to return to him. "Yes," he said, his jaw clenched again.

"Very well. You, Pelham, are a fool."

Will blinked. *That* was what she wanted to say?

"You had a chance at happiness, a chance very few people ever have. You had a chance at finding true love, and you threw it away with both hands. And why, I ask you?"

"You know why."

She waved her hand about, encompassing the room. "For a title, for family honor, for form's sake. Let me tell you something, Your Grace. Your title and your honor and your form will not keep you warm at night. It won't stave off the loneliness. It won't be by your side, holding your hand when you're old and frail as I am. It won't give you children or grandchildren. It won't make you laugh or cry or stare in wonder. But you hold your title close, Your Grace, because you'll never hold Juliette again." And with that, she turned on her heel and walked out of the room.

Will stood in the empty room with fists clenched and a thousand cutting ripostes on his tongue. He glanced at the empty spot where his father's portrait had been, lifted a vase on the table beside his couch, and flung it at the wall. He stared at the shards of broken pottery and the mark on the wall until his breathing slowed, and then he walked out of the drawing room and slammed the door closed behind him. Down the corridor, he could hear his servants working, removing another of his father's portraits. But it didn't really matter. Even if all the portraits were gone, his father was still here. Inside him.

Will's footsteps echoed on the hallowed floors as he walked through room after empty room. He found himself in his bedchamber—the last place Juliette had occupied. It was partially cleaned and straightened, but he must have called the servants to assist in removing his father's portraits before they could finish.

Will walked to the bed and touched the counterpane. Then he leaned down and smelled the pillow Juliette had slept on. It still carried her lavender scent. A pang of regret hit him so hard he all but doubled over. He stood beside the bed, jaw tight, and tried to obliterate the craving he had for her.

The problem was that it had grown over time. Yes, he'd wanted her the first time he saw her, but that desire was nothing compared to now. Now he didn't simply want her physically—though what sane man wouldn't want her physically?—he wanted her in every way. He wanted her smile, her laughter, her teasing. God help him, he even wanted her tears.

He knew what was wrong with him. The bloody countess was correct. He'd fallen in love. He'd broken his cardinal rule and fallen in love. And the devil take him if he still didn't think it was one hell of a good rule.

Love was not ordered or disciplined. Love was not logical or stately. Love made fools of everyone it touched. He hadn't thought he could fall in love—that was the chink in his armor. That was where love had found an entrance and pried it open. He thought that as the Duke of Pelham he was above the mundane act of falling in love.

And he had additional armor, as well. He'd never been loved. His father certainly hadn't loved him. His mother, if she had loved him, never showed it that he could recall. His friends might like him a great deal, but he doubted they loved him. No one loved him. No one had *ever* loved him. No one *would* ever love him.

Except Juliette.

And now he'd driven her away.

It was exactly as the countess had said. He'd driven away his one chance at love, at happiness. At one time he had thought his role of duke would bring him happiness. He had estates to oversee, parliamentary duties, social obligations. But for the first time in his life, Will wished he was not the Duke of Pelham. He wished he had never even heard of the man.

What was Juliette always saying? *You can make your own destiny.*

But could he? Could he really? Could he silence his father? Could he rid the man in his head as he'd rid the house of his portraits?

Will sank onto the bed, head in his hands. Juliette would accept nothing less than marriage. He knew that. Could he marry her knowing she had been a courtesan?

His family would be appalled. His servants would be appalled. His friends would be... mildly amused. Society would be all atwitter. He hated twittering.

But he loved Juliette more. He could not exist without her. Damn what she had been in the past, what she had done, whom she had known. He cared about who she was now and who she would become—the sixth Duchess of Pelham.

She would make a glorious duchess. She was born to be a duchess.

Will had one small problem. How was he going to convince *her* she should become his duchess?

⟡

Juliette did not go home to her town house. She could not bear to see the havoc Lucifer had wreaked in her bedroom and throughout the house as he searched for the lost diamonds. She would deal with it later. In the meantime, she would write to her servants and ask them to return, and try and find some way of paying them. She needed a protector. As much as she didn't want to endure a man's caresses, to have to close her eyes and pretend he or she was someone else, she had little choice.

She had fallen in love. She would love Pelham—the arrogant bastard—forever. But love would not pay Rosie or Hollows or keep a roof over Juliette's head.

She thought about going to Lily's or Fallon's. She knew both would welcome her with all their hearts, but Lily and Fallon had gone to Somerset. Or so she assumed. Their staffs would not allow her to take up residence while the ladies were away. It did not matter how close the three were.

But there was one place she was always welcome. There was one place she knew she would be granted entrance and a home for as long as she needed it. The Earl of Sinclair's residence.

And so when she arrived in London, she went to Sinclair House directly. She was pleased when their old butler, Abernathy, opened the door. He had not changed at all since she had last seen him. He still had the same white hair, the same crinkled brown eyes, and the same ruddy cheeks. She felt as though a hundred years had passed. Upon seeing her, Abernathy's face lit up, and he all but pulled her into a hug. "Miss Juliette! I am so glad you are here."

"You won't be when you hear all the rumors swirling about concerning me."

He waved his hand. "Pish posh. I don't care about rumors. Come in, come in. Lord and Lady Sinclair are not in residence."

"I know. I…" She bit her lip. "I was hoping I might stay here for a little while anyway. I will write to them, asking if they approve, of course."

"No need," Abernathy said. "You are always welcome here."

The words were like warm tea on a cold winter morning. Juliette could have cried with relief. It felt so good to be welcomed somewhere, so good to belong. She hadn't belonged at Rothingham Manor, as much as she wanted to. She would never have fit in there.

And that, of course, was a lie. But she needed to tell herself something if she was ever going to forget Pelham. What she really needed were Lily and Fallon to tell her what an ugly ogre Pelham was. How she could do so much better. How he was a complete and utter fool to let her go.

"I will have the housekeeper show you to your room," Abernathy said.

"Abernathy, do you know if Miss Lily or Miss Fallon is in Town?"

"I have not seen them, Miss Juliette. I could send a messenger to their residences with a note, if you would like."

They were probably still at Somerset. Still, the note would be waiting for them when they returned. "I would, yes."

And she sat down to ask her two dearest friends to come to her.

⁓

Will did not go straight to Juliette's residence when he arrived in London. He had planned to do so, but upon seeing the city, his bravery deserted him and he was left with a vague uncertainty.

What if she did not accept his proposal? He had

practiced and practiced the words he would say and the gestures accompanying his speech, but what if she did not like it? Good God, what if she no longer loved him?

He felt sick at that prospect. He felt ill at the idea she might refuse him. Perhaps he might stop at his own town house before calling on Juliette...

And when had he become a lovelorn schoolboy? It was pathetic.

And so he did not change his directions, and the coachman took him to Juliette's door. He sat in his coach for a long moment, gathering the courage he needed for the task ahead of him.

His heart pounded, his hands perspired, his knees were shaky. He stepped out of the coach, felt his legs buckle, but caught himself just in time.

He needed a strong drink. Perhaps two, he thought as he made his way to her door. Why had he not thought to stop at his club first? But he was here now. He must go through with it.

He cleared his throat and raised a shaking hand to the door. The knocker had been removed, indicating she'd left Town, but he didn't believe that. She had nowhere else to go. He knocked, but his hand slipped, and the knock barely sounded. Gritting his teeth, he clenched his fist and rapped harder, firmer, braver this time.

He stood and he waited.

And waited.

His heart beat harder, and he lifted his hand again.

Silence.

Could it be she was not in Town? Could it be

Juliette had not returned to London? His coachman had told him he'd taken her here. Had she promptly left after arriving? He stared at her door. Or might she be staying elsewhere?

And if she was, how would he ever find her? London was a sprawling city. If she didn't want to be found, she wouldn't be.

On the other hand, she was the Duchess of Dalliance—a notorious and exceptionally beautiful woman. Someone would know where she was. And he knew where to start.

❧

Juliette sat with Fallon, Lily, and the Countess of Sinclair in the sitting room of the countess's bedchamber. "You are not a fool," Lily was saying for perhaps the tenth time that day.

"He is the fool," Fallon said, also for the tenth time. "He doesn't deserve you."

"But I should never have fallen in love with him. I knew he didn't love me. I knew he would never marry a courtesan. And besides, he's an awful man—rigid, arrogant, demanding—"

The countess held up a hand, and Juliette quieted. One did not speak when the Countess of Sinclair was speaking. "The girls are right, Juliette. He is the fool. What's more, he is a bigger fool because he is in love with you, too. He has too much pride to admit it."

"But how can you possibly know that?" Juliette asked. "You don't even know him."

The countess gave her a long look, and Juliette

began to wonder if perhaps the countess *did* know Pelham. Juliette never ruled anything out when the countess was involved. She happened to glance at Lily and caught the look she flashed Fallon.

"What was that about?" she asked.

"Nothing," Fallon said. Juliette knew she would never be able to make Fallon tell her, so she fixed her gaze on Lily.

"Lily?"

"Nothing." She looked away.

"Lily, tell me."

"There's nothing to tell." But Lily's voice rose slightly, and Juliette knew she was lying.

"Tell me."

"Oh, you might as well tell her," the countess said. "She will find out eventually anyway."

"Find out what?" She grabbed Fallon's arm. "He's not dead, is he? Pelham's not hurt, is he? I thought Lucifer was on the Continent. Did he go after Pelham?"

"Juliette, Pelham is fine." She raised a brow. "A moment ago you said he was an awful man."

"That doesn't mean she wants him dead," Lily added. "The duke is fine, Juliette. He's in London."

"He's in London? He's here? How long has he been in Town?"

"Almost a week," the countess said.

"Oh." Juliette's heart sank. She didn't think it could sink any more than it already had, but she felt it drop into her belly. Hard. She supposed this would be her life from now on. She would hear of Pelham from other people. He would be in Town or in the country, and she would not be with him. She would hear or read secondhand accounts. Perhaps one day she would read of his engagement in the *Times*.

"Oh, bloody hell."

"Fallon!" Lady Sinclair admonished. "Language."

"I can't help it. Look at her. She's devastated. Juliette, he's been looking for you."

Juliette's whole body seemed to jerk in shock. "He has?"

"Yes, he came to my house and Lily's house."

"He even came here. You may be certain Abernathy did not admit him."

"Of course not." But Juliette was barely listening. Pelham was looking for her. Pelham wanted to see her.

"He will probably be back," the countess said. "I think he knows you are here. Do you want to see him?"

Juliette's first response was yes, *yes*! More than anything she wanted to see Will, hold him, kiss him. But she checked her impulse to say this. *Did* she want to see Pelham? What more did they have to say to each other? He had made his position clear, as had she. She could not accept being his mistress. But she was afraid if she saw him again, she might forget her principles and accept any offer he made. "No," she said finally. "No, I don't want to see him."

"Good!" Fallon said. "I hope he calls again when I am at home. I'll tell him to go to hell in person."

"Fallon." The countess sighed. "Language."

"I think you need to get out a bit," Lily said to Juliette. "You have been hiding for days and days."

Juliette spread her arms. "Where am I to go? I'm supposed to be a courtesan, but now I've lost my popularity. I need to find another profession."

Lady Sinclair patted her arm. "There's time for that yet, dear. Lily is right. What about a night at the theater? Mozart's *The Abduction from the Seraglio* is playing next week."

Fallon rolled her eyes, but Lily clapped her hands. "Oh, it will be wonderful to have The Three Diamonds back together again. Now, we must begin thinking about what we shall wear."

A tap on the door interrupted Lily, and Juliette was not sorry. She wasn't at all certain she wanted to brave the theater and the stares of half the *ton*. And she certainly did not want to think about fashion.

Lord Sinclair poked his head in the door. "I hate to interrupt, my dears, but I insist the countess rest."

The three girls jumped up. "Of course, Sin," Lily said. "You're absolutely correct. We will tire her out."

"I am not a child who needs a nap," the countess protested. The earl went to her side and helped her to rise. Juliette saw the countess did look tired, indeed. The earl, who was very busy, had taken time to make certain she rested so she would fully recover from her illness. She watched as he helped the countess to her bed, envious of the love between the two of them.

"Give me a kiss before you go," she told the girls. Dutifully, Fallon, Lily, and then Juliette gave her kisses on the cheek. The earl patted each girl's shoulder in a fatherly gesture.

"I shall see you at dinner," Juliette said, pecking the countess's cheek.

Both Lily and Fallon took their leave. They had balls to attend tonight and needed to begin their toilettes. Juliette had nothing planned. She had received several invitations, but they were all from the lowest, most notorious rakes. She was not that desperate.

She went to her room and stood at the window overlooking the street. Fashionable carriages clopped past, carrying the residents of Mayfair to and fro. She watched for a long time, wondering if the duke's carriage would come today.

And then she thought again of the love between the earl and his wife. Could she settle for less?

She closed the curtains and turned away.

Twenty-three

W ILL SAT AT HIS CLUB, STARING INTO THE FIRE AND drinking port. At some point he was going to have to admit she was lost to him.

Juliette was lost to him.

Her friends would not bring her a message from him, the stodgy butler at Sinclair House maintained he did not know a Juliette, and even the servants at Juliette's own town house would not do more than smile politely at him.

He wondered if she planned to go back to her home. Her servants had returned, but according to his sources, she was still ensconced at Sinclair House.

And Will had sources. He had men all over Town reporting to him if they even thought they saw a woman who looked like Juliette. He had men watching her friends' houses, her house, and Lucifer's Lair. He was spending a fortune, and it would be worth it to hold her in his arms again. But he was beginning to doubt he would ever speak to her again, much less hold her.

He tried not to think too much about where she

was staying or what she might be doing there. Had she fled back into the arms of the Earl of Sin? Was he warming her bed now? Will clenched his fists when he thought of another man touching Juliette. But what could he do? She was an independent woman. She could see whomever she liked. Somehow he had to convince her she wanted to see him.

But how, when he couldn't even get close to her?

Will heard a muffled sound and turned just as Fitzhugh took the chair opposite him. "What was that? You spoke into my deaf ear."

"I said you look like your favorite horse just went lame. Why the long face?" He signaled to a waiter and ordered a brandy.

Will frowned. "It's nothing."

"I don't think it's nothing. You've been moping around here for the last week. Is it Lady Elizabeth's death? Lord and Lady Nowlund are beside themselves with grief."

Devil take him. He'd completely ignored Lord and Lady Nowlund since arriving back in Town. He should call on them, pay his respects. His betrothal to Lady Elizabeth had not been finalized, so he was not breaking social custom by not mourning. But he owed them the courtesy of a call.

"I see that's not it," Fitzhugh said. The waiter brought his brandy, but he did not drink. Instead, he set the glass on the table and toyed with the rim.

"Stop trying to get inside my head," Will said. "I don't harass you about all of your private affairs."

"That's because I'm a better friend than you. I'm also in the business of knowing something about private affairs, and I have it on good authority that you have been trying to get an audience with the Duchess of Dalliance."

Will sat forward then forced himself to wait three heartbeats before speaking. "Her name is Juliette."

Fitzhugh shrugged. "Call her what you will. She apparently doesn't want to see you."

Will ground his teeth together. He had thought he was being rather circumspect in his efforts to see Juliette. How had the fact he was seeking her become known? And wouldn't the *ton* salivate for that information? Was he now going to be made a laughingstock in the *Morning Chronicle* again? "How did you find out?" he asked quietly.

"I like to know things. You can stop looking at me like you're going to throttle me. I'm not going to share your secret, and it's far from common knowledge. That's probably exactly your problem."

Will shook his head. Fitzhugh was one of the few men he knew who actually made sense, but he was not making sense today. "I don't have a problem. I was protecting Juliette. Apparently, Lady Elizabeth was murdered because of her connections to a man called Lucifer."

Now Fitzhugh leaned forward. "The Lucifer who runs Lucifer's Lair? I know of him. He's a dangerous man, not to be trifled with."

"Fortunately, my sources tell me he's out of the country. He fled after murdering Lady Elizabeth."

Fitzhugh's eyes narrowed. "And Juliette witnessed the murder. This is coming together now. But why would Lady Elizabeth have an acquaintance with Lucifer?"

"Apparently, she enjoyed the faro tables a bit too much. She racked up enormous debts. And then she made a fatal mistake. She stole Lucifer's diamonds."

"To pay the debts?"

"Possibly. Or perhaps she hoped to sell them and flee the country. Or perhaps she just enjoyed the thrill of stealing them. We will never know."

"She was a fool to believe Lucifer would not catch her."

"And when he did, she implicated Juliette. That is another reason I took her to Yorkshire with me. Lucifer was searching her town house for the diamonds before he fled the country."

"And where are the diamonds now?" Fitzhugh asked.

"I don't know. I've searched everywhere I can think of. I don't even know what they look like."

Fitzhugh crossed his arms. "I'd like to help you, but I'm on assignment."

"I thought you'd retired."

"I've been called back. One of the men I worked with on the Continent has been murdered. He was a friend, one of my diamonds in the rough."

"Do you think he was targeted?"

"I don't know, but I'm going to find out. I'll ask a few of my contacts to look into this business with Lucifer. I'd like to know exactly where he is."

Will nodded. "I'd appreciate that."

Fitzhugh raised his brows. "Would you? I think this is the first time you've ever thanked me for giving you assistance. I was under the impression dukes rarely expressed appreciation."

"There are a lot of things dukes should not do that I have done of late." He signaled for another port. He had a feeling he was going to need it.

"For example?"

"Searching all over London for Juliette. If word of this is made public, I'll look a fool."

"And I believe I said that is exactly your problem."

"Fitzhugh"—Will swallowed a large portion of the port the waiter put in front of him—"do endeavor to make sense."

Fitzhugh only smiled, which did nothing to improve Will's mood. "Allow me to make certain I understand the particulars of your situation. You are in love with the Duchess of Dalliance."

Will scowled. "I fail to see how feelings play any part in this."

"Good God, man. If you can't admit it to me, how are you going to tell her?"

That was a valid point, Will decided. "Fine." He clenched his jaw. "I'm in love with Juliette."

"A notorious courtesan."

"She was, yes."

"Do you intend to marry her?"

"Are you certain these questions are germane?"

"No, but it's entertaining watching you squirm, and I've had very little entertainment in my life of late."

"Fitzhugh."

"Answer the question, or I won't help you."

"I fail to see how you can help me, at any rate."

"Then you don't want to know how to win Juliette?"

Will narrowed his eyes at Fitzhugh. Could the

man really know how to get to Juliette? He'd known about Lucifer. Perhaps he knew where Will could get a quarter hour alone with Juliette.

"Fine. Yes, I intend to make her my wife."

Fitzhugh let out a low whistle. "Your uncle will not approve of that match."

"So he has made clear. Fortunately, I am the duke, not he. Get to the part where I win Juliette."

"One more question."

"Fitzhugh." Will's tone was one of warning.

"How much do you want her? Are you willing to risk what you hold most dear?"

Will reached across the table and grabbed Fitzhugh by the cravat. "What is this? A riddle? I told you I love her and want to marry her. I've already broken my cardinal rule by falling in love—and not simply with a woman but a courtesan, for God's sake. It's undignified."

"And that's what you shall have to risk."

Will furrowed his brow, and Fitzhugh unclenched the duke's fingers from his cravat.

"If you want to win her, you must give up your dignity. It's the only way to prove to her you really mean what you say."

Will leaned back in his chair and stared at Fitzhugh. He did not want to hear this. He knew he did not want to hear this. He'd do anything but what Fitzhugh was suggesting. Anything. He was the Duke of Pelham. He had a title and family honor to preserve.

"I don't know the duchess—I mean, Juliette—at all, but even I can see she's an intelligent woman. A courtesan marrying a duke? It will not be easy for either of you."

And yet she'd risked everything by falling in love with him—her pride, her livelihood, her heart. And what had he given her? He'd never even told her he loved her. Why should she believe him now? After the way he'd treated her, he would not be surprised if she slapped him. "I owe her an apology," Will muttered.

"Undoubtedly."

Will raised his eyes to Fitzhugh. "Dukes do not apologize."

"Perfect. It will show her how much she means to you when you do apologize. What else don't dukes do?"

"Marry courtesans."

"Right." Fitzhugh slapped the table. "You need to propose publicly. Apologize, tell her you are madly in love with her, and ask her to be your wife. In public."

Will thought he was going to be ill.

"What else is against the ducal code?"

Will stared at Fitzhugh. "Publicly humiliating myself is not enough? I must do *more*?"

"Do you want her or not?"

"How do I know all of this isn't simply for your amusement?" Will crossed his arms. "How is it you are the expert on women?"

"Have you met my mother?"

Will had. The Countess of Winthorpe was one of those Society mothers who could send even him running. If she got it into her head a man was a good match for one of her daughters, the man was as good as leg-shackled.

"She's married off three of my four sisters and both of my older brothers. I've made a study of her strategies. Not to mention, I've seen the hoops my brothers and my sisters' husbands must jump through to keep peace in their marriages. Trust me, Pelham, you're getting off easy."

"I can't think of anything worse than what we've already discussed."

Fitzhugh sipped his port and appeared thoughtful. He was silent for quite some time, and Will almost began to relax. Almost.

Suddenly, Fitzhugh sat forward. "I have it."

Will wanted to groan.

"You know, Pelham, it occurs to me I never see you dance."

"Dancing is undignified."

"Good." Fitzhugh clapped his hands together. "Then that's what you must do."

"You've failed to consider one crucial point."

"I doubt it."

"Juliette won't see me. I can hardly dance, propose, and—what was the other thing?"

"Apologize."

"Right. I can hardly do any of those things if she won't see me."

"She doesn't have to agree to see you. You must do this all publicly."

"But she's not going out in public."

"It's a good thing you have me, Pelham," Fitzhugh said.

Will begged to differ.

"I know where she is going to be tomorrow night."

"Where's that?"

Fitzhugh smiled. "The perfect venue."

❧

"I don't know why I'm so nervous," Juliette said once she, Lily, Fallon, and the Sinclairs were in the carriage on the way to Covent Garden.

"There's nothing to be nervous about," Lily assured her. "You look ravishing."

Juliette could not argue with that assessment. Fallon and Lily had spent all day fussing with her hair and gown. The three of them were dressed in flowing white silk covered with thousands of tiny spangles. Lily said if Juliette were to become one of The Three Diamonds again, she must look the part. And all three of them truly did look like sparkling diamonds.

Juliette had refrained from mentioning that she did not want to resume the charade of a glamorous courtesan, but since she did not know what she wanted to do instead, she said nothing. She thought the countess might have guessed her feelings. She'd caught Lady Sinclair watching her on several occasions, her expression curious, as though she wondered just what future Juliette was planning for herself.

Or perhaps she was waiting for Juliette to ask her advice. Juliette was not certain why she had not done so already. Perhaps because she already felt so indebted to the countess for all she had done for her.

Or perhaps because she feared she would burst into tears if she so much as thought about a future without Pelham. She didn't want to cry on the countess's shoulder any more than she had already done.

Juliette took a deep breath and tried to smile. Both Lily and Fallon wore concerned expressions, and they should be smiling and enjoying themselves. She had to admit she had never seen them look more beautiful.

Lily had scattered spangles in her auburn hair, and she seemed to glitter from head to toe. She wore some of Lady Sinclair's diamonds at her neck and in her ears and looked positively radiant.

Fallon was less ostentatious. Her dark hair was dressed simply and without decoration, save for a jeweled rose tucked behind her ear. The flash of red was exactly what Fallon needed, lest the white wash out her olive complexion.

Juliette had a similar flash of color in the form of an ice-blue ribbon about her neck. Dangling from the ribbon was a large square-cut diamond the countess had pressed into her hands. Juliette had stared in disbelief at the heavy jewel, and the countess had said, "Do not lose it, or Sinclair will have my head."

"No, my lady," Juliette answered.

"All four of you look beautiful," the earl said now. "I'm a lucky man." Indeed, the men of the *ton* would be excessively envious of the Earl of Sin, arriving with the three most celebrated courtesans in the country at his side. And yet, as he spoke, he patted the countess's hand and looked only at her.

Juliette doubted he'd ever had eyes for any woman but her.

But he would dutifully play his part at the opera as the most debauched man in Britain. If he didn't, he would have to answer to the countess.

They wound their way through the snarl of carriages also en route to Covent Garden, and after what seemed an eternity to Juliette, they arrived. Lily had already instructed her to make certain she was the last to exit the carriage. They all agreed it would heighten the suspense of those watching the arrivals.

And so when the carriage finally stopped and the footmen opened the door and lowered the steps, the earl was the first to descend, followed by his wife. She stood regally at his side while he held a hand out to Lily and helped her down. She took her place across from the countess, who did not look at her, and was then joined by Fallon. The earl made a show of bowing and kissing Fallon's hand. And then he paused.

Inside the carriage, Juliette's heart hammered. She knew he was pausing to build anticipation. The crowds would wonder who else occupied the carriage. They would speculate and conjecture, all the while staring at the magnificent, glittering gowns of two of The Three Diamonds.

And now Sinclair held his hand out again, and Juliette moved forward. She moved as if in a dream. She no longer felt like the Duchess of Dalliance, and this entire exercise seemed a ridiculous farce. But then the light caught the sparkle of her gown, and she heard the gasps of the crowd. She could not turn back now.

She took the earl's gloved hand, and he squeezed her fingers reassuringly. With as much grace as she could muster, Juliette stepped out of the carriage and paused so the earl could kiss her cheek. It was a grandfatherly kiss as far as Juliette was concerned, but the *ton* would make of it what they would.

And then Lily and Fallon were on either side of her, linking arms, and the trio of dazzling women stepped behind the earl and the countess. Juliette was thankful for the support of her friends, and as they moved through the arched portico, she was able to relax slightly. After all, this was a night at the theater. She had always enjoyed Mozart, and what opera was more appropriate for them to attend than *The Abduction from the Seraglio*?

She took a deep breath and attempted a small smile at a few gentlemen she recognized in the crowd. And then she felt Lily stiffen, followed by Fallon.

This was new. Those two were always confident and poised.

"What is it?" she asked between the clenched teeth of her smile.

"Nothing," Lily said. "Keep walking."

"Fallon, what is it?"

"Just keep walking."

"But why did you—?"

And then she saw him, and she knew why her friends had started. The Duke of Pelham, looking impossibly handsome in a vibrant blue tailcoat that matched the blue of his eyes, stood just inside the doors. He leaned negligently against the banister housing the steps that led to the boxes. His face was chiseled from granite, his cheeks and mouth sculpted by the finest master. His cravat was perfect, his trousers tight and unlined, and his boots shone. Only his hair showed any sign of rebellion. It was adorably tousled, and Juliette could not help but remember it looking so after a night of lovemaking.

His eyes were on her as she moved inextricably closer, and she felt the heat of his gaze burning through her. She did not know how her legs continued to propel her forward. Perhaps Lily and Fallon carried her.

And then she was past him, on the steps and ascending to the earl's box.

The duke was behind her, and, once again, he had allowed her to leave him.

Twenty-four

SHE WAS SO BEAUTIFUL HE ALMOST BELIEVED HE IMAGINED her. How could anyone look so completely stunning? Seeing her was like some kind of wonderful dream—only he wasn't dreaming. At least he didn't think so.

Fitzhugh clapped him on the back, and he lurched forward. "Breathe, Pelham."

No, he was not dreaming. Fitzhugh would make appearances only in one's nightmares.

"You lost your chance. Everyone was watching the two of you. This was the perfect moment."

It would have been perfect—if he could have spoken. But when he saw Juliette, his powers of speech seemed to desert him. How was he ever going to go through with this? He already felt the fool, and he hadn't even spoken to her yet.

Fitzhugh narrowed his eyes. "Don't tell me you've reconsidered."

Would it be so bad to think this through a bit more? Yes.

He had to act. The Dukes of Pelham had never been cowards. He would march to Sinclair's box, tell Juliette he was in love with her... and all the other rubbish Fitzhugh had told him. And if she didn't want him, that was that. He couldn't *make* her accept him.

God, he hoped she still wanted him. How was he going to live without her? What if he just picked her up, tossed her over his shoulder, and carried her back to his town house? It was a simple approach, not without appeal.

"Pelham?" Fitzhugh said.

"I'm going." He straightened his shoulders.

"Here." Fitzhugh handed him a flask. "Gin. It'll give you blue courage."

Will shook his head at Fitzhugh's play on the nickname for gin—Blue Ruin—but he took a long swallow, winced, and shook his head again. It was now or never. He mounted the steps to the boxes, his legs feeling like a team of horses was pulling them in the other direction. But he persisted.

Juliette was worth this. She was worth anything.

Of course, when he reached the boxes, he realized he didn't know which was Sinclair's, but he'd eat his arm before he asked. Instead, he walked the corridor and waited until he saw a crowd of inane-looking men. At the end of the corridor, toward the front of the theater, he saw what he was looking for. He was tempted to punch the first man he muscled out of the way, but it would have been a waste of time—time he could be spending with Juliette.

"I say!" the man exclaimed.

"What! Oh, pardon me, Your Grace," another said.

"It's Pelham," someone murmured.

Will moved through the group of men and stepped into Sinclair's box. The earl had a splendid view of the stage and the theater. Pelham glanced about him, taking in the large stage hidden by a rich crimson drapery and ornamented by an elegantly paneled arch. On each side of the arch rose two Grecian-styled female figures represented in relief. As the boxes were elevated, he also had a good view of the elaborate ceiling of the theatre, painted to give the appearance of a cupola.

And then Pelham turned his attention to the box itself. Sinclair had a subscription to one of the best available. It was spacious and separated from its neighbor by gilt columns. Each box was illuminated by chandeliers of cut crystal suspended from the tops of pillars, and the chandelier's glow provided the audience in the theater a splendid view. Will could all but feel the opera glasses trained on him. He wrenched his eyes from the audience in the theater to the occupants in the box. The earl and his countess were seated at the front of the box, and The Three Diamonds were arranged directly behind them. Juliette was between her two friends.

As Will stared at The Three Diamonds, shining under the diamond-cut crystal of the chandelier, something flickered in his mind. Impatient to speak to Juliette, he attempted to push it away, but it niggled.

Lucifer's Diamonds were jewels, were they not? He looked again at the three courtesans. *The Three Diamonds.* What if Lucifer's Diamonds were not diamonds at all but something else—something equally as valuable as diamonds, something rare, something sought after? What if he and Juliette had been looking for the wrong diamonds?

Will's gaze flicked back to Juliette just as a man he didn't know leaned over her chair, making her laugh. And then she saw Will, and her smile dropped.

"What is it?" the young man asked, turning to look at Will.

"Get out," Will said.

"Ho, now. Who the bloody hell—?"

"It's the Duke of Pelham, Gillivray. You'd better step aside," the dark-haired courtesan said. She was frowning at Will. The redhead was giving him an encouraging smile, and Juliette was staring at him as though she thought him a ghost.

"Pelham," the earl said, standing. "I don't recall inviting you to my box."

Beside him, the countess raised her eyebrows but remained silent.

"I need a word with Juliette," Will told the earl.

"Juliette?" the earl asked her.

"I… I don't think we have anything further to say to each other," she said.

Will's heart clenched hard in his chest. He had known this would not be easy, but he had not expected such coldness from her. Her eyes were frosty.

"I have something to say to you," Will persisted. "I—" No sense in doing things halfway now. He held his hand out to her. "Stand up."

"I'm perfectly happy seated where I am."

Will resisted the urge to haul her out of her chair. "Please," he said. Her eyes widened. She did not take his hand, but she stood. He moved beside her as her friends pushed their chairs aside. He and Juliette were plainly visible to the entire theater now. Was it only his imagination, or had everyone grown quiet?

"I want to tell you something. You needn't say anything back." Unless you want to, he thought. "I owe you an apology, Juliette. I owe you several." He took her hand. Her eyes were wide as saucers. "Madam, I am deeply sorry for any hurt I may have caused you. I am sorry for not defending you when others slandered you. I am sorry for my words at the prince's recent ball, and I deeply regret not having treated you in the manner you deserve. You are a lady in every sense of the word, and I vow I will never again treat you as anything other than a lady."

Juliette shook her head. "I don't understand. Why are you saying this?"

He knelt on one knee, still holding her hand. "Because I love you, Juliette. I think I fell in love with you almost the first moment I saw you. And since then my love has grown. You are the most remarkable woman I have ever met. You have made me a better man. I would be honored if you would become my wife, my duchess."

The crowd gasped, and Will did not imagine it this time. But he didn't care anymore. He cared only for Juliette. She was staring at him, her mouth working, and tears sparkling in her eyes.

"But I'm a courtesan. I can't be your duchess."

"Juliette, you are my love. No other woman could ever be my duchess. Please do not make me beg. I will, if that is what you require. God knows I deserve that and more."

"Will—" She put her hand over her mouth. Will's heart leaped. She had called him by the name she'd given him. He wanted to believe it was a good sign. But she hadn't answered him yet.

"Tell him yes, my dear," the countess said.

Juliette nodded, her hand still over her mouth.

"There's one more thing," he said, standing. "I believe I owe you a dance."

Her brow furrowed. "A dance?" Her voice was thick with emotion. She shook her head. "I don't think so."

"I do."

"There's no music."

Will looked down at the stage and the orchestra seated in the pit before it. "Conductor, now would be an opportune time."

"Yes, Your Grace." The conductor raised his baton, and the orchestra began playing a waltz. Juliette gasped.

"Did you plan this?"

Will held out his hand. "I would be honored if you would dance with me."

"I... I... there's no room."

At that, the countess rose from her chair, clapped her hands, and gave orders for the men standing about to remove the chairs. Then she joined the earl and the two remaining Diamonds in the entrance as Will put his arms around Juliette and began to lead her in a slow waltz.

❧

Juliette's head was spinning. She felt as though she were in a dream. She was back in Will's arms, and he loved her. He'd actually told her he loved her in front of everyone. He hated public displays of emotion. But now he was holding her, dancing with her, in front of the entire *ton*. She was used to having all eyes upon her, but she knew Will must hate it.

But he did it for her.

Because he loved her. He *loved* her! She wanted to shout it, to jump up and down, to twirl and twirl and twirl until she fell from light-headedness. Instead, she held Will tightly and willed this dream never to end.

"What are you thinking about, my love?" Will whispered in her ear.

She shivered. "How very happy I am. You have made me so incredibly happy." She leaned back, looked into his eyes. "Do you really love me?"

He kissed her mouth softly. "With all my heart."

"But all of this." She waved a hand at the audience and the theater. "You didn't have to do this."

"I believe I did." He glanced at the entrance to the box, and she spotted a tall, dark man she didn't know. He nodded at the two of them and melted into the crowd. "I wanted to show you how much I've changed. I wanted to show you how much you mean to me."

"Thank you." She put her forehead on his shoulder and smelled the clean scent of mint. His arms around her were warm and soft. She glanced up. "Do you know what I'm thinking about now?"

He raised a brow. "I might be able to guess."

"Take me home, Will. I want you to hold me, skin on skin."

He groaned softly. "I would like nothing better."

She stopped dancing and took his hand. "Then let's go."

"I can't. We can't."

She felt her happiness hitch and her dream begin to dissipate. How had she known this was too good to last? "Is there something wrong?"

"No. But I've decided we should wait."

"Wait? For what?"

"Until we're married."

She blinked. Had she heard him correctly? "But we have already…" She made a circling gesture with her hand. "There's no need to wait."

He tipped her chin up, kissed her lips chastely. "It's a sign of respect for my future wife. I want our wedding night to be special."

Tears rose to her eyes again, stinging the lids sharply.

"Is that all right?" he asked, his voice full of concern.

She nodded, unable to speak.

"Are you certain? You're crying." He looked slightly panicked, and she almost started laughing.

"I'm just happy," she said between sobs.

"Of course," he mumbled. "I always cry when I'm happy."

"Let's give the women a moment, old boy," Sinclair said, taking him aside. And then Juliette was engulfed by Fallon and Lily and the countess. She was surrounded by love. And tears.

And she had never been so happy in all her life.

❦

Will didn't particularly enjoy standing next to the Earl of Sin. After all, the man was his soon-to-be-wife's former lover. But he supposed it the lesser of two evils. Weeping women or a staid man who happened to be Juliette's former lover?

He'd take the man.

And then the countess broke away from the circle of women, and the earl abandoned Will. He patted Will on the shoulder. "Think I'll go for a walk."

Will frowned and turned to find the countess staring up at him. "I didn't think you'd do it," she said.

"My lady?"

She nodded to The Three Diamonds, who seemed a bit calmer and more composed now. They were whispering. In his experience, whispering women were never a good sign.

"I didn't think you'd do what it took to win her back. You broke her heart, Pelham."

"I know. I will make it up to her."

She nodded. "Yes. I think you will."

"It's the least I can do, considering I acted like a complete fool in Yorkshire."

"I am so pleased to hear you say so."

He raised his brows at her.

"Even at my age, it's uncomfortable to tell a duke when he's acting like a fool."

Will couldn't remember her mincing words before.

"If you don't mind my asking, Your Grace," the countess said, "why did you let her go?"

He raked a hand through his hair and watched Juliette. Their eyes met, and she smiled at him. He had to remember to breathe again. "Pride," he answered.

"Ah. Yes, I certainly understand what it is to have pride. And to have it injured." He gave her a curious look and noted she was watching The Three Diamonds. He shifted uncomfortably. No wonder Sinclair had fled.

"All the world thinks I am a fool," she said. "And I allow it because some things and some people are more important than pride. Why else would I allow the world to believe my husband is bedding those three women?"

Will started. "I…" He did not trust his ears and cleared his throat before speaking. "I'm not certain I follow, my lady."

"Then I shall speak plainly. My husband has never bedded your Juliette."

Will opened his mouth then closed it again. "Are you certain, my lady?"

She smiled. "Yes, quite certain. It was all a charade from the very beginning."

Will struggled to make sense of what she said. "Then Sinclair is not Juliette's protector?"

"Not in the sense you mean. I rather think he sees her as the daughter we never had. We were unable to have children, you see. These girls are our children."

"But why—?" He shook his head, tried to comprehend. "Why the charade? Why the pretense?"

"You shall have to ask Juliette, as that is her story to tell more than it is mine. Suffice it to say, she is not a courtesan, and she has never been a courtesan. But then that makes no difference to you now, does it, Your Grace?"

"No," he said and surprised himself because the words were true. "It doesn't."

"Exactly." The countess nodded. "When love fills one's heart, there should be no more room for pride."

Twenty-five

One month later

JULIETTE COLLAPSED ON THE BLUE VELVET CHAISE longue in the drawing room of Will's London town house and heaved a sigh of relief. Her white satin gown with the blue sash and beaded bodice felt as though it weighed three stone. "That is the last of them," she said. "I thought they would never leave."

Will, dressed in elegant charcoal gray, lifted her feet and sat beside her. "We're finally alone." He tugged off his gloves and set them neatly beside him.

Juliette knew that tone of voice and raised her head to smile at him. "*Married* and alone." She removed her gloves and dropped them in a heap on the floor.

"It was the longest month of my life," he said.

"I told you to get a special license."

He shook his head. "You deserved having the announcement in the *Times* and the banns called."

She smiled. "Thank you."

He coaxed one of her slippers off and then the other, and began to knead her feet. She groaned in pleasure.

"And now that we are alone," Will said, "and married, I want to ask you a question."

Juliette tried to open her eyes, but she couldn't manage it. "Hmm?" was all she could say.

"Why did you do it?" Will flexed her foot, and the motion felt heavenly. "Why would you choose to play the role of a courtesan?"

Juliette's eyes fluttered open. "So you *do* know. I wondered."

"It makes no difference to me."

She knew this, but it felt good to hear him say it again. "Who told you? Lily?"

"The countess. She told me that night at Covent Garden."

Juliette sat up. "And you're just now asking me?"

"I told you, it doesn't matter to me. The past is the past. Why didn't *you* tell me?"

"Would you have believed me?"

"Perhaps not at first."

She raised a brow, and he tickled her foot.

"Perhaps not ever." He smiled. It was so wonderful to see him smile all the time now.

She laid her head back on the arm of the chaise. "Are you certain you want to hear this? It's not exactly a celebratory story, and we are celebrating our nuptials tonight."

"I want to hear it."

She sighed. She would tell it once, and then it would be over. Will was right. She *should* have told him. "When it became clear to me I could no longer live with Oliver—rather, that he would end up killing me if I lived with him much longer"—she felt Will's hand on her foot tighten—"I went to my older brother and my mother and told them I had to get away." She ran a hand over her eyes. "I never thought of divorce. I simply wanted to escape. I was tired of living in fear. I'd spent three years doing everything I could to please Oliver, and nothing I did was ever good enough. He had begun beating me more frequently, and as I said, I really did fear for my life."

Will's face was white and strained, and she sat forward and took his hand.

"It's in the past now. I escaped."

"I should have killed him out on the moors," Will said. "I should have beaten the bastard until he was dead."

"Perhaps jail is a worse fate," she said. "In any case, my brother would not help me. You see, after my father died, I was a bit lost. I was so sad and lonely and missing my father. Oliver stepped in and wooed me. He made me feel so special, as my father had done. Oh, I was *so* young and so naive—only seventeen and really still a child.

"My brother and my mother rejected Oliver's requests to marry me. They did not think him a good prospect. In hindsight, they were right, but for reasons even they couldn't know at the time. But I begged and pleaded, and finally my brother relented and gave consent.

"When I wanted out, he reminded me how I'd begged him and refused to help. My mother relied on him to support her, and she could not go against his wishes. But she had a friend she knew would help me."

"Lady Sinclair?"

She nodded. "Yes. Lady Sinclair was the one who helped craft a scheme to convince Oliver to divorce me. When everyone thought I was cuckolding him, it became a matter of pride to him. It took another year, but I was finally rid of him. All of that time, I'd been living with the Sinclairs, and rumors were swirling that the earl and I were having an affair. It was completely untrue, but the rumors gave Lady Sinclair an idea. What if I were to become a courtesan? Not simply any courtesan, but one of the most sought-after courtesans in all of London?"

"It's a brilliant idea. What other options were open to you?"

"Exactly. I was a divorced woman, which is scandal enough, but I had no income, no family support, nowhere to go. I would have ended up on the streets. Instead, Lord Sinclair helped set me up in London. I don't know how he did it—I suppose he spent quite a deal of money—but he helped me build a reputation. By then, Lily and Fallon were also under the countess's wing, and she decided it would be better for the three of us to stick together. And so we became The Three Diamonds."

"And none of you are actually courtesans?"

"No. But what the countess gave us was freedom. Freedom to live our lives in relative security. Freedom to have fun, to enjoy life, to become someone new. I suppose we even had the freedom to choose the men we would bed, if we wanted to bed any at all. None of us had ever had that freedom before."

"I'm liking the countess more and more."

Juliette laughed. "I thought you might. And

incidentally, until I met you, I never met a man who interested me enough to take him to my bed."

"And you know that does not matter to me. You are mine now. You are no longer the Duchess of Dalliance but the Duchess of Pelham."

"It doesn't have quite the same ring."

Will frowned, and she laughed. She sat forward and cupped his face in her hands. "There is no other duchess I would rather be. I love being *your* duchess, Will." She kissed him softly and found his mouth more than eager for hers. Tingles of heat spiraled through her body from the tips of her toes to the ends of her hair. She had not realized how much she missed Will's kisses—how much she craved them. She pulled him closer and lost her balance, causing him to fall on top of her. She laughed and wrapped her arms around him.

He kissed her again then raised his head. "Why don't we go up to the bedroom? I have everything arranged."

She raised her brows, wondering what surprise he had in store for her. "Lead the way," she murmured into his ear. He stood and pulled her up, but her foot had caught in the hem of her gown, and laughing, she grasped the side table to keep her balance. Unfortunately, the Greek vase on the table toppled to the floor. She lunged for it but missed. It landed with a thud just short of the Aubusson rug and shattered on the wood floor. Papers scattered on the rug and littered the wood. "Oh, I'm so sorry. Is it authentic?" She bent to pick up the pieces and the slips of paper, but before she could lift anything, Will grabbed her hand.

"Wait."

"What is it?"

He fell to his knees beside her and lifted the largest shard of pottery. Beneath it lay a small folded scrap of paper. It was quality vellum and quite expensive. It would not have been used to jot a simple note.

"I assume that is not yours."

"No." He lifted the cream rectangle and flipped it open. He stared at the contents for a long moment.

Juliette, impatient to retreat to the bedroom, raised her brows. "Well, what is it?"

"It's a list of names." He angled the paper and she saw the names of four men scrawled in an elegant hand. At the top of the vellum, underlined twice, were the words *Diamonds in the Rough*.

She shrugged. "Should this mean something to me?"

"It means something to me. This is Lady Elizabeth's hand. I am almost certain of it. And, if I am not mistaken, these are the names of four spies for the British government, one of whom is already dead."

"Lucifer's diamonds," she breathed.

"Yes. They were never jewels, as we assumed. These names, these men's identities could be just as valuable as a handful of diamonds if offered to the right people or government. Obviously, at least one of the men has already been sold and disposed of."

She had no idea how he knew this, and she was not certain she wanted to know. She'd had enough dealings with Lucifer and his diamonds to last her a lifetime.

"And that's not all." He lifted some of the cheap papers and began thumbing through them.

"Lady Elizabeth's vowels?" she asked, scanning the parchment.

"Yes. Most of them issued from Lucifer's Lair."

He looked up at her. "Did she actually think she would get away with it? She must have known Lucifer's reputation."

"I don't know." Juliette gestured to the IOUs. "I would venture to guess she enjoyed taking risks."

Will folded the vellum along with the IOUs and placed the papers on the mantel in a mahogany box embellished with gold filigree. Juliette shivered with unease, glad to be rid of the papers. They felt tainted with Eliza's blood.

"I know someone who is looking for this information. I'll contact him in the morning," Will said, taking a small key from inside the box and locking it. He dropped the key in his waistcoat pocket. "Until then, they will keep." He held out his hand. Juliette took it, and he drew her close, kissing her fingers with his lips. She felt safe again.

"Let's go to bed, Duchess."

"A very good idea, Your Grace."

Will stood at his bedroom window and stared into the night. It was never truly dark in London, but his window overlooked the gardens, and so the view was darker than most. The scent of rose petals teased his nose, and he turned to glance at the bed behind him. Juliette lay on her side, her hand curled under her chin, the white counterpane pulled over her bare shoulders. Surrounding her were hundreds of pink, red, and white rose petals. During their lovemaking, a few petals had fallen on the rug and into the two champagne flutes on the floor beside the bed.

He lifted one of those flutes now, fished the petals out, and drank the last of the champagne. In a moment, he would climb in bed beside his warm, sleeping wife and hold her until the first pink light of dawn. He thought of his uncle, who had sent him a half-dozen letters, no doubt railing against his betrothal. Last night, Will had thrown them into the fire without reading them. He had thrown his unhappy childhood into the fire, as well. This morning he had begun over again. He was a different man, a different duke. He had Juliette by his side.

And she loved him.

He set the glass aside and took hold of the window drapes. He spared a last look into the garden. Lucifer was still out there somewhere—biding his time, waiting for his opportunity to take back the diamonds—the secret names of loyal men he had intended to betray. There had to be more than those names alone. Will was certain Lady Elizabeth's slip of paper was merely her insurance. What had she done with the rest of the information about the men? Whom had she sold them to? Had Lucifer killed her before she could sell all of them, or were the men on the list still in danger?

Will thought of the second name on the vellum.

Warrick Fitzhugh.

Will would arrange a meeting with Fitzhugh first thing in the morning. He didn't know anything about these Diamonds in the Rough, but he knew his friend was in peril.

And he knew Lucifer would not give up easily. The duke almost hoped he had a run in with this Lucifer. He felt he owed the man a few broken limbs for what he'd done to Juliette. He would make sure the man was hanged for what he did to Lady Elizabeth.

But Lucifer and the diamonds were a worry for the morning. He had the only diamond he wanted right here. And he lifted the counterpane and took her into his arms.

FROM

The Rogue Pirate's Bride

France, 1802

"THAT'S HIM," PERCY WHISPERED. "I'M ALMOST CERTAIN of it."

Raeven Russell glanced at Percy. There was a fine sheen of perspiration on his pale, freckled skin, and his white-blond hair stood up in all directions as though he'd run a hand through it half a dozen times. Which he probably had. Percy Williams was purser for the HMS *Regal*, and while Raeven knew Percy adored her, she also knew he abhorred any action that violated her father's rules.

She reached over and slung an arm around him in the jaunty way she had seen men do time and time again. "You look nervous," she said under her breath. "People will wonder why."

"I *am* nervous," he hissed. "You're going to get yourself killed."

"That's my problem." She shifted away from him and scanned the men around her. Which one was Cutlass? There were several likely candidates.

Raeven stood like a man—legs braced apart and hands on hips—to survey the seedy Brest tavern. Dockside taverns the world over were the same, she mused as she studied the crowd. They were filled with sailors looking for wine and women, ships' captains hiring additions to their crews, beleaguered serving girls skirting men's too-free hands, and whores working to entice any man with the coin to pay.

She didn't know why she should feel so at home. She certainly didn't belong here and had gone to considerable trouble to disguise herself as a young man before sneaking off her father's ship and onto a cutter with the crew members going ashore legitimately.

If her father knew she was here... She shook her head. She could hear his booming voice in her head. *The daughter of a British admiral should behave with more decorum, in a manner befitting her station in life.*

But what was her station in life? Her mother had died days after her birth, and from the age of four— when the last of her relatives had given her up as incorrigible—she'd been sailing with her father. This certainly wasn't the first tavern she'd visited. It wasn't even the first time she'd sneaked off the HMS *Regal*.

It was the first time she'd found Captain Cutlass. After six months of searching for the murdering bastard, she was about to meet him... face to face.

"It'll be my neck when your father finds out." Percy swallowed audibly, and she suppressed a smile.

"Then you won't be long in following me to meet our maker. I'll put in a good word for you."

He gave her a horrified look, which she supposed indicated he didn't think she'd be a very good envoy. He cleared his throat. "I prefer a little more time on this earthly world."

"I'm in complete agreement. Now, tell me which one he is again, but don't look at him or gesture toward him."

"Let's go sit at the bar," Percy said. "You can see him better from there, and we'll be less conspicuous."

"Fine." Remembering to play her role, she swaggered to the bar and leaned against it, trying to look belligerent. Percy ordered ale, and she did as well, though she had no intention of drinking it. She needed all her wits about her.

When the barkeep moved away, Percy studied his mug and murmured, "See the man in the far corner?"

Raeven allowed her gaze to roam lazily over the tavern until she focused on the corner he indicated.

"He's dressed as a gentleman in a navy coat, white cravat, buff breeches."

She saw him now and nodded. "A gentleman pirate." She shook her head. "Contradiction in terms."

"The rumor is he's a deposed marquis whose family fled France during the revolution."

She scowled at him. "Don't tell me you believe that rubbish. All the pirates concoct romantic stories. Just because one claims he's a duke doesn't make him any less of a thief and murderer."

"Of course I don't believe it. I'm telling you the rumor."

But she could hear in his voice he had believed the story, and now that she'd set her eyes on Cutlass, she could see why. The man did have the air of the aristocrat about him. It wasn't simply his clothes—any man could dress up as one of the quality, but there was something in Cutlass's bearing. He was sitting at a table, his back to the wall, facing the door to the tavern. That much told her he was no fool. There was a man seated across from him, and Cutlass was listening in a leisurely fashion to whatever the man was saying. Cutlass's arms were crossed over his chest, and his expression was one of mild interest. He had a glass of something on the table before him, but she hadn't seen him drink from it. Nor had she seen any whores approach him.

He was doing business then. It would have better served her purposes if he'd been drunk and whoring, but she didn't have the luxury of choosing when to strike.

Her gaze slid back to Percy. "He's handsome," she remarked and watched the purser's eyebrows wing upward. "I hadn't expected that."

The reports she'd had of him rarely mentioned his appearance. Captain Cutlass was known for his stealth, his agility, and his slippery escapes. It was rumored he'd boarded over a hundred vessels. That was obviously exaggeration, but even if his record was a quarter of that, it was an impressive feat. Of course, he claimed he was a privateer, and she knew he sailed under the Spanish flag and with that country's letters of marque. She didn't care for privateers any more than she cared for pirates, and made little distinction between them. Neither pirates nor privateers should dare attack ships of the British Navy. Neither should dare to kill a British naval officer.

She felt the anger and the blood pump through her and took a deep, calming breath. She couldn't afford to be emotional right now. She had to put emotion away. And she couldn't afford a schoolgirl crush on the man either. Yes, he was handsome. His dark brown hair was brushed back from his forehead and would have grazed his shoulder if not neatly secured in a queue. His face was strong with a square jaw, plenty of angles and planes, and a full mouth that destroyed the hard effect and hinted at softness. But the eyes—the eyes did not lie. There was no softness in the man. She couldn't quite see the eye color from this far away, but under the sardonic arch of his brow his eyes were sharp, cold, and calculating.

A worthy adversary, and she'd spill his blood tonight.

"I don't like the look in your eyes," Percy said. "Now that you've seen him, you can't possibly mean to challenge him. He's not a small man."

Raeven straightened her shoulders to give herself more height. She was well aware of her short stature, but size and strength were not everything. She was small and quick and deadly. "I do mean to challenge him," she said, brushing her hand against the light sword at her waist. "I'm only waiting until his business is completed." Though if it took much longer, she would have to interrupt. She wanted this over and done.

"I don't think that's wise. Perhaps if we wait—"

"I'm not waiting," she snapped. "I've waited six months, and that's too long."

"Timothy would not have wanted…"

Her glare cut him off. "Timothy is dead, and his murderer is sitting over there having a chat and sipping wine. Timothy would have wanted justice."

And because she knew Percy's next comment would be about justice versus vengeance, and because she did not want to hear it, she pushed off the bar and arrowed for Cutlass's table. It was a short trek across the tavern but long enough for her heart to pick up speed and pound painfully in her chest. She tried to calm herself with a deep breath, but she exhaled shakily. Her hands were sweating, and she flexed them to keep them loose.

When she stepped in front of Cutlass's table, he glanced up at her briefly and then back at the man seated across from him. Before she could speak, another man was beside her.

"Move away, lad. The captain's busy at present." The man was tall and lanky with a shock of red hair and pale, freckled skin. He was well dressed and spoke to her in fluent, if accented, French. English, she thought, and well bred. Probably Cutlass's quartermaster.

She stood her ground. "I think the captain will want to hear what I have to say." She said it to Cutlass, but he didn't acknowledge her.

"I'll tell him you wish to speak with him. In the meantime…" He made the mistake of taking her arm, and she responded with a quick jab to his abdomen. He grunted in surprise and took a step back.

"Problem, Mr. Maine?" Cutlass said smoothly. He had one brow cocked and a bemused smile on his lips. Obviously, he didn't see her as any sort of threat. "Is the lad giving you trouble?" He also spoke in French, but his was sweet and thick as honey. A native speaker, she surmised, and one with a polished accent. No wonder he played the deposed French marquis.

"No, Captain," Maine said, stepping forward again. "I'll get him out of your way."

Raeven put a hand on the small dagger at her waist. "Touch me again, and I'll slice your hand off." Her gaze met Cutlass's. "I want a word with you."

"Obviously." He lifted his wine, sipped. "But you'll have to learn some manners first. Come back when you've mastered the art of patience."

In one lightning-quick move, she drew her dagger, rounded the table, and pressed it under his jaw. "You want to talk about patience?" She pressed the blade into the bronze skin until a small bead of blood welled up. "I've been waiting six long months to slit your throat."

"Is that all?" he said, setting his glass of wine on the table. With annoyance, she noted his hand did not even tremble. "There are some who've waited far longer."

"I'm going to kill you," she said, looking directly into his eyes. They were cobalt blue and framed with thick brown lashes.

He raised a brow at her. "I don't think so." She should have seen it coming, should have seen his eyes flick down or his jaw clench, but he gave no indication he would move. And before she could react, he had her wrist pinned on the table, the dagger trapped and useless. Slowly he stood, his hand warm steel on hers. She watched him rise and rise and had never felt as small as she did in that moment. She realized the tavern had grown quiet as the patrons drank in the scene.

Percy's voice broke the silence. "Captain, the boy's had too much to drink. He's young. If you don't mind, we'll just be taking him back to the ship now."

Raeven scowled. She could imagine her father's men lined up behind her, Percy in the middle, his hands spread in a placating gesture. She kept her gaze locked on Cutlass's, saw him shrug and exchange a look with one of his men. Devil take her if he wasn't going to pat her head and shoo her away. She couldn't allow that. This was her last chance. Even now her father might have noticed her absence, and it could be months—*years*—before she had another opportunity to confront Cutlass.

"Coward," she said loud enough for her voice to carry through the tavern. "Too afraid to fight me, a mere boy?"

She saw the surprise in his face and then the irritation. "Look, lad, I don't want to kill you."

She laughed. "What makes you think you can? I'm good with a sword. Very good, and I challenge you to a duel." Now she did look away from him; she swept the room with her eyes, making sure everyone heard the challenge.

"Now you've done it," she heard Percy mutter. And she had. Cutlass could not back down from a direct challenge.

Acknowledgments

First of all, let me simply say I hate writing acknowledgments. I am deathly afraid I will forget someone important. Not to mention, I don't know all that many different ways to say thank you. So this time I am going to keep it simple.

Thank you to all of my friends and family. I am so fortunate to have you in my life. I know not every author has a great support group. Thank you to Tera Lynn Childs, my friend and a fellow in the trenches. Thank you for taking time away from your busy schedule and your deadlines to read this book and offer suggestions. I'm so glad I asked you if you knew of anyone looking for a critique partner. Know you are loved and appreciated.

Thank you to the Sourcebooks team. You do a wonderful job editing me, publicizing me, marketing me, and everything in between. I truly appreciate all you do to make my books a fabulous finished product. I especially want to thank Deb Werksman, because she listens to my awful pitches (and agrees they are awful), and buys the book anyway. Thanks for trusting me, Deb.

Thank you to Joanna MacKenzie and Danielle Egan-Miller. You clean up those awful pitches for me and have suffered through a few yourself. I really don't mean to pitch! Somehow, it just happens. Anyway, thank you for always being in my corner. That sounds cliché, but it's really true. I always know you have my best interests in mind.

And thank you to my writer friends—the Jaunty Quills, the Casababes, West Houston RWA, Christina Hergenrader, Elise Rome, Sharie Kohler, and Nicole Flockton.

Thank you, maddee at xuni.com, for all you do for me online.

Thank you to my readers. I love receiving your emails, your blog comments, your Facebook posts, and your Tweets.

Lastly, thank you to my husband for your love, support, and help with Baby Galen. Baby Galen, thank you for those two- and three-hour naps so I could finish this book!

About the Author

Shana Galen is the author of numerous fast-paced, adventurous Regency historical romances, including the 2008 Rita-nominated *Blackthorne's Bride*. Her books have been sold worldwide, including Brazil, Russia, Spain, Turkey, Japan, and the Netherlands, and have been featured in the Rhapsody and Doubleday Book Clubs. A former English teacher in Houston's inner city, Shana now writes full time. She's a wife, a mother, and an expert multitasker. She loves to hear from readers: visit her website at www.shanagalen.com or see what she's up to daily on Facebook and Twitter.

Lord and Lady Spy

by Shana Galen

No man can outsmart him…

Lord Adrian Smythe may appear a perfectly boring gentleman, but he leads a thrilling life as one of England's most preeminent spies, an identity so clandestine even his wife is unaware of it. But he isn't the only one with secrets…

She's been outsmarting him for years…

Now that the Napoleonic wars have come to an end, daring secret agent Lady Sophia Smythe can hardly bear the thought of returning home to her tedious husband. Until she discovers in the dark of night that he's not who she thinks he is after all…

"An excellent book, full of great witty conversation, hot passionate scenes, and tons of action."—BookLoons

"The author's writing style, how this story is built and all of the delicious scenes, and the characters themselves are just so rich, so enjoyable I found myself smiling and absolutely enjoying every single page."—Smexy Books

For more Shana Galen, visit:

www.sourcebooks.com

The Rogue Pirate's Bride

by Shana Galen

Revenge should be sweet, but it may cost him everything...

Out to avenge the death of his mentor, Bastien discovers himself astonishingly out of his depth when confronted with a beautiful, daring young woman who is out for his blood...

Forgiveness is unthinkable, but it may be her only hope...

British Admiral's daughter Raeven Russell believes Bastien responsible for her fiancé's death. But once the fiery beauty crosses swords with Bastien, she's not so sure she really wants him to change his wicked ways...

Praise for Shana Galen:

"Lively dialogue, breakneck pace, and great sense of fun."—Publishers Weekly

"Galen strikes the perfect balance between dangerous intrigue and sexy romance."—Booklist

For more Shana Galen, visit:

www.sourcebooks.com

The Wicked Wedding of Miss Ellie Vyne

by Jayne Fresina

❧

When a notorious bachelor seduces a scandalous lady, it can only end in a wicked wedding

By night Ellie Vyne fleeces unsuspecting aristocrats as the dashing Count de Bonneville. By day she avoids her sisters' matchmaking attempts and dreams up inventive insults to hurl at her childhood nemesis, the arrogant, far-too-handsome-for-his-own-good James Hartley.

James finally has a lead on the villainous, thieving count, tracking him to a shady inn. He bursts in on none other than "that Vyne woman"...in a shocking state of dishabille. Convinced she is the count's mistress, James decides it's best to keep his enemies close. Very close. Seducing Ellie will be the perfect bait...

❧

Praise for *The Most Improper Miss Sophie Valentine*:

"Ms. Fresina delivers a scintillating debut! Her sharply drawn characters and witty prose are as addictive as chocolate!"—Mia Marlowe, author of *Touch of a Rogue*

For more Jayne Fresina, visit:

www.sourcebooks.com

Lady Amelia's Mess and a Half

by Samantha Grace

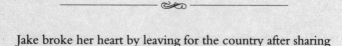

Jake broke her heart by leaving for the country after sharing a passionate kiss.

Lady Amelia broke his by marrying his best friend.

When she returns to town a widow—pursued by an infamous rake, Jake's debauched brother, and just maybe by Jake himself—Lady Amelia will have a mess and a half on her hands.

A sparkling romp through the ton, Lady Amelia's Mess and a Half *delivers a witty Regency romance in which misunderstandings abound, reputations are put on the line, and the only thing more exciting than a scandal is true love.*

"Clever, spicy, and fresh from beginning to end."—Amelia Grey, award-winning author of *A Gentleman Never Tells*

"A delightfully witty romp seasoned with an irresistible dash of intrigue and passion. Samantha Grace is an author to watch!"—Shana Galen, award-winning author of *Lord and Lady Spy*

For more Samantha Grace, visit:

www.sourcebooks.com

A *Publishers Weekly* Best Book of the Year

The Heir

by Grace Burrowes

---&⁊---

An earl who can't be bribed...

Gayle Windham, Earl of Westhaven, is the first legitimate son and heir to the Duke of Moreland. To escape his father's inexorable pressure to marry, he decides to spend the summer at his townhouse in London, where he finds himself intrigued by the secretive ways of his beautiful housekeeper...

A lady who can't be protected...

Anna Seaton is a beautiful, talented, educated woman, which is why it is so puzzling to Gayle Windham that she works as his housekeeper.

As the two draw closer and begin to lose their hearts to each other, Anna's secrets threaten to bring the earl's orderly life crashing down—and he doesn't know how he's going to protect her from the fallout...

---&⁊---

"A luminous and graceful erotic Regency...a captivating love story that will have readers eagerly awaiting the planned sequels."—Publishers Weekly (starred review)

For more Grace Burrowes, visit:

www.sourcebooks.com